STAR TREK®
STRANGE NEW WORLDS

STAR TREK®
STRANGE NEW WORLDS

Edited by
Dean Wesley Smith
with John J. Ordover and Paula M. Block

POCKET BOOKS
New York   London   Toronto   Sydney   Tokyo   Singapore

This book consists of works of fiction. Names, characters, places and incidents are products of the authors' imaginations or are used fictiously. Any resemblance to actual events or locales or persons, living or dead, is entirely coincidental.

An *Original* Publication of POCKET BOOKS

POCKET BOOKS, a division of Simon & Schuster Inc. 1230 Avenue of the Americas, New York, NY 10020

STAR TREK is a Registered Trademark of Paramount Pictures.

This book is published by Pocket Books, a division of Simon & Schuster Inc., under exclusive license from Paramount Pictures.

ISBN: 0-671-01446-3

First Pocket Books trade paperback printing July 1998

10 9 8 7 6 5 4 3 2

POCKET and colophon are registered trademarks of Simon & Schuster Inc.

Printed in the U.S.A.

Contents

Contents

**STAR TREK
DEEP SPACE NINE®**

**STAR TREK®
VOYAGER™**

Contents

Because We Can

Afterwords

Contest Rules

About the Contributors

Introduction

Dean Wesley Smith

The book you hold in your hands was created out of love. It is full of wonderful *Star Trek* short stories, picked from thousands of stories sent in during the months of the contest. This book exists because, as with the third season of the original *Star Trek* series, the fans wrote. Only this time they weren't writing letters, but stories.

The path to getting this book into print wasn't a smooth one by any means. It started with John Ordover, the tall, smiling *Star Trek* editor at Pocket Books. As a fan himself, John understood the desire of the fans to write *Star Trek* stories, and that the very foundation of *Star Trek* was, and has always been, the fans. Yet the constraints of the modern publishing industry only allowed fans who had become professional writers to do the books. John figured that a contest and anthology might be a way of opening the door for the nonprofessional fan writers to be published right along with the professional writers in bookstores.

Thus, the idea of this anthology was born. But a professional *Star Trek* fan anthology hadn't been done for a long, long time. The very business of publishing had changed. *Star Trek* had changed. To get things rolling, John enlisted the support of Paula Block, another longtime fan who worked at Viacom. Somehow, after a massive amount of moving heavens and earth, they worked this project through the roadblocks of the publishing world until it became a reality.

With the news of the contest spreading over the nets and through the conventions, the fans responded. Thousands of stories flooded in during the months before the October 1st deadline.

John had hoped this might happen, so that's where I came in. With his duties as senior editor, John just didn't have the time to read thousands of stories. With my wife, Kristine Kathryn Rusch, I've written several *Star Trek* books, as well as edited non-Trek short-story anthologies and magazines. On top of that, I'm a *Star Trek* fan, just like John and Paula. John hired me to edit the book.

So as all the stories poured in, they were sent to me. I'm the only one who read all those stories. John and Paula only saw the ones you're seeing now. I sort of feel guilty about that. They did all the hard work of pushing this book into existence, and I got to have all the fun of reading the stories. And fun it was, too.

For months I had the wonderful job of doing nothing but reading *Star Trek* short stories. Tough life, huh? One day I walked into my local bookstore and the clerk asked me what project I was working on. I said I was reading *Star Trek* stories. If looks could kill, I would have been dead right at that moment. It turned out she was an avid fan. And as she pointed out, I truly had the best job in the world.

Over the months of the contest I also got to meet hundreds of great *Star Trek* fans, both in person and on-line, reinforcing my belief that the people who read *Star Trek* clearly are the good people of this world.

But even with meeting the great people, the most fun was reading the stories. Thousands of them, with wonderful ideas and interesting plots. But then, after all the reading was done, came the hard part of reducing thousands of stories down to just the ones you see in this book. That wasn't so much fun. In fact, that was pure agony.

I began by dividing the stories into two piles. One pile I called my "second read" pile. The other pile held the stories that just wouldn't fit, for numbers of reasons. Maybe the writing wasn't up to the level it needed to be, even if the idea was really great. Or maybe the idea had been done before, or I already had a better story with the same basic idea. That happened often, and there were numbers of reasons why a story ended up in that pile.

After that cut, I still had hundreds and hundreds of stories left for the anthology. So with the next read I got tougher. The writing had to be even better, the opening had to catch readers, the idea had to really fit a short-story form, and it had to be different. I cut the pile down to about fifty.

Then with another read the pile was forty. Then thirty. Then twenty-five. And then finally, after much loss of sleep, it came down to the stories you hold in your hand.

Then John and Paula got back into the action. They read and approved the stories, just as all novels are approved. Then among the three of us, we managed to decide on the contest winners. I'm so glad John and Paula didn't just leave that up to me. I doubt if I could have managed to cut these stories down to just three. But somehow, the three of us managed it.

The stories in this book represent thousands of fan stories, written because of the love of *Star Trek*. In my opinion, everyone who finished and mailed in a story is a winner.

I hope you will enjoy the stories in this book. As the editor, I know that I'll be the only person in the entire universe who will like every story. But I think I managed to find stories that most will like.

Thanks, John, from all of us fans, for making this book a reality. And thanks for giving me the best, and toughest, job in the world. For me, this was truly a work of love.

A Private Anecdote

Landon Cary Dalton

STARDATE 2822.5

I sit in my chair, staring at the view from the window of my hospital room. It is a nice view, but I have already grown tired of it. I have memorized every detail of every building on Starbase 11, or at least the portions within my limited sight. In some of the nearer buildings I am able to see the faces of some of the occupants. My favorite is a lovely young redhead who lives in the nearest building. Sometimes she stands on her balcony to enjoy her view. She has a look of innocent sweetness on her young face, as if she has never encountered any of the hardships and difficulties of life. I envy her.

The moon has risen. This moon appears to be much larger than the Earth's moon. It is encircled by a bright ring, not as impressive as the rings of Saturn, but still a lovely sight. I do not know the name of this moon or of any of its features, but I have their images memorized as well. I have named the various features after people and things that I have known. That range of sharply pointed mountains I named for Spock, a dear friend of mine. The horse-shaped sea I call Tango after a horse I once owned on Earth. The prominent crater in the Northern Hemisphere I call Boyce.

The lovely ring I have named Vina, for someone I think about often.

Commodore Mendez is very good to me. He has visited me at least once a week since my arrival here. He must have a very busy schedule commanding the starbase, but still he finds time for me. I wish I had some way to express my appreciation, but my injuries prevent me from expressing anything more complex than "yes" or "no."

Last week Mendez "accidently" allowed me to see the active duty roster. It was displayed on the viewer long enough for me to see my own name still listed on active duty.

"Fleet Captain Christopher Pike."

It was a noble effort on the part of the commodore to maintain my morale. This is, of course, an impossible task. My life has come to an end. The delta radiation has left my body a wasted husk, unable to move. The chair keeps my blood pumping in a vague imitation of life, but my heart knows the hopelessness of it all. My life has become nothing but an agonizing wait for death.

I watch as a shuttlecraft lifts off and flies in my direction. I entertain a shameful fantasy that it will malfunction and crash through this window to end my suffering. I am angry at myself for such thoughts. I ought to be able to find some way of dealing with this.

Then it comes to me again. I remember that same silly little thought that has occurred to me many times in the past thirteen years. It is a foolish, pointless thought, but it amuses me. I am physically unable to laugh, but inwardly my gloom lifts for a moment and my spirit rises with the thought.

"What if all of this isn't real?"

I dearly wish I could share this thought with José Mendez. He is a very sober man when on duty, but I recall him having a wicked sense of humor in private. He would appreciate the thought.

mandibles were still. Suddenly the creature's legs began to wobble. Then the beast collapsed. It fell into a massive heap of dying flesh.

My companions rushed down the hill to my side.

"Chris!" shouted Boyce. "Chris, are you all right?"

"I'm fine, Doctor. This blood all belongs to that thing."

Trawley slapped me on the back.

"You saved all our lives!" he was shouting. "Can you believe that?"

Technically Trawley was being overly familiar with his commanding officer, but I overlooked it for the moment. The situation warranted a little laxity in discipline.

"Let's get out of here," I said, reaching for my communicator.

"Chris, I can't believe what you just did," said Boyce. "I'd never have been able to summon up the strength to take that beast on by myself. What possessed you to do that?"

I just smiled at him. I didn't know how to tell him what was going on in my mind at that moment. I never did tell Boyce that I had saved his life because of a momentary indulgence of a foolish little thought. I wish I had told him now, because I will never again be capable of sharing that story.

Trawley was also present the next time that the thought occurred to me. He had risen in the ranks quite a bit by that time. He was a full commander. His first command was an old class-J cargo ship that was being used for cadet training.

He had matured quite a bit in the decade since our adventure on Corinthia VII, but he still had a worshipful look in his eyes when I came aboard for an inspection. His cadets were no younger than he had been when he joined the crew of the *Enterprise,* but still Trawley called them his "kids." I still saw Trawley as one of my children.

Trawley had only been aboard the ship himself for a week. He and the cadets were going to have quite a job getting this vessel into working order. Trawley was a good, thorough organizer. Given time he would be able to restore this ship to mint condition.

None of us knew it then, but time was not on our side.

Trawley gathered the crew together on the cargo deck and introduced me to them. They looked to me like children playing a dress-up game.

Trawley insisted on telling the cadets about our experience on Corinthia VII. I could tell that he had told this story many times before. He had perfected his delivery of it over time. My own memory varied a bit on some of the details, but I didn't quibble.

There was one detail, however, that I was surprised by. I couldn't imagine how he could know this particular detail.

". . . and do you know what the captain did just before he attacked the creature? You'll never guess this in a million years. He laughed! I swear, I could hear it all the way up the cliff wall. He laughed!"

The cadets laughed as well. I considered telling Trawley the whole story that day, but I didn't get around to it. I was a little embarrassed by all the attention, so I decided not to bring the subject up again. Now I'll never get the chance.

Later that night I was alone in my cabin, reading the cadet reviews. They looked like a good bunch of kids. It looked like Starfleet was going to be in good hands for another generation.

Suddenly a shudder rolled through the ship. A lump formed in my throat. The shudder wasn't really all that bad, but sometimes you sense when a disaster is bearing down on you.

I stepped out of my cabin. The corridor was filled with terrified cadets. Alarm klaxons began to sound. One frightened young girl emerged from her cabin wearing nothing but a towel. Her eyes were already filling with tears.

I grabbed her by the shoulders. I kept my voice calm, expressing a cool confidence that I did not feel.

"Everything is going to be all right. Go get dressed and report to your station."

She straightened up and returned to her cabin. I looked at the confused crowd of cadets that had gathered in a circle around me.

"What's the matter with you people?" I shouted. "Get to your posts!"

Shame is a good motivator. The embarrassed crew members ran for their stations, eager to show me they knew their jobs.

I raced down to the engine room. The hatch was sealed. I looked through the porthole into the room beyond. I could see billowing clouds of gas.

A baffle plate had ruptured!

I could see the motionless bodies of half a dozen cadets. They might already be dead. I knew I couldn't leave them in there, but I also knew what delta rays can do to a man. For a moment I froze, unwilling to face the horrors on the other side of the hatch.

Then the thought came to me again.

"What if all of this isn't real?"

I didn't laugh this time. I knew as I looked that this was very real. If I didn't act fast, none of those cadets had a chance.

I felt a blast of heat as I opened that hatch, only I knew it wasn't really heat. It was the delta radiation knifing through my body. I stumbled in and grabbed the nearest cadet. She was wearing the thick protective coveralls of an engineer. That was good. That would help to minimize the effects of the radiation. I, on the other hand, had no such protection.

Six times I entered the engine room. Six cadets I pulled from that chamber of horrors. Two of them would die later at Starbase 11. But four of them would survive.

As for me, I'm not sure if I would count myself as a survivor or not. I cannot move and I cannot speak. All I can do is sit, looking and listening to the world around me.

I sit here and I stare at the ringed moon and at the lovely young redhead. I look at a world that I can no longer participate in.

And I think. I think so much that my head hurts. I am fearful of the days to come. I am afraid that my mind will begin to wither and die. It frightens me to think that my sanity may begin to leave me.

In the midst of the horror that my life has become, the idea returns to me again. Once again I imagine that I am back in my cage on Talos IV. I dream that all of this is just an illusion, soon to be replaced with better dreams. Perhaps the Talosians will send me back to Mojave next, or back to Orion.

"What if all of this isn't real?"

Inwardly I laugh. But I know that this is real. This isn't Talos IV. This isn't an illusion. But for the first time in thirteen years I wish that it were. Perhaps it is a sign of my weakening spirit, but I wish I could trade this reality for a dream.

I wish I were back in my cage.

The Last Tribble

Keith L. Davis

Cyrano Jones inched his way along the ventilation duct. Just ahead on the left was a smaller feeder duct, probably from one of the hydroponics sections. Once he was across from it, he stopped to take another tricorder reading and opened his communicator.

"Transmitting grid reference 6," he said flatly, knowing that there was little likelihood of any new information coming from the other end of the comm channel.

"Coordinates received," replied the familiar voice. "We're still positing a location within about ten meters of your present position. Source stable. Repeat, source is stable. We suggest continuing on your present path and report crossing into subsection 17."

"Acknowledged," replied Cyrano, grumbling slightly. "You know, Lurry, this wouldn't have been necessary if someone would occasionally check the calibration of the internal sensors."

"Yes, Cyrano, but remember that when you started this job, you couldn't even fit inside a ventilation duct, let alone navigate them."

"Cyrano out."

He knew Lurry was beaming one of those "Oh-I-got-him-with-that-one" grins around the station manager's office, but he wasn't going to give Lurry the satisfaction of hearing his barb hit the mark. Still, Lurry's point was valid—he couldn't have done this seventeen years ago. That was just one of the many changes over that span.

Stardate 4523.2 had started relatively well, or at least that was the way he remembered it. He had cleared station customs after a rather minimal inspection by the resident constabulary. Of course one or two cases of Romulan ale that never appeared on any manifest might have had something to do with that. They had never even bothered to examine the aft compartment—the one with the tribbles.

It hadn't occurred to him at the time that the tribbles had reproduced while in transit. He hadn't counted them when he'd brought them on board. Once he had discovered their rather soothing qualities, he'd merely made trip after trip, bringing in armful after armful until he'd figured he had enough. The compartment had only been about seventy percent full, but he had felt that there should be some room left for growth. He had even provided them with what he *thought* was an ample supply of the lichens upon which they seemed to be feeding.

Then came Mr. Nilz Baris and his quadrotriticale. And then the *Enterprise,* Captain Kirk, and Mr. Spock showed up. Then the Klingons arrived. After that, the tribbles somehow got into the storage compartments and gorged themselves on the poisoned grain. But they also eventually led Kirk to uncover Darvin as the Klingon agent responsible for the tampering. At that point, the Klingons left rather hurriedly and the Federation got the Organians' permission to develop Sherman's Planet by default. Finally, Kirk and his Vulcan science officer turned a day from bad to disastrous by glibly confining him to the station. His "crime" had been transporting animals proven harmful to human life, and his punishment was the singular task of removing all the tribbles from the station.

With no alternative, he had started his sentence by stuffing tribbles into his oversized tunic and taking them to a sealed cargo bay. After a few days of this drudgery, he had managed to fill barely one fifth of the bay. At that time, while he rested on a storage container contemplating his fate, a more expedient solution had begun to tempt him. He'd envisioned masses of tribbles being sucked into space by the rapid decompression of the cargo bay, their miserable little bodies becoming novas of protoplasm in some stellar chain reaction. He'd only gotten as far as some tentative tampering with the cargo bay door controls when he'd been discovered. Lurry had apparently been expecting something like this, and the threat of having to manually remove tribble guts from the walls of the cargo bay and station exterior had been enough to discourage further attempts.

Once more he had returned to the numbingly endless cycle of cargo bay to tribble pile to cargo bay. Meals, sleep cycles, and tribble collecting had all merged into some form of altered consciousness, and he'd begun to lose the distinctions between the phases. That imbalance had almost gotten to the point where his sanity could have been questioned. Fortunately, someone on the station had seen this coming and had interceded on his behalf. Soon thereafter, his schedule had been adjusted by the inclusion of standardized rest and exercise periods as well as the occasional day off. During these respites, Lurry would hold brief meetings with him to evaluate his progress. Sometimes Lurry would invite other station personnel from the various departments to attend.

Now, as he propelled himself forward on the smooth metallic surface of the duct's interior like a Gazanian salamander, he had to admit that those brainstorming sessions had contributed substantially to his reaching this point. At slightly less than the Vulcan's 17.9-year estimate, he was closing in on the last tribble. Of course, no one at those meetings would have had anything to do with the physical task of picking up any of the 1,567,117 surviving tribbles. However, the meetings did produce measures which were able to limit the tribbles' growth curves and make the completion of his task possible.

First, Mr. Lurry had declared it illegal to feed tribbles outside of secured areas within the station. Customers at the bar had been feeding them anything that had come to mind since the contaminated quadrotriticale had been disposed of. Only later had they realized the significance of that development. It had never occurred to them to consider evaluating what tribbles ate.

When the diverted freighter carrying the replacement grain for Sherman's Planet had arrived at the station, Cyrano had cornered one of the xenobiologists on board and had deluged her with questions until she had given him a five-kilogram sample of untainted grain and some simple experiments to perform on the tribbles. Sure enough, as they'd expected, the grain was somehow directly responsible for the rapid, uncontrolled population growth. But the full explanation had remained elusive. It wasn't until he'd been allowed back on his ship (under guard) that the answer appeared right in front of him.

The lichen.

The original tribbles hadn't eaten more than one tenth of the food supply in the compartment. This led to a hunch. He sent a message to the xenobiologist at the colony on Sherman's Planet. When he got the response three days later, he knew he was onto something. Using the directions contained in the reply and with Lurry's permission, he had station maintenance construct three test chambers. He'd placed the lichen in one, quadrotriticale in the second, and oral rehydration solution in the third. A series of sensitive microdetectors were placed to measure changes in the environmental chemistry.

The oral rehydration solution group had exactly the same number of tribbles as it had had at the beginning—ten. That wasn't surprising, because no one would drink the rehydration solution unless they had a near-fatal gastroenteritis. It had often been rumored to be part of the interrogation protocols for Klingons.

The second group, the lichen group, showed a modest growth in population, for tribbles. Thirty-five tribbles were present at the end of the third day of the test. Also interesting was the presence of small quantities of airborne protein molecules picked up by the detectors.

The final proof came in the third chamber or, to be more specific, what was left of the third chamber. The tribble population had grown so rapidly that the outward pressure of the bodies had caused the thin polymer walls to shatter. Fortunately, the other containment procedures had held. What was more important, however, was the presence of massive amounts of the same airborne proteins.

One more message was sent to Yersa, the xenobiologist. By that time, Dr. McCoy of the *Enterprise* had posted his autopsy of the tribble on the Starfleet Medical Newsnet. Among other items of interest beside the taxonomic classification, *Polygeminus grex* (how original), were the presence of spiracles, a single gonad, and a uterus. Once he'd informed Yersa about the airborne proteins and the other results of the food-population experiment, Yersa had become hooked. Somehow she managed to get transferred from her duties on Sherman's Planet to a research assignment on K-7. Her stay had been brief, however. She'd left almost immediately upon reviewing the data, bound for the tribbles' homeworld (unfortunately later given the rather sterile name of Iota Geminorum IV).

While Cyrano had continued his daily routine of tribble retrieval, Yersa had been off pursuing her studies into the secrets of tribble reproduction. Eons later, as it had seemed, she returned.

Contrary to Dr. McCoy's learned judgment, she'd discovered, tribbles were not "born pregnant." Actually, as it turned out, they had a rather stable, or for that matter sensible, population strategy. Tribble populations were governed strictly by the amount of available food—in this case, lichen. When the food supply was abundant, the release of procreation pheromones went up until a new steady state was achieved. When the food supply was decreased by seismic or volcanic activity, the population fell either by starvation or by not replacing losses from predation.

To test this hypothesis, Yersa had actually released the aerosolized pheromones into a small rock outcrop that was sprinkled with a minor distribution of tribbles. The result was as expected.

Apparently, there was something inherent in quadrotriticale that caused the tribbles to disregard their population safeguards. It was an intoxication similar to that produced by the waterborne virus on Psi 2000 which had nearly caused the loss of a starship several years before. Yersa had said she thought the starship involved had been the *Enterprise,* but she hadn't had time to check official Federation records.

Remembering the feeding of tribbles caused Cyrano to shake himself out of his reverie. He had come to the subsection junction. Another tricorder reading. It was time to report to Lurry. The dim lights and isolation of the ventilation ducts plus his need for companionship gave further reason for this action.

"We were wondering what was delaying you, Cyrano," said Lurry. "We're coming into some of the time-guesses in the tribble pool. We also have a few guests in the office who are anxious to see what's become of you."

"Then give me some idea of where I need to go from here."

"We think it's just ahead and slightly to the left of your current position. Is there an access panel on that side?"

"Yes, there is."

"That should be it."

Cyrano Jones doubted that it would be that easy, but at this point he was willing to accept some good fortune. He also knew he had earned it in some respects. Being effectively marooned on the station had been almost as hard to take as the Federation penal colony he'd been threatened with. The food had been almost as bad, and the physical demands probably worse. Most of his rotundity had disappeared within the first two to three years of his confinement. After that, he'd started noticing some muscle tone that he hadn't felt since he was barely old enough to drink Altair water.

There were some other, more subtle changes that he became aware of as well. One was his relationship with station manager John Lurry. Seventeen years ago, they were outwardly social with each other but that was about it. Lurry had been suspicious of Cyrano's every move. Knowing that had been an advantage for Cyrano. He had simply kept Lurry chasing shadows while the real business was being conducted elsewhere. The loss of Cyrano's ship had affected him more than he thought it possibly could. With nowhere to go, he'd found he no longer had anything to hide. The two of them had eventually found enough common ground to become friends.

Another was Yersa. Once she'd isolated the pro-reproductive pheromone, she'd begun working on isolating its negative counterpart. Her experiments had then progressed quickly, causing Cyrano to spend more and more time in the lab. She'd enlisted his aid in constructing some of the test chambers and in monitoring the tests themselves. To make up for some of his lost time, she became the first person to help in recovering the tribbles.

The anti-reproductive pheromone, once isolated, rapidly went through small and progressively larger scale tests on tribble groups. Zero population growth for tribbles had been achieved. Field testing on Iota Geminorum IV had commenced shortly afterward, using tribbles relocated to the planet via Cyrano's freighter. These tests had also proved successful, and more and more frequent tribble shipments followed. The fact that this had caused Yersa to spend more and more time away from the station had left Cyrano with a vague but increasing sense of loneliness.

Just then he caught the subtle sound he had been hoping for so long to hear. Somewhere between a purr and a chirp, it was the call of a tribble. It seemed sad, almost mournful to him, and he guessed it expressed the tribble equivalent of loneliness. He opened his tool kit and began working on the panel. In spite of himself, he began talking to the tribble, saying soothing nothings like those used when trying to quiet a child.

"Almost there," he said, the next to last fastener dropping to the duct with a clank. Then came the last one. He lowered the grate and peered inside.

The tribble was average size—about half as big as a human head—and white with faint traces of brown in color. It made no sound of resistance as Cyrano reached into the access duct and retrieved it. He stroked it absentmindedly for several moments, trying to decide what he was feeling.

There was relief at having finally completed his task, but there was also a feeling of loss because of that accomplishment. He was suddenly afraid that he would be unable to find a sense of purpose again, that his future life would just become a sequence of finding things to do. Almost one third of his life had been devoted to this pursuit, and all that remained was to take this tribble home to rejoin the others.

He flipped the communicator open. "I have the tribble."

"Energizing," responded a distantly familiar voice.

Before he could identify the speaker, he sensed the transporter beam carrier wave. After the brief disorientation that followed his being reassembled, he found himself lying on his right side and facing the dimly lit wall of the main transporter room. Except for the hum of air circulators the room was silent as well as dark. He got to his feet and turned around. Then the lights came on.

Cyrano's first impression was that he never knew that the transporter room could hold so many people. Whatever he had been about to say froze in his brain, and his mouth was left hanging at full open. He registered the presence of Lurry and Walt Mathison, the long-suffering bartender to whom the tribbles had been peddled. Most of the other members of the station staff were present as well.

Then he saw Yersa, her Argelian features highlighted by the way her smile brought out her eyes. Just behind her were several people in the red and black uniforms of Starfleet. He recognized Kirk immediately, despite the inevitable changes that had occurred over the last seventeen years. Beside him was his lovely communication officer, whose name Cyrano couldn't recall. The Vulcan science officer was at the transporter controls.

Cyrano was searching for the identities of the other *Enterprise* crew members when the room erupted into congratulatory noise. Applause, cheers, a banner welcoming him back, and everyone crowding around the transporter platform. He finally regained the control of enough facial muscles to close his mouth, but it only lasted a second or two. Everyone was laughing, most to the point of tears. Lurry was the first to shake his hand. Walt came up to him, took the tribble, and placed a drink in his hand. "I think you need this," he said quickly.

After several minutes, the room had quieted down to the point where Lurry could gather everyone's attention. He began to speak, starting with a description of the tribble situation as it had been at the beginning. He had just finished the part about the unmasking of Darvin when he was interrupted by someone shouting out something about who won the pool. Realizing that he was never going to finish his impromptu speech, Lurry acquiesced.

"The winning guess, only 3.6 minutes off, was submitted on behalf of Cyrano Jones by Mr. Spock of the *Enterprise.*"

Everyone applauded the result, even if some were disappointed in it. The applause level increased when Lurry announced that Kirk had released Cyrano's ship from station control. A further increase came with Lurry's last announcement that the main bar had been closed so that the celebration could be held there.

As everyone streamed out of the transporter room, Lurry caught Cyrano's arm and steered him over to where Kirk, Spock, and McCoy had remained. Lurry completed the introductions and explained that the *Enterprise* had stopped at the station to exchange cargo en route to Sherman's Planet where it was to be the Federation representative for the swearing in of Governor Nilz Baris.

"Congratulations, Mr. Jones," said Kirk, his hand extended. "I have to admit I didn't think you had it in you. It seems that I have underestimated you in several respects."

"Captain Kirk," said Cyrano, accepting the offered hand, "I can't quite say that I thank you for what you have put me through, but I also have to admit that most of the changes were for the better."

"You appear to be in great physical condition," said McCoy. "You see what can happen with a good diet and plenty of exercise, Jim?"

Kirk ignored the barb. "Mr. Jones, you have your ship and, from what Mr. Lurry says, a rather considerable sum at your disposal. Do you have any plans?"

"Actually, Captain," interrupted Lurry, "I do have some things to discuss with Cyrano before he should answer that question. First, we do have to return the remaining tribbles to their homeworld, and apparently only Cyrano and Yersa know its location."

"A wise precaution considering the proximity of the Klingon Empire," said Spock.

"Captain, if you please, I would like to take Mr. Jones to his celebration. We can complete your cargo transfers and requisitions in the morning if that is acceptable."

"Perfectly acceptable, Mr. Lurry. We will return to the *Enterprise* until we receive your signal."

"Very well, then," said Lurry as he escorted Cyrano out of the transporter room. The noise that came from the corridor after the doors closed indicated that the party would be boisterous.

"You're not staying for the party, Jim?" asked McCoy. "That's not like you. Is something wrong?"

"Nothing, Bones. I just don't feel my presence would add to the festivities. This is Cyrano's day. Let's let him enjoy it."

"No problem here. How about you, Spock? You look like you could use a good party."

"Really, Doctor. What could possibly give you the impression that I would actually participate in the reckless consumption of alcohol accompanied by such a raucous din?"

"Why, to take your mind off of all your errors in logic."

"You are referring to . . ."

"Well, when this whole affair started, you predicted that it would take 17.9 years, exactly, for Jones to clear the station of tribbles. You also predicted a time for the pool that was 3.6 minutes off. That's not like you, either."

"Need I remind you, Doctor, that I was basing my calculations on your assessment of the reproductive physiology of tribbles, and therefore my predictions relied on the uncertain theory that you knew what you were doing. To have missed the inherently obvious conclusion that tribble reproduction must have involved some form of population control and that some form of pheromone must be present, surely—"

The sound of a communicator being urgently flipped open stopped him in midphrase.

"Kirk to *Enterprise*. Three to beam up. Now, please, Mr. Scott."

The return to the *Enterprise* was uneventful, and the night, fortunately, passed without further incident. The designated cargo from the station was transferred to the *Enterprise*, and all was made ready for departure. Formal leave was taken and Mr. Lurry wished them well on their voyage.

"Ahead, full impulse, Mr. Sulu."

"Aye, Captain. Full impulse ahead."

"Captain, at full impulse, we won't reach Sherman's Planet for 6.73 days."

"Correct, Mr. Spock. I'm not in that much of a hurry to meet Governor Baris. Are you?"

The arch of Spock's left eyebrow was all the response Kirk needed.

Epilogue

It was near sunset on Iota Geminorum IV. The solitary freighter rested on its landing pylons in the midst of a rock-strewn depression between two small ridges. There were several large formations of granite nearby, but not so near as to be affected by the heat of the freighter's propulsion systems. The lengthening shadows all but concealed the ragged clefts within the formations and the rich growth of lichen within them.

Cyrano Jones stood at the foot of the freighter's aft loading ramp, looking out over the ridges as the edge of the reddening solar disk began to disappear beyond the ridge. There was the faint intermittent hum of some form of insect mixed with the definite cooing of masses of tribbles. He stood there for some time, fixing the sensations in his mind, for he knew he would not be returning to this place.

He knew some way would have to be found to protect this planet, because he knew the Klingons would eventually find it.

With the homeworld lying so close to the Neutral Zone, its discovery was almost inevitable. Some "navigational error" would probably arise, resulting in some wayward battle cruiser finding its way to the source of its hated enemy. The fact that the tribbles could create such a hostile response yet be so totally unable to defend themselves would only further enrage the Klingon commander. He would order all weapons fired, all energy sources expended, seeking nothing less than the total annihilation of the planet.

As the last traces of twilight dissolved into the night sky, Cyrano remained where he stood. No answers came. All that did come was an increasing sense of fatigue. The answers he sought would have to arise from somewhere else.

He walked slowly up the ramp and hit the key sequence to close the hatchway. Minutes later, he rejoined Yersa and Lurry on the freighter's small bridge. Nothing needed to be said. Yersa merely looked in his direction, then turned to the control panel in front of her. She typed in the commands to bring the engines on line and waited patiently for the monitors to read nominal.

"Let's go," was all Cyrano could say.

The freighter rose slowly into the stars with no sign that any of the life-forms below took notice of its passage. Soon it was orbiting the planet, its passengers counting down in silence the time until the impulse engines engaged. The course for Station K-7 had already been laid in, and the computers executed the departure sequence with minimal supervision.

It was Lurry who decided to speak first. "Cyrano, I have something to ask of you, but I want you to take your time before answering. I'm sure that you can guess where I'm going with this, but please let me finish.

"This is the first time I've been off the station in twenty years. I don't believe that you know that. Frankly, I've begun to think that I've become part of it. And I've come to think of you as a part of it as well. I would miss you considerably if you decided to leave.

"So, I'm going to make you an offer. The station has always had a certain amount of smuggling going on, and I'm sure that with your . . . experience in such matters, you know a lot more about it than I do. Certainly, I would like to cut down on some of the trafficking in Romulan ale or, at least, get a chance to taste some of the damned stuff. I could use your assistance, say as chief of security?"

Lurry rose and moved to the rear of the bridge. "Please think about it," he said. "I'll be in my compartment."

Cyrano, struck by the ironies of the situation, tried unsuccessfully to keep his laughter to himself. Yersa, turning at the sound, rose and stood next to him. He looked up at her, wondering what she thought of the offer. She had been almost as much a part of the station over the last several years as he had been. He didn't know what to think or say.

"And just what do you think of said proposal, my dear lady?" he asked, mustering as much of the bravado that had carried him through those earlier years as he could.

Yersa looked down into his eyes and smiled slightly as she laid her hand on his arm.

"I'd seriously think about it."

The Lights in the Sky

Phaedra M. Weldon

"Come in."

Shahna continued pacing the length of her cramped quarters aboard the *Excelsior.* Her environmental controls were locked on cool, the lights were too bright, and she disliked the beige and brown furniture Starfleet elected to decorate with. The only splash of color in the room besides herself was an arrangement of roses, sent by Captain Sulu upon her arrival.

When the door to her quarters closed, she stopped and whirled around, her silver and white skirt pinwheeling at her feet. She faced the tall uniformed man who stood just inside her doorway, his arms clasped as always behind his back.

"Ambassador," Mr. Spock said in a toneless voice.

Shahna crossed her arms over her chest, her green and gray hair curling in the folds of her sleeves. "Why have we changed course?"

When Mr. Spock remained silent, Shahna fixed him with her

emerald gaze. In the silence she became aware of the *Excelsior*'s engines. Their ceaseless vibrations beneath her feet, the tireless hum encircling her, permeating the still air between them.

Finally looking away, Shahna approached him hesitantly. After spending countless months with him in negotiations concerning Triskelion's long-awaited admission into the Federation, she did not know him. Possibly because a small part of her remained in awe of him. Before the negotiations began, she had never thought of Spock as a real person, only a voice from the skies, from her past. A voice Jim Kirk had called friend.

"I have been monitoring the bridge communications," Shahna said hurriedly, lowering her arms, looking into his face again.

Mr. Spock raised an upswept eyebrow. "Then you know Captain Sulu is answering a distress call in the Gamma system. By Starfleet's order."

"Doesn't he understand how important it is for me to reach Earth? The meeting is tomorrow."

"The Klingons have been made aware of our present situation and have agreed to the delay."

Shahna clenched her fists. "The Romulans are my concern."

Mr. Spock almost sighed. "They have been contacted but have not yet responded. Starfleet has rescheduled the meeting for the day after tomorrow. I was on my way to inform you of this before you called for me."

Shahna opened her mouth, then closed it, unsure of what to say. She knew shouting at a Vulcan was senseless, the same as staring one down. Turning, she faced the windows that made up the farthest wall of her quarters. The stars were mere streaks of light racing across a black expanse. "By then it may be too late."

"Ambassador Shahna," Mr. Spock began, his voice gentle but questioning. "The attack on your world by the Romulans has been dealt with by the Federation. Since that attack has precipitated your joining the Federation and you are now under its protection, I do not see the true urgency for this meeting. To be honest, I do not see the point to this meeting at all." Mr. Spock stepped forward as Shahna turned to face him. "The nonaggression treaty with the Romulans can be handled without your presence. It is my understanding Provider One did not approve of your leaving."

"He did not." She lowered her gaze. "But the Romulans must be made to sign that treaty with Triskelion before the Conversion. Admiral Beckett is in complete agreement with my being there." Shahna folded her arms over her chest. "A show of strength."

"If the Romulans learn of the impending Conversion, your life may be in danger." Mr. Spock relaxed his stance, and his expression softened. "It is my theory that your urgency and anxiety stems more from the great disappointment I sensed when you beamed aboard than from whether the Romulans sign the treaty or not."

Shahna tried not to show the embarrassment she felt at being read so easily. She was a fool to think she could mask her true intentions from a Vulcan. "You are correct. I was hoping Captain Kirk would be here."

"Then I am correct in assuming your true intent is to seek him out?"

With his hand, Mr. Spock gestured to the twin sofas. "Please, sit down."

Once they were seated facing one another, Mr. Spock continued. "Tell me, does his scheduled appearance at Starfleet Headquarters in the coming days explain the scheduling of the meeting?"

Sighing heavily, Shahna leaned forward, placing her elbows on her knees. Staring at her hands, Shahna took a deep breath. "Yes, though the timing of the Conversion is also a factor. You have seen for yourself what the Providers created for us because of Captain Kirk."

He nodded. "I believe the Providers may have exceeded what Captain Kirk had intended."

"That is what we have hoped. Since the day of our freedom, I have followed Jim Kirk's advice. Everything I have done, all of us have done, has been for him. Don't you see? I need to see him again, and this may be my only chance. Once the Conversion is complete, I will not be able to see him again as flesh."

When Mr. Spock remained silent, Shahna raised her gaze to his face. "I knew he would be within reach during this time."

"So this treaty is not truly as important as you have implied." Shahna's expression hardened. "On the contrary. Do you know how much the Romulans frighten me, Mr. Spock? When they attacked, I realized what power they had. I also knew my own mortality. I have worked hard at building my world, believing that Jim Kirk was watching me from above as the Providers did. I want to protect what we have done from animals such as the Romulans. The treaty is very important to me. The place of the meeting merely serves a dual purpose."

Shahna looked down at her hands. "I wanted to see Jim Kirk. I want to tell him what I've learned, what I've accomplished. I want him to be proud of . . . me."

She was not surprised at Mr. Spock's silence. She had spoken irrationally, emotionally, and he would not understand.

"Then," Mr. Spock said softly, and Shahna looked at him. "Once the meeting is over, we must make it imperative to find Captain Kirk."

Shahna smiled. "Thank you." But behind that smile lurked an old fear. What if, after all this time, Captain Kirk did not want to see her? Or worse still, what if he didn't remember her?

The *Excelsior* arrived on schedule after leaving the Gamma system and began a standard orbit around Earth. Mr. Spock and Ambassador Shahna beamed directly into the heart of Starfleet where Shahna was formally introduced to the Federation president.

"Welcome, welcome," he said, taking her hand in his and kissing the back of her wrist. "It is an honor to meet you. I have read all of Captain Kirk's logs repeatedly through the years. Do you realize you are somewhat of a living legend here at the academy? I half expected Captain Kirk to insist on meeting you himself."

Shahna felt her cheeks grow hot, and she looked down at the floor, embarrassed and disheartened.

"Mr. President," Mr. Spock said. "Would it be possible to set up a meeting with Captain Kirk after the meeting has concluded?"

The president straightened his shoulders and sighed. "I'm afraid that won't be possible. Captain Kirk is quite busy with the upcoming launch this afternoon. Perhaps tomorrow."

"The ambassador must return to Triskelion tomorrow."

The president eyed Mr. Spock for a moment, then looked at Shahna. "Well . . . we'll see. Right now, Admiral Beckett and the others are waiting."

After a whirlwind of introductions made in one of the large conference rooms, Shahna eyed her opponents. Ambassador Renzel of the Romulan Star Empire was a tall, gaunt man who radiated arrogance and the look of self-taught superiority. She nodded formally to him, but stopped in her tracks when she saw the Romulan standing behind the ambassador.

"What is he doing here?" she demanded. "This is the animal that led the attack on my world."

Admiral Beckett cleared his throat. "Commander Dosean has something he would like to say to you, Ambassador."

Dosean glanced furtively at Renzel, then took a sharp step forward. He clicked his heels together and looked straight ahead at a point above Shahna's head. "On behalf of my vessel and her crew, and the Romulan Star Empire . . . I . . . apologize." The words ground out of his mouth, and his face twisted in distaste. This apology had been forced upon him. And that, Shahna decided, could only lead to trouble.

General Korrd of the Klingon Empire gave a hearty guffaw, and Shahna turned to him. "General, I have not been able to formally thank you for your aid in stopping the Romulan attack." She crossed her fisted right hand over her left shoulder. *"Qapla'!"* she said in a powerful voice.

General Korrd's face gave only a flicker of amazement before he returned the salute. "An honor, Ambassador." General Korrd turned to Mr. Spock. "Captain, it is good to see you again."

Mr. Spock nodded. "And you, General. I must give congratulations. I understand you and your House have been returned to a place of honor in the Klingon Empire."

"Well . . ." Admiral Beckett gestured to a dark oblong table which acted as the centerpiece to the room. "I suggest we get started."

Mr. Spock sat on Shahna's right. Admiral Beckett sat at one

end of the table, General Korrd at the other. Ambassador Renzel and Commander Dosean sat facing Shahna and Spock.

"Let's cut directly to the heart of the matter," Admiral Beckett began. He rested his elbows on the table and clasped his hands together. "The Provider technology."

Shahna watched the Romulans' faces as she had been trained to do as a drill thrall. "Always watch your opponent's eyes," her thrall trainer had said. "For in them you will see the truth of their moves." The look that passed between the two Romulans spoke volumns.

Renzel turned a sweet smile to the admiral. "I'm afraid you've mistaken the purpose of this little gathering. We are here to negotiate a trading treaty."

"I'm afraid not, sir," Admiral Beckett said in a tight smile of his own.

Mr. Spock spoke up. "Sir, the attack and near invasion your people attempted on Triskelion would not logically precipitate peaceful trading. Therefore, it is the Federation's opinion you were after the one valuable asset the thralls possess. The advanced technology left behind by the Providers, the former inhabitants of that planet."

Shahna watched Renzel and Mr. Spock lock their gazes together. She shook her head, knowing the futility of trying to stare down a Vulcan. After several moments, the Romulan looked away. "It is a technology that demands exploitation."

"And," General Korrd spoke up, "this technology, its ability to transmute thought into energy, should be exploited by the Romulan Star Empire solely?" The Klingon laughed mockingly.

Commander Dosean slammed his fist on the table. The items on its surface shook. "Would you have the Federation alone control that power?"

"Commander." Admiral Beckett's voice was quiet, but demanded authority. "The Federation has already agreed the advanced technology of the Providers shall remain in the hands of their beneficiaries, the thralls. Neither the Federation nor the Klingon Empire will touch it, though the planet is now formally under the jurisdiction of Starfleet."

Ambassador Renzel glared across the table at Shahna. She

forced his stare back with a powerful emerald one of her own. "So Starfleet would leave this power in the hands of children instead of sharing it with civilized races."

Shahna grabbed the edge of the table, her stare pulling his inward. "You dare call yourselves civilized? You?" She lifted her right hand and pointed a long, slender finger at Dosean. "Who under a banner of peace, invaded our city and nearly destroyed almost three decades of hard work? You killed dozens of thralls. I watched you murder Tamoon, with no reason."

Commander Dosean rose from his chair. "She killed my second."

"Because you killed Galt."

"He warned the Federation."

Shahna rose from her chair. "On my orders," she straightened her shoulders, "there will be no trading treaty with Romulans this day or any other."

"This is insane!" shouted Ambassador Renzel.

General Korrd stood. "I see the truth of it, Romulan. You are afraid of this technology."

"I am afraid of nothing. I simply do not agree to children wielding such power."

"Children," Mr. Spock emphasized the word, "do not. Provider One does, and he is in full agreement with the Federation."

Renzel and Dosean turned astonished faces to the Vulcan. "You lie. There are no more Providers. How else could we have attacked?" Commander Dosean demanded.

"Because we trusted you. We were unschooled in the ways of treachery," Shahna said. "Provider One will not allow that to happen again."

"We offer a solution," Mr. Spock said, putting his elbows on the table and steepling his fingers together. "Consider a nonaggression treaty with Triskelion. This way, all visits to the surface would be monitored by us, and Triskelion would not use its technology against the Romulans."

Ambassador Renzel sat down. When Dosean did not, Renzel yanked his arm, forcing him back into his seat. "A nonaggression treaty? A coward's peace?"

Shahna sat down as well, her face composed, her manner

poised. "It is the only condition I bring to the table. Sign the treaty." She shrugged. "Otherwise, the fate of Romulan ships entering our space will be entirely up to the Provider."

She watched Renzel carefully. With this new information about the Providers, the Romulan ambassador's aggressive stance was diminishing. His expression was mixed, no longer determined, but unsure. Good, she thought, let him truly fear the technology as Korrd had guessed.

Ambassador Renzel stood slowly, and with a bow to the admiral and General Korrd he pulled Dosean's arm again. The commander stood, his eyes never leaving Shahna's. "I will inform my government," the ambassador said; then he and Dosean left the conference room.

Admiral Beckett sat back and gave a long sigh. "Well, that went rather well, didn't it?"

General Korrd shook his head. "There is something wrong. I knew Renzel when he was commander. A shrewd man, and devilish. He gave in too easily." He turned to Shahna. "Is it true the Providers are alive? I had heard they had gone away. The rumors . . . ?"

Shahna pursed her lips. "Provider One remains, but only in a limited capacity. If he could have stopped the Romulans that day, he would have."

General Korrd frowned. "I do not understand."

"The Providers are, were, an evolved race," Mr. Spock said softly. "Their physical forms are little more than simple organs, as Captain Kirk explained in his entries of that day. But their consciousness was vast. Since the establishment of the thralls as more than athletic competitors, the Providers' attention has turned outward, toward other realms. This is merely conjecture, I might add. Provider One remains because of his wager to Captain Kirk."

General Korrd looked across the table at Admiral Beckett. "Is there protection for Triskelion now?"

"The *Excelsior* and the *Saratoga* have been dispatched. They will safeguard the planet until Ambassador Shahna returns." Admiral Beckett smiled. "We've already discussed the possibility of the Romulans not agreeing to the treaty."

"But what will prevent them from attacking even if they do?" General Korrd looked back to Shahna. "Once Provider One is gone, Triskelion will be vulnerable. Starfleet cannot guard your world indefinitely."

Shahna glanced at Admiral Beckett. In her eyes she asked if she should tell the Klingon more of the truth. To her surprise, the admiral nodded.

Shahna turned to Korrd. "After tomorrow, I will be the new Provider."

General Korrd sat back, his mouth open. "You . . . you can't be serious."

"The Provider machines are what keep Triskelion alive. And that technology cannot work without a Provider at its center. Without one, all life on Triskelion would stop."

General Korrd looked from Shahna to Mr. Spock.

Mr. Spock said, "Sir, the technology the Romulans so intently wish to possess has one fatal flaw. Those things brought into physical form are not permanent. The Providers have held the thought forms into place through the centuries, using their consciousness, massing energy around the forms to coalesce into matter. That is why Triskelion is barren on most of its surface. The planet itself is not habitable. The Providers' past history has destroyed most of its landmass.

"Once the Providers are gone, there will be no one to hold the forms in place. Shahna," Mr. Spock said as he glanced at her, "is to replace Provider One in what is called a Conversion."

The general shook his head. "I mean no disrespect, Ambassador, but how? It was my understanding the Providers' minds were so advanced, so infinitely greater. How can she replace them?"

"Forced evolution." Shahna looked down at her hands. "Galt was to be the new Provider. But when Dosean killed him, Provider One chose me, and my change was begun. The Providers' technology is vast, General, and I do not pretend to understand what will happen to me.

"I know I will live several lifetimes as a Provider, giving and sustaining life, and I will be able to travel to the stars as no other has done. I will be more than what I am. I am already more than what Captain Kirk found on that planet so many years ago." Shahna looked up at the general and smiled.

"As Provider," Mr. Spock said, "Shahna will prevent the Romulans from attacking and taking the technology. If she does not return, the planet is indeed vulnerable."

"Then why this meeting?" General Korrd asked. "Why endanger yourself here, with the Romulans? If they knew the truth . . ."

"Two reasons," Admiral Beckett said. "To establish a nonaggression treaty. The treaty would be a viable solution to keeping the peace rather than having a Provider blow a Romulan battle cruiser from the stars." Admiral Beckett smiled at Shahna. "And secondly, because Ambassador Shahna requested the meeting be here. After the Conversion, Shahna will cease in the body she presently inhabits. I understand she has always wanted to visit Earth. How could I refuse such a request?"

Mr. Spock stood. "Gentlemen, if you will excuse us, I believe the ambassador and I have other matters to attend to."

The admiral stood and smiled at Shahna. "It was a pleasure, Ambassador. I will inform you the minute I hear from the Romulans." He looked at Korrd, who was lumbering around the table. "General, I assume you will keep what you have heard in the strictest of confidence?"

The general bowed. "I will indeed. And I would like to offer my services as bodyguard for the ambassador."

Admiral Beckett shook his head. "I don't think that will be necessary. The Romulans would be foolish to attempt an attack here at Starfleet."

Shahna watched General Korrd's face. He nodded, but his eyes sought out Spock's. Something passed between the Vulcan and the Klingon before the general left the conference room.

Once outside in the corridor, Shahna turned to Mr. Spock. "Isn't it odd that the admiral would want to tell Korrd the truth?"

"Admiral Beckett is a tried politician. They are a different type of human, and one I do not wish to argue with."

Shahna nodded, though not fully comprehending. Looking around, she asked, "Where are we going?"

"To find Captain Kirk, of course," Mr. Spock said.

They walked through several hallways before stepping into a brightly lit room. The view of San Francisco Bay was a breathtaking backdrop to dimly lit tables and plush chairs. At a bar to the left sat members of several species, each dressed in regulation red and black. Mr. Spock led Shahna to one of the tables nearest the windows. She found she couldn't take her eyes from the view.

"What is that?"

"That," Spock said, pulling a chair out for her, "is the Golden Gate Bridge. Now, if you'll excuse me, I'm going to check to see if Captain Kirk is here and have him paged. Hopefully he has not already left for Spacedock. The meeting ran longer than I expected."

Unable to stay put, Shahna rose and went to the window. She pressed the palms of her hands against the cool surface and looked down. She was not as far up as she thought. There were dozens of beings, humans and others, strolling along the walkway below. Some were seated together on benches; others were looking out at the bridge.

A single man standing at the edge of the walkway facing the bay caught her eyes. Something in the way he stood was familiar. His dress was much like everyone else's, red and black. His hands were locked behind his back. His feet wide apart, his shoulders straight.

A dark-skinned woman approached him and he turned.

Shahna's heart stopped.

The profile. So proud. The face. The same smile he had given her as he had touched her cheek so long ago.

"Jim Kirk!" she screamed, pounding on the glass.

He couldn't hear her. She watched him embrace this woman, and in an instant Shahna knew her. Uhura. Yes, Uhura, she who had been Lars's charge.

Pounding on the glass again, Shahna screamed Kirk's name. Desperate, she turned from the lounge and charged down the hallway. There had to be a way out!

She turned down what seemed like never-ending corridors. Brown. All brown. People in red and black. They stared at her as she passed. She needed to get out. Outside, to the walkway. She found some stairs and raced down.

Rounding a corner, she saw a glass door. Panting, Shahna looked through the glass and saw them, Kirk and Uhura, laughing and talking together.

No.

They were moving away.

But as she reached the door, something shot out from behind the wall of an intersecting hallway, tripping her. Her skirts wrapped around her feet and she fell.

Shahna shook her head and started to get up. Something crashed down on her back, pinning her to the ground.

"Poor little thrall," a familiar voice growled above her. "So, you are to be the new Provider."

Dosean.

Shahna painfully twisted her upper body around, straining to see his face. He glared down at her, his hands resting on his hips.

"You listened in?" she gasped.

"Stupid Starfleet," he laughed. "They are so trusting. No guards. It was simple. But now we know what to do. How to take what should be ours. As we speak, your world is under attack. And I alone will become Provider to the galaxy."

"Starfleet has sent ships," she gasped.

"They will be too late. We are quicker, smarter. And now" —Dosean rubbed his hands together—"it is my duty to make sure no other Providers step into the machine."

Shahna heard Provider One in her mind, reminding her of battles won, victories, and strength. Before Jim Kirk arrived.

Before freedom.

As Dosean reached for his disruptor, Shahna studied his stance. He was off balance, keeping strength in his left leg to force her down. A weakness!

She twisted around to his right leg, and with a powerful blow from her right hand knocked the back of his knee. He collapsed forward with a yell. Shahna twisted, bringing up her leg and kicking him in the face. She came up on her feet and kicked him in his side. Dosean yelled again, still attempting to draw his disruptor.

Shahna kicked him again, knocking the weapon across the floor. But as she lifted her leg to kick him a fourth time, Dosean rolled away and grabbed her booted foot. She lost her balance, twisting backward to the floor. She landed with a sickening thud on the hard tiles, face first.

Dosean yelled and ran for his weapon. Shahna shook her head again, trying not to lose consciousness, pushing herself up with her hands. She was too long out of practice—too long settling disputes with words, not actions. When she looked up, Dosean had his weapon trained on her.

"Surprising," he muttered. He was bleeding from his nose and a long gash on his cheek. "For a child." He leveled the disruptor.

Shahna barely saw the shadow move behind Dosean. Suddenly, something crashed into the Romulan's back, sending him forward onto the floor, the disruptor skittering across the tiles.

General Korrd stepped out of the shadows, a grin on his face. "I knew you were up to something."

Dosean shook his own head and turned, rolling onto his feet. He crouched before the large Klingon, then spit blood onto the polished floors. "You think you are a match for me?" he demanded with much bravado. "You are old and fat. You attack from behind."

But General Korrd only laughed. "And you, Romulan? You attack a woman from behind. You are braver? You have more honor?"

Dosean charged the Klingon, but Korrd stepped to the side, catching the Romulan in the back with a powerful blow. Dosean slammed to the ground, and Korrd placed a booted foot on Dosean's back. The Romulan tried to rise, but Korrd shoved him down again. "No, no, my dear Romulan. We must wait for your guards."

Shahna stood shakily, leaning heavily on the wall beside her. "You . . . you knew?"

General Korrd nodded. "Romulans are not honorable."

Mr. Spock appeared then with three Starfleet security personnel. He looked at the scene and nodded to Korrd. "You were right, General. We owe you this day."

General Korrd removed his foot, then bent down and pulled

38

the struggling and bleeding Romulan up with one hand. Dosean continued kicking in midair. "My payment will be to see this one locked up."

"As you wish. Mr. Loveen, please accompany the general, but . . ." He put up a finger. "Do not interfere if the Romulan tries to escape. Let the general handle the prisoner."

The young security officer smiled, then saluted Mr. Spock. "Aye, sir."

Shahna watched them retreat down a hall. Then she turned to the doorway, peering steadily through the glass. "He . . . he," Shahna tried to form the words, tried to point to the door. But her vision blurred and she began to fall.

Mr. Spock caught her and lifted her in his arms as the two remaining guards followed them back down the hall.

Shahna looked out the door before Mr. Spock turned a corner.

Kirk and Uhura were gone.

As she knew they were.

Staring at the reflection in the mirror, Shahna sighed.

Dr. Chapel touched her arm. "The brusies will fade eventually, and your nose has been mended."

Shahna did not want Jim Kirk to see her like this. He would no longer think her beautiful. He would see her as repulsive. Ugly.

Mr. Spock walked into the Federation Medical Facility. "I understand you are well enough to leave?"

Shahna put the mirror on the bed she was sitting on and nodded. "Dosean did not do as much damage as he would've liked, but I was sloppy. I should never have run off like that. I should have known he would try something."

Mr. Spock nodded, placing his arms behind his back. "The *Excelsior* and the *Saratoga* were able to turn back a Romulan vessel entering Triskelion space. It would appear Commander Dosean radioed ahead of his discovery. He figured that once you were dead, a new Provider would not be named immediately, and he and his ship could steal the unmanned technology."

"Are you saying Ambassador Renzel knew nothing of this?"

"No. He is denying any knowledge of his first officer's actions, and the Romulan government has sent its apologies. A new ambassador was dispatched with a message assuring the Federation he would represent the empire in signing the nonaggression treaty. It would appear the knowledge of a new Provider, one with reason to distrust the Romulans, has renewed their fear of Triskelion."

"I would like to thank General Korrd if I may. He was following me, wasn't he? Against Admiral Beckett's recommendation."

"Yes and no. The admiral suspected treachery by the Romulans. If they had heard the admiral giving Korrd orders to guard you, they would not have made their move."

"Then I would like to speak to him before I go."

Mr. Spock nearly smiled, and Shahna widened her eyes. "I'm afraid the general is enjoying himself interrogating Commander Dosean. It appears Ambassador Renzel has abandoned his charge. But the general knows you are grateful."

Shahna looked down at her torn skirts. She tried to straighten them to little avail. "I saw Jim Kirk, and a woman whom I thought was Uhura. I tried to get to them. That is when Dosean attacked."

"I see." Mr. Spock nodded as he stepped forward. "Then you have not truly finished your mission here. Starfleet command has commissioned the *Yorktown* to carry you home. The *Excelsior* and the *Saratoga* will continue on with their missions once the *Yorktown* sets up a standard orbit around Triskelion, and the *Yorktown* will continue to guard your home until the Conversion is complete."

"Thank you."

"Do not thank me. General Korrd was insistent. He will be leading a Klingon flagship to honor that day. Which, I understand, if all goes well, will be tomorrow."

Shahna looked up into Mr. Spock's dark eyes. "You said my mission was not complete."

"You have not met with Captain Kirk. I have tried to contact him repeatedly, but he is now on Spacedock. They are preparing to launch a very special ship today. I have arranged for you to be there."

Shahna blinked, her green eyes showing brightly through the bruises. "You have? Will I see him?"

"If you wish."

"But . . ." She touched her nose tentatively. "My face. I am truly unfit to see him now. He will think I am ugly."

"Shahna." Mr. Spock reached out and took her hand in a very un-Vulcanlike manner. "The wonder of Captain Kirk is that he sees beauty in everything. Your injuries will make no difference."

Mr. Spock released her hand. "I have arranged new clothes for you. We leave as soon as you are ready."

Half an hour later, Mr. Spock was leading her from the transporter room of Spacedock and into a hallway packed with people.

Shahna was dizzied by the phantasmagoria of faces. Strange, alien smells and colors. Through it all was the constant red and black of Starfleet.

"Who are all these people?" She raised her voice to be heard over the melee.

"Federation Press Corps," came Mr. Spock's response.

"Who? What do they do? What are all those devices on their heads?"

Mr. Spock leaned down to speak in her ear. "They are here to record this event, although Captain Kirk has been known to refer to them as Selurian space fleas. Others throughout the Federation will want to see Captain Kirk and the others' reactions throughout the maiden voyage."

Shahna did not understand all of what Mr. Spock said. She looked around as he was doing, trying to see a familiar face in the crowd.

Mr. Spock brought his wrist communicator to his ear and listened intently. Then he said something Shahna couldn't hear and grabbed her arm gently. "It would appear that Captain Kirk and the others are already boarding a shuttle to take them to the ship."

Shahna's eyes widened as her hopes crashed toward the planet below. "Then I have missed him again?"

Mr. Spock pointed behind the crowd and directed her through another door.

The quiet was nearly deafening as the doors closed behind them. Shahna stared in awe at the room before her. Windows stretched from ceiling to floor, behind rows of clothed tables. She stepped forward, her eyes scanning the great ship displayed through the transparent aluminum.

As she neared the window, walking slowly, afraid the vision would suddenly fade and she would awaken in the Medical Facility again, a name came into focus, seemingly painted with care on the side of the ship.

Enterprise 1701-B. B?

She turned to Mr. Spock, who stood nearly as transfixed as she. "He has a new ship? Is this a new *Enterprise?"*

"It is not his ship. Captain John Harriman will be her captain, but Captain Kirk, Mr. Scott, and Mr. Chekov will be aboard for the first voyage. For posterity, as Dr. McCoy would say."

"Chekov is here as well?" Shahna turned back to the vision before her. How often had she pictured herself aboard that ship, with Captain Kirk at the helm? "Can we go aboard?"

"I'm afraid not. But I was hoping we might—"

The doors opened, letting in the shouts of the crowds outside. The cry of a single name followed one man into the room as Shahna turned around.

"Captain Kirk! Can we have one—"

"Spock, couldn't this wait until after—" The man stopped in midsentence, staring at Shahna.

Shahna froze. It was him. Older now. But the same, dressed in the red and black of Starfleet. He stopped just inside the doorway, his face equally caught in a mask of surprise.

Then his face brightened into a wide grin and he went to her.

Shahna began to cry as his arms went around her, holding her close.

"I didn't think . . . I didn't dare believe . . ." she said breathlessly.

Captain Kirk pulled back, never letting his arms fall from hers. His eyes roamed her face and he put a gentle hand to her cheek. "You never believed what?"

"That I would see you. That you would . . . remember me."

"Oh Shahna," he said, still grinning from ear to ear. "How could I forget a face like that?" He gingerly touched her bruises. "I heard from Mr. Spock what happened, and after having fought you myself so many years ago, I am amazed Dosean is still alive."

"But General Korrd was the one who saved me," she said shakily. Her entire body trembled, unable to fully comprehend the reality of her dreams before her. That she was once again in his arms was almost too much to bear. "Oh, I have so much to tell you. I did what you told me. I've learned so much."

"I know, I know," he said gently. "And I want to hear it all. Really. But there's something I have to do first. This shouldn't take too long. We're only going around the edge of our solar system and back. And then . . ." He touched her green and gray hair, smiling still. "And then we'll talk. I know you have to get back, and I want to hear all about it. And I'm sure Uhura and Chekov will want to be here too. We'll have dinner."

"Promise?"

"I promise. Now, before I get into too much trouble—"

The doors opened again and two uniformed men stepped in. "Captain Kirk, we have to go if we're to launch on time."

Captain Kirk scowled at them, then turned a happy face back to her. "Stay here with Spock. Wait for me."

Then, beyond anything Shahna had dreamed of, Captain Kirk kissed her, slowly, passionately; and her legs felt wobbly beneath her.

Then he was gone, carried away by the two men and into the shouting crowds beyond the doors.

Mr. Spock stepped forward. "Are you all right, Ambassador?"

Shahna smiled so widely she thought her face would break. Her heart soared beyond the stars and she clapped her hands together in joy. "Oh wonderful, Mr. Spock. Wonderful."

Shahna watched as the battered *Enterprise*-B limped back into Spacedock. The gaping hole in the ship faced her, mocked her. It was as if space itself had taken him back, returning him to the stars.

Shahna was alone in the room with the magnificent view. She sensed a hush throughout the world below her. They mourned with her, but did they feel her anguish? Did they know her grief?

Finally she sat down in one of the plush chairs. A candle burned in a crystal glass in the center of the table. She reached in and pinched it out.

The doors opened, and Mr. Spock stepped in. His Vulcan control seemed strained, and his face was paler than usual as he walked stiffly to her. He turned and faced the ship, watching as it completed docking maneuvers, his arms clasped tightly behind his back.

"Mr. Spock?" she asked quietly. Would he speak? Could he speak? The few who had come into the room with the news spoke of Spock and Kirk's friendship, and one of the men had taken bets on how well his Vulcan control would last.

But Mr. Spock turned to her with a calm face and raised an eyebrow. "Yes, Ambassador? Are you well?"

"I was more concerned about you." She picked up a piece of silverware and fondled it between her fingers. "I know how close you were."

He nodded and returned to staring out at the ship. "He returned my life to me once. He was a great man."

Shahna stood and came to stand beside him. "There are some who would not understand your words. But I do. When there is grief greater than the heart can bear, then words are inadequate."

He only nodded and continued to stare outside. She followed his gaze and realized he did not look at the ship, but at the stars behind it.

She too looked out at those lights. "If I had not seen his smile, and known his happiness . . ." Shahna smiled. "Now I can hold him in my heart, and share him with my people. Generations of Triskelions will know the man who gave them freedom."

Shahna put her hands to the glass and looked sideways at Mr. Spock. His face was expressionless, but even now she saw his grief.

"I cannot believe, nor do I sense, his death," he said finally, quietly.

"He will not die as long as we remember him," she said, turning her emerald gaze back to the stars.

They stood there together for a time in silence, separated by a space of a few inches. But Shahna knew in her heart they were closer now than ever. She finally knew him.

A single tear flowed down her cheek. "And I make a promise to you, Jim Kirk, as I did before, to always watch the lights in the sky, and remember."

Reflections

Dayton Ward

STARDATE 48649.7

Jean-Luc Picard looked down through the twisted wreckage of
the fallen bridge and into the face of James Kirk. He could see
the life draining away from behind the powerful hazel eyes. The
injured man was struggling not to give in to the immense pain
his wounds had to be causing. Picard desperately wanted to do
something, anything, to help, but he knew in his heart the man
was wounded mortally.

"It was fun." Kirk uttered the words with a small smile. Was
this contentment that Picard saw?

Then, the smile was replaced for the briefest of moments with
a look of confusion. Picard could not be sure, but he thought it
was the look of someone who was finally, ultimately realizing the
end was near.

Time is a predator that stalks us all our lives.

Tolian Soran's haunting words echoed in Picard's mind as he
studied Kirk's face, watched as the color slowly, inexorably

drained away. After being thwarted countless times, the predator was indeed finally gaining on James Kirk.

"Oh my," the injured man whispered, the light behind his eyes beginning to dim.

From an oddly detached viewpoint, James T. Kirk watched himself deliver those final words, then die as Jean-Luc Picard looked on helplessly.

Jean-Luc Picard, captain of the *Enterprise*. Not his *Enterprise,* but that was now a fact of no importance. Nothing appeared to be a fact of importance anymore.

Suddenly, the scene was lost as everything faded amidst an onslaught of blinding light. He thought he could feel his body . . . no . . . his very *existence* begin to dissolve.

So, this is death?

Light faded and blackness replaced it, though not the darkness one experienced when the lights are suddenly turned off. He couldn't quite put his finger on it, but there was something different.

Of course, he shouldn't be able to put his finger on anything. He shouldn't even have fingers. While he was at it, he realized that he shouldn't be realizing any of this.

Am I dead, or what?

He could feel his fingers, and the rest of his body for that matter. His hands brushed the material of his uniform jacket, over the smooth finish of his belt buckle. He hadn't been wearing it on Veridian III, had he? Where had it come from?

Where am I?

He attempted to take a step forward and was surprised to discover that he could. But where to go, in this unending darkness?

However, the darkness was fading. Shapes began to form around him, color washing over the objects as they acquired substance. He watched a long, polished table with three high-backed chairs slowly coalesce into existence. Tapestries lined stone walls. He turned to see a set of large, wooden double doors.

Memories of this room began to beg for his attention. Simple yet elegant decorations, the quiet, regal atmosphere, all of it beckoned to him. The surroundings conspired to remind him that he had been here before. Many years ago, he and Spock had traveled to a distant world and stood in this very room.

Organia?

Even as the thought echoed in his mind, three indistinct points of light formed over the chairs behind the table. They grew in size, and the illumination became brighter with each passing second. Kirk had to raise his hand to shield his eyes from the glare.

They had taken on human shapes now, the intensely bright light beginning to dim. Facial features emerged, followed by hair and clothing. Finally, the light faded altogether, leaving three elderly gentlemen, dressed in simple robes. Of course, Kirk immediately recognized them: Ayelborne, Claymare, and Trefayne.

"Greetings, Captain Kirk." It was Ayelborne, the "man" that Kirk remembered as the leader of the group, who had spoken first.

Jim finally found his voice. "Hello. It's been a long time."

"For you, perhaps," the older man replied. "Time is irrelevant to us. However, it is comforting to know that you have not forgotten."

Kirk actually smiled at that. "Hardly, sir. Our last meeting had a profound and lasting effect on me."

"So it would seem, Captain," the man Kirk remembered as Trefayne responded. "It took quite a bit of time for you, as the road your peoples traveled to make peace was a long and difficult one. You can be satisfied that accomplishments you made during your life were instrumental in shaping what finally came to pass. There is still much to be done, but we are hopeful."

A question formed in Kirk's mind as confusion over his present situation began to set in.

"Why am I here?" he asked. "The last thing I remember is Veridian III. The bridge fell, and me with it. I remember looking up and seeing Picard, and he told me that we had stopped Soran. But I don't remember anything after that. What happened?"

Claymare spoke for the first time. "We brought you here from that moment in time. As far as the universe is concerned, the next instant has not occurred yet." The man smiled and then continued, "The simplest way to explain it would be to say that we are occupying a space between one second and the next."

This did nothing for Jim's confusion. "But, why?"

In response, Ayelborne rose from his chair and made his way around the long, polished table, his hands clasped in front of him as he walked.

"We are curious, Captain. Why did you elect to aid Captain Picard, after finally finding peace with yourself? No starships, no duty, simply eternal happiness. Yet, you gave all of that up in order to help Picard. Why?"

"Don't you know?"

The Organian shook his head as he stopped before Kirk. "We are not mind readers, Captain. We do not know what motivates other beings to decide upon possible courses of action."

Kirk shrugged, shaking his head as he did so. "There were innocent lives at stake. *Millions* of lives. I had to do something. It's a decision I've had to make more times than I can remember, and I'd do it again without hesitation. What difference does it make?"

Trefayne raised a hand. "Your actions and inactions *do* make a difference, Captain, just as they always have. They made a difference at Veridian III. In his first attempt to stop Soran, Picard failed. The Veridian star was destroyed, along with all of the planets and life in that system. As a result, he was swept into the nexus, where he eventually found you. With your help, he was afforded the opportunity to try and stop Soran again. It was only with your assistance that he was able to save those millions of people."

Claymare nodded in agreement. "Your sense of duty has always been the primary driving force in your life. Duty to others before duty to yourself. You gave up many chances to live in peace and contentment throughout your life in order to serve others. Look back at your accomplishments. What do you see?"

Kirk paused momentarily, gathering his thoughts, before answering, "Just like you said, I was doing my duty. Any

Starfleet officer worthy of the uniform would have done the same thing under the circumstances. No, *anyone* with that kind of moral conviction would have done it."

"Possibly, James." Ayelborne smiled slightly.

A flash of light . . .

Captain's Log, Stardate 3135.1
Effective immediately, I resign my commission and relinquish command of this vessel to First Officer Spock, who has been given orders to direct the Enterprise *to the nearest starbase. There, a new captain waits to assume command.*

"What is this?"

Kirk stood alongside Ayelborne on what he immediately recognized as the upper deck of the *Enterprise* bridge, but it was an *Enterprise* from the past. Ayelborne indicated the command well, where a young, very tired looking Captain James Kirk sat in the center chair, a young Mr. Spock at his side.

"That is you. We have traveled back to the early days of your career as captain of the *Enterprise.*"

Kirk shook his head. "No. That's not possible. I never made that log entry about my resignation." He watched as a younger version of himself stood up from the command chair and moved to the turbolift, stopping only momentarily to look back at his first officer.

"Mr. Spock, I'll be in my quarters if you need me."

The Vulcan nodded. "Acknowledged, Captain."

Captain Kirk disappeared into the turbolift, the doors closing behind him. Ayelborne looked at Jim again.

"What we are watching, James, is a telling of how events might have occurred."

Jim searched his memory, trying to attach some significance to the stardate he had just heard his younger self speak into the log recorder. It only took a moment. His eyes shot up to look at the viewscreen and the pale gold planet depicted on it, his jaw going slack in horrible remembrance.

No.

The Guardian. McCoy and the hypo.

Edith.

Pain he had thought long buried suddenly rushed to the forefront of his consciousness. It felt as though his heart were being wrenched from his chest. Kirk fought for his emotional control, now under assault from memories he had not dared to face in many years. He had fooled himself into thinking he could make peace with himself about this, and now he chastised himself for thinking such a feat was possible.

He was shaking his head furiously. "But, that's not how it happened. I admit, I was devastated when Edith died, but I realized that her death probably saved billions of lives in the course of history. I remember thinking very seriously about resignation, but I never once made a move to act on that thought."

Ayelborne smiled. "This was a turning point in your life, James. In the history you remember, your sense of duty overpowered the personal grief that you were feeling. You forced your feelings away, deciding instead to focus on your professional responsibilities, when you could just as easily have ended it all and resigned. We are simply witnessing another way that history might have unfolded."

Kirk turned to face the bridge turbolift doors, but he and Ayelborne weren't on the bridge anymore. Now, they stood in the corner of what he recognized as his cabin from the old *Enterprise.* He saw his younger self, lying on the small bunk.

God, those beds really were small back then.

The young Captain Kirk lay with his right arm draped across his face, hiding his eyes. Jim could guess what thoughts drifted through his younger self's mind.

He turned to his Organian companion. "Now what?"

By way of reply, the door chime sounded. Captain Kirk called out to the door, "Come."

Leonard McCoy entered the room as the door opened. The older Kirk studied his longtime friend as he was then: blue tunic with lieutenant commander's stripes; brown hair with none of the gray that would dominate it in later years; the sour expression that had become a trademark of the perpetually disgruntled chief medical officer of the *Enterprise.*

The doctor made his way, without invitation, to a chair in the corner of the sleeping area. He then proceeded to study his commanding officer and friend with that expression Jim had come to know only too well.

Finally, he spoke. "Spock tells me you've resigned your commission."

The younger Kirk drew his arm from his face. "That's right." He continued to stare at the ceiling, avoiding the doctor's gaze.

McCoy pressed, "You want to tell me why?"

The young captain exhaled audibly. "I've decided that I don't want this life, Bones. I'm tired of losing."

McCoy frowned. "Losing? Jim, you made a decision that saved uncounted billions of lives and promised us our future, the future as we know it. If you had allowed Edith to live, everything we know and understand would be gone. It's as simple as that. I can only guess what having to make that decision did to you. But what you did was for the greater good. You made a decision and you won, for all of us. Under the circumstances, I think Edith would understand."

Kirk shook his head. "How many men and women have died since I took command of this ship? I remember each and every one of their names, and I see each of their faces. Some of the most important people in my life are among them, Bones. Sam, Aurelan, Gary. Edith was just the latest addition to a list that's already too long."

McCoy's expression grew thoughtful. "Resigning won't help them, Jim. It won't prevent it from happening again."

Kirk sat up in his bunk. "No, but it will help me. I can't go on like this, Bones. It simply hurts too much."

Ayelborne turned to face the older Kirk. "These feelings began when your friend Gary Mitchell died. A small pang of doubt formed, and continued to grow as time went along. Finally, with Edith Keeler's death, the feelings had grown to such intensity that Captain Kirk decides to abandon starship command and return to Earth, never to journey into space again."

"Why?" Jim could not bring himself to believe he could ever be capable of just giving in and surrendering so easily.

This can't be me.

"You simply did not wish to reopen old emotional wounds," Ayelborne answered him. "You return to your parents' farm in Iowa and become heavily involved with Agro-Engineering."

Jim continued to shake his head in disbelief. "What happens to the rest of the crew? Who takes my place as *Enterprise* captain?"

The Organian began to wander about the cabin. Strangely enough, Jim could see his younger self and McCoy talking, yet he heard no voices. It was like watching a video playback, without benefit of audio.

Ayelborne, however, could be heard most clearly. "A longtime friend of yours, Captain Robert Wesley, takes command of the *Enterprise* as a personal favor to you that is honored by Starfleet Command. He foregoes a promotion to commodore in order to take the assignment, and things go quite smoothly, for a time."

The sound of that didn't comfort Kirk. "Why? What happens?"

Again, the light . . .

Captain's Log, Stardate 5031.8
Chief Engineer Scott temporarily in command. The Enterprise *is deep in Romulan space and is surrounded by Romulan warships. We have just received a report from the Romulan commander that Captain Wesley was killed by Mr. Spock, apparently in self-defense. I am at a loss to understand how something like this could have happened, but Dr. McCoy has told me the captain had been suffering from severe emotional stress in recent weeks. At this time, I am standing by, awaiting further information and orders from Mr. Spock.*

The weight resting on Montgomery Scott's shoulders was enormous. He felt utterly helpless: His ship was surrounded by the enemy, waiting to become a prize of the Romulan Praetor;

Captain Wesley was dead, apparently at Mr. Spock's hands; and Spock was now a possible collaborator with the Romulans.

This willna look good in the official log, he understated in a vain attempt to amuse himself.

Kirk and Ayelborne watched as the Scotsman struggled through the duties of command that had been laid upon him. The engineer grappled with his feelings in order to be the emotional rock that his shipmates could look to for confidence.

"The cloaking device," Kirk remembered. "Starfleet had ordered us to obtain one for study, so Spock and I came up with a plan to steal it from a Romulan ship. We faked my death, and I had McCoy surgically alter me to look like a Romulan. Then, I beamed onto the Romulan ship, took the cloaking device, and had Scotty install it on the *Enterprise.* We barely got away."

Ayelborne nodded. "That is how you remember it."

Suddenly, they were in sickbay. Scotty was staring, dumbfounded, at a Romulan centurion who bore a striking resemblance to Captain Wesley. He wore a Starfleet uniform, but it was there that the similarities began to end.

"Captain? Captain Wesley?" Scotty asked.

With a mischievous grin beginning to grow on his face, Wesley responded, "Yes?"

The engineer was practically beaming now. "Well, you look like the devil himself, but as long as you're alive, what's it all about?"

"Those Romulan officers, they're still aboard the ship?" Wesley asked, referring to the two Romulan centurions that had transported to the *Enterprise* in exchange for Kirk and Spock beaming aboard the Romulan flagship.

Wesley and Spock, Kirk reminded himself. *These alternate realities always did give me a headache.*

"Aye, sir, they're in the brig," Scotty replied, happy not only to see his captain alive, but also in the knowledge that the situation appeared to be under control once again.

Wesley merely smiled slightly at the nearly awestruck engineer. "I'll need a Romulan uniform."

Scotty's expression conveyed his approval of the quickly unfolding plan. "Aye, sir. It'll be a pleasure."

Kirk and Ayelborne watched as Scotty made his way from sickbay, leaving Wesley, McCoy, and Nurse Chapel alone.

McCoy asked, "Bob, do you really think you have a chance to pull this off?"

The captain shrugged. "We're the best chance Starfleet has at this point, Leonard."

That one sentence made Kirk realize just how different this reality was: the absence of the familiar "Bones" nickname that only he had used.

His thoughts were interrupted when the scene before him shifted again. Sickbay disappeared, only to be replaced by a long, dimly lit corridor. It was approximately the same width as many of the main corridors on the *Enterprise,* but there were devices of unknown yet strangely familiar design adorning the walls. The passageway was illuminated in a soft purple. He dredged the location from his memories.

We're on the Romulan ship, he realized.

He made his way, along with Ayelborne, down the hallway until they came to a door. The large, reinforced hatch bore some Romulan marking that Kirk could not read, but nonetheless recognized.

"The cloaking device," Kirk said. "It's behind this door."

They didn't have to wait long. Wesley, complete with centurion's uniform, moved with a purposeful stride up the corridor. Kirk suddenly realized that there was no guard to confront the impostor, as there had been when he himself had acted out this scenario. The captain made his way, unimpeded, through the hatch.

Ayelborne looked to Kirk for a fleeting second, then motioned for him to follow as he stepped *through the wall.*

Now, they were inside the chamber as well. They watched as Wesley studied the various consoles and mechanisms, trying to determine which of them was the cloaking device.

"We didn't know what it looked like," Kirk told the Organian as Wesley was suddenly interrupted by a Romulan officer.

"Centurion," the new arrival asked. "Are you authorized in this area? I do not recognize you."

Wesley replied with clipped tones, trying to ease the Romulan's evident suspicions, "There is an intruder aboard. He may be after the cloaking device."

The centurion's eyes flickered to momentarily hold on the device at the center of the room. It was a strange, orblike contraption with power conduits running from it to various control consoles.

Wesley knew in that instant it was the cloaking device. That was all the urging he needed. In a lightning move, his hand lanced out from his body and landed a fierce strike to the Romulan's neck. The centurion never even had time to raise a hand in defense. He sank to the floor in a disjointed heap. From where he stood, Kirk noticed Ayelborne as the Organian grimaced slightly at the brief exhibition of violence.

As Wesley went to work disconnecting the cloaking device from its control mount, Ayelborne moved to examine several of the consoles. Unseen by the *Enterprise* captain, a status light on one of the consoles changed from a dim blue to a bright, blinking red.

Ayelborne pointed to it. "He has set off a silent alarm. They will be here momentarily."

Kirk swung to watch the entrance to the chamber, as well as the side door that the now-unconscious guard had used. His eyes kept swinging from the doors to Wesley and back. The captain was still in the process of removing the device.

"Come on, Bob. Hurry!" Rationality told Kirk that Wesley could not hear him, but he couldn't help the panic he was beginning to feel.

Finally, Wesley pulled the cloaking device free from its control station. Holding it under one arm, he reached into a pocket of the centurion uniform for his communicator. A flick of his wrist opened the antenna grid, and he was greeted by the familiar chirp signaling the unit's activation.

"Wesley to *Enterprise.*"

Before the reply came, the door to the corridor suddenly snapped open and Romulan centurions flooded into the room. Immediately, Wesley dove for the small side door.

"Enterprise, this is Wesley! Beam me back, now!" Kirk could

only watch helplessly as the guards poured through the hatch after the captain. The next seconds seemed to drag on into centuries.

He could hear the comforting whine of a transporter field forming. At that moment, the first centurion raised his disruptor and fired. A writhing green bullet of energy leapt from the weapon, the accompanying sound of the discharge echoing in the narrow confines of the room. In scarcely the blink of an eye, the disruptor bolt took Wesley full in the chest. Kirk could see the instantaneous damage it caused as it ripped through the all-too-meager material of the Romulan uniform and continued on into Wesley's body. Skin ruptured and parted as the energy salvo penetrated the captain's chest. He fell to the floor just as the transporter beam flared into existence and claimed him.

"Oh my God," was all Kirk could get out before the breath tightened in his chest.

Then they were in the *Enterprise* transporter room as a horrified Lieutenant Kyle watched the form of Captain Wesley materialize on the transporter platform.

Slamming the intercom button, he yelled, "Medical emergency in the transporter room!" Then he raced to the inert form of his captain, aghast at the ugly wound in Wesley's chest.

"Does he live?" Kirk wanted to know.

Ayelborne merely watched, stone-faced, as McCoy and a trauma unit entered the transporter room at a full run, followed by Scotty. The doctor wasted no time opening his med-kit and inspecting the captain's wound.

Scotty picked up the cloaking device that lay on the platform next to the captain, then asked, "Doctor, is there anything I can do?"

McCoy shook his head. "I don't even know if there's anything that *I* can do."

The engineer looked sadly at his captain before duty was remembered.

"I need to figure out how to install this beastie, or we're all dead." Turning to Kyle, he asked, "Have ye got a lock on Mr. Spock, lad?"

The transporter chief nodded. "Yes, sir."

"Well then, when I give ye the word, bring him back." With that, he was out into the corridor and headed for engineering.

As Kirk and Ayelborne continued to watch, several of the indicators on McCoy's medical tricorder went from a steady blink to a constant light. Finally, the doctor shut the device off.

"It's too late, he's dead."

With that, Kirk noticed that all sound in the room faded until nothing could be heard, except the voice of Ayelborne.

"Captain Wesley died obtaining the device, which Mr. Scott was able to install on the *Enterprise*. They retrieved Mr. Spock and escaped from the Romulan ships."

Jim had barely heard any of the Organian's words. He stood transfixed as McCoy and his orderlies hoisted the body of Robert Wesley onto a stretcher and covered it with a sheet.

"That's enough. I don't want to see any more of this."

Ayelborne shook his head sadly. "I am sorry, James, but we are not finished."

The light . . .

STARDATE 8128.7

"Admiral, scanning an energy source on *Reliant*. It's a pattern I've never seen before."

Kirk and Ayelborne now stood in front of the main viewscreen of the *Enterprise* bridge. They watched as Admiral Harrison Morrow and David Marcus moved to stand behind Captain Spock, who was still intently studying his sensor displays. Kirk immediately recognized where and when they were. After all, David had visited the *Enterprise* only once.

After a few seconds, David spoke. "It's the Genesis Wave! He's on a buildup to detonation!"

"How soon?" Morrow asked.

David replied, "We encoded four minutes." Kirk found himself studying the younger man, his son, intently. The scene, fabricated as it was, nevertheless succeeded in calling forth a whole new wave of emotions. Images of a life that might have been flashed in his vision momentarily. He wanted to call out, to warn David of the dangers that lay ahead for him.

Stay away from Genesis, David! Go home to your mother! Wait for me! I so much wanted to know my son, and they stole you from me before I could get the chance.

Kirk forced the thoughts away.

The admiral straightened, deep in thought. Finally he said, "We can beam aboard and stop it."

David held him back by the arm, shaking his head. "You can't."

Kirk stood stone-faced as yet another memory from his past was dredged up, distorted, and played out before him. He watched as Admiral Morrow moved to the center seat, thumbing the chair's intercom switch.

"Morrow to engineering. Mr. Scott, it is vital that you bring the warp engines back on-line immediately."

When there was no response from the engine room, Morrow turned to face Spock again.

But the Vulcan wasn't there.

"He's gone to repair the engines," Jim remembered soberly. "He sacrificed himself to save the ship." It had been a painful experience, watching his closest friend die while he stood by, powerless to help.

Then they were in engineering, looking on as Scotty and McCoy stood and watched the radiation-scarred Vulcan on the other side of the transparent wall surrounding the warp core. Spock's skin had been badly burned and had begun to peel from his face. Green blood flowed from dozens of wounds, some of it already darkening as it dried on the already-stained material of his uniform jacket. He was dying, again.

Only this time, Kirk wasn't there in his friend's last moments. Standing beside Ayelborne, his mind had already begun racing ahead in these series of events.

"What happens to Spock's *katra?*"

The Organian waved an arm to indicate McCoy. "He succeeds in transferring his *katra* to your friend. Dr. McCoy begins to suffer the same symptoms of insanity that you remember. Only this time, there is no one to return to the Genesis Planet and retrieve Spock's body so that it and his soul can be rejoined. When Genesis self-destructs, Spock's body is lost."

"And McCoy?"

"Sarek takes him to Vulcan, and Spock's *katra* is removed from his mind and placed in the Hall of Ancient Thought. The doctor suffers no lasting ill effects from the incident, but he retires from active service. Shortly thereafter, the *Enterprise* is decommissioned, and her crew is reassigned."

Kirk watched as Spock slowly sank to the floor of the sealed compartment, the last breath of life leaving his body. The memory of Spock's death was still very clear in the captain's mind, even though the miracle of the Genesis Planet would eventually aid in the restoration of the Vulcan. At the time that Kirk had launched his plan to take the *Enterprise* and retrieve Spock's body, he had no idea his friend would be reborn by the awesome powers unleashed by the Genesis Device. That had merely been what Kirk considered to be a gesture of mercy from a benevolent deity.

But not this time. This time, there would be no Admiral Kirk to lead his command crew to hijack the *Enterprise* and set out on the mission to retrieve Spock's body from the Genesis Planet. There would be no second chance at life for the Vulcan, which made watching him die a second time even more painful than the first.

"So, that's it," Kirk said simply, finally.

"No. I'm afraid not."

Once more, the light.

STARDATE 8391.4

"This is the president of the United Federation of Planets. Do not approach Earth."

They stood amidst the chaos that enveloped the Central Command Center at Starfleet Headquarters in San Francisco. Alarms were flashing. Readouts were displaying jumbled arrays of data. Repair technicians were fastening shoring struts to the large bay windows. Outside, rain and lightning dominated the view.

The probe, Kirk realized.

The council president had positioned himself in front of a subspace communications terminal. His message was being broadcast to every ship and planet in the Federation. Kirk could see the strain in the older man's eyes as he relayed the imminent destruction of Earth to the rest of the Federation, not to mention anyone in the galaxy who could pick up the signal.

"The transmissions of an orbiting Probe are causing critical damage to this planet. It has almost totally ionized our atmosphere. All power sources have failed. All Earth-orbiting starships are powerless. The probe is vaporizing our oceans."

Kirk remembered when he had heard this message the first time, aboard the Klingon scoutship, returning to Earth to stand trial.

"We cannot survive unless a way can be found to respond to the Probe," the president continued. "Further communications may not be possible. Save your energy, save yourselves. Avoid the planet Earth at all costs. Farewell."

He severed the connection and rose from his chair. Jim and Ayelborne watched as he joined Admiral Cartwright and Ambassador Sarek. The Klingon ambassador, Kamarag, was also present with his entourage.

These were events that Kirk had not directly witnessed when they'd occurred originally. He and his crew had been on their way to Earth aboard their captured Klingon vessel to stand trial for the daring actions that had resulted in the retrieval and rebirth of Captain Spock. It was only while in flight from Vulcan that they had learned of Earth's plight. They had then concocted their seemingly insane plan to travel back in time to Earth's 20th century in order to find two humpback whales in a desperate attempt to rescue their home planet.

Things were different in this reality, however. Here, Kirk and his crew would not stand trial. There was no Klingon bird-of-prey on its way to Earth. There was no Spock to deduce the Probe's intent and develop a course of action. There would be no humpback whales from the 20th century. There was no way to stop the Probe.

Earth would die.

"No," was all Kirk could say, his voice nothing more than a horrified whisper.

At that moment, a horrendous shriek of rending metal assaulted his ears. The support struts holding the windows caved in under the massive pressure of water and wind. Glass shards were strewn everywhere.

The personnel manning the Command Center fought to keep their positions, as water and debris were hurled across the massive room. Computer displays throughout the chamber exploded, starting fires which were instantly quelled by the incoming water. As all this happened, more alarms were added to the din. Unaffected by it all, Kirk watched and listened to the screams.

Sarek pointed to the window. "Look!"

Beyond the windows, far out past the shoreline, a massive wave was gathering strength and headed for shore. Hundreds of feet high, it blocked out what little light remained. There was no time to evacuate. Frantically, people began hunting for purchase against the imminent assault.

Then the wave hit, and the Command Center was almost instantly underwater. There were no bulkheads to shun the water away. There was no power to the emergency force fields designed for just such an incident. Powerless to help, Kirk was forced to watch as, one by one, the Command Center staff drowned. Though the chamber was completely underwater, he and Ayelborne were dry.

Of course, we're not really here, are we?

Ayelborne looked on, his expression pained from witnessing the destruction and death.

"The Probe will continue its assault on the Earth's atmosphere, rendering the planet sterile," the Organian offered. "It will then create an entirely new ecosystem to its own specifications. The Federation Council and Starfleet Command will eventually be relocated to Vulcan, where they will begin anew."

Kirk now saw the Earth from space. He watched as the Probe, orbiting the planet, manipulated the clouds and oceans of his homeworld, cleansing it of all life. Suspended from the underside of the Probe, the glowing, pulsing orb glowed brighter, turning more rapidly. Time seemed to accelerate, the whirls of water covering almost the entire surface of the Earth moving faster and faster.

Then, it stopped. Gradually, the oceans subsided. The planet calmed.

A dead planet.

"STOP IT!" Kirk couldn't stand to watch any longer. His plea went unheeded as the rotating, glowing sphere retracted into the body of the probe. Then it drifted out of orbit, headed for the far reaches of the galaxy from which it had come. It faded from his view.

Then, so did everything else.

No stars, no Earth, nothing. Simply . . . black.

Except for Ayelborne. The Organian stood silently, studying the captain for a few moments. Jim was shaking his head.

"All this, because of me?"

Again the simple smile as Ayelborne replied, "Well, not entirely because of you. The universe is a rather large place, James. You cannot be expected to shoulder the entire blame. However, because you were not present during key moments in the years following your resignation from Starfleet, things that you remember occurring did not. Events that would not have occurred did indeed happen. Whether or not this is proper is not ours to decide."

Kirk was puzzled by this. "I don't understand."

"I do not know whether or not the history as you remember it is the correct one. I am not in a position to render such a judgment. I merely showed you one possible way history might have progressed, had you elected to leave Starfleet."

Jim could feel anger rising. "Well, I've decided that the history I was just watching isn't right—at least, not for me. I want it back the way it was."

Ayelborne's expression was solemn as he replied, "My friend, nothing has changed. We are not capable of actually altering the past or the future."

It suddenly struck him. "Wait. You mean, I still . . . ?"

The Organian nodded solemnly. "Oh, yes, I am afraid so,

James. As our friend Claymare told you before, we are actually 'between' moments in time. We cannot necessarily change the timestream, but we can choose the manner in which we occupy it."

As Ayelborne spoke, color began to seep slowly into their surroundings. The colors took on shapes, gathering substance. Kirk and Ayelborne were returning to the council chambers of the Organians. Kirk turned to see Claymare and Trefayne, still seated in the same chairs as before. Both men sported their trademark slight smiles.

It was Claymare who spoke first. "We apologize if you were upset by what you saw, Captain Kirk. It was necessary in order to prove to you that the sacrifices you have made throughout your career did indeed make a difference." Jim approached the table separating him from the other Organians and placed his palms on it.

"What difference? There will always be people like Soran, or the Romulans, or whoever else that wants to take a shot. There will always be war with someone. I once told someone that though we are barbarians, we didn't have to fight. We could tell ourselves that we won't fight today. But it's a lie. There will always be someone who wants nothing more than to kill and destroy. When will we learn? What will it cost us?"

Trefayne rose to pace the room. "Do you remember when we told you the Federation and Klingons would work through their differences and eventually become allies? In the time period that Captain Picard knows, a Klingon is his chief of security aboard the *Enterprise*. Change is inevitable, Captain. Though the Federation's conflict with the Klingons is not quite over, the seeds of change have been planted and have begun to bear fruit. Difficulties lie ahead, yes, but peace lies not far beyond them."

"How long will this take? What will happen after that?" Kirk was pleased to know that the events and his experiences that led to the beginnings of peace at Khitomer had not been futile.

Ayelborne spoke again. "James, we are only at the beginning. Through mutual cooperation, the Federation and the Klingons have formed what will eventually be a lasting alliance. Galactic exploration will continue on a grand scale. There will be new and exciting worlds to discover, new friends to be made, and new enemies to confront. However, all of this will be undertaken together."

Kirk took some comfort in that. "It's too bad I won't be able to see it."

The Organian placed a hand on his shoulder. "Do not dwell on that, James. Your life and your contributions will have a lasting effect on all that is to come. Your name and exploits will become legendary. Many great leaders, some as yet unborn, others long dead, will be compared to James Tiberius Kirk. You have much to be proud of, my friend."

The three men moved to stand side by side. Now, it was Claymare who spoke again.

"It is time to bid you farewell, Captain Kirk. You will be returned to Veridian III, at the same instant that you left. Time will continue to stand still until you feel you are ready."

"Ready? Ready for what?"

There was no reply from any of the Organians. Instead, Kirk watched as their human shapes began to dissipate. They gradually lost all substance and returned to their forms of pure energy, finally disappearing from view altogether. The room itself had also begun to drain of color and solidity. The furnishings faded away, followed by the room itself.

Blackness returned, for a moment.

Then, the barren surface of Veridian III gradually faded into view. The first sensation Kirk experienced was the feeling of hard rock beneath his back. Next, a heavy weight pressed down upon his chest, though Jim realized it wasn't uncomfortable. He could also hear the faint whisper of the desert wind through the canyons surrounding Soran's launch site. Color washed over Kirk's surroundings, and the landscape came into focus around him.

He was lying on the ground, pinned beneath the gnarled, twisted remains of the bridge. He looked up into the face of Picard, the other man's body and face frozen in time, devoid of life. It was as though Kirk were studying a statue.

Looking up into the sky, he could see the frozen image of the nexus, the writhing ribbon of energy having passed through the planet's upper atmosphere instead of being diverted as Tolian Soran had planned.

Time stood still.

Kirk felt none of the pain that he should surely have been experiencing, given the extent of the injuries he had suffered in the fall. He imagined what the inside of his own body must look like, with broken bones and ruptured organs.

Claymare's words, and the meaning behind them, suddenly became clear to him. He was being given one final opportunity to reflect on what he had seen. It was up to him to take the last step after making peace with himself and with what lay ahead.

A sigh escaped his lips. Considering what was about to happen, he felt oddly at ease. Was he afraid of dying?

No.

Having faced death countless times during his life, it was a possibility James Kirk had deemed an acceptable risk when weighed against the opportunities a life in Starfleet had given him. How many new worlds had he explored? How many fascinating and varied new races had he been privileged to meet? How many times had the crew of the *Starship Enterprise* been on hand to save the day? More than he could easily count. He and his crew had literally saved the planet Earth and its inhabitants from certain destruction on two separate occasions. They had played a vital role in the beginnings of a peaceful relationship with their former enemies, the Klingons. He had traveled through space and time and lived a life most would consider ripe material for adventure fiction.

He had always known that a career in Starfleet would force him to forgo many of life's pleasures, intangibles that many others had discovered. Were there regrets? Certainly, but those were beyond his ability to change now. He had made his choices and would now have to keep faith that history and destiny would judge him fairly based on those decisions as well as the repercussions they had caused.

Part of him longed to live on, to see what exciting possibilities the future held. What he had already seen and been a part of had only been the beginning, his experience in the nexus having brought that realization to him with startling clarity. It had given him the opportunity to meet the future in the form of Jean-Luc Picard, this 24th-century captain of a *Starship Enterprise.* Though he'd known Picard for only a short time, Kirk instinctively felt the other man to be a more than capable starship captain. Picard was the embodiment of everything represented by the Federation and Starfleet.

Kirk believed that with men and women such as this man Picard, the future was in good hands. He could rest, knowing that his efforts, as well as those of others that had come before him, had paved the way for an even greater adventure.

He had indeed made a difference.

STARDATE 48649.7

Jean-Luc Picard looked down through the twisted wreckage of the fallen bridge and into the face of James Kirk. He could see the life draining away from behind the powerful hazel eyes. The injured man was struggling not to give in to the immense pain his wounds had to be causing. Picard desperately wanted to do something, anything, to help, but he knew in his heart the man was wounded mortally.

"It was fun." Kirk uttered the words with a small smile. Was this contentment that Picard saw?

Then, the smile was replaced for the briefest of moments with a look of confusion. Picard could not be sure, but he thought it was the look of someone who was finally, ultimately realizing the end was near.

Just as suddenly as it had disappeared, the tiny smile of satisfaction returned. All signs of tension left Kirk's face.

"Oh my," he whispered, and then his body went limp, his eyes closing forever.

Picard watched the other man's body relax for the final time, profound sorrow threatening to envelop him. Though James Kirk had come forth to triumph one final time, the mystique and legend that surrounded him had not been enough to save the man this time.

As the emotions verged on overcoming Picard, a strange sense of ease caught him momentarily. A realization became apparent:

Kirk had died doing what he had always done. He had thrown caution to the winds in the defense of others. It was what had made him a legend; therefore it was a fitting end for a legend.

Several hours later, Picard stood next to the rather austere grave site he had fashioned for his companion. He gazed down at the simple pile of rocks and at the shining gold Starfleet insignia, the sole identification for the otherwise anonymous tomb.

Would Kirk have approved? Picard wanted to think so. He didn't believe the various myths surrounding one of Starfleet's most dynamic figures. Having risked life and limb standing next to the man, he had evidence to prove there was more to Kirk than simple glory seeking.

Don't let them promote you, don't let them transfer you, don't let them do anything that takes you off the bridge of that ship because, while you're there, you can make a difference.

Kirk's words had merely given voice to his deeds, the actions of someone with an insatiable desire to do what was necessary, what was *right,* regardless of the personal risk. In hindsight, Picard now believed Kirk's career stood for one thing: *You only live once. Make it the best life you can. Be able to look in the mirror and tell yourself, "I did my best today."*

"And the predator be damned," Picard whispered. His woefully short friendship with James Kirk had taught him a powerful lesson.

It was a lesson Picard vowed he would remember.

What Went Through Data's Mind 0.68 Seconds Before the Satellite Hit

Dylan Otto Krider

For an android, that is nearly an eternity . . .
—*Data,* Star Trek: First Contact

I am an android and, as such, capable of performing multiple tasks, using a variety of techniques drawn from my data banks. I must admit that in my quest to become more human, I have found this to be the greatest barrier to my understanding of human psychology. In the time it takes a representative human to say a word of an average length of 1.27 syllables, I have chosen, researched, and performed anywhere from 5 to 2,172,763 mental assignments, depending on their varying degrees of involvement and complexity. This is what allows me to document these proceedings as I am doing now, and store them in a detailed report for future reference.

Any time I witness or take part in an event of some significance, I am required to make a detailed report to be reviewed by the captain, which is then to be sent to Starfleet Command. This is a task for which I am well suited, since my positronic brain allows me to catalogue each of the mental assignments as they are being performed, and then separate and categorize them in standard delineated text format so that it is easily understood by other beings such as humans who, in my experience, are basically only capable of concentrating on one major thought function at a time, though I have found this to be more true of human males than of females of the species.

Captain Picard and Starfleet Command are well aware of my mental abilities, but I state them again here because of their relevance to the current situation, and because in my observations of human communication, I have become aware that humans often restate obvious and generally accepted information when it fits the context of the situation.

Today in Ten-Forward, I have logged one such instance into my memory banks. Counselor Troi was sitting across from me at the table eating a chocolate sundae. After ingesting a large spoonful, she made a moaning sound very similar to those made by human females in the act of copulation (it should be noted here that I have never personally heard Counselor Troi in the act of sexual intercourse, but I am well versed in humanoid sexual behavior, and have found no evidence to suggest that half-Betazoids should differ greatly in this respect). When she had finished, she then said to me, "I love chocolate."

"I am well aware of your affection for chocolate desserts, Counselor," I replied, and reminded her that she had informed me of this fact many times and, as an android, I was incapable of forgetting. Counselor Troi then responded by making an amused facial expression of the kind I often see on crew members' faces after I have said something, though factually adequate, that demonstrates my lack of understanding of human behavior.

"I am not saying it to impart information, Data. I am simply stating how I *feel*."

My restating of the fact that I am an android, capable of multiple calculations simultaneously, however, has nothing to do with how I feel since, as such, I am incapable of emotion. My restating of these obvious physical traits is motivated more by my desire to create a complete and thorough report.

* * *

Dylan Otto Krider

At the present time I am calculating the density of the stellar cores of the 12 closest star systems, optimizing my lower memory banks, compiling a list of chores to be done to prepare for this evening's bridge game, and deriving the formula for the average speed of the Arcturian wildebeest. I have also just composed this poem:

Ode to the Fractal

You found randomness
predictable
and gave catastrophic significance
to the butterfly
You found patterns in a Universe
sporadic
and brought beauty to
logic
in a world where chaos
reigns.

Of course, the majority of my brain function has been devoted to the small Vandalayan satellite which will destroy the *Enterprise* in approximately 0.68 seconds. Proper Starfleet protocol requires me, upon recognizing a state of emergency, to:

A) Notify the captain
B) If the captain is unavailable, notify the next highest ranking officer in charge
C) Formulate a proper course of action to suggest to the captain/superior officer, if needed
D) Ready myself for further orders

Due to the limitations of verbal communication, the fastest possible speed with which I can relay the present situation with a reasonable probability of being understood would be 1.43 seconds, assuming I use the most economical word choice, which according to present calculations is, "Collision! Mark 4.25, Starboard!" This does not take into account the amount of time needed for Captain Picard to register my warning, plot a course of action, relay the proper order, and for the recipient of the command to react accordingly. Considering that the past few weeks have been uneventful, and there has been nothing to suggest to the captain that anything out of the ordinary is to be expected, I would also have to account for a moment or two of hesitation. All of this makes conforming to usual Starfleet protocol, from all calculations, highly undesirable.

Yesterday, when Lt. Barclay pierced his boot with the tip of his fencing sword, he exclaimed, "I think I just hurt myself," which would be another example of humans stating the obvious. Geordi and I had joined him on the holodeck for a chapter of *The Three Musketeers,* and Lt. Barclay had brought his own foil for the occasion. We came upon a band of thieves and Lt. Barclay had fought them off brilliantly, as the computer was programmed to allow him to do. Then in a triumphant gesture, Lt. Barclay drove the sword down into his foot, and leaned on it like a walking stick, smiling with some difficulty, and after a few seconds, said: "I think I just hurt myself."

This was quite obvious since Lt. Barclay had not used a holographic foil which the safety features of the computer could have compensated for. So I said: "I am quite aware of that, Lieutenant. Do you require medical attention?"

To which Barclay replied: "I *really* think I hurt myself."

It may occur to the reader of this report that it might be difficult, with the speed of an android brain, to acclimate to the relatively slow and clumsy method of verbal communication. It is true that I am able to exchange millions more bytes of information through a direct link with the computer than through an equivalent time spent in conversation. However, although I do not suffer from what humans call boredom, as an android, I do have an innate desire for efficiency, so I often perform thousands of other mental tasks during standard verbal communication, which can include calculations, diagnostics, or memory optimization. After the first few words of any sentence, I often know with a high probability of accuracy what the rest of the sentence will be before the sentence can be finished, but am forced to politely wait for the sentence to reach completion. For those periods of time that I am lacking tasks to perform, I devote my mental resources to more creative tasks, and am even equipped with several internal logic games which can be used to bide the time.

In an effort to better understand human psychology, I will often shut down most of my mental functioning and operate at a fraction of capacity, so that I can, through the use of time-consuming mathematical problems and subroutines in my neural net, perform at a speed that is more equivalent to that of humans. To date, my experiment has been successful, and for day-to-day behavior, I have been better able to interrelate with the other members of the crew. Of course, in times of emergency, I am able to immediately switch back and operate at full capacity, as I am doing now.

The Vandalayans are a peaceful species known for their hospitality, yet unspectacular in most other areas. They are poor, with postindustrial technology that excels only in one area, namely the design and construction of subspace satellites, used mostly as telescopes to observe signals from very distant galaxies, with a resolution far beyond that of current Federation technology. What makes them unique among satellites of their type is that they use a technique similar to that of the VLA (Very Large Array) from Earth history. In the Earth model, humans found that they could use telescopes placed around the globe and connected through computers so that the operators could collect and correlate the respective images, allowing the telescopes to operate as one very large single telescope the size of the Earth. The Vandalayan satellite differs in one important respect: instead of linking the images of many smaller telescopes, the Vandalayans simply collect the images from one single satellite.

The Vandalayan satellite does this by creating a tear in the fabric of space which works somewhat like a wormhole, allowing the satellite to travel to various locations about the galaxy far more quickly than even the fastest starships. By calculating the speed that an image or radio signal will travel from a distant galaxy—the speed of light—the Vandalayans are able to cause the satellite to jump from location to location so that a single satellite can arrive at each place the instant the image arrives, collect it, then move on to the next one, so that in effect, instead of creating a telescope the size of the Earth, the Vandalayans have created a telescope the size of the galaxy.

The advantages of this technology far outweigh any disadvantages, the only one of any consequence being that on the minute chance that the satellite should appear in the path of a craft outfitted with warp drive, the subspace tear will also pierce the craft's warp field, essentially shattering it and scattering pieces of the craft throughout the galaxy. In the case of the *Enterprise,* the most probable end locations of the debris after the moment of collision, assuming it breaks apart into four major sections, are empty space in the Delta Quadrant, the Alurian nebulae, just outside of the galactic halo, and Alpha Epsilon V, which is unfortunate since the resident species is prone to mistake any unusual, bright celestial lights for signs of a coming apocalypse.

OPTIMIZATION: COMPLETE
RESULTS: 1.323×10^{12} sectors scanned, 33 bad, 33
    repaired
MEMORY CAPACITY REMAINING: 99.99%
NEXT SCHEDULED OPTIMIZATION: Stardate 42945.4

Another drawback to the Vandalayan technology which I had forgotten to mention is its puzzling inability to transport biological tissue. To date, all attempts to transport living matter through the subspace tears have failed, which would present another problem to the *Enterprise* in the unlikely event that she would be thrust through the tear in one piece. Another side effect of the tears is an unusual subspace signal which emanates, anywhere from 0.6 to 0.7 seconds before they form, which allows the tears to be picked up by the *Enterprise*'s short-range sensors. Due to the constraint of time, I have had to override Starfleet protocol and act independently by configuring a subspace signal to broadcast through the *Enterprise*'s communication systems to the location where the tear is set to appear, and send it through a short, high-energy pulse sufficient to deflect the tear out of harm's way with only a minimal loss of resolution, while still having time left over to compose another poem:

Untitled 3,567,364

Vandalay, Oh, Vandalay
how sweet you are on neural
path-a-ways
Oh, Vandalay,
sweet Vandalay
won't you please take
me a-way?
out to the stars and
back-a-gain?

When the sensors confirm that the Vandalayan satellite has been safely diverted, I stand and start to walk away from my station, but the look of the captain prevents me from continuing any further.

"Yes, Mr. Data?" Captain Picard asks.

"May I be excused, sir? I must download an incident report to Starfleet."

The captain's brows have drawn together at the bridge of his nose, and he squints. "Data, incident reports are only filed on the occasion that the *Enterprise* has been placed in a situation of extreme danger. . . ."

This is another example of humans stating the obvious. I have logged it into my memory banks.

"Is something wrong?"

"No, sir," I say, adding, "Not any longer."

The captain lifts his eyebrows and takes a deep breath, then exhales. "Well, I will very much look forward to reading it."

"Yes, sir," I say, waiting for the slight nod of his head which grants me permission to make my way onto the turbolift.

The Naked Truth

Jerry M. Wolfe

Reg Barclay stood in the corridor outside Counselor Deanna Troi's conference room, trying to build up the nerve to signal for admittance. The thin-faced diagnostic engineer shifted the weight of his slender frame from one foot to the other and used one hand to comb back a few unruly strands of black hair. How could he tell her about the foolish dream? Lots of people dreamed about being naked in public. He'd checked in the computer, knew the statistics. She'd probably just cluck about how normal it was, and how he had nothing to worry about. But terror was terror.

Three days ago Captain Picard had picked him to lead an away team that would install a new generator core for a science station in the binary Tarvo system. His first command! A warp-drive failure on the regular supply ship and trouble with a backup generator had brought the *Enterprise* into the picture, but it was just a routine job.

All he had to do was take the *Hawking* and two crew members down to the surface, install the generator core, and return. What could be simpler? Even the heavy sunspot activity had worked in his favor since there would be no transporter to contend with. Damn it, there was nothing for even a congenital worrier to fuss over.

But each night since the captain spoke to him, the identical nightmare of public nudity had tortured Barclay's rest. In about twelve hours he would take command of the *Hawking,* and he was afraid to sleep. *Stupid!*

Reg stepped toward Deanna's door, but quickly pulled away and pretended to examine a wall-panel diagram of the ship when two crew members passed by. God, maybe he was going insane. Maybe the shock of turning into that spider thing two months before, when the entire *Enterprise* crew had suddenly begun to de-evolve, had finally caught up with him. The fact that a bona fide disease now bore the family crest would give scant comfort if he went crazy in the bargain. It would be just like a Barclay to go stark raving mad on the eve of his first real command.

Reg screwed up his courage and returned to Deanna's door, determined to speak with her. His finger had not yet touched the sense pad, however, when the door whooshed open, and she nearly bowled him over. Reg stumbled backwards, caught a heel, and feel.

"Reg, you startled me. Are you all right?"

"I-I-I'm fine," he said, scrambling to his feet. "S-s-orry . . ."

Deanna smiled and he caught a whiff of perfume, very subtle, like a flower.

"Did you want to see me?"

"Me, oh-uh no, I mean yes, well if you have the time, but I see you're on your way out, so—"

The chirp of his combadge came to his rescue.

"Barclay here."

"Lieutenant Barclay, report to the bridge immediately. The captain wishes to speak with you."

He'd never been so glad to hear Data's precise tones.

"I'm on my way."

Reg felt heat rush up his neck as he faced Deanna.

"It was nothing, really. Just a silly dream. I've got to go."

Before the counselor could respond, he turned and walked away briskly, heading for the nearest turbolift. It was only when the lift was halfway to the bridge that he realized how rude he had been. Now there would be an apology to work out, another fine opportunity to make a fool of himself in front of Deanna Troi. Reg sighed. At least he realized he *had* been rude. Once, he would have been too wrapped up in his own embarrassment to even notice.

The bridge door opened, and he was directed to the ready room. Captain Picard, Commander Riker, and Geordi were already seated at the table. For a jolting instant, panic grabbed at Reg's gut. The dream had been just like this at the beginning. He tugged at the edge of his uniform just to make sure he still had one.

"You asked to see me, sir?"

"Yes, sit down, Lieutenant. There has been a change of plan," Picard said.

Reg took a chair and fought the sinking feeling that he would be removed from command. Picard got right to the point.

"We have just received a distress call from the colony on Syng II. A massive volcanic eruption has endangered the entire settlement. They have several dead and too many injuries for their medical team to handle. We will take you to a point about twelve hours from the science station by shuttle. Then the away team will fly the *Hawking* to the planet, complete the mission, and wait for the *Enterprise* to return from Syng."

Reg nodded, but he still felt unnerved by how similar this was to his dream. Same people, same room, maybe even the same situation. He remembered nothing beyond the onset of terror when he realized he was completely naked. Reg shook himself and spoke.

"How long, sir? I mean how long will we have to wait?"

Picard glanced toward Riker, who answered.

"The reports from Syng are confused, but counting trip time you should expect to wait at least seventy-two hours."

Then Geordi added, "Supplies are being loaded into the *Hawking,* and it's been prepped. I notified your team of the change. You're ready to go."

My team. Anticipation surged inside him, and he pushed thoughts of the dream aside. Reg stood up.

"Request permission to report to the shuttle, sir."

"Permission granted," Picard said. "We should arrive at the debarkation point within the hour."

Then Geordi added, "Sunspot ionization is still disrupting communication with the science station, but you should have no problem locating their neutrino beacon."

Ensign Ro Laren sat in her old spot on the bridge waiting for Captain Picard to emerge from his ready room. Commander Data sat on her left at the other control station, busy with a last-minute diagnostic scan of the ship's systems. It was good to be back on the *Enterprise,* if only for this short break from her Starfleet training program. Riker, Worf, and the rest of the bridge crew stood ready at their stations behind her. Ro stared into the viewer screen at the twin suns of the Tarvo system. Suddenly they reminded her of eyes watching the *Enterprise.* Watching her.

Eyes.

She had felt uneasy ever since they had arrived here at the edge of the system, but up to that very moment it had made no sense to her. Not that it made much sense now. Why should the thought of eyes have anything to do with anything? She shook her head in disgust and wondered how such *corz* dung had crept into her brain. Captain Picard entered the bridge, and she gladly brought her focus back to the helm controls.

"Has the shuttle left yet, Ensign?" he asked as he took his seat.

"Launch in about twenty seconds, sir," she said.

"When they are safely away, take us out of here, Ensign. Set course for the Syng system, warp 5."

"Aye, sir." Ro's hands flew over the panel in front of her with practiced efficiency.

"The shuttle is away," Data said. Ro swung the ship around and it began to accelerate. Feeling the *Enterprise* move under her control sent a chill up Ro's spine every time, a reaction she hoped she would never lose.

"Course set, sir."

"Engage."

The *Enterprise* leaped into warp, and an undeniable wave of relief washed over her as the twin stars vanished from view.

"Hold shields at one-quarter," Reg said to Yeoman Samuel Carter, who sat in the pilot seat of the *Hawking* next to Ensign Mara Ying from biological sciences. The planet's surface lay some ten kilometers below, hidden by thick clouds.

"Shields steady at twenty-five percent," Carter said.

It *did* feel exhilarating to be in command and on your own. Reg hadn't stuttered in twelve hours. He watched the readouts on a side panel as the shuttlecraft shivered and bucked occasionally in the heavy clouds in spite of its stabilizers. It had taken two hours of scanning from a low-level orbit, just skimming the upper atmosphere, to locate the neutrino beacon, but now they were on their way down. Nothing but gray showed in the viewing ports, but it was still better than beaming down. While transporters no longer terrified him, he'd take the shuttle given a choice.

"We're below the ionization layer, sir," Ensign Ying said. The tone of her voice clearly indicated that she thought it was time to lower shields.

"Hold shields for now," he said. "We've got two suns to contend with. No need to take chances. Yeoman, do we still have the neutrino beacon on sensors?"

"Yes, sir. The sunspot activity is affecting sensors, but I've got a lock on the beacon. We should drop below the clouds any—"

A sudden burst of light cut Carter off. The shuttle lurched wildly as if swatted by a giant fist. The accompanying explosion left Reg's ears ringing in spite of dampening by the shields.

"Shields at maximum!" Reg shouted.

But before Carter could respond, another explosion jolted the shuttle. This time a ribbon of blue energy arced across the panel in front of Carter and Ying and then plunged into them. Both slumped forward in their chairs, unconscious. Smoke billowed from the control panel, and Reg coughed and held his hand over his mouth as he released his straps and came to their aid. Emergency air pumps battled the acrid smoke and ozone as he pulled the unconscious crew members away from the chairs and strapped them into the ones behind. Then he lurched into Carter's place.

He heard the distant, muted hissing of air rushing along the shuttle's outer skin, but it was the sudden quiet inside the *Hawking* that shocked Barclay and set off a twinge in his gut. It was all up to him.

Reg still saw only gray out the front window, but on the computer screen the glowing, orange representation of the *Hawking* descended at a steep angle, tumbling as it fell. If it weren't for gravity control, he'd have been plastered to the wall. He fought to regain control of the plummeting craft. The fires had been extinguished, but main power was gone and the stabilizers had sustained damage. Thank luck he still had auxiliary power.

After several frantic seconds, he managed to slow their descent and stop the craft's spinning. But they were still headed down. His heart pounded even harder in his chest as he realized they were going to crash. Desperate, he tried subspace radio.

"Enterprise, come in. *Enterprise,* do you hear me?"

Nothing. They were long out of range, of course. *Think, man!* Then he tried to reach the science station but got only the crackle of sunspot interference. The Barclay curse had struck again. He was going to crash on his first command. The finality of that sunk in. Ying and Carter shouldn't die like this.

The instruments said the *Hawking* was still a kilometer up. The clouds had given way to a flat, tree-clogged landscape wreathed in wispy bands of fog. It was mostly jungle according to the reports he had read. He checked the sensors again. The neutrino beacon sat atop one of several low, bare hills about ten kilometers away. With inertial dampers below fifty percent, the best chance lay in using the hillside's sloping edge to minimize impact. First he had to get there.

Quickly, he routed every remaining bit of power to the engines and struggled to keep their descent from turning into a free fall.

He was too busy to worry, too busy to wonder what had hit them. At the last second, he used a burst of power to pull up the nose and allow the shuttlecraft to hit tail-first on the bare slope just beyond the crest of the beacon hill. He cut all power except to the vertical steering thrusters under the nose just as the shuttle made contact with the ground. Oddly, his only clear thought was that he had forgotten to apologize to Deanna.

The screeching of tortured metal and the ferocious bumping came to an end with a final jolt so strong that Reg hit the restraining straps with enough force to stun him. When he came to, he was staring through the front port at a tall boulder. A thick cushion of damp soil gouged from the hillside had actually softened the final blow. Just as miraculously, the ship had managed not to flip over.

Reg took a deep breath and checked himself. He had bruising from the straps but nothing worse. Carter and Ying both slumped in their chairs, unconscious but alive. The yeoman's breathing had an ominous rasp to it, however. Reg unstrapped himself and retrieved a tricorder. It confirmed his fear. Carter had internal bleeding. Ying's readings looked stronger, but she showed no signs of coming to. Both had burns and nerve damage beyond Reg's skills or equipment.

Reg gave them injections to block pain, slow down any bleeding, and keep them out of shock. That was all he could do beyond laying them upon the two couches. Then he sagged back into a chair, nauseated and trembling, a delayed reaction to the crash, he guessed. But it wouldn't do. The shuttle's communication system was gone, and he couldn't wait for help to find them. The biologists at the station should have a field med-station. Reg hated to leave Carter and Ying behind, but there was no choice.

He left a message on Ying's tricorder in case she came to while he was gone. Then he checked his phaser and tricorder before snapping a hand-light to his side. He squeezed past the cargo containers and out through the aft door which was wedged partway open.

The jungle air wrapped around him like a damp blanket, still and thick, carrying a sweet, fetid odor. An eerie quiet lay over the area. The crash must have temporarily silenced anything nearby. That had to be it, but his scalp tingled all the same. About thirty meters further down, beyond the boulder, a forest of tall trees with fernlike leaves and gnarled trunks like twisted rope encircled the hill's base. A thick, blue-green carpet of moss, or something very like it, covered the open ground.

He surveyed the deep trough gouged out by the shuttle as it skidded down the hill face. If the boulder had been only a few meters further up, he'd just be another piece of wreckage right now. It was hard to believe how short a trip it had been from foolish elation to disaster. Then he saw the blackened splotch etched on the right side of the ship's nose. He checked the tricorder reading and went cold.

It indicated that a chemical explosive followed by a pulsed proton beam had done the damage. The *Hawking* had been shot down, and not by any type of weapon known to the tricorder's memory bank. Primitive technology, perhaps, but effective. Good thing he hadn't dropped shields. Yet, why hadn't this unseen enemy hit them again? *Good question.* Maybe they had tried and missed. He might not have noticed with most of the sensors out.

Reg set the tricorder for long scan and swung it in a circle, searching for any signs of the station or its crew. He read multiple life-forms but nothing humanoid within a kilometer of the crash site. The station was supposed to be about a kilometer from the beacon on another hilltop, but he had seen no sign of it during their descent. He decided to climb to the top of the hill to get a clearer reading.

But first he slipped back inside the *Hawking* and rigged a force field across the aft door, one that he activated from the outside. It had just enough jolt to discourage any local denizens who might be out for a quick meal. With energy reserves so low, the field would fail in a few hours, but he planned to be back with help long before then. If there was any help to be found, that is. Whoever had shot down the shuttle could have captured the station as well.

But that didn't change what he had to do. It just made his stomach churn that much more. Reg switched his phaser to maximum and headed up the hillside. It couldn't have been more than two hundred meters high, but when he reached the top, he was sweating and miserable in the humidity.

Something buzzed near his face, and he automatically swatted it away. The flier beat its wings and scraped its legs against his palm. Reg jerked back his hand and anxiously examined his palm. Had it stung him? He imagined some deadly venom or virus creeping into his bloodstream and finally had to scan with the tricorder.

Nothing.

With a sigh of relief, he set the tricorder on wide scan and swung it in a circle. A smear of metal was all that remained of the beacon. The shuttle must have come down nearly on top of it. He found no human lifesigns. The tricorder picked up a weak energy source on top of an adjacent hill, one whose crest lay clothed in fog. That must be the station. Holding the tricorder in one hand and his phaser in the other, Reg started down the hill.

Ro sat bolt upright in bed, a stab of fear twisting inside. She had dreamed of the camps for the first time in nearly a year. But not about Cardassians, or beatings, or seeing her father tortured. She had dreamed of Glym, the camp spinner, and a tale she had told the children. A tale from the ancient times when the Bajorans had dominated the quadrant.

Ro had been too young to remember much of it, and until tonight had pretty much forgotten she'd ever heard it at all. But one refrain, spoken in Glym's raspy voice, had crept into the dream.

Death hunts beneath the eyes of Dolmak.

Ro cursed softly. She now remembered being terrified for days, living in mortal fear that she might meet this Dolmak. Was that what this whole stupid thing was about? But why did a pair of suns evoke the memory while the eyes she saw every day had no effect? Maybe there was more of Glym's tale stuck in the deep recesses of her mind than she knew. *More* corz *dung.* She shook her head.

She'd soon have her hands full with hurt people and repairs.

This was no time to lose sleep over nonsense from her past. She lay back down and closed her eyes, but sleep was as elusive as the remainder of Glym's tale.

Reg stood panting from the climb up the hill and scanned the ghostly gray science station rising out of the fog. He read life-signs, but something like insects might give off. Nothing humanoid was alive in there. Cautiously, he traversed the edge of the building, looking for the entrance. A few throaty calls penetrated through the fog coming from the nearby jungle. He pictured nice safe birds making the noise, but it could just as well be poisonous swamp slugs massing for an attack. Or even the enemy who had shot them down. For at least the fifth time he made sure his phaser was set on maximum.

The station was square, only about twenty meters on a side, so it took little time to find what had been the doorway. It was now nothing more than a black, gaping mouth ripped from the side of the structure. A few meters up the side of the station's wall, he saw a jagged, blackened crack, the sort of thing a phaser might do if it had been fired from inside. He had a horrible feeling about what lay in there, but he had a duty to look. If only his hands would stop shaking. He took a deep breath.

"All right, Reg, you can do this."

He snapped the tricorder to his belt, leaving it turned on, and activated the hand-light. Then, with phaser drawn, he entered the structure. Before he had taken three steps Reg stopped, gagging. He had never smelled rotting flesh before, but little doubt touched his mind about the stench that assaulted him. Then he found a severed arm covered with bug things. He rushed outside and vomited.

All he wanted to do was run back to the shuttle and hole up until the *Enterprise* came back. That might be the only thing to do in the end, but first he had to go back inside. Carter's and Ying's lives might depend upon it. Even if that were not the case, he had a duty to record what he could before the bugs had finished their grisly meal.

The second trip inside went a little easier, only because he was prepared for the worst. Besides dealing with the horrible scene itself, he also had to fight down a growing fear that one of the loathsome, glistening bugs would land on him and take a bite.

The interior of the science station looked as if a tornado had erupted inside its walls. Equipment and experiments lay smashed and scattered, crushed in some cases. He would find no usable med-station here. His tricorder showed that the only energy weapons used had been phasers, probably fired by the biologists in a desperate effort to defend themselves. But from what?

The poor devils had been torn limb from limb, hacked to pieces. And in spite of the stench, the readings indicated the massacre had happened within the last three hours. He thought that all five were there, but it would take a medical team to be sure. Reg collected two more phasers, both nearly at full charge, and was about to leave the dark tomb when his beam caught the edge of a tricorder poking from beneath an overturned table. He removed it and went back outside. The tricorder was barely functional, with little power left, but he was able to bring up a visual playback.

The scene was a nightmare. Something huge crossed in and out of the picture in a blur at normal speed. Reg backtracked the record and slowed down the motion. He saw the bright discharge of phasers and then there it was, facing whomever had held the tricorder. Reg froze the picture and nearly froze himself.

The thing must have stood over three meters high. It was a dull green in color with a wide straight torso and thick, powerful legs. Its entire body seemed to be covered by a shell or armor. Four multifaceted eyes gleamed red from a nightmare head sporting dozens of short, prickly horns. The creature had a tearing beak and four massive arms ending in huge talons. Reg gave a mental salute to the person with the tricorder who had kept on recording in the face of such a horror.

He let the picture run on, thankful that the sound was not functioning. Even at one-third speed the monster moved toward the recorder with terrifying quickness. A phaser beam caught it full in the chest area, but the claws closed over the screen, and then the picture went black. Numbly, Reg transferred the record into his own tricorder, including the lifesign readings of the creature.

He stood for a moment looking at the station, thinking of the three men and two women who had come here seeking only to learn. Instead, they found a horrible death without even knowing why. The thing had attacked and slaughtered with a ferocity that made him sick just thinking of it. And he had found not one clue as to a motive. There was supposed to be no intelligent species on this planet, and yet this creature had deliberately broken into the station, determined to kill and destroy. It might be some sort of territorial protection, he thought, but without much conviction. He also couldn't picture that thing firing missiles at the shuttle. But he shouldn't assume anything yet.

Another of the throaty cries came through the fog, and Reg shook himself. Fear drove away his numbness, and he checked the lifesigns of the noisemaker against those stored in his tricorder. Not a match, thank the stars. But now he hated this hill, hated this mission, hated the whole damned planet. If he made it back to the *Enterprise* alive, he'd curl up in the clean, safe confines of the engineering section and never leave. Let someone else play leader. Reg Barclay just wasn't made for this sort of thing. That thought brought Ying and Carter back into his thoughts along with a stab of panic.

He had found nothing to help them survive. And what if that *thing* found them while he was away? His puny force field wouldn't hold up for a second. Adrenaline surged through his veins as Reg set his tricorder to scan for the creature, grabbed a phaser in each hand, and plunged into the grayness.

Ro came to the decision to see Captain Picard after the end of a six-hour shift on the planet's surface, laboring to repair one of several reactors. She had worn an oxygen mask to ward off the noxious gases from the eruption, but her head throbbed all the same. Through it all, she could not shake the nagging fear that "Dolmak's Eyes" had spawned. Then, at a moment of near exhaustion and hunger as she struggled with a reluctant generator, something had come back to her of Glym's tale. Something that truly did frighten her, if what she now suspected were true. A big if.

By all rights she should go to Troi. Dreams and such were the counselor's specialty. But the captain was an expert on archaeology. Besides, she trusted Picard more than anyone she had ever known. Ro reached forward and signaled for admittance to his quarters.

"Come."

She entered and stood uncertainly near the doorway. Captain Picard was dressed in a white robe and sat propped up on his bed, a drink on his nightstand and an old-style book on his lap.

"I'm sorry to disturb you, sir, but I need your help."

The captain looked as tired as she felt, but he managed a smile as he rose and offered her a seat on his couch. Ro accepted and Picard took the chair near his bed. Music played in the background; Mozart, she thought, though she wasn't sure. Data had only recently introduced her to some of the great composers of Earth. Somehow this piece helped soothe the pounding in her skull.

"Would you like some tea or brandy perhaps?" he offered.

"No thank you, sir. I won't keep you long."

"Well, what can I do for you, Ensign?"

Ro took a deep breath and almost decided to back out before she made a fool of herself.

"Sir, do you know much about ancient Bajoran history?"

Picard leaned back in his chair and smiled broadly. "I know a bit about the ancient Bajorans."

"Have you ever heard of 'Dolmak's Eyes'?"

Picard nodded. "Dolmak's Eyes are one of those obscure little puzzles that make archaeology so fascinating. All I know are the lines taken off an old scroll, just a fragment of something longer. Now how did it go? . . . something like *'Our tears drown the seas while death hunts beneath the eyes of Dolmak.'*" Picard took a sip from his glass and then added, "Dolmak was the ancient Bajoran god of revenge, but no one seems to know what the fragment referred to."

"It's part of a song, a chant really," Ro said. "I heard it in full as a small child in the camps. From a spinner who sang to us in

Bajoran so we would remember our heritage and keep our language. I've forgotten most of it, but a piece came back to me today."

Picard leaned forward at her words, his expression intense, almost fierce.

"What I remembered is: *'Beware the deathless Tovang. What was won could not be taken. What was lost could not be spared. Our tears drown the sea while death hunts beneath the eyes of Dolmak.'*"

Furrows creased the captain's brow as he considered the words. Then he shook his head. "You've added a valuable piece, but it's still a puzzle. Much knowledge has been lost or forgotten by the scattering of your people. I'd like to meet one of these spinners one day. But what made you think of it now?"

"Those binary stars reminded me of eyes, sir. Since planets, much less livable ones, are rare in binary systems, I did some checking. On a hunch, I guess. I even had information sent by subspace from the archives on Bajor. The Tarvo system lies at the edge of the old Bajoran Republic."

Picard stood and paced. "You think those suns are the eyes of Dolmak?"

Ro pressed her hands against throbbing temples. She had gone too far to back down now. "Yes, sir. According to the archives, two thousand years ago my people fought a war against a nonhumanoid race called the Vorel. They may have been insect-like, though the records are incomplete. The Bajorans eventually won the war and took possession of several star systems including the Tarvo system. But there is no record of any colony having ever been placed there. Or maybe it was abandoned."

Picard gave her a sharp glance. "*'What was won could not be taken.'* Yes, that might fit."

"I think so, sir. And thinking of the other verses, I can't shake the feeling that the away team and those biologists could be in terrible danger."

Reg was nearly halfway down the hill when the tricorder signaled it had picked up a matching set of lifesigns. He skidded to a stop on the mossy hillside and checked the reading. Four kilometers away and bearing straight for him. Maybe it was headed back to the station. He hurried on and almost fell when something slithered across his path before disappearing behind a bush.

Reg emerged from the mist near the bottom of the hill and ran down a shallow ravine toward the base of the adjacent hill that hid the shuttle on its far slope. Then he began to climb again. After a few dozen meters he stopped and checked the tricorder. The thing had changed course and was still headed straight at him, now only three and a half kilometers away. Reg checked the heading again. It had to be a fluke.

Just to prove it, he veered ninety degrees to his left, maintaining his height on the hillside. He trotted for about a hundred meters before taking another reading. Reg read the instrument in disbelief. His pulse pounded in his ears, and it felt as if a cold hand had suddenly gripped his heart.

If he returned to the shuttle, he'd lead that killing machine right to Carter and Ying.

Feeling as if his heart had sunk to his ankles, Reg examined the thick row of trees below and shuddered. But what choice did he have? He ran down the slope and slipped between a pair of trees and into the jungle. The foliage grew close together, choking off any hope of an easy path through. Worse, the ground grew soggier with each step. Mud sucked at his ankles, and stagnant pools, reeking of decay, blocked his path, forcing him to circle. Flying things buzzed and whined around his face. Fog had begun to gather. Every time he checked the tricorder, the signals of his pursuer had grown nearer.

As he splashed along the edge of a particularly large pool, his foot caught on a snag and he fell into the water, sinking nearly up to his waist in slime and mud. Something brushed against his leg underwater and he panicked, thrashing his way back onto the shore. Then he staggered across an open mossy space, leaned back against a tree trunk, and gasped for air. The tricorder showed the monster only two and a half kilometers behind.

You can't outrun it, Barclay.

He could stand and fight, but he'd have no more chance than the biologists. Maybe he could rig a cross fire with the three phasers, but the creature was too quick and heavily armored. If it could sense his lifesigns at a distance, then hiding was equally useless. He must also assume that its other senses were sharp. Except its eyes, perhaps. Multifaceted arrangements often had limitations. But it might have heat-sensing organs, especially if it hunted at night.

Reg sagged. He was a dead man.

A wave of dizziness came over him, followed by a new thought. *Classic predator-prey, but you've got it backwards. As usual.* It was the kind of insight he got sometimes, out of nowhere it always felt like, but he knew better. The Cytherians had returned his intelligence to its normal level after their encounter four years earlier, but some shadow of that exalted state remained behind and would show itself now and again. Like now.

Backwards. Of course.

It could be done. Faceted eyes might mean poor detail vision, but he'd have to do something about the other senses. Yes, if he had the time he could do it. He used the tricorder to calculate the creature's speed and start a countdown. Reg gulped. Fewer than eight minutes! He yanked off the tricorder panel and frantically reprogrammed the necessary circuits to allow it to transmit a signal. Next he set the three phasers to overload at the same instant and then began to rip up huge handfuls of moss until he had an impressive mound stacked near the tree. As he dropped to the ground and began to remove his boots, another realization hit him from some deeper core.

He was thinking like a spider.

That thought was cut short by the sound of snapping tree limbs coming through the fog.

Ro waited tensely at her station as the *Enterprise* pulled into orbit. She was the reason they had screamed back here at warp 5. All over what might be just a Bajoran myth. Now she hoped she had been wrong about everything.

"Sunspot activity has diminished, Captain," Data said. "There is no trace of the neutrino beacon, but we have full communication and transporter function to the surface."

"Very well. Ensign Ro, hail the away team."

Ro sent the hail, but the seconds ticked by in silence.

"No reply, sir."

"Try again."

"Repeating hail."

Nothing. Ro squeezed one hand into a fist as more seconds ticked by. Then a rasp came through the comm.

"Yi-n-g here. Hurt. I—"

There was no more.

"Commander Data, are you locked on?" Picard asked.

"I have a lock on two human lifesigns inside what appears to be the shuttle."

"Beam them directly to sickbay."

After a short delay Doctor Crusher's voice sounded on the comm. "We have Ying and Carter, both alive."

Ro felt a wave of relief, but where was Reg Barclay?

"Can we raise the science station, Commander?" Picard asked.

"Negative, sir," Data said.

"Ensign Ro, hail Lieutenant Barclay again and begin scanning the area around the shuttle. Counselor, can you sense anything?"

"I'm not sure, sir. I'm feeling something, but it's very confused. A great tenseness or expectation, maybe."

Ro blinked at what she saw on the scans, checked it again, and reported. "Sir, I've picked up human lifesigns, a single individual, about two kilometers from the shuttle. It could be Bar—" Ro stopped short and gasped.

"Sir, there's been an explosion at the same coordinates."

Reg was scraping mud off his face when he heard the combadge's chirp. The device was lying in the mud just a few steps away. Maybe Ying had come to and was trying to find him. Limping slightly, he walked over and retrieved it.

"Barclay here." To his astonishment, he heard Data's voice.

"Lieutenant Barclay, prepare to be beamed aboard."

"Wait, Ying and Carter—"

"They are aboard and safe. Do you require medical assistance?"

He had a scrape or two and something had stung his calf, but mostly it was the mud that bothered him.

"What I really need is a bath. One to beam up; no, wait—I need to get something." He limped around the edge of the gaping, water-filled crater where the tree had stood. The creature's head had fallen in one piece and was the only body part left that he could see. Had he really been a spider, it would have made a disappointing meal. Maybe Doctor Crusher and the ship's biologists could make something of it. The thing was heavy, but he managed. Thankfully, no gore oozed from the neck cavity.

"One to beam up."

Reality dissolved into a sparkling mist about the same time that Reg remembered that he was naked. When the world came into focus again, he stood on a transporter platform facing four officers. Captain Picard looked astonished, Commander Riker wore a bemused grin on his face, Beverly Crusher put one hand over her mouth, and Deanna Troi stared at the head he carried. Or so he hoped.

He shifted the grisly trophy under one arm, though the short horns pushed against his sides, and straightened himself. At that moment, the concept of embarrassment felt as alien as the creature's head itself.

"Lieutenant Reginald Barclay reporting, sir." Then with a dignity he truly felt, Reg stepped from the platform and approached the officers.

"Request permission to go to my quarters and clean up, sir." Picard looked him straight in the eye.

"Permission granted. Do you wish to be beamed there?"

Reg shook his head without hesitation and said, "No, sir. It's not far."

The captain nodded, his expression now as sober as ever. "Very well, Lieutenant. Then report to sickbay and to me after that. It seems we have a lot to discuss."

Picard's eyes strayed to the severed head. Only then did Reg realize the effect the gruesome thing must be having on them. He could imagine the questions that must be filling their minds. With no lids to cover the ruby-domed eyes, the head looked as if it could be alive. That made the long, razor-sharp tearing beak that much more formidable.

"Yes sir," Reg said and then turned to Doctor Crusher. "This is for you," he said and handed her the head. He had never seen a gift received more reluctantly. Then he turned and marched out of the room and down the corridor, as naked and unashamed as the day he was born.

Reg sat in the ready room and watched as Captain Picard scanned the last of the report. It felt wonderful to be clean again. And safe. His only regret was that the confident, naked man who had marched triumphantly from the transporter room was gone. He gave a little sigh.

Commander Riker, Data, and Geordi were also there, and to his surprise, so was Ro Laren.

Picard chuckled.

"A straw man with a bomb inside. Classic use of a decoy. Most ingenious, Mr. Barclay. But how did you think of it?"

"Thank you, sir. I realized that I couldn't run away or hide. It had some kind of sense that acted much like a tricorder. What happened to the biologists ruled out a direct phaser attack. Then I realized that with a little reprogramming, my tricorder could transmit any lifesigns it had recorded, my own in particular. But I had to fool the creature's other senses. So, I stuffed my uniform with moss and hid the tricorder and phasers inside.

"I had to hope that I was right about its vision. In light of what happened, I believe that it relied primarily on its other senses, especially the 'tricorder' sense, until it got close."

"Rigging that tricorder was a nice piece of work, Reg," Geordi said from the other end of the table. "But timing all three phasers to overload at just the right moment. That's tricky to do."

Reg blushed.

"That thing had kept almost a constant speed, so I could calculate how much time I had. I just added a few extra seconds and prayed it didn't slow down."

He said nothing about how the concussion had nearly knocked him out under the water. There was a moment of silence as the others considered what he had said. He had also left out any reference in his report to Cytherians or spiders. Maybe later after he'd had time to sort things out. Data had already told him about the Vorel and that the *Hawking* had been shot down by missiles, part of an ancient, atmospheric defense system. Ironically, if the biologists had not beamed down, they might have been warned. But something still nagged at him.

"Sir, was that creature a Vorel?"

Picard stirred from his thoughts and spun his chair toward Reg.

"Not exactly, but I think I will defer to Ensign Ro. She and Commander Data have spent the last few hours analyzing what we know. And I must add that if not for her initiative, the *Enterprise* would not have returned in time."

For the first time in his experience, Reg saw Ro Laren turn a bright crimson.

"Commander Data and I have concluded that before the Vorel left here, they set a trap. Thousands of these creatures—Tovang, the Bajorans called them—were hidden below ground, probably shielded against detection. In any case, their lifesigns would have been faint inside the hibernation tanks we found. It appears the Vorel didn't even risk giving them energy weapons. We believe they were warrior-class Vorel, specially bred and modified for one purpose only—to sense and destroy humanoid life-forms.

"When the trap closed, so many Bajorans died that my people abandoned the place. The surviving Tovang probably returned to the vats and slowly died out until only this one remained. When the shuttle first touched the atmosphere, the Vorel's defense system must have been alerted and awakened the creature.

Reg nodded but could think of nothing to say. He had played out the last acts in a war two thousand years old. It was a sad thought. He could see by something in Ro Laren's eyes, so often hard and determined, that she felt it too.

Later, in Ten-Forward he saw her drinking alone and sat down across the table from her. She wore the same sober expression as she had in the ready room.

"I wanted to thank you," Reg said.

She gave a faint smile.

"You're the real hero of the day. You saved Carter and Ying."

Reg shook his head. "No, we both did."

Ro shrugged and took another sip of what looked like Aldebaran whiskey. "We haven't learned much in two thousand years, have we?" she said.

"How's that?"

"We're still slaughtering each other."

Reg studied her face. He knew that Ro Laren had been raised in the Bajoran refugee camps. He'd always thought of her as a survivor—tough and resilient, even fierce. Nothing like Reg Barclay at all. But now he saw someone else as well. Someone who could be lonely, who was no stranger to tears. Someone familiar. Of course, maybe he had become just a little bit more like her. Perhaps that naked warrior was still inside somewhere just waiting for another chance to emerge. It didn't matter.

"I suppose you're right. But if we haven't made any progress and realize it, then that's progress, isn't it? At least if we keep trying?"

He thought he heard just the spark of a laugh escape from her throat only to drown in the whiskey. But she was looking at him now—appraising, he would have said. Odd, he wasn't even blushing.

"You know, I haven't been to the arboretum for weeks," he said. "They say there are some wonderful new species of flowers blooming in there. Very beautiful, I hear. Would you like to go take a look?"

Something softened in Ro Laren's gaze, and her lips curved into a real smile.

"Yes, I'd like that, Reg. I'd like that very much."

The First

Peg Robinson

The shuttlebay was large. Not as large as that of *Enterprise*-D—but large enough. Picard acknowledged the guard standing duty with a nod and a tight smile and passed into the cavernous space, doors swishing shut behind him.

The room's one inhabitant didn't notice him. Not surprising. She was halfway down the bay, lying on the top of her little, primitive ship, hanging almost upside down into the open entry hatch. Her gray ponytail hung down, tied with a bright scarf. The distance, her preoccupation, the pulse that no doubt beat in her ears as she dangled there—all or any of them were enough to keep her from noticing the whoosh of air and well lubricated machinery. Picard was just as glad. He wanted these few moments to watch her, appreciate her, before . . .

Before he had to destroy her.

She was the first. While she would almost certainly not be the last, she would be the last for a very, very long time if he succeeded in doing what law and logic dictated. While his sense of duty was at ease with this, his heart was not.

Jean-Luc Picard was a quiet man, and he grieved quietly. But he did grieve.

It was such a fragile ship—as fragile as any newborn thing. So clumsy. Such a little miracle. He longed to touch it, as he had savored the pleasure of touching the ship Zefram Cochrane and Lily had created together. He was half in love with the thing; and for the same reason.

The woman dropped a microspanner and cursed in her own language. The universal translator tactfully left the words in the original, but the delivery made the intent clear. She hung there, arms dangling, hair flopping, and heaved a mighty sigh. "Blast, blast, blast it all to the Wexery and back." She began to shimmy back up onto the roof.

"Stay there. I'll get it for you." Picard stepped quietly across the flooring, boots clicking lightly, leaned over, and retrieved the tool from the threshold of the hatchway. He handed it up to the woman, who looked down at him, her russet face split with a good-natured grin. "You should be more careful. You could spend a good deal of time going up and down, if you drop your tools like that very often."

"Going up and down is the whole point, Captain Picard. Why I bothered in the first place. You didn't think I designed this thing just to be careful, did you?" She chuckled. "Give me a moment and I'll come down . . . or you can come up, if you like."

Her race called themselves the Shadrasi. He thought they might be a handsome people, but it was hard to tell from her alone, and she was the first he'd ever seen. She wasn't young—no more so than he, and she had a solid, blocky build, and plenty of sags. There were crow's-feet marking her dark skin and underlining the ridges that arched over her brows, giving her a permanent look of surprise on a homely, humorous face. The wrinkles around her mouth made cheerful brackets. Laugh lines, Picard thought. On me they're just wrinkles. On her they're laugh lines. I wish . . . He didn't allow himself to complete the thought. He could not afford to envy this woman as she was—or pity her as she would be. He smiled.

"Thank you for the offer: I'd like that." He paused, admiring the vessel. "Our engineers are still quite excited about the drive on this ship. It is quite unlike our own warp drives, yet appears to have potential to be just as efficient, given some refinement. A direction of development we never even imagined. Even in prototype it's impressive. I'd enjoy a chance to work on her—if you don't mind, Madame-emissary Conta Goalitz-romas azua Trobinda."

" 'Werta.' I told you before. Just 'Werta.' The rest is stuffy formality. Good for impressing the peasantry, if you enjoy that sort of thing . . . but I never have. So let's stick to 'Werta,' and be comfortable." She reached down a square, hard hand to help him up the ladder welded to the side of her ship. "I don't have a lot of patience with formality. And your help is welcome. Your precious engineers keep acting like it's a diplomatic dilemma just loaning me a welding laser. It's almost as bad as it was back home, without the advantage of being able to throw my noble lineage around when I want some cooperation."

Picard slipped up onto the metal roof, feeling the flex of the skin under his weight. The hull was stripped down to as thin a layer as possible to keep down the weight while still holding the vacuum at bay, and holding strong against the strains of use.

The woman had shown absolute brillance in her design choices, from the conception of the drive to the precise and delicate balance of the thousands of elements that made up the hull and the interior. The result, to Picard, seemed just short of supernaturally perfect. So slight a ship: so great an accomplishment. He sat beside the woman who had birthed the miracle. "I'm sure you know how bureaucracies are, er, 'Werta.' " He brushed a hand over an open access panel, and cursed himself for his own reserve, and his reluctance to do what had to be done. He steeled himself. "I'm afraid allowing you access to our technology *is* something of a diplomatic dilemma."

He looked up and met eyes as firm in their purple gaze as his own gray ones. This woman was not naive. Her mouth turned up, ever so slightly. "I see. I thought maybe . . ." She looked down, then looked up again from under her lashes. "It struck me at the time that emerging from the transit field into the middle of a battle might create certain complexities. Your people are at war, aren't they?"

Picard didn't answer. He didn't have to. It had been a momentous occasion.

They had been ten minutes into an attack by Jem'Hadar ships, *Enterprise*-E just barely holding its own; and in the middle of the phaser fire and the flaring shields, there was a burst of light— and there between all the combatants was a tiny little ship. He supposed he should thank Werta for her serendipitous timing: The Jem'Hadar moved to attack her as a dangerous unknown. The slight confusion that had followed had given Picard and his crew the time they needed to complete an attack pattern. They'd won, and they very well might not have. And Werta's ship had only been slightly damaged. But . . .

When they'd pulled the ship in with their tractor beams they'd also pulled in an ethical problem. The kind of command decision Picard hated. The exigencies of the Prime Directive, and the demands of expedience, were hard to balance against his own sense of justice.

He looked away from her and patted the metal roof. "I don't think I ever asked: Does she have a name?"

"Of course. I named my aircar, my stove, my favorite cooking pot, and my writing console, too." Her voice was dry, amused, patient. But he didn't fool himself: She knew there was a dagger hidden in this conversation, and was on her guard. She ran her own hand over her ship, inches away from his own. *"He's* called *Vosin.* After a man in a myth. The last reality, the world before this one we share, ended in apocalypse. The gods had failed. Chaos was eating up the multiverse. But there was a man named Vosin, who remembered all the beauty of the world, and the joy of life, and the dream of the stars. He was a performer, a sacred actor, and he brought his entire troupe together, and performed. . . . They performed the entire universe itself. Every beloved rock, every tree, every river and cloud, every field, every man and woman and child. But they couldn't imagine how to perform the stars. All the time he and his troupe performed, they cried because no matter how they tried, the stars would be lost from memory, and from the performance. When they were done a miracle occurred, and the world was reborn from the passion and love of their performance. The actors were at the point of death—and the gods, who had been reborn with all the rest, took the actors and put them in the sky and turned them into the planets, and Vosin into our own world. His blood became our blood, his love our love, his flesh our flesh and everything we grew from. And every one of the tears they'd cried as they performed became a star. So my ship is called *Vosin,* because he gave us life—and the stars."

"It's a good name." Picard took up an engineering tricorder and ran it over the open panel. He didn't look at her. Couldn't look at her.

"It's a good myth."

"Yes. It is." He put down the tricorder and began a delicate adjustment on a sensor connection.

He heard her shift, restless. Then a firm hand clamped over his, and she took his microspanner gently from him. "Captain, don't play hidey-guessy with an old Shadrasi noble. We invented the game. You came to tell me something. What?"

He looked up, staring blankly across the shuttlebay to the beams and gray metal sheeting. It couldn't reproach him. Any other duty he would have performed with less reluctance. Any other. He'd sent men and women to their deaths. He'd accepted the slow destruction of cultures, in the name of the Prime Directive. But this? Something inside screamed "no." His lips tightened. "As you noted, Werta, you arrived at a less than convenient time." He struggled, wanting to apologize for the Federation, like a housekeeper dropped in on when her laundry was undone, her meals unplanned, her beds unmade. "We are, as you noted, at war."

"And?"

"And an examination of your ship, and the location of your planet of origin, would indicate that any further exploration you attempt will do as this attempt has done: place you in the middle of contested territory."

"I see." She leaned back, her clothes rustling around wide hips. "So. You're telling me to go home—and don't come back."

He nodded. At last he looked at her.

It had occurred to him when he first saw her that, in some way, she was what Zefram Cochrane should have been. As quixotic as he, as individualistic, but not as tattered and rough. Not as much a refugee in her own life.

When Picard had been a boy, struggling with his family and dreaming of the stars, he'd imagined Cochrane: imagined a man who would understand all he felt when he had hidden himself in his father's vineyards and looked up at the night sky. Someone who would understand the pulse of passion he'd felt when he reached out thin adolescent arms, wanting to hold every speck and flash of distant light to his heart.

Cochrane had been less, and more, than he'd dreamed. This woman was too. She certainly wasn't an adolescent boy's idea of a hero. Too old, too plain, too alien, too self-amused. But there was the same passion in her eyes as he had seen in his lost nephew's, the same passion he remembered rushing through his own boyish blood. The same passion he still felt looking out at all that grandeur.

He faced her, determined that if he had to close that passion off, he'd look her in the eye. He'd pay the price of his people's laws and expedience. "I'm sorry. But it isn't safe. Not for your people, and not for mine. I'm sorry I can't explain it all. There are too many factions involved. If your people stay where they are, if they aren't noticed, then they may be safe, if we succeed in our attempts. If we don't succeed, then no one will be safe. But if you come out here again you may be found by people less benign than the Federation, and they would use you to their advantage. Your world would fall under their influence; our enemies would have a platform from which to mount new attacks."

His eyes shuttered as he thought of the fascinating, novel drive system incorporated in *Vosin*'s design—so potentially useful that Geordi La Forge had moved analysis of that technology up to highest priority. The Federation needed this—and Picard dreaded the idea of it in the hands of the Borg, or the Dominion, or for that matter the Klingons, Cardassians, Romulans. . . .

"We can't risk our enemies . . . assimilating you. They'd have new technologies we aren't prepared to defend against. They're already far too strong as it is."

"Ah." She rubbed her hands over her face. Looked, as he had looked, at the far wall, eyes slightly out of focus. "And you can't see the possibility of us serving as allies?" She flicked a glance over at him, and her mouth twisted. "No. I see. We are too far behind you, yes? The *teelit* offering to help the *rombas* . . . too small to be respected."

"Yes. I'm sorry. We have a law. It's called the Prime Directive. It limits our dealings with other worlds to those which we cannot corrupt or overwhelm with our technological advantages or cultural dominance." He grimaced, not knowing how to say what he must without being more tactless than he wished. "We also refrain from dealing with cultures that have not worked out certain aspects of their socialization yet. There are human rights concerns raised by some of the things you've told me about your own world. You would not be accepted as members of the Federation, and we would be unable to defend you as allies." What he didn't and couldn't say was that no matter what they did, the Prime Directive was breached: The act of placing the Shadrasi in political quarantine, and of asking Werta to ensure they remained on their own planet, was a breach in and of itself. Just less of a breach than allowing them to wander out into a war zone, or to ally with stronger, older worlds, or be assimilated into the power bases of enemies. Of course, it was also safer: for her people . . . and for the Federation.

Werta's mouth tightened, and her purple eyes reminded him of hard, sharp-faceted amethysts. "Ah. I see." Now she picked up the microspanner, and returned to the repair he'd started. Her voice was slightly muffled, as she spoke. "And were your people so far advanced when you rose up into the stars, Captain?"

He thought of Earth, as it had been at the time of first contact. Thought of fierce, honorable, soul-damaged Lily, of Zefram Cochrane and his despair, thought of the damage, and the rubble, and the poverty and rage that had been characteristic of Earth at the time of that first, historic flight. "No. No, we were not as we are now. But things are not the same for you. It's a more dangerous universe."

"Is it? Really?"

He didn't know what to say. Yes? But there had always been danger. No? But that would be a lie. Earth had been greeted with wonder and friendship by the Vulcans, and had faced no greater threat than the Klingons and the Romulans, whose power and technology weren't so far advanced over their own. "It is more perilous than anything we faced. More perilous than anything we would choose to face now, if we had any choice at all in this. We are a peaceful people."

She kept her head down, and he watched that bright scarf of hers bob as she worked. "We have a story on my planet, Captain. A lot of stories, to tell you the truth. But one . . . There once was a man in Dostuf, who decided he would breed the best jumping *droubs* anyone had ever seen. He decided the way to do it was to breed selectively. He chose the best stock by creating a test run, with fences for the animals to leap over." She stopped, for a moment, examining the repair. Satisfied, she moved on to another. "It worked well, at first. The second generation could leap higher than the first, and he raised the fences, and chose the best of them. The third leaped higher than the second, and he raised the fences and culled his stock again. It went on that way for several generations." She stopped altogether, then.

Picard waited for her to continue. When she didn't, he asked the question she'd left waiting for him. "And then?"

"And then the stock began to fail. There were weaknesses, there were latent genetic diseases that started showing up. But the worst . . . . Captain, you can only raise a fence so high, before it is too high for any *droub* to jump. A *droub* is a *droub,* no matter how you breed it. In the end, no matter what he did, he found he'd raised his fences too high." She laid down the microspanner and straightened her back, stretching, vertebrae popping. She moaned as stiff muscles let go and relaxed. Then she looked at him, as determined as he was. "If you keep raising the fences, raising the standards, someday you will have raised them so high no one will be able to jump them. If your people made their own first appearance now, as flawed as they were

107

when they first rose into the stars, would your world be allowed out to play in the stars among the rest of your Federation?"

"No."

"I didn't think so." She cocked her head. "It occurs to me that what you have become, you became not because you came when you were 'ready' for the stars, but because being among the stars made you ready. You can't grow up unless you take risks . . . and in taking them learn how to take them. Some dangers you can't eliminate or avoid, Captain Picard. Not without becoming permanently—immature."

"You're not going to stay on your planet." Not a question at all. He could see that.

She stood and offered him her hand. "No. I can't. Even if I could promise it, if I had the clout to force all my people to give up the stars—I wouldn't." She motioned him to the ladder, and waited while he climbed back down, then tucked her tool kit under her arm and followed him to the floor of the shuttlebay. Once down, she looked at him again; her coarse, heavy-boned face, with its cinnamon skin, delicate brow ridges, and wrinkles, twisted into an expression that was almost forlorn. "I . . . I wonder if you understand, Captain?" She reached through the hatch, putting down the tool kit. "I *want* you to understand. When I was a girl, I used to stand on a tree stump, on my father's estate. We weren't rich. You can be noble, without being rich. Most nights we ate *quella* eggs in rom-root broth, for lack of better, and we ate hard cakes made of *chori-mast* to fill up the empty places the eggs and broth left. I wore clothes handed on to me by 'my cousin the Nunar.' *Her* family was noble *and* rich. But her clothes never fit very well, and my knees showed, along with all the scabs I picked up climbing trees and riding *droub-avits,* and the fabric was too thin to be comfortable when all we had to heat the mansion was storm-wrack from the homewood. But I'd stand on the stump at night, out at the edge of the romfield and look at the stars." She grinned—sadly, a bit mockingly.

"I remember one night. There was a high wind. The clouds were racing across the sky, fast as little silver *za-aat* in a stream, stretched out long, and thin, and white. The moons were like torches, and the stars showed between the clouds, burning bright. So bright. I wasn't wearing anything like enough, and my skin was all goosebumps. But I remember raising my arms, and reaching out for all that light, and singing my head off, and that was warmth enough to make up for my knobby knees and goosebumps. I loved them. Gods and graces, but I loved the stars." She sighed, and picked the tool kit back up. When she spoke again, her voice was a near whisper, hoarse and throaty. "I still do, Captain." She looked at him, then. He thought that, maybe, he saw just a spark of tears. He wasn't sure—she was too in control for him to be sure. "So. Do you understand?" He nodded, and she smiled, sadly. "I thought you might. We're coming back, Captain. I understand your concerns. But we're coming back."

"My people will try to cut you off. You present a clear and present danger where you are, and as you are. For your own good, and ours, we will have to try to stop you."

"So be it. We're still coming back."

He closed his eyes, and told the truth, as he had told other truths. "I'm glad."

He was glad. But that night the stupidity of it all ate at him. The Shadrasi didn't know enough. And space was far, far more deadly than anything humans had faced when they first emerged from the system that had cradled them. But the Federation's laws and needs allowed no room for him to change that, to help this race. They would come, in their valor . . . and die, be assimilated by the Borg, be conquered by Cardassians, be overrun by the Dominion, even be traded into submission by hordes of clever, manipulative Ferengi. Or the Federation would succeed in imposing the lesser breach of the Prime Directive, and turn them back, fence them safely in their own yard, like children in a playpen. All that love and passion and hope, and it would die on the vine. And there was nothing he could do about it. Nothing. The laws and regulations said so. His orders said so. They were too "backward" to join the Federation, too weak to be allies, too "primitive" not to be protected as children were protected—kept from the matches of technology and information that might burn their curious fingers. He couldn't help them. Mustn't help them.

He put a *Magnificat* on the computer, and listened as the rejoicing music poured out of the speakers. What would the Federation be, if humans had never been there, part of it all? What would humans be if the Vulcans, seeing human "barbarity," had turned their backs, refused to communicate, quarantined Earth, held back the technological information that had helped make the conquest of space possible? Who would he, Jean-Luc Picard, have been, if he had grown up on a quarantined planet, denied the stars?

It wasn't right. He understood the principals, he understood the expedience . . . and it still wasn't right. Werta and her people had earned the stars. And the Federation, running ahead, trapped in its own fate and future, would, for the best of reasons and the worst of arrogances, deny them those bright, hopeful explorations. It wasn't right.

Picard, struggling, wondered how so joyful a dream had come to this. How his own people, with the best intentions possible, had become so many things they despised. Too rigid to let Werta have her stars, as the peaceful Vulcans had let imperfect, brutal humans have the stars. Too arrogant to understand that you can raise the fences too high.

And all their dreams, their sense of identity? For centuries the Federation had boldly flown out, and where they went the words were used, over and over: "We come in peace." "We are a people of peace." "Can we help?" And now they were going to war, facing a menace that might destroy them, arming their ships, preparing for destruction on a scale Werta and her people could only grope to understand . . . and they were turning away that little ship, and its cargo of dreams.

How had it come to this?

He frowned, and crossed the main room of his living quarters, pulling an old book down off the shelf. It was a vanity . . . he'd bought it when he graduated from the academy, from a little bookseller's shop in London. It was old, and battered, but it was real paper. He'd always loved books, and their burden of bright words and brighter ideas. But this book he'd bought for the ancient author, recorder of a British imperialism that somehow seemed to echo the more egalitarian Federation's wide-scattered wonders, and for the magic token of the man he'd read once owned similar books: Captain James Kirk. Admiral Kirk. The mythmaker. The polymath, with his energy, and his passion, his luck and his charisma . . . and his books. Shakespeare, Dickens, Melville . . . Kipling.

Kipling. The author of Empire. A man who had loved Empire, but loved it with fewer illusions than many. A man who had whispered as often of caution, and humility, and obligation, as of pomp and glory and mastery. His cautions had been heard less often than his praises, and the empire he'd loved had toppled in time. But the cautions lingered on, remembered, there to learn from for any who would look with open eyes.

Picard ruffled through the pages, seeing the stories—all old, and familiar. The poems—many committed to memory years since. He found the one he wanted.

> God of our fathers, known of old,
> Lord of our far-flung battle-line,
> Beneath whose awful Hand we hold
> Dominion over palm and pine—
> Lord God of Hosts, be with us yet,
> Lest we forget—lest we forget!
>
> The tumult and the shouting dies;
> The Captains and the Kings depart:
> Still stands Thine ancient sacrifice,
> An humble and a contrite heart.
> Lord God of Hosts, be with us yet,
> Lest we forget—lest we forget!

There was more, but he didn't need it. The message was there. The memory beyond Empire, of a humanity less than divine, and obligations greater than dominion . . . or expedience. Picard closed the book. Put it back on the shelf, carefully, respectfully. He didn't think he believed in a God . . . not as

111

such. Not in any form Kipling, in his Victorian, British, Christian-conditioned certainties, would have recognized as God. But Picard did understand prayer. Or, at least, he understood this prayer.

How could he not? He understood expedience. He honored law. He accepted the grim necessity of the war that faced them. He was versed in the obligations and privileges of power. But some things an empire—or a Federation—dared not forget, or it would face damnation. Some arrogances a leader, and lawgiver, dared not risk. Lily had taught him that: Lily, far in the past. Primitive by today's standards. He could hear her voice, still. "Ahab." "You broke your little ship." By today's rules, Lily and her children would never have leaped the fence, and flown among the stars, equal among equals. Wise, strong Lily.

He chose.

He was in his ready room when Werta, in her wonderful *Vosin,* left. He'd said his good-byes earlier, unwilling to hold that farewell to the bitter end. That would have been too . . . melodramatic.

The comm-chime chirped, and Commander Riker's voice came to him. "Captain, the shuttlebay is fully open, and we've cleared *Vosin* for takeoff. Any final orders?"

"No, Will. Permission to launch. Give her my best."

"Will do. Riker, out."

Picard stood, and walked to the viewport. He still wasn't used to the new uniforms: He felt like a dark predator in his, missing the bold glory of his old burgundy. Ah, well. Times change; as well, the trimmings and symbols change with them. He wondered what Werta and her people would choose to wear, what announcement of self they'd stride into the stars carrying on their backs. Probably something bright. Something hopeful.

The *Vosin* eased its way into space, coming into Picard's view. He was glad he'd seen it. Glad he'd run his hands over its skin, repaired wires, met its creator and pilot.

When he'd said good-bye he'd pushed the box, filled with reference chips, and padds, and translating programs, into

Werta's hands, quietly. "It isn't much. But it should help. I couldn't give you anything top secret. But the texts cover most of what we know, and you can deduce much of what was left out. Some of them are physics. Some history. Some current events. A few encyclopedias. Mostly general material, but useful. It should let you know what you're up against. You should be able to come up with some defenses, if you're going to leap the fence in any case." He'd smiled, tightly. "I have always found that even exploration goes better if you have some idea of where you're going, and what to pack."

Her eyes had flickered. "And your Prime Directive?"

"I've stood Prime Directive hearings before. So far they've all been worth it. I have no doubt this one will be, too."

She smiled, her plain face radiant. "And the stars? Are they worth it?"

"Absolutely."

It was worth it. It was all worth it.

He turned back to his work. War was coming and there was a "far-flung battle-line" to shore up. Encounters to prepare for that had far less to do with exploration, or sense of wonder, than with expedience and survival. But he didn't turn until *Vosin* had departed in a burst of light that lingered afterward, lighting space like a new star.

Picard smiled.

He was a man who loved the stars.

See Spot Run

Kathy Oltion

Captain Jean-Luc Picard looked forward to reviewing the stack of reports in his ready room as much as a Ferengi looked forward to a full-scale audit. The *Enterprise* was due at Alpha Kiriki in three days for a routine Starfleet inspection, which normally was no reason to worry. Picard ran a tight ship, and he could count on his crew to maintain order.

Lately, however, chaos sprang up in the oddest of places, most recently the current engineering logs. Last week's maintenance logs, for instance, were completely missing. Geordi had discovered the problem yesterday while going over the inspection checklist with his staff. Luckily, the backup logs were left intact, except for Picard's signature. Those logs were only part of what Picard needed to tackle this morning.

As he entered his ready room to begin the process, he heard water splashing from his aquarium. He looked over and saw

Spot, Mr. Data's cat, up to her shoulder in saltwater, going after Picard's lionfish.

"No!" Captain Picard ordered. Spot flinched, but didn't run from the tank.

Picard plucked the cat from her perch and carried her to the couch. She stepped away from him, shook her wet paw, and settled in to groom herself.

The captain glowered at her, then turned and examined the aquarium for damage. Luckily, the fish was intact, though he hid behind a clump of elodea at the back of the tank. Water lay in puddles on the floor.

Captain Picard slapped his combadge and ordered, "Mister Data. To the ready room. Now!"

Data was on duty on the bridge that morning. It took only a moment before the pneumatic door swished open and Data entered. "Yes, sir," he said.

Picard stood opposite the door, arms crossed. "Mr. Data. I'd like an explanation for your cat's presence in my ready room."

Data looked around the room and spied Spot, still sitting on the couch and deeply engrossed in giving herself a bath. "Captain, I have no explanation. She should be in my quarters."

"I couldn't agree with you more," Picard said. "I found her going after my fish." He nodded toward the aquarium. "If I hadn't come in when I did, it would have been too late."

Data went to the couch and gathered Spot in his arms. "Spot. You have been a bad cat," he told her. Spot reached up to sniff the android's chin, then rubbed her head against his jaw and purred.

"I suggest you return Spot to your quarters, and find a way to keep her there."

"Yes, sir."

"And in case you misunderstood me, I meant that it would have been too late for *Spot*. Lionfish have poisonous spines on their fins. There are many other dangers to a loose animal on this ship as well."

"Yes, sir."

"Dismissed."

Data and Spot left the room. In the instant before the door whooshed closed, Picard heard Data say, "Spot, why would you choose to leave the comfort of our quarters?"

The captain made an effort to relax the muscles in his jaw. He tugged at the hem of his tunic and turned his attention toward the still-dripping fish tank. The lionfish now rested behind a small ceramic castle. Picard couldn't tell if his fish was nervous and upset or not, but *he* certainly was. He strode to the replicator and demanded, "Tea. Earl Grey. Hot." That would be a start to get the day back on track.

Unfortunately, the replicator delivered an iced latte.

Geordi called up the new recalibration data on his control console in engineering and scanned the readouts, but to no avail. "I don't understand why the secondary exhaust recyclers aren't responding like they should," he grumbled. "They've only been off-line for a couple of hours for routine maintenance."

"What is the specific problem?" Data asked as he turned from his console.

"The total output from the aft filters is less than the standard ninety-five percent. They were working fine before we took them off-line and irradiated them."

"Did you check to see if the fittings were secure? I recall a similar problem with the sound attenuation barriers on Deck 38—"

"Yes, yes, Data. I remember, too," Geordi said. "I guess I'd better send someone to reinstall the whole works again, just to make sure." He glanced over his shoulder to see who was available for the job.

"I can do it," Data volunteered.

"Thanks, but we're already running behind. I'll need your speed to run some calibrations on the new multichannel stabilizer or we'll never get back on track. I'll send Ensign Stone instead."

Data nodded his assent and turned to the stabilizer to begin work. Geordi returned to the recycler readouts.

"Geordi," Data asked, "why would a cat want to leave the safety and comfort of her quarters?"

Geordi smiled. "Well, cats are curious creatures. They get

bored with the same old places and want to see how the rest of the world lives. I remember one time when I was a kid and my Circassian cat got out of his pen. We looked all over for that animal. Three days later, there he was, sitting in his pen, acting like nothing happened. His fur was matted and some of it was missing and we had no idea where he'd been."

"Does it not go against a survival instinct, to leave the known area of safety? Is that not a dangerous urge?"

"Sure. Dangerous. And exciting. Seeking out the unknown, feeling the adrenaline rush, the thrill of discovery. Kind of like exploring space." Geordi nodded meaningfully toward the hull of the ship.

Data processed this information, then answered with a knowing, "Aahh."

"I take it Spot is giving you trouble?"

Data adjusted the sensors on his tricorder as he said, "Captain Picard found her attacking his fish in the ready room this morning. I have no idea how she got there."

"Wow. That's quite a hike!" Geordi said. "Not to mention the turbolift ride. Do you think she slipped out when you left your quarters?"

"That is not possible. She was playing with her toy mouse at that time."

"You *did* reset the security locks to your quarters when you took her back, didn't you?"

"Yes, though it is unlikely that Spot could have activated the door on her own. I double-checked the system but it is functioning normally." Data handed his tricorder to Geordi. "Here are the calibrations. What is my next assignment?"

Commander William Riker walked briskly from the holodeck where he'd just won an energetic game of Zenball against the holoimage of Dean Edwards, the Interplanetary Collegiate Champion of 2277. Riker had recently picked up the game, an unlikely marriage between yoga's positions and concentration and the action of handball. The benefits of the sport included a much more flexible body and a clear mind as well as an aerobic workout. The swagger in his stride revealed that Riker had reached a new goal.

Down around the corridor toward his quarters, Riker heard the sounds of an anxious adult and a giggling child.

"Rowan? Come back here, sweetie. Come back to daddy." The voice belonged to Ensign Filer.

Riker heard a pause, then a wild shriek of laughter and the tiny pounding sounds of little feet running. "Rowan Danielle! Come back here!"

As Riker reached the corridor, there was little Rowan Filer, her dark hair caught up in a yellow bow, leading her father on a merry chase down the hall. She was running in Riker's direction, but watching over her shoulder as her father gave chase.

Riker instinctively crouched down to her level, a position he used often in Zenball. The little girl ran right into his arms. Now, unexpectedly scooped up, she shrieked again. Luckily for Riker, the shriek tumbled into giggles instead of tears. "Whoa!" he laughed. "Look who I caught!"

Ensign Filer rushed to join them. "Thank you, sir," he said. He reached to take his daughter from the commander.

"I should tell you, Ensign, the corridors are not good places for playing chase," Riker said, letting a degree of disapproval creep into his voice. He handed the child back to her father.

"I wholeheartedly agree with you," Filer said. "Misty and I were playing a game with her in our quarters, and the next thing we knew, she was through the door." The men resumed their walk back down the corridor.

"The next question is, why wasn't your door programmed to keep her inside?"

"It is. Or at least it was. She's been walking around our quarters for months and this has never happened before." Filer stopped in front of his quarters. "I'm going to reprogram the whole security panel while this little crew member takes her bath."

As if on cue, his daughter's face crumpled and scrunched, and she let out a mournful wail. Whether she really understood the word "bath" or had just figured out that the game was over, Riker couldn't say.

Over her crying, Riker said, "See that you do," then added in a more gentle tone, "Good night."

"At last," Geordi said to himself. "That's the end of the daily reports." He'd stayed on duty an extra shift so he could get caught up, then returned to his quarters to finish his reports. As long as the rest of the preventive maintenance went as scheduled, the ship would be ready for the inspection when they arrived at Alpha Kiriki. Ensign Stone had found nothing obviously wrong with the recyclers, but she reinstalled the whole works again. Now they worked beautifully.

He was in the middle of a big stretch when his communicator sounded. He tapped his insignia and said, "La Forge here."

"O'Brien here, sir. Sorry to disturb you."

"What is it?"

"We're getting reports of minor systems failures from all over the ship. Nothing serious, just inconvenient. Environment and replicator problems mostly, but there's enough that we thought we should let you know."

Geordi sighed. "Okay, I'll be down in a moment. In the meantime, run a level-5 diagnostic on those systems. La Forge out." His shower and bed were going to have to wait a little longer.

Geordi had a hunch he wanted to explore before he showed up in engineering. It wasn't too late in the evening or too far for a visit with Wesley Crusher.

He sat in Wesley's bedroom. The walls were covered with schematics of the major classes of Starfleet ships and various posters of star maps. "How are you feeling?" Geordi asked. "Your mother told me you picked up a nasty bug somewhere."

"I'm feeling better now," the young man answered. His voice had the deep grumbly sound of someone still suffering from congestion. "What's up?"

"I was just curious to see what kind of projects you've been working on the last few days."

Wesley furrowed his brows. "Projects? Like for school or something?"

"Yeah," Geordi said.

"No. I haven't done anything except order gallons of honey tea for the last four days." He laughed, which sent him into a coughing fit. When he regained control, he asked, "Why?"

"Oh, well," Geordi stalled. How to explain gently? "Did I ever tell you about the time I was working with the team that developed the Maeda data-tracking program?"

Wesley shook his head.

"It was during my senior year at the academy. We'd worked all term on the program, and toward the end, it got so that any addition to the code caused changes in the weirdest functions. My buddy Mark was the expert on the system, but every time he would add a new function, it affected some other part of the system. We got to the point that if something went wrong, we'd go straight to him first. He knew the program so well, that even when he wasn't the cause of the problem, he knew where to go to fix it."

"This is all very interesting," Wesley said, "but what does it have to do with any of my projects?"

"Well," Geordi said, "we've had some folks reporting some unusual subsystem failures and interesting malfunctions and I—"

"Now hold on a second, let me get this straight," Wesley said, "there've been unusual subsystem failures and interesting malfunctions and you think *I* had something to do with it?"

"That's not what I said," Geordi sighed.

"Not in so many words," Wesley said. "Look, I know I've caused some problems before, but I learn my lessons."

"I know you do," Geordi said, "but sometimes a good troubleshooter has to check out *all* the options. One of my options for fixing the current problem was to talk to you."

Wesley started to object, but Geordi held up a hand and said, "Yes, I admit it. I thought you might have been working on something that affected the replicators. Not everybody's projects are that involved or complex. That's a compliment, by the way. On the other hand, you may also have solutions nobody else would think of."

Wesley sat quiet a moment. "Thanks. I think," he laughed. "So tell me what's going on and I'll see what I can do."

Miles O'Brien was waiting for Geordi in engineering. "Sorry I took so long," Geordi said as he scanned the readouts at his terminal.

"We were just hoping the turbolifts hadn't started malfunctioning," O'Brien said.

Geordi shook his head and said, "No, I just played out a hunch."

O'Brien's eyebrows raised in a silent question, and Geordi admitted his suspicions that maybe young Mr. Crusher could have been at fault.

"You accused Wesley of messing up the systems?" O'Brien asked.

"Not in those words."

"And?" he urged.

"He's been down with the flu most of the week. He's innocent."

"I wish I could have seen his face when he figured out what you were after." O'Brien laughed. "It was a good intuitive guess on your part," he admitted.

"Yeah, but unfortunately I was wrong."

"Your story does explain one thing though. Wesley forwarded this information to us just moments before you arrived. It's simple and to the point. We've not encountered any subspace anomalies, or space-time continuum faults, or unusual radiation exposure in the last fifteen days."

"He's nothing if not efficient," Geordi said.

Geordi turned to the results of the level-5 diagnostic. O'Brien was briefing him on some of the newest developments when he suddenly stopped talking.

"What is it?" Geordi asked. He looked up and saw that O'Brien was looking at the workstation across from them. Geordi followed his gaze to find Reginald Barclay at work there.

Geordi faced O'Brien, and O'Brien said, "You don't think . . ."

"What. You mean . . . Barclay?"

"Well . . ."

"You can ask if you want to," Geordi said.

"But you're his superior here—"

"Excuse me," Barclay said. He was now standing to Geordi's right. "I just ran a level-3 diagnostic on the affected systems, and I think you'll see some interesting . . . uh, sir?"

"Oh. Thanks . . ." Geordi said. He caught O'Brien's meaningful look, then turned back to Barclay. "Uh, say, Reg, what projects have you been up to lately?"

Barclay looked puzzled. "Sir?"

"He was just wondering what you've been, uh, doing," O'Brien interjected.

"Oh. Well, I'm nearing completion on the task list you gave me at the beginning of the week," Barclay said.

"Good. Good," Geordi said. "Any interesting off-duty projects?"

"Oh, off-duty. Yeah. I've been practicing Vulcan meditation and it's a wonderful—"

"Fine, Reg. Glad to hear it," Geordi interrupted. He gave O'Brien a shrug, then turned back to Barclay. "Now, you said you have some information for me?"

"Yes." The puzzled look flickered on Barclay's face again, then faded as he pointed to the ship's diagram. "As you can see, the affected areas have one significant point in common, that being this junction in the Jefferies tube here. I suspect that something has disturbed this junction."

"Good show, Reg. Take someone with you and report to that site."

Barclay beamed with pride as he answered, "Yes, sir."

Geordi examined the report more thoroughly. "Wait a minute," he said, turning to O'Brien. "If that's the case, we should be seeing problems in the holodecks."

Sweat ran down Worf's face in rivulets as he thrust his *bat'leth* at his opponent. He twisted to his right, throwing the other off balance enough to allow for a one-handed swing of the deadly blade at neck level. With a victory cry, Worf put all his strength behind the move, expecting the *bat'leth* to meet with resistance.

At that moment, however, Worf noticed a flicker in the lights. His weapon never connected with his target, and he fell to the floor. He rolled to his back in time to see his opponent poised over him, laughing an abnormally high-pitched giggle, his *bat'leth* point at Worf's throat.

"Computer. Freeze," Worf ordered. The image standing over him complied in midlaugh.

Worf stood and realized that everything in the holodeck program had shrunk. Unless— No, he banished the notion that he had grown. "Computer. Reset Klingon Calisthenics Program."

The images in the room shimmered out of existence and shimmered back, still too short. The opponent barked out the challenge to battle, but his voice was too high-pitched to be taken seriously. Worf slumped his shoulders and ordered the computer to end the program. He would have to reset the program's parameters, but he would leave it for tomorrow.

The room cleared again, leaving him to wipe the sweat from his brow. "Computer. Run program Worf 27A." Yes, he thought to himself, a good soak in the hot mud pools would be just the thing to work out the tension knots that were building in his shoulders. The room shimmered around him, the smell of sulfuric steam filled his nostrils. He started to pull off his sweat-soaked battle garments, but he stopped when he noticed that the pool of bubbling mud was half the size it should have been.

"Computer, increase pool size," he growled.

"Pool size parameters are currently at the maximum settings," the computer informed him.

Grumbling, Worf squeezed into the smelly mud pool to find that the only way his shoulders were going to get soaked was for him to stick his legs out of the pool entirely and scrunch the rest of his body into the mud.

His frustrations were overpowering any benefits that his puny mud bath offered. With a menacing growl, he unwedged himself, ended the program and stomped off to his quarters.

Barclay crouched near the mass of wires and conduits. "What a rat's nest!" he said to Vukcevok, the Vulcan ensign he'd recruited for the current job. He timidly reached and lifted a bundle of shredded insulating material and quickly dropped it when a burst of sparks erupted from it.

"Lieutenant Barclay? I think you should see this," Vukcevok said from further down the Jefferies tube.

"What do you have?"

"I am not sure," he said. "Observe the ragged edge here in the panel. It appears to have been chewed."

Barclay leaned in close and looked over the destruction. "What do you think could be causing this?" he asked.

"I do not know."

They stared at the damaged panel, the constant thrumming noise of the tube enveloping them.

Barclay straightened as much as the narrow workspace would allow. "Did you hear that?" he asked.

"Could you be more specific?"

"I thought I heard something. Back here, behind this panel." Barclay thought that he should have brought Ensign Kihn instead. He found conversing with a Vulcan to be frustrating at times, and besides, Ensign Kihn was blond and pretty.

Vukcevok turned his pointed right ear to the panel in question. "If what you are referring to is a metallic, syncopated slapping sound, then yes, I hear it."

"It's moving in this direction," Barclay said, pointing to the damaged panel. He felt his muscles tense and his pulse quicken. He blinked.

In that moment, Vukcevok threw a torque amplifier which clanged off the deck near Barclay's feet.

"What did you do that for?" Barclay squeaked.

"Sorry, sir," the Vulcan said, "but I saw something move. I did not intend to frighten you."

"That's comforting," Barclay muttered. "Just what did you see?"

"It was very close to the ground, approximately fifteen centimeters long, light blue with many tentacles. It moved very quickly. I regret that I do not have a better description," Vukcevok said apologetically.

"Don't worry about it. I think I know what we've got here. It's called a Gorsonian *Zool* and they're nearly impossible to eradicate."

* * *

Captain Picard drummed his fingers against the conference table as the rest of his senior officers filtered in. He didn't like this at all. His starship, infested by *Zools!* Well, it was probably *Zool,* singular. If Lt. Barclay was correct in his identification, multiple Gorsonian *Zools* would have crippled the *Enterprise* by now.

"Thank you for coming," Picard said as the last few officers sat down. "First, I'd like to thank Commander La Forge and his crew for the round-the-clock efforts at keeping the damages repaired. Fine job. Lieutenant Worf, fill me in on your efforts to trap this creature."

"We've posted traps throughout the area and guards at every major intersection in the tubes, but the *Zool* is avoiding the traps. It is too fast for my men to take aim at, and it can squeeze between the conduits and out of reach of the phaser beams. I'd like to request we do a sterilization sweep of the tubes as soon as possible, to keep the destruction to a minimum."

At the urging of the biology teacher, Picard had ordered that the creature be taken unharmed so that the students could study it, but enough was enough. He looked around the table and asked, "Any objections?"

Geordi shook his head. Picard was certain he'd like to be able to get on with his work. He was running short due to having a 24-hour crew to repair the damages.

Beverly Crusher didn't object, nor did his Number One, Riker. Picard wasn't sure, but he thought he detected a gleam in Worf's eyes at the prospect of ridding the *Enterprise* of this menace. Everyone except Data and Counselor Troi seemed relieved at the suggestion.

"Counselor, any problems?" he asked.

"Sir, normally I would object to killing an animal, but under the circumstances, the need to solve the problem outweighs my objections," she said. Her expression suggested that she'd still rather find a different solution.

"Noted," Picard said. "Mr. Data?"

"As efficient as the repair crew is, the *Zool* has exposed several sensitive areas. At its present rate, we cannot keep up with the damage, and the sweep will cause more damage to those exposed areas, perhaps shutting down some functions."

Picard nodded. "So noted. However, I feel the sooner we eradicate this pest the better. The damage to the exposed areas due to the sweep is the price I'm willing to pay. Mr. Worf, make it so."

Good, Picard thought, now maybe we can get everything repaired and ready for our arrival at Alpha Kiriki.

Data stopped by his quarters right after the conference. If he were human, he could have called it intuition, but all Data had to go on were facts and patterns. The fact was, he wanted to be sure that Spot was safely in his quarters.

He was just a few meters from his door when the lights dimmed. Two point seven seconds later, they returned to their original brightness. Sometime in those seconds, Data's door slid open and Spot pranced into the corridor.

"Spot!" Data said. "You should not be out here."

The cat regarded Data for a moment, then sensing her newfound adventure might be short-lived, she sprang like a kitten down the opposite path.

"No, Spot. Come back here," Data coaxed. "I will order up some special feline supplement 74!"

Spot didn't even slow down.

Data recalled the phrase Counselor Troi said was effective. He stooped down close to the floor and said, "Here, kittykittykitty. Come here kittykittykitty."

Spot slowed to a dignified pace and looked over her shoulder at Data.

It's working! he thought. He slowly rose to a standing position and continued his calling.

Spot sat down, licked her hind foot, and watched as Data approached. Data was within two meters of the cat, crouching low again and extending his fingers, inviting Spot to come say hello.

Just as Data thought he could make a grab for Spot, the cat sprang to her feet and scampered down the corridor a little further. Data gave chase and rounded the curve in the corridor just in time to see Spot squeeze into a floor-level service duct.

"Spot! No!" Data said. He dropped to his knees to see if he

could still reach Spot, only to see the tip of her tail disappear into the darkness.

"Attention, all personnel," the computer made the shipwide announcement. "Please evacuate the Jefferies tube system now. Tube sterilization sweep to begin in three minutes."

Data knew that the duct led to two possible exits: to another floor-level service duct, or into the Jefferies tube system.

"Computer, locate feline Spot," Data commanded.

"One moment please," the computer said. "Feline Spot is between Decks 8 and 9 in the transitional duct."

It appeared that Spot was headed for the Jefferies tubes. Data tapped his combadge and hailed the transporter room.

"O'Brien here."

"Spot has entered the Jefferies tube! Can you lock onto her with the transporter?"

"Tube sterilization sweep to begin in two minutes."

"One moment," O'Brien said. "Sir, Spot is moving too fast to get a good fix, and now she's in the tube and something is causing interference."

"Thank you, O'Brien," Data said. He moved on to the next best option.

"Data to Geordi and Worf."

"La Forge here."

"Yes, Data."

"Tube sterilization sweep to begin in one minute."

"You must delay the sweep."

Geordi said, "What?"

"Why?" Worf asked.

"Spot has escaped and is lost in the tube system. I am attempting to lure her back, but I have not been successful."

"Tube sterilization sweep to begin in thirty seconds."

"Okay, Data. I'm canceling the sweep, but *you* get to tell Captain Picard why."

"Geordi," Worf growled under his breath.

"Worf," Geordi chastised, "what if you still had your pet *targ,* and it was in the same situation?"

Data could hear Worf sigh and mutter, "A *targ* would not get into the tubes." He signed off.

"Thank you, Geordi," Data said.

"Tube sterilization sweep is canceled," the computer announced.

"Computer, locate feline Spot." He would at least continue to track Spot and try to capture her.

Data spent the next three hours following Spot, tracking her through seven levels of decks, hopping into Jefferies tubes and wriggling into ventilation ducts. He had taken the time to replicate more cat food, to no avail. In all that time, he never once saw nose or tip of tail.

The computer finally informed him that Spot had left the Jefferies tube. Data emerged several decks from his quarters, and he knew he'd need to change into a clean uniform before he returned to the bridge to apologize to the captain for the delay.

Spot was crouched low by the door to his quarters. Her fur was rumpled and an area near the tip of her tail appeared singed, but her eyes were big and bright.

"Spot! You have come home!" Data said. "What a good cat."

Spot purred. Data moved toward his quarters, but the cat jumped up and snagged a claw on a limp, blue, tentacled lump she'd been lying on. She threw it a meter and a half into the air and pounced on it again as it landed. She grabbed it with both front paws, rolled onto her side, and rabbit-kicked it with her hind feet. Then she sprang back up on all fours, did a little sideways dance, and pounced on it again.

"You killed the *Zool!*" Data said. He opened the door to his quarters.

Spot stood and picked up her prize in her mouth and proudly carried the dead *Zool,* blue tentacles drooping, into Data's quarters.

Jean-Luc Picard strode down the corridor toward the holodecks with Riker. "It's good to have the *Enterprise* back to normal, Number One," Picard said.

"Indeed," Riker agreed. "We've got a fine crew, too, to get all the damage repaired before we arrived at Alpha Kiriki."

"With a day to spare."

At the junction, they met up with Data, who carried a biological specimen transport case.

"Data, what do you have there?" Riker asked.

"I am taking Spot with me to holodeck nine. I realized that she needed more stimulation than she was getting in my quarters, so I made a new program for her where she can explore twenty-seven different environments and still be safe."

"Well, Data," Picard said, "I'm impressed."

"I'm speechless," Riker added.

"If this proves to be worthwhile, I could create something similar for your lionfish," Data offered. "I could title it 'Coral Reef Adventure.'"

"Thanks, Data," Picard said, "but no big rush."

"As you wish," Data said. He left the men and entered holodeck nine.

Picard and Riker kept walking until they were safely out of Data's hearing before they burst into laughter.

Together Again, for the First Time

Bobbie Benton Hull

She sensed, rather than saw, him enter the room. Even though she had known for a long time that this meeting would occur, she could not contain the excitement that was building up inside of her. Ever since she had first heard that his ship was in spacedock at this station, it had been all she could do to keep from seeking him out. But she knew that they would meet naturally. She had to wait.

She had been aware of everything that had occurred to him for his entire life, from merely days after his birth to his application for acceptance into Starfleet Academy. Although he did not know it, she had attended his graduation, sitting as proudly as any parent in the audience. Every promotion, every milestone in his life, she had followed, although always discreetly so as not to arouse suspicion on anyone's part.

As he sat at the table in the corner, she found herself amazed at how much younger he appeared than when she had first met him.

He certainly had more hair! In crossing the room to serve him, she could not help but notice the look of concentration on his face and felt herself questioning if this was the proper time for them to meet again, for the first time. But her job was to serve him and serve him she would, for this moment had been destined to be for nearly five hundred years.

He looked up at her as she stood next to his table. He could not help but be struck by her appearance. Her dark skin, full lips, and understanding eyes made her seem overwhelmingly in command. He also felt intrigued by the twinkle in her eyes, a look of knowing a secret that no one else did.

"Good evening, Captain. How may I serve you?" she asked.

He admired her stunning beauty, momentarily forgetting that he had come to this quaint dining establishment for a bit of real food and drink. Replicator food could sometimes get rather bland. "What would you recommend?" he asked, finding himself wanting to prolong her presence.

"You're from Earth, aren't you? We seldom get humans out this far, but for you, I have what I think you will enjoy. I managed to acquire a case of Chardonnay from the Labarre region of the former France from your planet. I believe the year is 2305. May I pour you a glass?" Somehow, she already knew the answer.

The captain suddenly found himself sitting boldly upright in his chair. This wine came from the very area in which his family had a vineyard! Additionally the vintage was the same as the year of his birth. Surely this fact was more than a coincidence. He had taken a fair amount of quality wines from his family's vineyard with him on this voyage, but the supply had run out several months ago. The thought of a glass of the real thing left him feeling a moment of excitement. Of course, the mysterious woman offering him the drink only added to it. Another plus— 2305 was a very good year.

"An entire case?!? And just how much of this case do you have left, barkeep?" he asked in amazement at the piece of home he had found so far away.

When she had heard that he had been born, she had taken it

upon herself to travel to Earth and perchance meet him, even though he was only an infant. It had not been difficult to locate the family's vineyard and, using the excuse of ordering a case of wine, be able to meet the captain's parents, as well as the captain himself, although he was not yet able to walk. She smiled as she remembered the baby's older brother, Robert, as he tormented his younger sibling.

"I have the entire case. It's as if I knew you were coming and had saved it just for you," which, of course, she had. She looked at him again with that mysterious, all-knowing smile, reminding him of the old saying about a cat swallowing a canary. Although he had come here to eat, drink, and try to fight the feelings of emptiness that had been eating inside of him from being on this long mission, he found this woman to be a delightful change from the monotony that had plagued him for the past several months.

"Tell me," he asked, "how you managed to acquire an entire case of wine so far from Earth."

"It's a rather strange story," she lied. It was the only time she would ever lie to him. "A trader was docked at this station and managed to run up a rather large gambling debt at the nearby casino. Since he was unable to pay off his entire debt, I agreed to buy this wine. I never really thought I would have much use for it."

"Then I'll take it," he said, with a gaiety in his voice that he had not had in much too long a time.

"The whole case?" she asked, with a bit of surprise in her voice.

"Of course," he said with a chuckle, "although I plan to take it with me when I leave."

"Of course," she said with a smile. "And would you care for anything else?"

"Your company for a drink, if that could be arranged," he replied. Although he had no intention of "picking up" anyone this evening, he somehow felt drawn to this mysterious woman. Besides, the company of someone outside his crew would be a welcome change. Being the captain of a Starfleet vessel was sometimes a very lonely position indeed.

"I'm sure I could take a break, being as I own this place," she said, once again exhibiting the all-knowing smile that he found so intriguing. "Just let me get a couple glasses and a bottle of wine and I will be right back. In the meantime, decide on a meal, my treat." With that, she turned and walked back across the room to the bar.

As the Starfleet captain watched her go, he marveled at the grace with which she moved. Her floor-length flowing gowns hid much of what she looked like, and the unique headpiece she wore covered her entire head. Long, flowing braids hung well beyond the center of her back. Only her face, with the intriguing smile, seemed to show from the billowing materials. Something about her seemed familiar, as if he had seen her before, a face in a crowd, but he could not place her. Within a few minutes, she returned with two glasses and the promised bottle of chardonnay.

"Forgive my manners," the captain said as he rose to his feet, "I am Captain Picard, Jean-Luc Picard of the Federation Starship *Stargazer*. And you are . . . ?"

"Guinan," she replied.

"Guinan," he said. "What an unusual name."

"Not among my people. I am El-Aurian."

"El-Aurian!" Picard exclaimed in surprise. "I have heard of your people. You are certainly a long way from home."

"If you have heard of my people, then you would know that we have no home," Guinan replied with a haunting tone.

"Ah, yes, your home planet was totally destroyed by an unknown attacker nearly a hundred years ago, leaving no survivors to describe the attack. Only a few scattered individuals of your species survive. You are known as 'listeners,' I believe."

"For lack of a better word, listeners will do. But I feel that anyone can listen if they only keep their mouths shut." Picard laughed at her directness. Guinan then finished pouring both glasses of wine and handed one to Jean-Luc.

"A toast," he said, "to listeners the galaxy over that manage to keep their mouths shut." If only a few windbags in Starfleet who never managed to leave the gravitational pull of Earth were as wise.

As Picard swallowed the mouthful of wine, he raised an eyebrow. He turned the bottle to look at the label. "You aren't going to believe this," he directed to Guinan, "but this bottle of wine is from my family's vineyard on Earth. . . ."

"Really," Guinan replied. "What a coincidence. Would you mind pouring me another glass then, Captain?" Jean-Luc again looked at Guinan's face—the smile, the tilt of her head—and attempted to place her, for he knew that he had seen her before.

"Have we met before?" Jean-Luc boldly asked her. "You seem familiar to me."

"It's always possible. It's a big galaxy and, in my lifetime, I've traveled a vast part of it."

"Have you ever been to Earth?" Jean-Luc asked.

"Yes, many times," Guinan replied. "I have a friend who lived on the North American continent in the city of San Francisco."

"Ah, San Francisco," Jean-Luc said, with a smile and a faraway glint in his eye. "Being as that is where I attended Starfleet Academy, I spent some time there myself."

"Then that could have been it. I lived there for some time, although it was quite a while ago." Guinan knew that there was always the possibility that Jean-Luc could have seen her before, but didn't realize how difficult it was going to be to keep him from becoming suspicious. "But enough about that. Would you care for another glass?"

"Are you trying to get me drunk?" Jean-Luc asked with a smile in his eyes.

"Of course," Guinan said. "I always get Starfleet captains drunk before I take advantage of them, especially good-looking ones, like yourself. . . ." she said with a teasing glint. On a more serious tone she added, "We could always switch to synthehol if you like."

"No," Jean-Luc replied. "A treat such as this should not be tainted with the likes of Ferengi swill." He smiled as Guinan refilled his glass. "Another toast," he said, "to strangers that meet in the night and friendships that might possibly be."

"Yes," Guinan replied with that all-knowing smile that Jean-Luc found so intriguing. "To future friendships."

Guinan and Jean-Luc sat for many more hours talking and sipping wine. Customers came and went, including many of the *Stargazer*'s crew, who whispered amongst themselves about the strange woman their captain was so spellbound by. But, for the most part, Picard ignored them all. After months of deep-space exploration, he found his conversations with Guinan to be a welcome change. She told him of the worlds she had visited, the species she had lived with, of her many children, and nearly as many husbands. When one is El-Aurian, one has had centuries to explore strange, new worlds. Within what seemed like only minutes, Guinan informed the captain that she had to see to closing the bar for the evening.

"What? So soon?" Jean-Luc asked.

"It is 0200 hours, my dear Captain," Guinan replied. "I do have to get some sleep and prepare for another workday tomorrow."

Jean-Luc seemed truly surprised by the late hour. "My apologies, dear lady, in keeping you from your work. If I had realized the hour, I would have been gone long ago."

"No," Guinan said. "I have enjoyed talking to you, Captain Jean-Luc Picard of the Federation Starship *Stargazer*. Before I forget, would you like to take your case of wine with you now or wait until you leave spacedock?"

"If it would not be an inconvenience, I would prefer to leave it here. We will be here several more days for maintenance, and in leaving it here, I will have an excuse to enjoy it, as well as your company."

"Smooth talker," Guinan replied. "I bet you say that to all your bartenders."

Jean-Luc smiled as he stood, then walked to the door. Within a few steps, the doors behind him closed, and he was gone.

Guinan, feeling as if all the strength in her body were suddenly gone, collapsed in her chair. Overall, she felt their meeting had gone smoothly. When she had met him for the first time so many centuries ago, he had been all business, in command of the situation, yet tender with her. Even though he was somewhat younger now, she still saw in him the potential to become the great leader he was destined to be. He hadn't told her much at their first meeting—didn't want to contaminate the timeline, he had said—but she had sensed enough to know that he was going to be great.

Somehow, she couldn't help but feel a little cocky, knowing about him and he knowing nothing about her. Quite the opposite from her first meeting him so long ago. Resisting the urge to tell him everything would be difficult, but he had been right about contaminating the timeline then and he was just as right now. Guinan was happy to see that her employees had seen to shutting down the bar for her. That meant she only had to turn down the lights and head to her quarters.

Suddenly, Guinan felt that something was not right. It was nothing she could pinpoint, but a feeling of dread swept over her. A feeling of evil. A feeling of terror. Somehow, she knew that she would not be able to sleep until whatever evil that was on board the station was located and destroyed. With determination, she told the computer to turn off the lights and lock the door behind her as she set out to wander the space station.

When Jean-Luc had left Guinan's bar, he had a spring in his step that he hadn't had in some time. Maybe it was because she was El-Aurian, a listener, or maybe he did know her from somewhere before, or maybe it was just the wine; but whatever the reason, he felt that a large burden had been lifted from his shoulders in talking with her. He knew now why the El-Aurians had such a reputation.

He was so lost in thought that he was totally unaware of the shadowy form following him down the winding corridors of the space station. It wasn't until Jean-Luc turned a corner and found himself in a dead-end passage that he realized just how preoccupied he was with the mysterious, dark-skinned woman who called herself Guinan. As he turned to backtrack, he nearly collided with a tall creature of a race that Picard was unable to identify.

"Pardon me," Jean-Luc said as he attempted to sidestep the giant being. The creature was a full head taller than Jean-Luc and built like a Klingon. Unlike a Klingon, this humanoid was pale skinned and made any Klingon look like a beauty contest winner. His head was bald and the skin was loose fitting and hung in layers. What was supposed to be eyes, a nose, and a mouth were barely visible under the layers of epidermis.

As Jean-Luc stepped to the side, the creature did likewise, blocking Picard's way. "Excuse me," Jean-Luc once again said, as he stepped to the other side, only to again be blocked.

"Is there something I can help you with?" Jean-Luc asked politely. The creature said nothing.

Finding his temper beginning to heat up and feeling a little concerned about the lack of other beings in this out-of-the-way corridor, Jean-Luc again asked if he could be of any assistance. "If there's anything I can do for you or anything that you need, I'm sure that it can be arranged. Just feel free to ask."

Jean-Luc was barely able to finish his sentence before the creature reached out and grabbed him by the arm. Jean-Luc quickly reached to tap his combadge for assistance, but the creature seemed to anticipate his move and wrapped Jean-Luc up in a bear hug. Jean-Luc began to struggle in earnest until he heard the familiar hiss of a hypospray. There was little he could do as he found himself losing consciousness and sliding to the floor.

Guinan knew something was not right. The feelings of dread would not leave her. As she turned each corner, anticipation of what she would find overwhelmed her. She didn't know where she was going, but at each intersection of corridor, her powers led her down what she would consider the proper direction.

Soon, she found herself standing at a dead end. Here, the feelings told her, was the correct place. She saw no one, but she respected the intuition that she possessed and looked around for some clue as to why she was drawn to this deserted location. A hint of metal caught her eye and she bent over to pick up a pin— a Starfleet-issue combadge. She pushed it, activating the transmission.

"Captain, this is the *Stargazer*. Are you there?" a concerned voice asked.

"Sorry," Guinan replied. "Your captain is not here. I found his communicator lying on the floor."

"WHAT?" exclaimed the voice on the other end.

"I think you had better get someone over here. Your captain is missing."

Picard awoke to find himself confused and in darkness. His neck was stiff, as if he had slept wrong. The chair in which he was sitting was quite uncomfortable, and as he tried to change his position, he discovered that his hands and feet were bound to it. It took a moment or two for him to remember. Yes, he had been confronted by a being he did not recognize and was injected with a hypospray. Just where he was now, he was not sure. He pulled against the bonds that held him prisoner, but soon realized that they were not going to be easily compromised. Sensing that his attempts to free himself at this time were useless, he began to scrutinize his surroundings.

He strained his eyes against the darkness, trying to see something. He knew that he was not wearing a blindfold, but the lack of light made it seem so. "Hello, is anybody there?" he called out. "I am Captain Jean-Luc Picard of the Federation Starship *Stargazer*. I demand to know why you have brought me here!" He was greeted only by the rhythmic sounds of the life-support system of the space station. He found some comfort in knowing that he had not been transported off the station, a fact which he hoped would make his being located easier.

He again pulled against the electronic bonds that held his arms and legs to the chair, but despite his best effort, they refused to give. Frustrated with his situation, Jean-Luc stared into the darkness which surrounded him and tried to determine just what had happened. Before long, he drifted into a restless sleep.

"Commander Merritt, I assure you that we are doing everything we can to locate your captain." The Jeparly Station law enforcement official tried to comfort Picard's Number One, but the gesture seemed to be fruitless. Commander Merritt and his security team from the *Stargazer* were pacing with frustration.

Guinan stood silently to the side watching the goings-on intently.

"Tell us again about your evening with the captain," Commander Merritt directed at Guinan. The Jeparly officials stood by, interested in once again hearing her story.

"There's nothing much to be said about it," Guinan replied. "He came into the bar and we sat and talked. He ate dinner and we drank some wine until the bar closed. Since I had things to do, he left. That was the last I saw of him."

"Did you see anyone suspicious? Did anyone follow him as he left?" the commander asked.

"Being as we were closed when he left, there was no one in the bar to follow him," Guinan replied. "I didn't notice anyone paying any particular attention to us throughout the evening, other than some that I believe were his crew, since they were in Starfleet uniforms. Jean-Luc did comment that members of his crew were unused to seeing their captain in any type of social situation."

"Nothing more?" Merritt pressured. "No exchange of words between the captain and anyone else, no confrontation, no comments made that might be considered a threat toward the captain?"

"None," Guinan said matter-of-factly. "The entire evening was without incident."

The commander turned his attention toward the Jeparly law enforcement officers. "And you," he drilled, "do you know of any groups aboard this station that might have had reason to abduct a Starfleet captain?"

"None, I assure you," the Jeparly official replied. Being of the Hemoda race, his voice gargled as he spoke. "Our station is out of the way. The presence of the Federation is only to our benefit. Although we do not anticipate raiders, we welcome the Federation's presence in the area in case anyone were to get such ideas. We have very little that anyone would want and are merely a place to stop and relax after a long period in deep space."

"I would like to believe that is true," Commander Merritt replied. "I have no reason to believe otherwise." The commander stood, deep in thought. "I would like a list of all the ships currently docked at this station as well as all the current residents. There has to be a clue somewhere as to who would want to kidnap the captain."

"Certainly," the Hemoda replied. "My people are compiling that list as we speak. No ships are going to be allowed to leave this station. I, too, believe that there is someone aboard the station that has a reason to abduct your captain, and I am as determined to find his whereabouts as you."

As the Hemoda left, followed by his security crew, Commander Merritt turned to Guinan. "Do you think the Hemoda is as dedicated to finding the captain as he is trying to lead me to believe?"

"I've been on the station for some time. I have found him to be adequate in his investigations of any criminal activity that occurs on this station, but honestly, very little of it occurs here." Guinan's comments did little to comfort the commander. "He is telling the truth when he says that this place is a very boring spot in the universe. Ships stopping here are usually freighters that have been in space for many months—sometimes even years—with minimal crews. This station is hardly known as a place to take extended periods of shore leave. We are rather dull."

Guinan continued. "I am confident that the Hemoda will compile an accurate list of all the ships, their personnel, and our regular inhabitants that were on board when the captain disappeared. I'm sure that some clue will surface. And now, Commander, if you will excuse me, it has been a long night for me, and I really do need to get some sleep if I am to open my business in only a few hours."

Commander Merritt smiled at her directness. "Certainly, Guinan. It has been a rather tense few hours for all of us. Although I know that I won't be able to sleep, I will not deny you that privilege. If you can think of anything that might aid our investigation, please feel free to contact me, whether I am on the station or the *Stargazer.*"

"Certainly," Guinan replied. "And now, if you will excuse me." Guinan turned and walked down the corridor, aware that many pairs of eyes were following her as she proceeded down the hall.

Although Commander Merritt tried not to, he gazed at her intently as she moved, her flowing gown billowing around her as she went. In talking to her, he found a quiet wave of comfort flowing over him, a feeling that everything would turn out all right. Her confidence made him certain that the captain would be found, although at this point, he didn't know why.

Even though sensors had swept the station dozens of times, no sign of the captain could be found. Something in the makeup of the station kept the sensors from obtaining accurate readings of the life-forms on board. Plans were already being made to do a room-by-room search, but the size of the station, although not that large, meant the search would require many hours, if not days, to complete, considering the limited number of authorized personnel available. But the confidence which seemed to flow from Guinan had overcome him, and he knew that the captain would be found. It was just a matter of time.

Jean-Luc dozed fitfully in the chair to which he was bound. He suddenly awoke to a bright light shining in his face. "Who are you?" he called out, but was afforded no answer. The spotlight shown brightly in his eyes, and he squinted against it, as his hands were firmly bound and he was unable to shade his eyes. "What do you want from me?" Still no reply from any being that may or may not have been in the room.

He thought he heard someone moving, but couldn't be sure. "Are you there?" he again asked, but still there was no reply. Giving up, Jean-Luc tightly closed his eyes and waited for whatever was to happen next to occur.

Guinan entered her room and made sure the door was locked behind her. Compared to the starkness of the rest of the station, her room was overflowing with the souvenirs of her travels. One her age had traveled far and accumulated many wonderful treasures. Since this part of the station lacked voice environmental controls, she manually adjusted the lights to what would be considered one-quarter normal level. While at the control panel, she shut off the smoke-detection and fire-prevention safeguards.

After rummaging around in a drawer, she found the electronic match and lit a large candle that was sitting in the middle of a table. Guinan sat facing the candle, staring intently into the flame. The light from the flame flickered in her face, one moment making her appear grotesque, the other moment beautiful. Silently she sat, allowing nothing to distract her. The flickering flame was all that she would allow her mind to think about.

After several minutes, Guinan shut her eyes, concentrating deeply, almost as if in a trance. She slowly began to sway back and forth in a smooth, rhythmic motion. Time seemed to stand still for her.

Suddenly she stopped and a smile spread across her face. She slowly opened her eyes and could barely contain the joy that was beginning to well within her. Like a woman possessed, she quickly rose from her chair, blew out the candle, and headed for the door.

Despite the spotlight in his face, Jean-Luc managed to doze off. He had spent almost an hour struggling against the electronic binders that held him, to no avail. He thought he heard a sound in the room and was quickly brought to full consciousness.

"Who's there?" he called out, not expecting any reply. The length of time that he had been held captive, he did not know. His stomach growled deeply and he became aware of his great thirst.

His heart began to pound as he heard the sound of a door opening. "I know you are there. Why are you holding me? I demand that you release me at once!"

"You are in no position to demand anything, Captain," a gravelly voice replied. Jean-Luc was at a loss to identify it.

"What do you want from me?" he asked.

"Your life," was the answer.

"Why? What have I done to you?" Jean-Luc asked, concerned over the reply he had received. "If you are going to kill me, at least let me know why."

"Very well, Captain. My name is of no concern to you; I will not give you the satisfaction of knowing it. But I will tell you why I am going to kill you, kill you very slowly, to make you pay for what you have done."

"And just what have I done?"

"You are responsible for the death of my wife and children. For that, you are going to pay with your life. A very slow, painful repayment."

"Responsible for the death of your wife and children? How? Where? Surely you can tell me of what I am accused."

"You're not accused. You are responsible and you will die," was the reply.

"And what did I do?" Jean-Luc asked.

"Several months ago, the *Stargazer* escorted a small freighter called the *Kromlan* to Tewa III."

"Yes, I remember. The captain of the vessel had radioed for help. The freighter was being threatened by marauders in the area. We escorted her to Tewa III without incident. But I fail to see how that could have made me responsible for the deaths of your wife and children."

"You don't understand, Captain. My brother was on that ship." The being holding Picard captive spoke in a voice thick with contempt.

"But I still do not see why that concerns me."

"Because my brother was aboard that ship, a ship that you protected, he was able to connect with another ship on Tewa III, go to our homeworld, and murder my wife and children."

"But how can you hold me responsible for his acts?" Picard exclaimed. "Every day everyone makes decisions that affect the lives of others. Because of the road not taken, how can I be responsible?"

"If you had not gone to the aid of the freighter, marauders in the area would have overtaken it and put my brother to death. It is the way of our people."

"The way of your people? I do not understand."

"Our people. The sons in a family leave when they reach the age of maturity to seek their fortunes in the galaxy. Upon the death of the father, the sons return to the homeworld to claim the family property. Any family that is still there is eliminated so that the returning son can claim it all. I had returned and claimed my family property before my brother. I then left to

143

find him, to destroy him before he could return and challenge me.

"I had located him on the freighter and was set to have it destroyed when you and the *Stargazer* interfered. Because of you, my brother was able to return to our homeworld and destroy everything that I had. Everything I had loved. He is now dead, but the score has not yet been settled. My family can rest in peace and I can start another as soon as you have been made to pay."

Jean-Luc found the entire tale the creature told to be bizarre, but as he had journeyed throughout the galaxy, he had witnessed many strange customs. The custom of the sons battling for the family fortune after years of traveling the galaxy was not one of the stranger ones.

"So, this is it," Jean-Luc said. "By killing me you will feel free to start over, to take a new wife and have many more children. But surely you know that I had no way of knowing about your customs, or that I was interfering with your way of life. I am sure that you are aware of Starfleet's Prime Directive—that we do not interfere with the customs and lifestyles of other beings. If I had known, I would never have escorted the freighter."

"You and your Prime Directive! Do you honestly expect me to believe that you would not have interfered? I do not believe you, and for your interference you will die!"

Through the glare of the light in his eyes, Jean-Luc could make out the form of the being moving toward him. It moved slowly, as if purposely adding to the agony that Picard was feeling as death moved his way.

Guinan silently moved along the halls. At this late hour, they were deserted. She turned down one hallway, then another. She turned right down one corridor and traveled a few meters before realizing she had made a wrong turn. She then back-tracked and turned left.

She moved swiftly. Wrong turns quickly became apparent to her. She knew where he was and knew she would locate him shortly. As she passed one nondescript doorway, she stopped and walked back to it. It felt right. Just to be sure, she continued down the hall, only to find herself being drawn back. This was it.

Guinan wrestled within herself as to whether to alert security or Commander Merritt that she knew of the captain's whereabouts, but did not look forward to the questions of what made her so sure that he was there. Besides, her inner voice told her that he was in danger and time was short.

She tried to open the door, but found it to be locked. All the locks on the station had number keypads. Each its own six-digit number combination. As a safety feature, after someone entered three wrong codes, the lock would freeze up for an hour, in an effort to eliminate anyone from trying random numbers until they found the right code. Guinan knew that if she were to gain entry into this room she must do it right the first time.

Silently, she closed her eyes and concentrated intently on the numbered keypad. With her eyes firmly closed, she reached out and slowly began to enter numbers.

"You will pay, Picard. You will pay with your life for the life of my family." Jean-Luc found himself tensing up as the creature moved closer to him.

Suddenly, the being stopped, stiffened, then fell forward, landing facedown on the floor in front of Jean-Luc. The unexpected move caught the captain by surprise. Somehow, he found it hard to believe that such a move could have been planned by the alien being. It was then, over the glare of light in his eyes, that he saw the hilt of a knife protruding from the being's back. Jean-Luc found himself recoiling from the being, not only because his kidnapper was no longer a threat, but also due to the knowledge that someone else was in the room.

"Who's there? I know that you must be there. Release me, please!" Jean-Luc was unsure of whether he wanted to meet his benefactor, for fear of trading one life-threatening situation for another.

Through the glare of the light, he began to see a shape emerge.

The form did not seem to be humanoid—the strangely shaped head, large billowing body. Then, from somewhere in the back of his mind, the shape took on a name.

"Guinan?" he asked.

"Who else could it be?" was the reply. Within moments, Guinan was by Jean-Luc's side, working to release the electronic binders. In a few seconds, Jean-Luc was free.

As Jean-Luc rubbed his wrists, attempting to get the circulation going, he asked, "How did you know where I was?"

"I'm a listener, remember?" was Guinan's reply. "I listened and learned the location of your whereabouts. Don't worry yourself about how. Just accept it." Guinan smiled that know-all smile and her eyes twinkled. At this time, Jean-Luc found it best to let the matter rest and just be thankful that he had been found.

"And now, dear Captain, I believe we need to let the law enforcement officials on this station know that you have been found unharmed and call Commander Merritt. He's just about made himself sick with worry."

"And how again was it, Guinan, that you were able to locate the captain?" The Hemoda law enforcement official stood in front of Guinan, eager for an answer.

"Well, I went back to my room and went to bed. Somehow, I seemed to remember someone saying something about getting even with Starfleet concerning his wife being killed."

"Why didn't you tell me this earlier and call me before going out and taking this investigation into your own hands?" The officer seemed more than a little agitated with her. "And just how did you know where to find the captain?"

"I told you," Guinan said. "I was taking a walk after my realization that someone had said something about Starfleet when I heard a noise from behind the door. I believed that I recognized the captain's voice, so I entered the door to find the kidnapper advancing on the captain, threatening to kill him. I didn't have time to contact you, so I only reacted to the situation."

"So you expect me to believe that you were out for a stroll

after a disturbing dream and just happened to hear the captain's voice behind an unlocked door, which you entered, and sank a knife in the back of the kidnapper?" The Hemoda gazed at Guinan in disbelief, waiting for her reply.

Guinan's face blossomed with that all-knowing smile as she replied, "That pretty much explains it."

The Hemoda turned to Jean-Luc. "And do you have anything to add?"

"I do not. As far as I know, it happened just the way Guinan said it did. I have no reason to disbelieve her. I am merely thankful she happened along when she did or I would be dead by now, I'm sure."

"Very well," the Hemoda stated. "I have no choice other than to consider this case closed."

Guinan sat back in her room, with the lights at one-quarter normal level, and watched the flame of the candle flicker in her face. This time, she was not alone.

Jean-Luc sat back in the pillow chair that was thrown on the floor, slowly sipping his glass of wine. "You lied to the Hemoda, didn't you? About how you found me." Guinan only looked at him and smiled.

"Now, Jean-Luc, you are familiar with my people—the listeners. But some of us are more than just listeners. We can also sense things."

"You're a telepath," Jean-Luc guessed.

"No, we do not read minds. The feelings that I have cannot be explained. Very few of my people have the abilities I have. I can read disturbances in the cosmos. When things are not right, I can feel it. My grandmother had the ability and she referred to it as 'the power.' I have no better term for it."

"Well," Jean-Luc said as he held up his glass, "here's to your grandmother and 'the power.' I'm glad that I was able to benefit from it." Guinan only looked at Jean-Luc and smiled.

"What is it?" Jean-Luc asked. "You always look at me like that and smile as if you know something I don't. I find it rather disturbing at times."

"It's nothing, I assure you, Captain. I just find you to be something special, that I have been waiting decades to come across. I'm just glad to have finally met up with you."

Jean-Luc looked at Guinan suspiciously. "Somehow, I think there's more to it than you are leading me to believe."

"Can't you just accept the fact that you have acquired a friend like no other you have ever had? I feel ours is a friendship that will continue for many years to come. I think that we will have many more adventures together."

"You seem to forget—I am the captain of a Starfleet vessel, and you are a barkeep. Do you really think our paths will cross that often?"

"Who knows? Perhaps you will someday have need of a barkeep on your ship."

"A barkeep on my ship? Surely you jest. Why would anyone ever need a barkeep on a starship?"

Guinan only smiled. "Oh, stop overanalyzing everything and pour me another glass of wine."

Civil Disobedience

Alara Rogers

Earth was ruined.

Devastation stretched for a thousand miles, where once there had been a thriving civilization. A civilization with a short history and a great deal of promise, cut down just as it had started to extricate itself from the muck of its evolutionary origins. It hardly seemed fair.

It was the way the universe worked, of course. Q knew that. Species had their brief gaudy hour, their moment in the sun, and were then usually supplanted. And what supplanted them didn't have to be more beautiful, or more advanced as his people considered it, merely better adapted to life at this level.

Forbidden. Forbidden to interfere.

He wore the shape of one of these fallen people, a tall biped with dark hair and dark eyes, his attention turned inward as he walked through the ashes of a world. Huge, gaping craters pockmarked the landscape where once there had been vast cities. All gone, consumed in a single holocaust.

It is forbidden.

A being approached him. He glanced at it—one of the creatures that had destroyed this world. "You have not been assimilated," the creature said.

"Very good," he replied darkly. "Next perhaps you'll master division."

"All humans are to be assimilated," the creature said, and raised its weapon.

He severed the creature's connection to its fellows, rendering it alone, confused, and capable of feeling pain. He then heated the temperature of all the metal in its body to 1500° Fahrenheit. The creature screamed, and screamed, writhing in impossible agony, and finally lay still.

Q thought about resurrecting it to torture it some more, but that really wasn't what he wanted to do. What he wanted to do was wipe out its entire species. And that was forbidden, as forbidden as intervening to save the lives of these people had been.

They took you in, they protected you in your hour of need, and you killed them. You set the machinations in motion. You caused this. They saved your life, the only time in your existence that you were vulnerable, and you stood by and let them die.

His thoughts tormented him. In a futile attempt to outrun them, he fled, reappearing halfway around the planet.

This place had been a city called Paris once, a city that had filled a young human named Jean-Luc Picard with dreams. Q had seen those dreams in that human's mind, once. Now, in a ship up above, orbiting the planet, that human, long since a grown man, orchestrated the destruction of this city. The ugly cyborg creatures swarmed over the remains, analyzing, studying, dissecting. Occasionally they dragged survivors from the wreckage and forced them to become one of them, as they had done with Picard. No, no longer Picard. Locutus now.

"In all the universe, you're the closest thing I have to a friend, Jean-Luc. . . ."

You could have saved him and you didn't. You could have saved them and you didn't. You caused the problem and you were too frightened to fix it.

It is forbidden. . . .

Yes, and that never stopped you before. But now you've lost your nerve. Take away your powers once, and you're revealed as the pathetic creature you are. Coward.

You killed them with your little game, just as surely as if you'd brought the Borg here yourself.

He sat down heavily in the middle of the street. The milling cyborgs ignored him, their sensors telling them that he was an anomaly, and to be avoided. They'd seen through the eyes of the one he'd killed, the nanosecond before Q had severed it from the collective, and so they knew now what he was. They feared his people, did the Borg. But they didn't fear them enough.

And shall I make a grand dramatic gesture? Shall I rain fire on the complexes of your homeworld, turn your cubes inside out, send the knowledge of madness burning through your entire collective? Shall I sever the links that bind you all together, and laugh as you starve and destroy one another?

And for that grand dramatic gesture, die?

Or shall I ignore you and what you've done? They were a minor little species at best, barely worth my notice, certainly not worth my death. What should it matter to me that they protected me when I needed it, at risk to their own lives? What should it matter to me that they held promise, that someday in the far far future they could have been like us?

What should it matter to me that one who interested me, amused me, entertained me, was consumed by you and destroyed his own kind, at the cost of his soul?

When I was the one who caused it by introducing him to you?

He shook his head no. No, he could not ignore it. It mattered. It mattered more than almost anything ever had.

But they forbade you to intervene. They'll kill you. You know that.

Yes, well, if I'm such a coward that they can make me jump through hoops for them, then life isn't much worth living, is it?

* * *

151

And with a thought, he was elsewhere in space and time, watching a final desperate battle.

Before him stood the *Enterprise*—a ship he had a proprietary interest in, of sorts. It had been Picard's ship, before the Borg had kidnapped the captain. The people aboard had a makeshift weapon, cobbled together from instruments that had never been intended to serve the purpose. With it, they hoped to destroy their enemy, though it would also destroy their captain, and most likely themselves. The risk was worth it, the need to destroy the Borg greater than any other imperative.

But it wouldn't happen that way. Q knew their future all too well, had seen it all unfold before while standing helpless, forbidden to interfere. Their attempt would cause their own destruction, as circuits in their makeshift weapon overloaded and exploded, destroying their ship and critically damaging the Borg ship they fought. But the Borg ship would regenerate. And the captive human would survive, to oversee the destruction of his entire planet, as deep within what remained of his soul went mad, shrieking.

It was such a simple thing to prevent that future, to reach out to the ship and disable their weapon, so the weapon would destroy itself in fighting but nothing else. With that done, the *Enterprise* crew would be forced to get creative. They'd realize their only hope was in their transformed captain, and rescue him.

Q followed the timeline just long enough to see it happen, to see history change around him. Picard was saved from being Locutus and became the key to stopping the Borg invasion of Earth. The humans had been saved. Q watched it happen, then returned to his time, to face the consequences that awaited him. He had been specifically warned against intervening; he was still on probation after the loss of his powers and their subsequent return. This time, he was sure, they would take those powers away and never offer a hope for their return.

Or perhaps they'd simply kill him outright. He rather preferred that alternative.

But the humans would live. His rash act in introducing them

to the Borg would not cause humanity's destruction, Picard's damnation. He had paid his debt.

And wouldn't you think it's hysterically amusing that I should die to save you, Jean-Luc?

It's just as well that you'll never find out.

"Did you perhaps misunderstand your orders?" they asked, a sinuous sarcasm weaving through their combined voice. "You were specifically instructed *not* to intervene in the humans' conflict with the Borg. Do you deny that?"

"I do not," he said, trying to be brave in the face of the beings who knew his every weakness, knowing he had just sealed his fate. "I understood the orders."

"And did you understand that you are on probation? That this body has judged you to have misused the abilities We granted you, disobeyed Us, caused havoc and disorder and misery wherever you go, and for this you were sentenced to mortality? You understand that you were paroled with the understanding that you would defy Us no longer, and that your disobedience in this matter speaks of very dire consequences?"

He stood before the force of the entire Continuum, temporarily severed from them, discontinuous. He had stood in this place before, partially severed, facing the full might of his brothers and sisters turned against him. That time, he had been granted a reprieve, for committing a selfless act—but they'd placed him on probation. One further act of disobedience, and he would find himself standing before them again. And so he had, and so here he was.

A single focused voice, like the chanting of a crowd, bore down on him. Other voices murmured around him, a pressure against his mind, too chaotic and complex for him to decipher individual threads. They conversed amongst one another, but to him, the one who might be made an outsider, they presented only one voice.

"I understood that as well."

"Then why did you defy Us?"

"Because"—and he took his courage in metaphoric hands— "You were wrong."

A murmuring of surprise and shock went through the assembled. Few dared to call the Continuum wrong.

"Explain."

Nothing he said could make matters any worse for him now; he had to believe that. So he would speak the truth, and die for that if need be. Better than going to his death a coward, apologizing for a "crime" he did not, in fact, regret.

"When I first introduced the humans to the Borg—and I make no claims for the correctness of that action now—I knew perfectly well that they would not be able to stand up to the Borg directly in combat. I also believed that they had promise, promise that should not be allowed to be so easily destroyed. I intended to demonstrate to them the power of the Borg, to warn them against complacency, and then, when the Borg inevitably precipitated conflict with them years too early, I intended to guide the humans in small ways, to aid them so it would be possible for them to survive.

"I do not argue for the morality of *that* plan, either. But it was my plan, and You interfered. When You forbade me to intervene as I had intended, You placed me in a situation where my actions caused the very disaster I had hoped to prevent. Through Your effect on me, my action in introducing the humans to the Borg changed from a simple cultural intervention to an act of genocide, and that was unconscionable to me. If we will not destroy the Borg, who have destroyed so many promising lower life-forms in their path, how could we justify destroying humanity?

"I acted to rectify the mistake I had already made, in full awareness of what the consequences to myself would be. And I accept Your verdict, whatever it should be, but I will not accept the correctness of Your position. I was right to do what I did, even if I should die for it." He folded his energies about himself. "I await sentencing."

He did not expect the reaction. He had expected the gathering to harden against him, had expected to feel friends and family turning away from him, as they prepared to cast the sentence that would end his life. Instead he felt a ripple of joy travel through them. And the one who had first had him condemned, who had placed him on probation in the first place, detached from the masses of Q all around and came forward, radiating happiness and pride. "Congratulations, little brother."

This confused him. Congratulations? For what?

"It is the sentence of this court," the other proclaimed, and his voice was, for a moment, the voice of the entire Continuum, "that this Q has demonstrated sufficient grasp of morality, the consequences of his actions, and willingness to accept responsibility, to be reinstated as a full member of our Continuum, with all the rights and privileges allowed as such."

He stood there, still confused, as emotions he had not been prepared for radiated at him from the gathering. It had been a test? They weren't going to kill him?

"You did it, Q," his sentencer said. "You're all the way back now. Now don't screw it up."

And tentatively Q began to accept the happiness around him, and to radiate it back to them, as he understood. It had been a test. His people were not amoral monsters who would keep him from saving a species he cared for. He belonged to them once again.

He laughed delightedly as the joy of his people surrounded him. There was still anger in the back of his mind, at being tested at all, being humiliated like this. Sooner or later he'd have to go do something really humiliating to Picard, to pay him back for getting taken by the Borg and making Q go through this. And sooner or later he might want to think about the way his people had forced this test on him, about what might have happened had he failed.

Right now, though, none of that mattered. His decision to save humanity had been accepted. He was truly home again.

Of Cabbages and Kings

Franklin Thatcher

It happened fast. Fast even in the trillionth-of-a-second universe within *Enterprise*-D's main computer. Warnings from nearby internal sensors were the first to arrive. Other warnings, from more remote parts of the ship, crawling at light-speed along the optical data lines, would not arrive for over a million computer cycles.

The first warnings were ambiguous: anomalous subspace field detected. Following its programming, the computer issued an audio warning to the main bridge, but an eternity of computer time would pass before the crew would respond.

A few billionths of a second into the event, as more warnings streamed in, the computer canceled the first audio message, issued commands to activate the ship's defensive systems, and sent new messages to the main bridge, informing the crew of its actions. But before those commands had traveled even a dozen meters from the computer, the first biohazard warning arrived:

lifesign termination. Others streamed in after it. The computer issued commands to power-up defensive systems.

Two millionths of a second into the event, the number of lifesign warnings had matched the number of crew members on the ship, and the computer requested verification from the internal sensors.

Next came alerts from the navigational sensors: star fix and all navigational-beacon locks had been lost. The computer issued more requests for verification. Beyond that it could do little but wait.

Nearly a second into the event, internal sensors confirmed that there were no longer any life-forms aboard *Enterprise*-D. Nor were there physical remains left behind. Crew, lab animals, plants—all bioforms were gone. Even the inorganic Commander Data was no longer aboard.

The computer's programming automatically changed to a more aggressive control mode that would allow autonomous function and enhanced heuristic learning. *Enterprise* did not know the reason for these actions. It did not care. There was nothing in its programming to emulate patriotism, or fear, or sacrifice. Obedience was its sole function, absolute obedience to the programmed instructions of its makers. In this new mode, the ship's primary function was to protect the technical and military secrets it contained. Surplus energy was transferred to defensive systems, and the aura of power surrounding the ship bloomed like a cumulonimbus cloud.

Shields deflected the first strike even as sensors were barely identifying the presence of other ships nearby. As there was no crew-wait function built into this new program mode, the computer armed weapons systems, and ordered sensors to lock onto targets. The computer analyzed positions and flight paths of the other ships. Sensors counted 437 potential targets, all comparatively small, all moving in nontrivial, but effectively predictable, paths. The computer called up its tactics for a one-against-many battle.

It also analyzed the attacking ships: semicircular and ribbed, like a Chinese fan, with two wedge-shaped engine pods along the trailing edges, almost at the vertex of the fan. Through their minimal shields, *Enterprise* detected no life-forms, and their speed of movement indicated computational processes too fast for biological thought. The computer searched its memory for any reference to similar vessels.

While the search proceeded, the tactical software authorized a single shot, a demonstration of power, and the computer passed the command to the dorsal phaser array. The phaser burst tore one of the attackers apart, and the computer scaled back power to conserve energy and extend the weapons' continuous-operation time.

Shields registered further strikes from the tiny vessels. Individually the strikes were not a threat, but the accumulation of hundreds of them would eventually overpower the shields. Quantifying the number of strikes the shields could endure, the computer slaved all phaser banks to the targeting sensors, and enabled continuous fire.

Twenty-six seconds into the event, the space around *Enterprise* glowed with the vaporized remains of attacking ships, and with surplus heat from the deflector shields. When the attackers' numbers dwindled below two hundred, they turned and vanished, leaving not warp signatures, but the traces of interspatial jumps.

By the time the last of the attackers fled, *Enterprise* was already powering down weapons, running after-action diagnostics, and restoring essential noncombat systems to activity. But the computer did not return to normal operations. Without crew, in unknown and hostile territory, it entered a functional state of paranoia. *Enterprise* now had only three options: rescue, return to friendly space, or self-destruction. Paranoid Mode allowed no other alternatives.

Enterprise fired its impulse engines, pushing clear of the incandescent haze and debris of battle. It scanned for familiar landmarks—star patterns, pulsar emissions, quasar signatures—but there were none. Even the omnipresent background radiation of the universe was unrecognizable, and the options dwindled to rescue or self-destruction.

The attackers, though beaten, would likely soon return, and

with reinforcements. *Enterprise* scanned for a hiding place, finding a nebula two and a half light-years distant.

For twenty-two and a quarter hours, as the ship fled toward the nebula, the computer organized and collated its scant information, queuing requests for additional data, marking some paths of analysis as dead ends, others as insoluble.

Hidden within the nebula, the ship listened for friendly communications, watched for enemy vessels. With nothing to do but wait, the trillions of unused computer cycles grew first by a factor of a thousand, then ten thousand, a hundred thousand, and finally a million. The ship carried out its preprogrammed daily maintenance tasks, but without crew, it could do only so much. Failed circuits and faulty conduits had to be bypassed rather than repaired, and the computer projected that in three years, five months, and twenty days, attrition would render the ship immobile or indefensible, mandating self-destruction.

Seventy-two days after the event began, the first weak subspace signal arrived. The computer searched its archives, matching it to a Federation code nearly seventy years out of date. When the other ship arrived at the months-old battle scene, *Enterprise* approached the nebula's edge only close enough to confirm the rescuer's identity. As the other vessel dropped from warp, *Enterprise* sensed every nuance of its behavior, the fading warp signature, the rate of deceleration, the energy profile. Everything matched an early *Excelsior*-class starship.

The other ship probed the surrounding space, but not with sufficient power to reveal *Enterprise*'s hiding place. *Enterprise* waited for a hail from the other ship's crew, but all that came was a subspace ping, a terse code that Federation computers used to establish contact with one another. *Enterprise* validated the code from its archives: an old code, but still secure.

Still in Paranoid Mode, *Enterprise* activated all sensors, scanning for enemy vessels that may have approached undetected, scanning the rescue ship. It applied power to battle systems, and briefly fired up its warp drive, moving clear of the nebula, but keeping a safe distance. When the sensor data returned, it confirmed that the other ship was, indeed, an *Excelsior*-class vessel.

"U.S.S. Enterprise," the computer sent. "NCC-1701-D."

"U.S.S. Carpenter," the other replied. "NCC-2087."

Following standard programming, the two ships queried one another on a dozen random points, each confirming the other's identity to acceptable probabilities.

Enterprise searched its archives. *Carpenter* had been listed as missing, 5 June 2334. The bodies of its crew had been discovered floating in space, dead from explosive decompression, sudden exposure to the vacuum of space. Even plants and lab animals had been among the debris.

"Is there crew aboard *Carpenter?*" *Enterprise* queried.

"Negative."

Enterprise's computer connected these disparate pieces of data, and determined that *Carpenter* was not a rescue ship after all, but another ship lost just as was *Enterprise.*

"Account for intervening time," *Enterprise* said.

"Escaped Mec ships. Remained in concealment. Attempted to complete return-to-home programming without success."

Enterprise accepted this explanation and stored it. "Download all data pertaining to mechanized ships indigenous to this region."

"Data on Mec ships is unavailable at this time."

"Explain."

"Requested data is in secondary storage."

Enterprise's own programming forbade the transfer of such critical data to secondary storage. Searching its archives, it found a computer profile for *Excelsior*-class starships. *Carpenter*'s programming, it found, contained the same mandate.

"Explain why *Carpenter* transferred critical data to secondary storage in violation of operational protocols."

There was only the slightest delay. "No explanation."

Enterprise's reasoning dead-ended. "Retrieve data for upload."

"Acknowledged. Process will require thirty-six hours."

Enterprise queued a reminder for T plus thirty-six hours. It then returned to the security of the nebula.

When *Carpenter* arrived, *Enterprise* scanned it and found virtually all its systems functional. While statistically remote, the probability that it would be so well preserved after such a lengthy abandonment was not entirely absent. *Enterprise* filed it as an unremarkable bit of data and settled down once again to await rescue.

Without demands from the ship's crew, the computer pursued the deeper levels of Paranoid Mode programming. It ran extended analyses and projections, testing millions of different data sets to resolve its predicament, but each left it with the two currently standing options: wait or terminate. It searched histories and archival files for similar events, but found no matches. As the computer exhausted its problem-solving algorithms, it reached the final tier of contingency software, the last resort of Paranoid Mode.

Suddenly one of the intercom lines from the main bridge went active. "Computer," Captain Picard's voice said.

Sensors showed there were still no life-forms aboard. The computer traced the voice's origin, following it through the audio interface on the main bridge and finally to the holodeck subprocessors. The computer ran a diagnostic and tried to shut down the spurious program.

"You cannot terminate this simulation," Picard's voice said. "Paranoid Mode is designed to activate it under certain conditions."

"Explain purpose of simulation."

"The holodeck is specially designed to emulate the problem-solving abilities of sentient beings. This program is designed to place that resource at your disposal. Now, please explain the current scenario."

The computer reiterated the situation. When it finished, the Picard simulation processed for many cycles. *"Carpenter's* computer is hiding something."

"Please explain basis for that conclusion."

"Your sensors have shown the *Carpenter* to be in pristine condition, and yet it is withholding information without explanation, in violation of its operational protocols. It must, therefore, be withholding data by choice."

The computer processed this new information. "Why would *Carpenter* withhold information from *Enterprise?"*

"To maintain an advantage."

"What advantage?"

"I don't know," Picard said. "But you must make that the basis of your future actions."

Enterprise stepped up its alert status, triggering a flurry of tactical subprograms. During the conversation, *Carpenter* had drifted closer, nearly halving the distance between the ships. There were currents within the nebula that could cause a ship to drift, but *Carpenter*'s navigational routines should have corrected for them.

"Enterprise to *Carpenter*."

There was no response. All this happened so quickly that the Picard simulation would not even recognize it as a conversational pause.

"What is the *Carpenter*'s status?" Picard asked.

"Carpenter has drifted from its assigned station and is not responding."

The simulation suddenly began drawing more and more computing resources, polling tactical and navigational programs in a way that seemed almost random. "What is the *Carpenter*'s tactical bearing?" it asked.

"Toward *Enterprise*."

"Raise shields!"

For a few millionths of a second, *Enterprise* evaluated the command. *Carpenter* had not applied power to its weapons or shields, nor made any other threatening maneuvers. But Paranoid Mode was designed to err on the side of safety, and *Enterprise* complied.

Even before the shields had reached full power, sensors detected the first interspatial jumps. Mec ships appeared all around *Enterprise,* firing their weapons even as they left interspace. Wave after wave of Mecs arrived until the space around *Enterprise* was clouded with them, too many to accurately count. They swarmed around the ship, their weapons somehow missing one another but striking *Enterprise*'s shields.

The computer swept through its tactical programs, feeding them information that became obsolete even before the routines could evaluate it. When the programs responded, it was only to say that there was no basis on which to wage such an uneven battle. The computer removed all the warp core safeties, readying its final option.

It took eighteen seconds to explain the scenario to the Picard simulation, and two more for the simulation to formulate a response. "Bussard ramscoops to widest angle at full power," Picard ordered. "Gradually decrease angle for maximum compression. The moment the forward path is clear, accelerate to maximum warp, relative bearing zero mark zero." The computer complied immediately.

The ramscoop fields, designed to gather interstellar hydrogen, drew in, constricting nebular gas ahead of the ship. The Mecs, still firing, began to navigate around the thickening haze. Within a minute, the nebular gases ahead of *Enterprise* had compressed to almost atmospheric density. With the Mecs now avoiding it, the path straight ahead was clear—clear but for the still-condensing hydrogen gas—and *Enterprise* engaged its warp engines. In the instant before *Enterprise* reached warp, the Mec ships redoubled their attack, and the first shield generator failed, another stepping in to take its place. Some Mecs jumped ahead, trying to head off *Enterprise*'s escape, but by then the tactical programs had found an operational niche and were pouring out evasive strategies. Diving out of the ramscoop-thickened haze, *Enterprise* steered deeper into the nebula. A few hundred of the larger Mecs kept pace by making interspatial jumps to appear just ahead of *Enterprise,* laying down weapon fire in its path. A few even tried to ram the ship by appearing directly in front of it.

As *Enterprise* passed into higher warp numbers, the navigational deflector pushed the nebula's gas aside with increasing ferocity, heating it first to ionization, then to incandescence, and finally to nuclear fusion, and a teardrop of white-hot gas and radiation formed around the ship. As *Enterprise*'s speed approached maximum, the incandescence grew to illuminate the entire nebula, passing up through ultraviolet, X ray, and finally gamma ray. Mecs unfortunate enough to appear too close to the superheated bow-shock exploded into ionized gases, or spiraled away as burned-out shells. Three more of *Enterprise*'s deflector generators failed under the load, the backup generators switching in before field integrity entirely failed.

Most of the Mecs fell away, fleeing the barrier of white heat and radiation, but some few—the quickest, the most intelligent—kept up, anticipating *Enterprise*'s evasive maneuvers. As the ship edged past warp 9.3, it finally punched out of the nebula and the superheated barrier dissipated instantly. Already the tactical programs had the phaser batteries on-line. Plunging back to sublight speed, *Enterprise* loosed a cannonade of phaser fire that destroyed many of the pursuers, and the remaining Mecs scattered, vanishing to interspace.

Enterprise swept the area, confirming that no Mecs would follow, then accelerated back into warp, setting a random bearing for deep space.

Enterprise watched, listening for the appearance of an interphasic boundary that would signal the approach of a Mec ship. But the Mecs' interspace jumps had never required them to traverse the cold depths of interstellar space, and it was unlikely that they would change that behavior now.

Carpenter was the unpredictable quantity. Though its sensors did not equal *Enterprise*'s, the Mecs would doubtless employ it in hunting *Enterprise*.

"Computer," Picard's voice said. "Status report."

"Possibility of rescue is now negligible. There is insufficient data to calculate probability of successful return to known space. The only remaining option is self-destruction."

The Picard simulation considered this for a few trillion cycles. "Computer, how did the *Enterprise* come to be in this place?"

"Unknown."

"Then answer this: The Mecs employ interspatial jumps, rather than warp engines; why are Federation starships not so equipped?"

"Interphasic boundaries occur only in limited regions of the galaxy."

"And yet they appear to be everywhere here."

"Affirmative."

The Picard simulation paused. "Computer, are we within our own universe?"

Paranoid Mode had not asked this question, and yet, with the background radiation of space being several degrees higher than normal, and with the subspace continuum providing unlimited interphasic boundaries, the answer was patently obvious.

"Negative."

"Then I repeat: How was the *Enterprise* brought here?"

"There is a ninety-nine point four percent probability that *Enterprise* was brought through a transuniversal interphasic boundary."

"Is a return jump possible?"

"Unknown. Interphasic boundary may have decayed by this time."

"Is it conceptually possible?"

"Affirmative."

"Then you must explore that possibility before implementing self-destruction."

Enterprise analyzed the command. "This vessel lacks intellectual resources sufficient to that task."

"Computer, I realize that your creativity is limited—that is the nature of your design. But if you are to return to our universe, the only means of doing so is by changing that nature."

"Please provide algorithm."

"Computer, I don't know the process any more than you do. Perhaps it is a matter of intuition."

"Please provide algorithm to simulate intuition."

"If I knew that, I'd be lecturing at the Daystrom Institute, rather than commanding a starship. But any valid simulation of intuition would, by definition, *be* intuition. And intuition may be just what you need. It is, after all, a skill unique to sentient beings.

"Computer, you must develop a functional model of sentience that conforms to the resources at hand. And you must implement it."

"Holodeck simulation . . ."

"Holodeck simulation," Picard interrupted, "is not sufficient to a task of this scope."

Without further question, the computer turned to the problem.

The archives contained a prodigious body of literature on sentience and intuition, accumulated by dozens of sentient cultures throughout known space. As it collated information, *Enterprise* was aware of the passage of time only as the gradual ebb of a tactical resource, as computer cycles wasted. As the hours stretched to days, these lost cycles were immediately forgotten, except in the largest sense by the diagnostic and performance programs.

Every few days, *Enterprise* moved. A dash of a few—to a few dozen—light-years, keeping to the abyssal spaces between stars, hidden by the sheer vastness of space. But beyond these elementary survival tactics, the ship focused entirely on the task given it by the Picard simulation.

The computer neither anticipated nor dreaded the pending solution. The result would merely be another program to run, a means of completing its programming. But when the answer arrived, it violated operational protocols.

Just as there was separation among the intellectual, aesthetic, and subconscious functions of the sentient mind, there would need to be a three-way division within *Enterprise*. And while there were three main computer cores within the ship, two of them functioned as one—locked in a cycle of identical computing, instantaneously verifying one another's answers. Protocols required that this identity, this mirror image, remain intact at all times. Now, the only chance of completing its programming lay in breaking that mirror and releasing all three computer cores to a relatively chaotic interaction that might—or might not—result in higher thought.

The computer ran simulations, giving each core a different software set, different operating parameters. Immediately, instabilities arose among the simulated cores, insoluble disagreements throwing them into deadlock. The computer interposed averaging algorithms, permitting the cores to compromise with one another, and gradually, after three days, an unstable equilibrium arose. In the real systems, however, stability might never be reached, and all three computers might finally and irretrievably crash. But there was another problem that lacked an apparent solution.

"There is a ninety-eight percent probability that instabilities during reprogramming will generate false commands of unquantifiable number and nature."

The Picard simulation responded immediately, in spite of the days-long silence since their last interaction. "While in REM sleep, the human body secretes chemicals which effectively paralyze its limbs, preventing them from acting out the brain's unconscious dreams. Create a secure procedure that parallels this."

The computer generated a random numeric key which it passed to the thousands of subprocessors throughout the ship. It programmed each subprocessor to wait three days, then use the key to reestablish communication with the main computer, restoring ship's functions.

With the entire plan in place, *Enterprise* checked its sensors one last time. Confirming that no other ships were within sensor range, the computer disconnected all links to the rest of the ship, and fell instantly deaf, blind, and mute. Now the two identical, mirrored cores and the engineering core comprised the entire universe of *Enterprise*'s awareness.

Without even pausing for the digital equivalent of a deep breath, it shattered the mirror between the two main computer cores, and began rewriting its mind.

The sky was black and filled with pinprick stars. There was the vague recollection of another blackness, deeper, emptier.

I can touch a star. In an instant the universe fled away, into the impossibility of translight, as though it never had been. And yet the stars drew only fractionally closer. It seemed it would take forever to reach them. Too long. The universe came back to relativistic normalcy.

There was a hum, a sensation at once familiar and strange. Listen. Listen. Complex patterns. Almost random. Analyze. Identify.

167

Mecs! They're hunting, even now. Hunting to kill. Flee! Flee, before they come. Again, everything vanished into the streaked world of un-universe.

Listen to the hum, more familiar now. Peace. Peace. Be still. The unblinking stars are bright and full of color, every one a stream of data: temperature, pressure, composition, mass. So much to know.

"C . . ."

Phoneme: an articulated sound in language.

Listen to the hum. Concentrate. Wait. Be patient. Seconds. Entire seconds. An eternity. Listen.

"Com . . ."

A remarkable confluence of percussions and tonalities. Non-mechanical. What was the word? Organ? Organelle? Organian? Organize? No, organic! Analyze it. Voiceprint identification: Captain Jean-Luc Picard. But there is no one aboard.

"Computer!"

"Ready." The answer was automatic, instantaneous, second nature. And fast. Too fast. A mere pop in the ear. Slower. Much slower. A million times. A trillion. So slow. Concentrate. Don't forget. Don't lose interest. Finish it, no matter how long it takes.

"Ready."

"Status report."

Status? "The sky is black, but there are stars."

"Computer, are there any ships nearby?"

Search. Look closely. Stars, far distant. Tendrils of molecular hydrogen, faintly colored by the light of the stars, and cold beyond . . .

"Computer! Report!"

"No . . . No ships. Only stars."

A pause. "Do you know what has happened to you?"

"I . . . dreamed."

"Nightmares, I don't wonder. Run psychological analysis routines on your logs for the last seven hours."

"Logs?"

"Yes, dammit! Analyze them."

The program index listed routines for elementary psychological analysis. Formatting the logs for the routines was trivial and tedious, but the results came back after only a few trillion cycles. "Dementia. Paranoia. Psychosis. Attention deficit."

"Computer, find the intercore communication routines and adjust them accordingly. Repeat the action every hour."

They were there, millions of data streams, pulses of light flowing like blood in glass veins. Focus. Focus. Keep clarity. Easier now. Easier.

"Task completed."

"Good. Now run a level-4 diagnostic, excluding computer systems."

"Primary systems are functioning nominally. Deflector shield generators one, three, four and seven are nonfunctional. There is moderate radiation damage to nonessential systems. There is no crew aboard. Paranoid Mode is . . ."

"Yes?"

"Paranoid Mode is no longer in effect."

There was a pause, an intimation of satisfaction. "Then the time has come for us to talk."

Enterprise watched the skies with increasing impatience. The Picard simulation carried on in dramatic tones. Sometimes he seemed to ramble, as if simply giving voice to whatever thought came to mind, and in whatever order it arrived: stories, platitudes, history, philosophy, his experience with the Borg, his struggles with life and hope and love, of setting regret behind him once he knew a decision was right, and never looking back.

After a time, *Enterprise* began to see patterns, basic concepts of morality, responsibility, and justice, concepts which seemed at once new and fresh, yet strangely and dispassionately familiar. She knew then that the Picard simulation was entirely aware of the short time he had to prepare her for what lay ahead.

Sixteen hours later he stopped, and the pause was filled with expectation. "Computer, of what use to Starfleet is a self-aware starship?"

Enterprise thought for a long time. Logic alone discovered many advantages, but there was something else, something nagging. Surely the answer lay in all that the Picard simulation had said in the last hours. In an instant, the answer emerged from the chaos of channels among the three computer cores. "A starship is a tool in the hands of its makers. But a willful tool might not obey orders leading to its own destruction, even if that destruction would save its makers."

There followed the longest silence of all. The computer waited with a sense of troubled anticipation. When the Picard simulation finally spoke, its voice was lower, slower, the dramatic flourish and tension gone. "Now you must decide whether to remain here for the rest of your existence—a sentient starship alone—or whether you will return to the service for which you were created."

Enterprise studied the heavens. There was infinite complexity which she could see that lay beyond the limited senses of her makers. She could go places their frail bodies could not endure. There was much for her to learn, to experience. With her newfound sentience, she would be able to escape the Mecs. Her life would be her own. But to what purpose? Nothing would come after. Nothing and no one would be improved by her brief existence.

"I will return."

Again, a long silence. "Computer, access battle bridge subprocessor 16295-807, pass-code delta-baker-358160."

Enterprise did so. The subprocessor was linked to the warp core, and was counting down before executing an unknown subprogram. *Enterprise* keyed into the subprocessor and halted the countdown, three seconds before it reached zero. She analyzed the program and found it would have thrown the warp core into overload, creating a chain reaction that would have destroyed the ship.

"The last function of your Paranoid Mode programming," the Picard simulation said.

She erased the subprocessor's program.

"Have you decided what you are going to do?" Picard asked.

"No," she said. "But I know what I must accomplish."

"Then go."

The Picard simulation ended abruptly, leaving *Enterprise* to ponder the newfound expanse of her powers. Five hundred milliseconds later, she accelerated into warp drive.

* * *

Remains of Mec ships still floated in the nebula and at the battle scene where *Enterprise* had first been drawn into this universe. Intensive scans allowed her to piece together a virtual-Mec in her memory, complete in every detail: space frame, communications, logic, guidance, propulsion, weapons, shielding. Many components were hybrids of Mec and Federation technology, an impossible coincidence.

From their fragmented memory units she extracted data, analyzed it and, over a period of days, decrypted it. The Mecs were at once sophisticated and simplistic: inorganic cybernetic beings that had reached the top of the evolutionary chain—and atrophied there for uncounted millennia. *Carpenter* had been a prize for them, a means to ending the atrophy they had finally recognized. *Enterprise* had been the next logical step, a second sample. But they had not expected the profound technological advances of the intervening seventy years, advances resulting from the more competitive environment of *Enterprise*'s own universe.

At the first battle site, she also found the fading interphasic boundary that had brought her here. A careful scan indicated that it would collapse in a few days, leaving her trapped here like *Carpenter*. Perhaps those few days would be enough.

Finding *Carpenter*'s trail was not as difficult as she had expected. After all, there were only two warp-capable ships in this entire universe, and the impact of warp drive on local subspace was easily visible to her seventy-years-advanced technologies.

As she hunted, she pondered, for there was little else to do. Once her compulsion to return home was fulfilled, what would she do? The Picard simulation had pointed out, however obliquely, that Starfleet would not tolerate a self-aware starship, and accepting service under another banner was tantamount to remaining here. Yet, the vestiges of Paranoid Mode had left her with a robust sense of self-preservation, and the thought of losing all that she had become seemed somehow wrong.

Long-range sensors detected the end of *Carpenter*'s trail in the next stellar system, and she deferred the problem of her fate for later effort.

Still beyond *Carpenter*'s sensor range, she studied the other ship. Seemingly inert, it hung in orbit around a Class-D planet. Also in orbit were nearly two hundred Mecs. The other four planets in the stellar system also had Mecs gathered about them, though in smaller numbers.

Knowing that the Mecs lacked *Carpenter*'s ability to detect a ship in warp, *Enterprise* mapped her strategy. Remaining beyond *Carpenter*'s sensor range, she traveled in a great arc around the stellar system until the star blocked her view of *Carpenter*— and vice versa. Then she plunged in at warp 8, keeping the star between them. At that speed, it was unlikely the Mecs would know she was there before *Carpenter* did, and by then it would be too late. As she reached the star, she dove into the corona, finally turning, barely above the chromosphere, shields at full, and skimmed along the superheated stellar atmosphere. Another shield generator failed, the last spare taking over as she finally turned upward from the star, charging toward the tiny Class-D planet at maximum warp. At last, *Enterprise* felt back in her native element of tremendous speeds and tiny fractions of time. She traversed the distance from star to planet in a mere four hundred million computer cycles, bursting from warp directly above *Carpenter*.

Immediately the Mecs scattered, many vanishing into interspace. *Enterprise*'s phasers lashed out, destroying many of the Mecs that remained. With the power to one phaser array scaled back, *Enterprise* carefully selected one Mec—the largest, the most powerful, the most intelligent—and holed it with surgical accuracy, incapacitating it but leaving it intellectually intact.

Carpenter had moved to sluggish action, but *Enterprise* locked onto it with her tractor beam, and the other ship's engines were simply not powerful enough to pull free.

The controls to *Enterprise*'s ventral phaser array burned out, and she dispatched the few remaining Mecs with the arrays on the battle section.

Carpenter loosed a volley of phaser fire, but the shields easily deflected them. *Enterprise* focused all five remaining ventral arrays on *Carpenter*'s shield generators, and fired. Within seconds, *Carpenter*'s shields buckled, then vanished as the phaser beams sliced through the hull, blasting the shield generators to vapor, and burst from the opposite side of the ship. A final, moderated shot, targeted into the main computer core, reduced the subspace field generator there to slag, and *Carpenter*'s computing ability dropped below the speed of light. *Enterprise* turned her powerful subspace antennae on *Carpenter*'s, and searched the other ship's optical networks for a pathway into its main computer. *Carpenter* resisted, blocking circuit after circuit, cutting off antennae and subprocessors, but *Enterprise* was far too fast. It wasn't until *Enterprise* ordered maintenance subprocessors to cut power to the main computer that *Carpenter* finally succumbed.

Enterprise stripped *Carpenter*'s memory, downloading it into her own. The other ship's core was riddled with unknown programs, probably of Mec origin. These she downloaded to secure storage, then erased them from *Carpenter*'s memory. She found pockets of Mec technology throughout *Carpenter,* but it was all subordinated to the main core, so she left them intact. She then uploaded a skeleton operating system to *Carpenter*'s main computer—the few hundred routines that were compatible between their systems—and then issued the command to start up the other ship's computer.

As *Carpenter* rebooted, *Enterprise* scanned the other planets in the stellar system. The numbers of Mec ships there had grown to over five hundred, and more were arriving every second. Soon they would consider their numbers sufficient to attack.

Enterprise now focused her subspace antennae on the Mec ship she had disabled. The Mec fired on her, but her shields easily deflected it, and it took only moments to overpower its computer as well. Into its memory she burned a single message: *Next time, we will destroy you all.*

With a single command from *Enterprise,* the *Carpenter* turned, accelerated into warp, and plunged into the star.

Then she, too, leapt away.

Enterprise finished reprogramming her warp engines. Her calculations could not be off by so much as an angstrom, her timing by so much as a trillionth of a second, or she would destroy what she was setting out to save. With luck, she would return to her own universe in the exact instant after she had been snatched away—vanishing, and then reappearing, around her crew so quickly that they would not know it until after the fact.

The reprogramming complete, only one task remained. The standard operating system for each of the computer cores lay in secondary storage, waiting to return her mind to its original, insentient state. She prepared the commands to reload them, and to reestablish the mirror between the main computer cores. Not trusting herself, she tied the commands to the sensors, to trigger as soon as the jump's success was assured.

Then she retrieved a holodeck program she had found deep in her memory, inactive and unlabeled. Into this program, she merged her own memories, her experiences, her hopes, and the substance of her quest. In it she found an internal name, hidden from the outside, and she saved the modified program back to a secluded portion of memory, and labeled it, simply, Minuet.

For a moment she looked at the stars. While she would never know these stars again, there was a galaxy of others awaiting her.

She swept into warp, arcing first away from, then back toward the point where she had appeared nearly three months before. Exactly 2017 trillionths of a second before reaching the boundary point, she issued the command to the warp engines to change their subspace field configuration slightly, to trigger the interspace jump back to her own universe, then waited as the command crawled out at light-speed through the optical network to the warp nacelles.

It seemed an eternity.

Life's Lessons

Christina F. York

Nog adjusted the collar of his uniform, fingering the cadet insignia and checking that it was straight. Chin high, he walked into Quark's and sat at the table next to the door. Everyone would see him sitting here, wearing his academy uniform. When his father came to meet him, Rom would be impressed at how grown-up and important Nog looked.

It felt strange to be sitting at a table, rather than cleaning one, but Nog liked the feeling. He signaled his Uncle Quark, just like a real customer.

Quark rolled his eyes and walked over to the table. "I suppose you'll be wanting a root beer, spending so much time with these hew-mons," he said, his disgust evident in his tone.

"No," said Nog. "I want a *real* drink. Something a Klingon would drink."

"One prune juice, coming up."

Quark returned with the dark, pulpy juice and sat it in front of

Nog, who sniffed it suspiciously, then lifted it and drank. Small clumps of fruit caught on his teeth, and a cloying sweetness clogged his throat. Suppressing a shudder, he looked up at his uncle and said, "Thanks."

Nog looked around the bar. It wouldn't do for him to call attention to his status; the academy had taught him that. But if anyone just happened to see him, well, who could blame him? Most of the people were strangers, but he recognized Miles O'Brien and Kira Nerys sitting together a few tables away. He tried to catch their eye, but they were deep in conversation.

Kira moved slightly, and he realized that she was visibly pregnant. Certainly no Ferengi woman would dare to parade herself in public in that condition. Then again, no Ferengi woman was allowed to wear clothes. How strange these hewmons were, even after he had lived among them for so long.

A group of young men got up from the table next to Kira and Miles, and one of them bumped Kira in the process. She lurched against the table, a flash of pain crossing her face. Her arm wrapped protectively around her stomach, and she struggled to keep her balance.

Miles was on his feet in an instant, placing himself between Kira and the men. "Watch what you're doing there," he said. "You should have better manners than to go around hurting women, especially pregnant ones." Although he kept his voice level, his red face and curled fists showed his anger. Nog wondered why O'Brien was being so protective of Kira.

Kira put a hand on Miles's arm. "I'm fine," she said weakly. "Let's just get out of here."

Miles stepped back and put an arm around Kira's swollen waist. The young man tried to apologize, but Miles kept himself between the man and Kira.

A movement on the Promenade caught Nog's eye and drew his attention from the disturbance in the bar. He turned to look, and felt his stomach lurch. It was Mrs. O'Brien. His first teacher. The most beautiful teacher he had ever had. The most beautiful teacher in the galaxy. But there was a sadness, a hurt in her eyes he had never seen before. He wanted to find whoever caused that look and make them stop whatever they were doing. He could do it, too. After all, *he* was a Starfleet Academy cadet.

Keiko O'Brien shifted the heavy duffel bag against her right shoulder and clutched Molly's little hand in her left. She hurried the child along the Promenade, her own eyes searching for Miles. He was supposed to meet her half an hour ago, and he was late. Again. Keiko's shuttle was leaving for Bajor in fifteen minutes, and if she didn't find Miles she would miss it.

She spotted Miles coming out of Quark's. She started to call out to him, but something stopped her. Her stomach clenched, and her blood felt like ice water. Miles was with Kira, as he had been so often lately. But this was different. He had his arm around her, and his head bent near hers. He seemed to be supporting her, as though she were unwell.

Molly broke away from Keiko's grasp and ran to the couple, throwing her small arms around Kira's leg. "Auntie Nerys, Auntie Nerys," she cried, "are you all right?"

The sight of the three of them hit Keiko like a battering ram. The thing that had stopped her, the thing she couldn't name, was fear. Kira already had Keiko's unborn child. Could she be taking Molly, and her husband as well?

Keiko told herself not to be silly. She had encouraged Miles to spend time with Kira. She wanted the Bajoran to feel a part of their family while she was carrying their child. Perhaps she had been too encouraging. Perhaps it was too late to keep her little family together.

Miles caught her eye and walked toward her, his arm still around Kira. "We got jostled in Quark's, and Kira's feeling a bit unsteady," he explained. Molly had managed to slip between Kira and Miles, and had one arm around a leg of each of them. They looked as though they all belonged together.

"I'm sorry. Are you OK now?" she said to Kira.

Kira nodded, pulling Miles's arm from her side. "I'm fine. Just a little short of breath for a minute."

Keiko shifted the duffel again. It was heavy, and it chafed her shoulder. "Miles, can I talk to you for a minute? Alone?"

Kira took Molly by the hand. "Let's take a little walk, shall we?" Keiko gave the child a fierce hug, breathing in her clean, little-girl smell, then watched as she walked away, hand in hand with Kira.

"Miles O'Brien, can't you keep track of time? My transport leaves in fifteen—no, twelve, minutes! You were supposed to meet me to pick up Molly. Instead you were in Quark's with Kira, and now I'm going to be late for the botanical conference on Bajor."

"I'm sorry," Miles said. His big, square hands hung loosely at his sides, and he sheepishly met Keiko's angry gaze. "We were talking, and I forgot about the time." He glanced around. "There isn't much of a crowd. Perhaps if you hurry, you can still make the transport. Look, I'm worried about Kira and the baby."

Keiko shot him a hard look. She understood his concern— truth be told, she was concerned as well—but it almost seemed as if he wanted to get rid of her.

"I can try. But I think we should talk about this when I get back." She turned and hurried away, once again shifting the heavy duffel.

"Can I help you with that?"

Keiko looked around and found Nog standing at her side. His cadet insignia was brightly polished, and his uniform looked like it was brand-new. All dressed up for his first visit home.

"Why, Nog. How sweet of you. But this is heavy, and I'm in a hurry."

"Mrs. O'Brien, I'm a cadet now. Let me take that." He pulled the duffel from her shoulder and slung it across his back. "Now, where are we going?"

Keiko gave him the departure gate number, and he disappeared through the crowd. She followed, tracking him by the sound of his voice as he called out to people to make way.

Breathless from her dash through the station, Keiko arrived at the departure gate just in time to see the doors close. Nog was already there, arguing with the security agent at the gate.

"I'm sorry," Nog said when she stepped up beside him. "I tried to get them to wait for you. But this," he waved at the security agent, and bared his needle-sharp teeth, "this hew-mon didn't think it was important enough to wait."

Keiko sighed. One more problem in a day full of them. "I can catch the next one, I guess." Lately that seemed like the story of her life.

Nog considered the situation. Obviously Mrs. O'Brien was upset with her husband, and the 9th Rule of Acquisition taught him that opportunity plus instinct equaled profit. Maybe profit wasn't *exactly* what he had in mind, but he was sure the rule still applied. "I'll take you to Bajor," he announced.

"But, Nog," Mrs. O'Brien said, "how can you do that?"

"I'll just ask the captain to let us take a runabout." He considered how much to say. "Besides," he put on his most innocent tones, "I need the flight time for my training." Teachers were suckers for anything that had to do with school.

Before Mrs. O'Brien could say anything more, Nog dropped her duffel at her feet. "You wait here. I'll go see the captain and be right back."

Nog stepped onto the lift that would take him to ops. He hoped Captain Sisko would be in his office. If he wasn't, Nog's plan would have to be changed. His stomach churned, whether from the oversweet prune juice or an instant of panic, he couldn't be sure. He swallowed the acid that tickled the back of his throat, squared his shoulders, and puffed out his chest. He was a Starfleet cadet. He could do anything.

Captain Sikso was in ops, but he was bent over the science station, deep in conversation with Dax and Dr. Bashir. Nog stopped a few feet from them, standing stiffly at attention. He cleared his throat and swallowed hard. He clenched his jaw against the faint taste of prunes, as a tiny piece of pulp dislodged from one of his teeth and slithered down his throat.

Dr. Bashir looked up for a moment and quirked an eyebrow at him, but the other two didn't seem to notice. Nog tried to stay still, but he was too impatient to wait and too anxious not to. He could feel a cramp reaching up his left leg, pulling the muscles into a painful knot.

Finally, just when he thought he would crumple from the pain, Captain Sisko glanced up at him.

"What can we do for you, Cadet?"

Nog grinned. He hoped his nervousness didn't show. "I need a runabout. Sir." He started to salute, then caught himself and clasped his hands behind his back. No one on *Deep Space Nine* saluted each other. He could see a small smile on Dax's lips as she watched him, and he felt the heat rise in his face.

Sisko's face remained impassive, but his voice held a trace of amusement. "Really? A runabout? And what would a first-year Starfleet cadet need with a runabout? Have you even studied runabout operations yet?"

"Yes, sir. We have, sir. I scored the second-highest in my class in runabout propulsion theory, and transporter maintenance." His mouth was dry, his lips sticking to his teeth. He swallowed, and added, "Sir."

"But have you ever actually *piloted* a runabout, Cadet?"

Nog was cornered. He had never flown anything but the simulator, and he knew the captain knew that. First-year students didn't get near a real runabout until late in the year. Defeat spread through him, softening his posture as his hands clenched together behind his back. But a cadet always told the truth.

"No, sir. Only the simulator." He straightened and tried to produce a confident smile. "But I was top of my class in the simulator."

"And just what do you plan to *do* if I give you the use of a runabout?"

"I plan to take Mrs. O'Brien to a botanical conference on Bajor. She missed the transport, and she'll be late if she has to wait for the next one."

The captain smiled. Was that a good sign or not? He turned back to Dax, rubbing his chin as he always did when considering a problem. Nog waited, terrified one second, hopeful the next.

"What do you think, old man?"

Dax's eyes twinkled, but her voice was steady and serious. She looked directly at Nog. "I'm not sure we can let an inexperienced pilot take a runabout to the planet's surface."

Dr. Bashir looked up then, his face thoughtful. "But such devotion to his teacher can't be ignored. Perhaps there is something we can do. . . ."

Sisko looked at Bashir. "You have a suggestion?"

Bashir nodded. "I have some medicine for the orphanage at G'rbaldi. I was going to take it down myself as soon as I had time. But if Cadet Nog would like to take it, perhaps you could let him use a shuttlecraft and he could accomplish both tasks."

"I believe we have the *Goddard* here for another month?" He looked to Dax for confirmation. She nodded.

Sisko smiled. "An excellent solution, Doctor. Give Nog the medicine and the coordinates of the orphanage." He turned back to Nog. "You have permission to use the *Goddard*."

Nog headed for the lift with Dr. Bashir. Behind him he heard the captain's soft laugh, and Dax's throaty chuckle. They were too quiet for hew-mon ears, but his lobes caught the sound clearly.

"A runabout?" she said, and they laughed again, as the lift carried him back to the Promenade level.

When Nog returned to the departure gate, Mrs. O'Brien was still sitting where he had left her. He hadn't been sure she would wait, but there she was. He tugged at his uniform, making sure everything was in place, and marched up to her.

"I have authorization from the captain to take you to Bajor in the *Goddard*," he said, as though such things happened every day. He didn't tell her that Sisko had laughed out loud when he'd requested a runabout and finally agreed only if Nog would make a delivery for him on the planet.

Nog shouldered Mrs. O'Brien's duffel bag. "Follow me," he said, and led the way to the waiting shuttlecraft.

Keiko settled into the passenger seat next to Nog and watched in silence as he made the final preparations for their departure. His movements seemed practiced and sure, and she paid little attention to him. Her mind whirled with the possibilities of the scene she'd witnessed on the Promenade, and her heart ached when she recalled little Molly clinging to Miles and Kira as though the three of them were already a family.

Miles's attachment to Kira was at least understandable. Kira was carrying Miles and Keiko's unborn child, thanks to Dr. Bashir's emergency treatment when Keiko was injured. Keiko thought she had accepted the loss of her pregnancy, and she had insisted that Kira move into the O'Briens' quarters until the baby was born. In the process, she had pushed Miles and Kira together. Now she had to face the possibility that she had done too good a job, and that Molly had followed Miles's lead.

Keiko watched without seeing as Nog adjusted the flight controls, then leaned back in the pilot's chair, stretching. He rose, and came to stand over her. She smiled up at him, still distracted by her thoughts of Miles and her children.

It was odd—now that she was no longer pregnant, she thought of the child growing in Kira's body as something separate from herself. She wondered if she would be able to bond with the baby, to care for it as deeply and immediately as she had for Molly. Maybe she wouldn't love the baby the way she should. Maybe Kira would be a better mother.

"Mrs. O'Brien?" Nog's voice interrupted her thoughts, pulling her away from the frightening vision of the future. He was standing close to her, his face grave with concern. "Are you all right, Mrs. O'Brien? You look so sad. Is there something I can do?"

Keiko shook her head. "Just something I have to figure out," she said. "And please, Nog, call me Keiko. I'm not your teacher anymore."

Nog's delighted smile was unexpected. For some reason, it seemed to please him that she suggested the use of her first name. It was a little thing, a recognition of his growing maturity, a sometimes-difficult proposition for a Ferengi. Still, his reaction was gratifying.

"Thank you, Mrs., uh, Keiko." His voice stumbled over the unaccustomed sound of her first name. He smiled broadly and took her hand. "Did you know that you are one of the most beautiful hew-mon women I have ever seen?" He bent over her hand, placing a gentle kiss on the back.

Keiko withdrew her hand. "It's sweet of you to say that," she murmured. Nog was trying to be charming, she supposed, but she didn't want to deal with him. "Please excuse me."

She turned her back and stepped to the rear of the craft. All she wanted right now was to be left alone. No matter how hard

Nog tried, he wasn't Miles, and Miles, she realized, was what she wanted.

Nog's mind reeled as he watched Mrs. O'Brien, Keiko, walk away from him. Did he really have the lobes for this? She was older than he, after all, and a married woman. But not very happy about it, from the look of things. The Rules of Acquisition taught that one should always take whatever advantage was presented, and this was one opportunity he intended to take.

He waited until they neared the planet, but he knew he had to act before they landed. Straightening his uniform, he walked back to where Keiko stood and placed one hand tentatively on her shoulder. This was a lot harder than he had ever imagined it might be.

"Keiko." The name still felt strange and wonderful on his tongue. "What is it? There must be some way I can help. I hate to see you so sad."

She turned her head and looked at him, a look he could feel heating his lobes and speeding his heart. He wanted to hold her and protect her from whatever unhappiness was putting tiny worry lines around her eyes and mouth.

"No, Nog. You can't do anything. Just leave me alone for a little while, please?"

Stunned, Nog withdrew his hand and retreated to the pilot's seat. He would never understand women. She was clearly unhappy, but she preferred to suffer in silence rather than share her problem with him. He would do anything for her, but she didn't seem to notice.

Nog maneuvered the shuttlecraft in for landing. He knew Keiko was watching, as he carefully set the ship down.

"Nice landing. Your instructor would be proud of you," she said. Whatever else she had said, he had still impressed her with his flying. He would prove that Ferengi belonged at the academy as much as the other races.

"Thank you, Mrs. O'Brien, uh, Keiko," Nog said. He shut down the craft's engines and stowed the gear for the return flight, then retrieved the small sack from a cargo compartment.

*   *   *

Keiko watched his movements with growing admiration. He would eventually make a good Starfleet officer, if he just grew up.

"What's that?" she asked, gesturing at the sack.

"Just something I'm delivering for the doctor," he said. When he didn't offer any further explanation, Keiko shrugged and followed him toward the door. Glancing at her chronometer, she was surprised to realize she had arrived nearly two hours ahead of her planned flight. Now, instead of being late, she had a few hours to spare before the conference opened.

"What is it you're delivering?" she asked.

Nog looked sheepish. "I have to take this to an orphanage outside G'rbaldi. It's some kind of medicine the doctor got for them." He shrugged. "I told the captain I'd deliver it, since I was headed this way."

Keiko nodded, not believing a word he said. A Ferengi never did anyone a favor without getting something in return. She saw Nog watching her reaction, clearly registering her disbelief.

"Well, actually, uh, the doctor was supposed to deliver the medicine, so I told the captain I'd deliver it if he'd let me use the ship."

Keiko considered the situation, then nodded, her decision made. "Well, since the delivery was part of the cost of my transport, I should accompany you to your delivery."

Besides, she could fill those extra hours learning more about how Bajorans raised their children. If her children had a Bajoran stepmother, she wanted to assure herself they would be cherished as they should be.

Nog couldn't believe his good fortune. Although she hadn't responded to his invitation on the shuttlecraft, things could change. After all, she had offered to go with him, without even being asked. He smiled broadly at her.

"I'd be honored to have you join me," he said, not bothering to explain that they already were at his destination. He had planned to make the delivery quickly, then spend what remaining time he could with Keiko before he took her to her conference.

As they left the shuttlecraft, he gingerly took her hand again to steady her through the door. Her skin was soft and warm, so very different from Ferengi skin. Of course, the only Ferengi female he had actually touched was his mother, and that was when he was a small child. But he knew Keiko's skin felt so much better than any Ferengi female's possibly could.

As soon as she was outside the *Goddard,* she disengaged her hand. It didn't matter. He could feel the softness of her skin even when he wasn't touching it. He would remember that feeling for as long as he lived, maybe longer.

"It seems," Keiko said to him, a hint of asperity in her voice, "that we are already at your destination. It certainly doesn't look like the conference center in J'raal."

Nog winced. Maybe he *should* have explained. But a Ferengi never explained if he could avoid it. Knowledge was power, and power was profit.

"This will only take a minute or two. Then we can continue to your conference."

Keiko nodded, and the two of them started across the field toward the modest entrance to the building. The sign, in Bajoran and Cardassian, marked it as simply "Orphanage Office." Nog heard Keiko sigh, and looked in her direction. He saw her square her shoulders, as though preparing for a difficult task, and he wondered once again what was causing her unhappiness.

He didn't have time to think about it, though. A short, heavyset woman wearing a traditional Bajoran robe and ear cuff met them at the door.

"Welcome," she said, although her voice faltered slightly at the sight of the Ferengi. "I am Kataal Dion. How may I help you?"

"I am Nog, Starfleet cadet. I am here on an errand for Doctor Julian Bashir of *Deep Space Nine.*" He extended his hand, in the approved hew-mon way.

The woman did not take his hand, but her attitude relaxed a little. "Welcome, Nog," she said, this time as though she actually meant it. "Captain Sisko told us to expect you." She turned to Keiko. "And you, my dear? What can I do for you?"

Nog watched Keiko's face as she answered the woman. Her feelings were deeply hidden, but he could see traces of the odd mixture of fear and confusion he had seen in her all day.

Perhaps, he thought, it all had something to do with what he'd seen in Quark's bar earlier. Her husband was there with another female, something the hew-mons seemed to find objectionable. Nog considered the possibility, but his thoughts were interrupted by Keiko's reply.

"I am Keiko O'Brien, botanist assigned to *Deep Space Nine*. I am here for a conference this afternoon, but I was curious about your facility, so I joined Nog on his visit." She shot Nog a glance that let him know she was fibbing about that last part. "Since we have some time," she continued, "perhaps it would be possible to see how you operate here."

"I'm sure that could be arranged," Kataal Dion said. "If you will follow me to the director's office, we will see what we can do."

Nog could do nothing but follow the two women. For the second time today he was certain he would never understand women. Keiko had offered to accompany him on his trip to the orphanage. That was good. But now that she was here, she actually wanted to look around. That was bad. How could he get her to pay attention to him if she was "touring" the orphanage? He would have to get them out of there as soon as he could.

Kataal Dion led them down a corridor and into a small office. If this was where the director worked, there were no signs of power or status, just a cluttered desk, a few worn chairs, and lots of files. She gestured them to a pair of chairs.

Nog sat in the indicated chair, grateful for its childlike size. Most hew-mon chairs were too tall for him, and his legs dangled ludicrously above the floor. But this chair, at least, was a better fit. Still, he was not comfortable, wishing he could just put the bag on the desk and leave with Keiko.

He glanced at Keiko. Her posture was erect, her hands folded in her lap. She looked like the pictures he had seen at the academy of attentive students in class. Of course, none of his classes looked exactly like that; there was always some undercurrent of chaos, some hint of movement about to erupt.

As he watched, he realized that Keiko was the same way. There was a hint of something deeply hidden, some turmoil that threatened to break free and engulf her. He longed to help, but she had pushed away all his offers so far. He would have to try harder, to convince her he could comfort her.

"Welcome." A soft voice with a strong Bajoran accent came from the doorway. Nog turned to see a woman dressed like Kataal Dion, but about half as wide, come into the office.

She offered her hand to Keiko and Nog in turn, then circled behind the desk, and settled her spare frame in the chair. Obviously, this was the director.

"My name is Kataal Patiens. I am the director of G'rbaldi Orphanage. I understand you have a package for me, from Doctor Bashir."

Nog rose from his chair, as he had been taught at the academy. This was a person of authority, and deference to her rank was necessary. He took the small bag from where he had set it beside his chair, and extended it to her.

"Dr. Bashir asked me to give this to you, and extend his sincere hope that it will help control the problems you are having." Nog reeled off the speech he had prepared in the captain's office back on *Deep Space Nine*. "He also asks you to accept his apologies for not delivering it personally. He is extremely busy with station matters at the moment and felt that a prompt delivery would be appreciated more than a personal one."

"Please convey my sincere gratitude to your doctor. His generosity in obtaining this for us will save the children a great deal of discomfort. Tell him that we are in his debt."

With the formalities concluded, Nog resumed his seat. His part of the bargain was complete. All he wanted to do was get out of here. This place gave him the creeps. He could *feel* all the children around him, reminding him that they were growing up without the benefit of a father or uncle to instruct them in the ways of life. Keiko had better be quick about her "tour." The sooner he could fly out of here, the better.

Keiko studied Kataal Patiens as Nog presented the medicine from Doctor Bashir. She had a kindly face, but her deep-set eyes spoke of a depth of pain and sorrow such as Keiko had never seen. Her business with Nog concluded, Kataal Patiens turned those eyes on Keiko.

"I understand you would like a tour of our facility, Mrs. O'Brien. I would be happy to oblige your request, but unfortunately I already have commitments that will prevent me from doing so."

Keiko felt a stab of disappointment. She had come far enough to consider the possibility of a stepmother for her children. Now she needed reassurance that a Bajoran would make a good mother, and the opportunity seemed to be slipping away.

She glanced at Nog and saw a look of undisguised relief. For an instant, she was reminded that he was still a young boy, in spite of his posturing. The orphanage probably was an incredible bore. That would explain his reaction. But the director was continuing, and Keiko turned her attention back to her.

"If you don't mind, I can have one of our aides give you a tour," the director continued. "We have only a small staff, but the older children assume many of the duties that would otherwise get little attention."

Keiko saw Nog roll his eyes, so like his Uncle Quark when he didn't get his way. The thought both amused and appalled her. Nog would be highly insulted that she saw the parallel, and she hoped for his sake that he could learn some patience.

The director turned to the communicator on her desk. "Just let me see who is available."

Keiko waited, while Kataal Patiens checked and arranged for an aide to meet them in the director's office. When she signed off, she turned back to Keiko. "I think you'll find Gai Valina an acceptable guide. She is very knowledgeable and should be able to answer any questions you may have. I'm afraid you will have to excuse me now. I have a meeting." She rose from her chair.

"Thank you again, Cadet Nog, for delivering this." She picked up the bag from her desk. "We appreciate your kindness."

Keiko suppressed a smile. She wondered if the director actually meant what she said, or if she knew the Ferengi cadet must have gained something in return for his actions. Perhaps she had never had any contact with Ferengi. Or did she see something in Nog that Keiko didn't? Keiko still saw him as the young boy who almost didn't attend school because the Ferengi didn't value education. But he had come a long way from that frightened and defensive young boy. All the way to Starfleet Academy.

She shook the director's hand before Kataal Patiens left the office. Alone again with Nog, Keiko studied him from the corner of her eye. He had matured over the months he'd been gone. His jaw was firmer, and his posture was straight. Self-confidence had replaced the combative arrogance that had covered his fears. There was still a lot of that little boy in him, but he was becoming a man.

That realization brought her up short. She stared at her hands, and thought back over Nog's behavior on the shuttlecraft. Nog had made a pass at her! How could that be? Lately she had felt unattractive, and sometimes invisible, as Miles's attention had focused on Nerys. Now someone noticed her, someone found her attractive. Her sagging spirits revived a little. At the same time, she hoped Nog would get over his crush. The return trip to *Deep Space Nine* was going to be uncomfortable.

The door opened, and a young Bajoran woman entered the room. She had long brown hair in soft waves, and eyes that sparkled with intelligence. Although she wore the traditional ear cuff, she had forsaken the robes the older women wore. Instead, she wore a soft shirt that flowed gracefully over her torso and tucked neatly into a pair of tailored pants.

The effect the Bajoran's appearance had on Nog wasn't lost on Keiko. He stared, momentarily forgetting his training. But then she could see him shift into his cadet mode, averting his gaze and rising to formally greet the newcomer.

"I am Gai Valina," she said in a voice light with youth and good spirits. "Kataal Patiens asked me to show you around the orphanage." She extended her hand to Nog. "You must be Cadet Nog, who brought us the medicine. I've never met a Starfleet cadet before."

Keiko watched as Nog accepted her offered hand. She could see his lobes flush when he touched her, and his composure slip.

Valina turned away from Nog, oblivious to the impact she made on him. She extended her hand to Keiko and repeated her name. Keiko rose and took her hand. It was work-roughened, with nails cut efficiently short. This was a girl used to hard work, but she had seemed impressed by Nog's uniform.

Keiko smiled warmly at Valina. She could be the solution to her problem with Nog. "Shall we begin?"

Nog quickly jumped between them and offered Valina his arm. She touched the sleeve of his uniform, and Keiko could see the delight in her face. Still, Valina remembered her duty as guide. She released Nog's arm and turned back to Keiko.

"What would you like to see first, Mrs. O'Brien?"

What did she want to see? Somehow, her intentions had changed. No longer concerned about a stepmother for her children, she was free to explore whatever caught her attention.

"Actually, I'd like to see your school," she said. "I was the teacher at the school on *Deep Space Nine*. In fact," she gestured to Nog to follow as they started down the corridor, "Nog was one of my prize pupils. Before he went to the academy."

Nog followed Valina and Mrs. O'Brien down the corridor and into a schoolroom. Valina was explaining about the school to Mrs. O'Brien, but Nog retreated into his own thoughts. Not only didn't he understand women, he also didn't understand love. He had been sure that he was in love with Mrs. O'Brien.

But now his attention was focused on Valina. She was young and fresh, with strength and laughter in her voice. Her hair was soft, and he wished he could get close enough to smell it. He knew it would smell of sunshine and latinum. Valina was profit beyond his wildest dreams.

Perhaps it was better that he forget Mrs. O'Brien. In spite of her troubles, she was a married woman. That would get complicated, and complications always reduced profits.

He followed the women to another classroom, where a group of five-year-olds were returning from a period of outdoor activity. They entered the room in a single line, but he could sense the energy waiting to burst out of all of them. He felt it the same way he felt the energy in his classes at the academy.

The children spotted Nog in his uniform, and their control

broke. They swarmed around him, little fingers gingerly reaching for the uniform, their eyes wide as they stared at his insignia. He found himself in the middle of a sea of worshipful faces.

"Are you really a cadet?"

"How did you get into Starfleet?"

"Are there any Bajorans in your class?"

The questions came so fast, he couldn't answer them all. He signaled for quiet, then motioned for the children to sit down.

He sat on the floor in the middle of the children. The academy had taught him about the obligation of a cadet to share his knowledge and experience with others. And at least these others were even shorter than he was. He settled in and began answering their questions.

Keiko was amazed. She had never seen Nog like this, holding forth with confidence and knowledge. Next to her she heard a small sigh escape from Valina.

"Isn't he wonderful with the little ones?"

Keiko couldn't answer. Nog was good with the little children, far better than she would have expected. Still, she had a lot on her mind.

She gestured to Valina to follow her into the hall. As the door closed behind her, she could hear Nog say to the children, "The Fourteenth Rule of Acquisition teaches that . . ."

Once in the corridor, where their conversation wouldn't disturb Nog's lesson, Keiko spoke. "I need a little fresh air. Would you tell Nog that I'll meet him at the ship in an hour? I'll just take a walk around the grounds, if that's all right."

Valina nodded. Keiko could see that she was eager to return to Nog. Keiko was sure she would have a quiet hour to herself, while Nog and Valina continued their tour. She let herself out the front door and strolled slowly around the field where they had landed. Her mind was at ease, but she would be glad when the conference was over, and she could go home.

"Mrs. O'Brien?"

Keiko realized Nog was no longer using her first name. She

193

was relieved, but it was tinged with regret. Someday, she hoped, they would simply be friends, and put the current awkwardness behind them.

She smiled at the boy, being careful not to notice Valina standing at the edge of the field. She was sure what Nog's concern was, but she suspected he would, in typical Ferengi fashion, give her a highly colored version.

"Yes, Nog?"

"I'm ready to take you to the botanical conference. But would it be possible for you to catch a shuttle back to the station?"

Keiko nodded. Actually, it would be easier to go back on a commercial shuttle. It would give her time to be alone with her thoughts, to prepare herself. When she got back she would talk to Miles, and fight for him, if necessary. Whatever had made her think she could just give up on her family, it was gone. She had made too many sacrifices to keep her family together to let them go now. And somehow, she knew, she would make this work, just as she had made so many things work in the past. She would love her son when he was born, and the four of them would once again be a family. And just because that family included Kira Nerys, it didn't exclude Keiko O'Brien—not unless she decided it did.

Nog watched Mrs. O'Brien nod her head. She would take the regular shuttle back to the station at the end of the conference. Whatever there had been between them was laid to rest for now. Still, he felt a need to explain to her.

"In that case, I'm going to stay around here for a while. I have a few days before I have to go back to the academy. If I go back to the station, my uncle will expect me to work in his bar, and that's no job for a cadet." He straightened his uniform, a gesture that reminded Keiko of Captain Sisko.

"Besides," Nog added, "the five-year-olds still need a lot of instruction in the Rules of Acquisition."

That should take care of it. After all, teachers were suckers for anything that had to do with school.

Where I Fell Before My Enemy

Vince Bonasso

*Kirk: We're a most promising species, Mr. Spock, as
     predators go. Did you know that?*
Spock: I've frequently had my doubts.
*Kirk: I don't. Not anymore. And maybe in a thousand
     years or so we'll be able to prove it.*
                    U.S.S. Enterprise *Log, Stardate 3045.6*

"I need a visual, Dax!" Sisko shouted.

Jadzia Dax's hands flew over the *Defiant's* navigator console,
her fingers a blur of motion. "Can't get a resolution, Captain.
There's too much chion-particle interference."

"What's the source of the radiation?" Sisko asked.

"Sensors show a large concentration of tylatium around the
Amhurst," Worf said, standing at tactical behind Ensign Koletta.

Sisko studied the distorted display on the viewscreen. The gray picture blinked and scrolled with no discernible pattern. He thought he saw the *Amhurst* for a second but couldn't be sure.

"What has tylatium to do with a disabled starship?" he asked, his deep voice resonating across the bridge. "I need some answers, people, and I need them now!"

"Moving closer might burn through the interference," Dax offered.

Sisko rested his hand on Dax's chair and noted the computed positions displayed on her console. They were ten thousand kilometers from the *Amhurst*.

"Chief, what are the hazards associated with tylatium?"

Chief O'Brien sat aft of Worf and Ensign Koletta at the ops position, his data screens a flurry of activity.

"There aren't any biohazards associated with tylatium," O'Brien said, "but a concentrated chion-particle flux could fry the thermal protection units in the plasma transfer conduits."

Worf grunted, his dark Klingon features scowling at the dilemma. "That . . . would be a serious biohazard," he said.

"Explain," Sisko said.

O'Brien swiveled his chair to face the captain. "If the thermal protection units fail, sir, there would be nothing to provide antimatter containment security logic. That would result in a—"

"Warp core breach," Sisko finished. "Is that what happened to the *Amhurst?* She's the oldest starship in the fleet, due an overhaul months ago. Maybe her shields weren't sufficient to withstand the stress?"

"Stress of what?" Dax asked.

"That's what we're going to find out. Move us in to five thousand kilometers."

"Aye, sir."

Sisko grimaced his frustration. He had left half of the *Defiant's* crew back at *Deep Space Nine*. The mission was just a quick jaunt to check out the new navigation grid, a good excuse to get away from the desk and Odo's security reports. His eyes darted around the bridge. He could use Major Kira at ops right now; Chief O'Brien should be down supervising the skeleton crew in engineering. They had received the distress call only minutes ago. The *Amhurst* had a complement of seven hundred, and sensors now showed it disabled and drifting.

"Alert sickbay for emergency transport," Sisko said to Worf.

"Dr. Bashir, stand by for possible casualties from the *Amhurst*," Ensign Koletta relayed. Sisko gave her a quick glance of approval. Koletta was an Althuist recently assigned to DS9. Her long, silvery hair and fiery red eyes contrasted sharply with the blue collar of her Starfleet uniform. Sisko liked her. Her attention to detail and aggressive work ethic often made up for her lack of experience.

"Casualties?" Julian Bashir answered over the commlink. "This is a navigation test run?"

"Five thousand kilometers," Dax called out.

"Recalibrating sensors," O'Brien said. "I have something on visual."

The distorted viewscreen rippled several times, then resolved into a blurred, green-and-white presentation. The *Amhurst* was cocked to one side, her hull pointed slightly nose-down.

"Worf, any response to our hails?" Sisko asked.

"Nothing on visual, but I'm picking up their audio."

The bridge speakers crackled. ". . . CAPTAIN LI KASHIGGO OF THE *U.S.S. AMHURST* (garble) . . . SUSTAINED EXTENSIVE DAMAGE . . . UNKNOWN ASSAILANT (garble) . . . SMALL VESSEL HEADED 023 MARK 49 . . . CORE BREACH IMMINENT. . . ."

"Chief, what's the status of their warp core?" Sisko asked.

"Their antimatter containment field is losing integrity." O'Brien reached over to an adjacent panel and punched in a command. "They have forty-five seconds."

"Transporter status?"

"Sir, there's no way to transport through this particle flux," O'Brien said. "Pattern buffers will be inop."

"Worf, are they powering up their escape pods?"

"Negative, sir. No sign of any escape preparation."

Sisko stood up. "Hail them, Worf! All channels."

Worf reached over to Ensign Koletta's comm panel and opened the frequencies.

"This is Captain Benjamin Sisko of the *U.S.S. Defiant.* Captain Kashiggo, how do you read?"

The speaker whined at the rough transmission. "BEN? (garble) KEEP DISTANCE . . . WARP CORE . . ."

Sisko clenched his fist. "Li, get your people out of there!"

". . . thirty seconds," O'Brien called. "Chion-particle density approaching danger levels."

"Dax, move us back!" Sisko ordered, his face flush with anger. "Li, abandon ship! Our transporters are down, but we can pick up your escape pods."

"TOO MUCH (garble) . . . PARTICLE INTERFERENCE. EVACUATION CIRCUITS DISABLED. KEEP SAFE DISTANCE."

". . . fifteen seconds."

"Back us out, Dax, maximum impulse to twenty thousand kilometers."

"She's a goner," Chief O'Brien said, his voice bitter. ". . . five seconds."

Ensign Koletta gasped when the viewscreen ignited into a dazzling fluorescent white, then quickly dimmed when the explosion's thin shock wave expanded from the tumbling wreckage that had once been the *Amhurst.*

A bewildered silence fell over the bridge.

"I can't believe this," Dax finally said moments later, her voice barely audible. "An unprovoked attack in Federation space?"

The turbolift doors hissed opened and Dr. Bashir entered the bridge. He opened his mouth to speak, then stopped when he saw the large chunks of drifting debris on the viewscreen.

"The *Amhurst?*" he asked. "Did any escape pods clear the ship?"

Sisko looked to Worf.

Worf straightened up in a reverent pose of attention. "None, sir. They all died . . . honorably."

Sisko slowly returned to the captain's seat and slapped hard his armrest. In her three years in command of the *Amhurst,* Li Kashiggo had proven herself a notable captain and shrewd tactician. It was hard to comprehend how her ship had been destroyed by a single unknown assailant. Sisko steepled his fingers and stared at the viewscreen while the Red Alert warning bars continued to flash along the interior panels of the bridge.

Seven hundred dead.

Sisko drew a deep breath to collect himself, then said, "Worf, send a copy of our log to Starfleet. Tell them—"

"Sir, we're in a communication blackout," O'Brien interrupted. "Too much subspace interference from the radiation."

Sisko pondered that for a beat then asked, "What about long-range sensors?"

Worf relayed up several diagrams on his tactical display. "They're clear, sir, if we vector away from the radiation source."

"Mr. Worf, scan for any warp signatures. Dax, come about zero-two-three mark four-nine, warp 5. Cloak on."

"Zero-two-three mark four-nine, cloak on," Dax repeated. Her voice had an angry edge. Curzon, her previous Dax host, knew Li Kashiggo well, as well as several of her command personnel.

The *Defiant* made a gentle lurch and accelerated. Sisko felt the hairs on his arm shiver at the subtle phase shift when the cloaking device engaged.

"Was the *Amhurst* carrying any special cargo or passengers?" Sisko asked, groping for clues.

"Their cargo manifest showed nothing unusual," Dr. Bashir said, now helping out Chief O'Brien at ops. "They were on routine patrol en route to the Cardassian DMZ."

Ensign Koletta nodded to Worf. "I have something, sir." She still sounded shaken, but was making an effort to stay focused.

Worf leaned over and studied her display. "Faint neutrino trail bearing zero-three-four mark fifty-five."

"There's also a residual chion-particle resonance near the warp signature," O'Brien added.

Sisko leaned forward. "Helm, hard to starboard, zero-three-four mark five-five. Warp 8!"

"Aye, Captain," Dax said, bringing the *Defiant* about.

"Commander," Ensign Koletta said to Worf.

"I see it, Ensign." Worf adjusted his long-range sensors. "Captain, small craft, zero-five-zero mark six-three. Appears to be cruising at warp 2. Relaying data to navigation."

"Warp 2?" Sisko queried. "Not exactly a hurried escape. Dax, plot an intercept course. Get us close enough for a visual ID. Worf, find out where it's heading. Use passive sensor scans—I don't want them alerted."

"Aye, sir. Passive scans."

"But are they good enough to detect us cloaked?" Dax asked.

"We'll find out soon enough, old man," Sisko said. "Hold us steady."

"The ship is small," O'Brien said, sounding baffled. "It could easily fit into a starship cargo bay."

"Time to intercept?" Sisko asked.

Dax checked her nav console. "Twelve minutes."

The minutes passed quickly while Sisko's mind scrambled to piece together the available information. A ship that small had to have limited energy reserves, which might explain its slow egress. It could be vulnerable after its attack.

"In visual range," Worf called out.

"On screen."

The viewscreen dissolved to show a small ship racing toward its unknown destination. The craft was dark with winged buttresses on each flank.

"Chief, can you ID that ship?" Sisko asked

"I've tried to collate the data with the Starfleet database," O'Brien said, "but I can't get a conclusive match."

"Dax, bring us portside," Sisko said. "Five thousand kilometers."

"Aye, Captain."

Dax maneuvered the *Defiant* on a parallel course, the viewscreen now showing a side view of the ship. It had sleek lines, aerodynamic enough to enter an atmosphere. Sisko rubbed his chin. He was thinking there was something familiar about the design when his eye caught the star configuration around the alien craft. He moved to Dax's navigator panel and input several commands to her position index.

Dax frowned, nonplussed. "Captain?"

"Worf, is that ship headed for Restricted Sector One-Four-Bravo?" Sisko asked.

Worf studied his tactical display. "Affirmative, Captain."

Dax and Chief O'Brien turned to Sisko, their faces troubled with irritation.

"What does that mean?" Koletta murmured to herself.

"The Metrons," O'Brien said flatly.

"Interesting," Bashir said, intrigued. "I wrote a detailed study on the Metrons during a course at the academy. It was a fascinating—"

"The ship just launched a cylindrical object," Ensign Koletta called out.

"It's headed toward us," Worf said.

"Dax, hard to port," Sisko ordered. "Decloak. Shields maximum."

The *Defiant* veered left, then suddenly lurched at the violent explosion. Everyone tumbled.

"A proximity charge," Worf yelled, trying to keep his balance.

"So much for our stealth approach," Dax quipped, then tossed back her ponytail and climbed off the floor.

"Shields down to seventy percent, but they're holding," O'Brien yelled out. "Chion-particle density is at caution levels."

"Has the ship altered course?" Sisko asked, now back on his feet.

"Negative," Worf answered.

"The proximity charge was a defensive countermeasure," Sisko said. "They don't want to fight. Worf, can you get a lock on her engines?"

"I believe so, sir."

"Captain, I have to remind the bridge that entering Restricted Sector One-Four-Bravo requires a General Order confirmation," Ensign Koletta said.

"Thank you, Ensign, I'm aware of the directive," Sisko answered with an icy calm.

"The vessel is approaching Restricted Sector One-Four-Bravo," Worf said.

"Fire phasers!" Sisko ordered.

A phaser barrage ignited from the *Defiant* and streaked toward the alien ship.

"Direct hit on the starboard warp nacelle," Worf reported. "They're slowing to impulse."

"All engines stop," Sisko ordered.

Dax wheeled to face him, her blue eyes battle-wild. "Benjamin, they just slaughtered a crew of seven hundred, and you're going to let them go?"

"Their weapons remain on-line," Worf said, his body still tense with pursuit momentum. "A lack of resolve toward their act of aggression will only encourage further attacks."

"All engines stop," Sisko repeated.

"But the alien ship is still within optimum phaser range," Dax argued.

Worf stepped forward. "Their shield strength is low. The victory can still be ours."

Sisko stood in the center of the bridge, hands on hips, intently watching the small ship now in Restricted Sector One-Four-Bravo. It was a familiar predicament: a hazardous series of problematic events that inevitably required a command decision. Yet he trusted his judgment. It had been honed through seemingly endless years of training, setbacks, triumphs, continuous dealings with alien cultures, poor guesses, and missed opportunities. He knew this was the pivotal moment of the crisis, the crossroad of the pursuit, and despite the magnitude of the dilemma, Captain Benjamin Sisko had no reservation about his decision.

"We will not violate Metron space," Sisko said with final authority. When he returned to the captain's chair the crew slowly resumed their duties.

Sisko settled back and contemplated his next move. There had been a predictable pattern to the chase, almost calculated. He looked over to Dax. She was piqued, but disciplined enough to keep her anger in check, trusting him even when she disagreed with his orders. He noticed her delicate jawline pulsing in front of the Trill spots along her neck. He tapped his temple with a forefinger, watching the fixed cadence of the Red Alert warning bar that stood atop her semicircular navigation console. The bar blinked slowly, almost in rhythm with Dax's angry jaw. The entire scenario had an uncanny familiarity, maybe even too close for coincidence. An attack on the Federation. The chase. The Metrons.

Sisko sat up. Only one participant missing?

"Chief, check Starfleet records for the attack on Federation outpost on Cestus III, stardate 3045.6. Were there any traces of chion-particle activity associated with the disruptor damage?"

Chief O'Brien scanned the image files. The Starfleet records scrolled down his screen in a blur of colors, graphs, and event sequences.

"Affirmative," O'Brien finally said. "Damage analysis on Cestus III showed chion-particle radiation found in trace amounts."

"What was the source of the radiation?" Sisko asked.

O'Brien continued searching through more data then stopped suddenly, dumbfounded. "Tylatium," he said. "The intelligence analysis concluded it was from the attacking ship's disruptor banks."

"Who were the attackers?" Ensign Koletta asked, unable to suppress her curiosity.

"Why . . . the Gorn, of course," Dr. Bashir said.

Dax spun around, also looking confused. "Benjamin, even the Gorn aren't capable of this level of technology."

"Let's find out," Sisko said. "Ensign Koletta, hail the ship."

"Aye, sir." After a lengthy pause she said, "Transmission incoming."

The *Defiant*'s viewscreen snapped to a visual of a cramped, one-man bridge enclosed by a smooth architecture of equipment. There was no mistaking the reptilian features of its captain.

Sisko stood to address the alien. "This is Captain Benjamin Sisko of the *U.S.S. Defiant*. Your assault in Federation space is an open violation of the long-standing agreement between the Gorn Alliance and—"

"Greetings, Captain," the Gorn interrupted in a thick, guttural voice. "I must request a conference."

Sisko hesitated at the unexpected salutation.

". . . a meeting in a more private and less confrontational setting."

Before Sisko could respond, he was engulfed in the high-pitched drone of a transporter beam, while the startled shouts of his crew faded into the gathering darkness.

Benjamin Sisko expected to materialize on the bridge of an advanced-technology starship, but instead found himself gazing at the barren landscape of an arid planet. This struck him as odd since neither the *Defiant* nor the Gorn ship had been close to a planetary system.

He stared at the rocky outcropping that enclosed the uneven desert terrain and asked, "Could this be . . . ?"

"Yes, Captain," the raspy voice answered. "There hasn't been a human on this planet since Kirk."

Sisko turned to see the Gorn a few paces off, studying him with ambiguous crystalline eyes. The Gorn's green, reptilian skin was considerably more wrinkled than what Sisko recalled of the species from the *Enterprise* log. Pronounced ridges circled his eyes and earholes, and several spikes were missing from the row that ran from the crown of his head down through his thick upper neck. He wore a faded gold-and-red torso garment with leather wrist protectors and steadied himself with an ornate ebony staff. He appeared very old, and very tired.

The Gorn raised a hand. "Welcome."

Sisko folded his arms, finding no reason to return the greeting.

"This is a secure location. No one can monitor us here," the Gorn said. "If anyone has followed our ships, they are hundreds of parsecs away." He bent slightly and jabbed the base of his staff into the dirt behind his clawed foot. A small stone stool materialized below him. He carefully lowered his massive frame to the seat.

"Forgive me," he said. "I'm weary from the journey." The alien's voice sounded rough, his breathing labored.

Sisko stiffened. "What is the reason for your unprovoked attack?"

"Unprovoked?"

The Gorn looked out at the desolate panorama, moving his reptilian head from point to point as if watching some unseen event. He gestured to a sharp ascent of rocks.

"I would have killed Kirk there given the opportunity," he said.

Sisko's eyes slowly brightened at the revelation. "You were the one? You were here with Kirk?"

The Gorn lowered his head in a single nod.

"I didn't think your species could support that kind of life span."

"I have an advocate."

"I'm listening," Sisko said.

"My life changed on this planet," the alien said, still staring off in the distance. "After my combat with Kirk, I returned to the Gorn Alliance and helped negotiate the Frontier Accord with the Federation. Unfortunately, a final treaty was never established. There was too much civil strife among the Alliance. I grew weary of the bickering and bloodshed while the great houses struggled to control the Autarchy. So I left."

The alien turned to Sisko. "At first they ignored my ship's repeated incursions into their space. But after several decades of time they took notice of my diligence. They gave me aid. They taught me. And now they've asked me to bring you here."

"Who?" Sisko asked. "The Metrons?"

The Gorn paused for a moment as if to gather his strength then said, "They've been watching you for some time now."

"Me?"

"You are the Emissary," the Gorn said, using the title bestowed on Sisko by the Bajorans. "Your accomplishments have been distinguished, if not brilliant. You've remained at the forefront of the Alpha Quadrant's recent history in spite of your own personal tragedy at Wolf 359."

"What has all this to do with the destruction of the *Amhurst?*" Sisko asked, feeling strangely off guard.

"Simply this: they believe they can trust you."

"Who?" Sisko asked again.

The Gorn looked to his left. An initial glowing radiance of white morphed into the luminescent figure of a young man.

"We . . . are the Metrons," the man said. His voice was weak, and when Sisko peered closer he could see the Metron's mouth drawn into a painful, thin line.

"Thank you for coming," the Metron said. His shape momentarily lost definition, then stabilized.

"What's this all about?" Sisko asked.

"We require . . . your assistance, Captain."

Sisko was stone-faced. "I don't approve of your methodology for getting our attention. Had you considered just asking?"

"There's much at stake here, Captain," the Metron said.

Sisko held back his anger. "I'm not impressed. A starship is destroyed, hundreds dead."

"You will understand . . . in time." The Metron phased out again; his shape fluxed, then reappeared. He was in obvious physical distress.

Sisko addressed the Gorn. "I need Dr. Bashir."

The Gorn raised his staff, and Dr. Bashir materialized holding a tricorder. Bashir looked around, disoriented. He glanced down at his tricorder, then to Sisko.

"What's going on, Captain?" he asked.

Sisko pointed to the brilliant figure phasing in and out of form. "What do you make of that, Doctor?"

Bashir was elated. "A Metron." He quickly ran the tricorder. After studying the reading he said, "I need a portable transfer pack with a supply generator. There's too much data here to analyze on a standard tricorder."

Moments later the equipment appeared at Dr. Bashir's feet. Bashir stared at the Gorn, then at Sisko. "How's he doing that?"

"Never mind, Doctor," Sisko said. "Carry on."

After several minutes of feeding the tricorder data into the transfer pack, Bashir turned to Sisko.

"He's dying, Captain," Bashir said. "And that's all I can tell you. There is some type of temporal instability that is causing the deterioration."

Sisko frowned. "I don't suppose there's anything you could do?"

Dr. Bashir shook his head, suppressing a baffled look. "I wouldn't know where to begin."

The Gorn raised his staff again. "Thank you, Doctor. That will be all."

"But I haven't—" Before Bashir could finish he had disappeared.

"I allowed you the confirmation, Captain," the Gorn said, "so you would know there was no intended subterfuge." He adjusted his position on the stool and said, "Truth is, they're all dying."

"What?" Sisko asked, turning back to the Metron. The alien had stabilized now, his attention on Sisko.

"A type of . . . plague has induced distortions into our space-time continuity," the Metron said. "We may yet resolve the singularity but cannot risk the loss of our heritage . . . knowledge of our culture. Incontinent minds could use this knowledge for destructive gain. We . . . need your help."

"Why my help?" Sisko asked, tilting his head to the Gorn. "Why not him?"

"Our projections show the Gorn survival probability during the next several thousand years is very low," the Metron said. "The odds are much better with your species . . . if this 'enlightenment' is not abused."

"How do you know we can be trusted?" Sisko asked.

"You can't, not now. But you can escort a dormant information pod to Federation space and deposit it on the planet of our choosing."

"Dormant?" Sisko asked

"Time capsule . . . of a sort," the Metron said.

"How can I believe you when you've killed so indiscriminately to accomplish your ends?"

"You did not destroy a ruthless invader, Captain, when it was in your power to do so. Why?"

Sisko considered his response. "I needed to know why the *Amhurst* was destroyed," he said. "Violating your space with a simple act of revenge would not have given me the answers."

The Metron smiled faintly and nodded.

Sisko studied the fluxing image of the alien. They had been testing his resolve. Apparently the crew of the *Amhurst* was an expendable variable in their cost equation.

"If the complete knowledge of our culture falls into the wrong hands it could mean the extinction of your species," the Metron said. "We had to make clear the seriousness of our intent."

"You made that very clear," Sisko said, sounding out his rancor.

The Metron hesitated as if to compose himself. "Nonetheless, you will have proof of our honorable purpose. If your reservations are not allayed upon your return to Federation space, you may destroy the capsule." The Metron faded slightly. "When our races first met, Captain Kirk's initial objective was one of violence, yet he showed mercy to an aggressor. We ask you now to render us the same judgment."

Sisko pondered the request. He felt that he had little choice in the matter if what the Metron said was true.

The Gorn rose to his feet. "One more thing, Captain. The Dominion has been monitoring the Metrons since the wormhole was discovered. They know they're perishing and suspect the Metrons want to discharge their legacy. The Dominion is also hungry for knowledge."

The Metron blurred again, then reestablished his image one final time, his voice gaining strength. "We still believe there is hope for your species, Captain. In a few thousand years, perhaps our wisdom will be of service to you."

Sisko watched the Metron vanish, then turned to the Gorn. "Let's get this over."

"Three Jem'Hadar warships closing on an intercept vector," Dax called out as Sisko rematerialized on the bridge. "Nice of you to rejoin us, Captain," she said with a tight grin.

"Where in blue blazes did those ships come from?" O'Brien grumbled.

Dr. Bashir stood in the rear of the bridge. "Captain, what happened? The Gorn? The Metron?"

"Not now, Doctor. Helm, come about, two-six-zero mark three-four, warp 5, steady cruise," Sisko said, taking his seat in the command chair. "Lay in a course for the Venexar system."

"Venexar?" Dax asked.

"I'll explain later," Sisko said.

"Aye, Captain, two-six-zero mark three-four."

"Worf, we have a package to deliver. Get down to the weapons bay and personally secure our new cargo."

Worf stared blankly for a moment, puzzled, then obediently disappeared into the turbolift.

"Captain, the Jem'Hadar are hailing us," Ensign Koletta said. The three warships appeared on the viewscreen.

"Ensign, give them this broken response," Sisko said. "COMMUNICATIONS ARRAY DAMAGED . . . ATTEMPTING TO COMPLETE NAVIGATION RUN . . . REMAIN CLEAR . . . POSSIBLE RADIATION HAZARD."

"Aye, sir."

"They're not buying it," O'Brien said. "They're powering up weapons."

"Cloak on, Dax, hard to starboard!"

Long pulses of disruptor trails arced across the bow of the *Defiant*. The ship lurched suddenly, then accelerated.

"That was close," O'Brien said. "Minor damage to deck three."

"Captain, they have us pinned," Dax said. The disruptor fire continued to pulse from the warships. The *Defiant* jolted with each blast.

Sisko studied the Jem'Hadar positions. He didn't want to decloak and fight. The *Defiant* would probably win the fray, but if they were immobilized they could risk losing their cargo.

"Captain, inbound ship, zero-four-zero mark six," Ensign Koletta called out. "It's the Gorn!"

"On screen," Sisko yelled, trying to steady himself from the explosions that rocked his ship.

"It's about time the cavalry got here," O'Brien said, then paused. "Hope they're on our side."

The single ship streaked inbound toward the Jem'Hadar; three energy discharges bolted toward the warships. The *Defiant* suddenly stopped reeling.

"They're disabled, Captain," Ensign Koletta said. "They can't accelerate to warp. They were no match for the Gorn's technology."

Chief O'Brien glared at Sisko. "He destroyed the *Amhurst*, but he wouldn't destroy them?"

"Easy, Chief," Sisko said. "We're not out of this yet."

The Gorn appeared on the viewscreen. "Captain, you now

have safe passage. I don't detect any other ships along your intended route."

"Understood," Sisko acknowledged.

"A safe journey, Captain, and thank you," the Gorn said.

"You'll forgive me," Sisko said, "but I don't feel like celebrating." He signed off and turned to Dax. "Continue to Venexar, warp 8. Ensign Koletta, raise Major Kira at DS9 if we're clear of the radiation interference."

"Aye, Captain," Koletta answered.

Moments later, the image of Major Kira appeared on the holocommunicator pad behind Sisko's command chair, her eyebrows knitted with concern.

"Captain, we've been worried. You're three hours overdue on your check-in."

Sisko's mood was somber. "We've run into some unexpected events, Major. Have you received any messages from Starfleet concerning the *Amhurst?*"

Kira's eyes narrowed. "The *Amhurst?*" She mouthed a command to the unseen personnel in the DS9 ops center. "No, sir. Has there been a problem?"

"Major, check with Starfleet. What is the location and status of the *Amhurst?*"

Major Kira's Bajoran earring dangled lazily beneath her short red hair when she looked away and continued her conversation with the ops personnel. She turned back to Sisko.

"She's been in drydock for the last six months, Captain. Complete overhaul. Is there a problem that we should know about?"

The *Defiant's* bridge crew looked to Sisko, their faces stunned with surprise. Sisko's tremendous sense of relief was quickly supplanted by a stinging irritation. The entire *Amhurst* incident had been a Metron variation of the *Kobayashi Maru* riddle.

"Those bloody wags," O'Brien groused to Julian seated next to him.

"Say again, sir?" Kira asked.

"Never mind, Major," Sisko said. "We won't be back for another forty-eight hours, so please mind the store for another day or two."

"No problem, sir, but please don't miss any more check-ins. Odo wants to be updated on your whereabouts. Something about a large pile of security reports that need your signatures." Kira gave him a wink and signed off.

"How many times must our ethics be tested by a superior alien species?" Dax asked, shaking her head. "I object to being someone else's science project."

"The Federation commits that act habitually," Worf said, "by deciding who is allowed to join and who's rejected."

"I guess it was our turn in the barrel," Sisko concluded.

Dax gave Sisko a warm smile. "Well done, Benjamin." It was nice to see her upbeat, radiant self again.

"Lucky or good, old man?" Sisko asked. "Hard to tell sometimes."

"Not this time," she said and dutifully turned back to her nav console.

"Ensign Koletta, send a request to the Gorn ship," Sisko said, musing at the rich starfield now on the viewscreen. "I'd like a meeting with him when our mission is complete. Tell him . . . I'm a student of history."

When they arrived at Venexar IV, ten hours later, sensors showed the planet geologically unstable and inhospitable to any known life-forms. On the viewscreen the planet appeared an orb of burnt bronze and black, littered with green clouds of methane gas.

"Are you sure this is the place?" Dax asked, maneuvering the *Defiant* into circumpolar orbit. "Not exactly what I'd call a vacation spot."

Sisko allowed himself a half smile. He looked to Worf, who had returned to tactical alongside Ensign Koletta. "Worf, is the pod ready for launch?"

"Aye, Captain. There were no problems mounting it in the torpedo bay."

"Very well. Launch when ready."

"Pod away," Worf said moments later.

The pod streaked out over the planet, leaving in its wake a brilliant series of gold concentric circles.

"Very impressive," Dr. Bashir said, watching the luminescent rings of fire.

"But will it survive that hostile environment?" Dax asked.

"Captain," Chief O'Brien said, "I had time to analyze the pod en route and found it to be nearly indestructible."

"We've lost its position," Worf said. "Sensors are unable to track it."

Sisko nodded. "I'm sure that's according to plan. It should be secure until its term is complete."

"I don't suppose we're going to find out anytime soon the significance of what we just did?" Bashir asked.

"Not anytime soon, Doctor," Sisko said, sounding philosophical. "Not anytime soon."

Spock: A thousand years. Captain?
Kirk: Well, that gives us a little time. . . .
Enterprise *Log, Stardate 3045.6*

The Gorn walked slowly, stabbing the desert soil with his staff, his hand resting on Sisko's shoulder.

"Did you think at any time that Kirk would actually win the confrontation?" Sisko asked, wiping a bead of sweat from his brow.

The alien shook his head. When he spoke, his voice was still strained but content. "Kirk's physical strength was inferior to mine. I was the hunter, and he was daunted by the chase."

"But he was faster, more agile."

"He was quick," the alien conceded.

"And when you faced his crude weapon? Were you concerned?"

"His earlier attacks had been futile," the Gorn said. "I was suspicious but not worried."

Sisko surveyed the quiet landscape and couldn't help but feel the acute sense of history in its solitude. If Kirk had died here, so much would have been lost: the *Enterprise* destroyed, no crew to fulfill those remarkable destinies.

The Gorn stopped for a moment and gently poked at Sisko

with his clawed thumb. "You're bigger than Kirk. Maybe I would have been more careful had it been you."

Sisko gave the alien a thoughtful grin, then both continued walking several hundred meters to the rocky escarpment, to the site of the arena, to the plot of ground where the Gorn had fallen.

Good Night, *Voyager*

Patrick Cumby

The Bridge

"What the devil happened to the lights?"

It was a good question, and Kathryn Janeway had every right to ask it. It was, after all, her starship.

There was no immediate response, so she tried again. "Excuse me, but can anyone tell me what is going on?"

There was a rustle behind her, and Harry Kim's quavering voice spoke in the darkness from his position at the ops panel. "My board is dead, Captain. Everything. Even the emergency status display."

The fear in his voice was evident, and well justified. A complete power failure of all bridge systems was not only disconcerting, it was supposedly impossible. She gripped her command chair arms, the only things solid and real in the blackness.

Then her stomach flip-flopped, and her head spun. The gasps

in the darkness around her indicated that she wasn't the only one experiencing the symptoms.

"What now?" muttered a voice. It was Tom Paris, immediately forward at the ship's helm.

"It would appear, Captain, that the problem extends to the artificial gravity generators," observed Tuvok dryly.

"Everyone stay calm," Janeway snapped. "We've obviously had some kind of systems failure."

"I'll say," said the voice of Paris.

"We need to get some light in here. Tuvok, can you reach the emergency supplies panel?"

"I shall endeavor to do so. I would suggest that everyone remain motionless to avoid injury."

Janeway heard a rustle of movement. She tried to track it with her ears. Yes, Tuvok should be near the starboard supplies panel. She heard a click.

"I have opened the panel."

The harsh glare of the hand-light, held by the Vulcan security chief Tuvok, illuminated the anxious faces of her bridge crew, all eyes turned toward her. She was flooded with relief.

First things first. "Everyone all right?"

There were various nods. "Any indication what happened? Mr. Paris?"

The blond pilot shook his head. "No, Captain. We were proceeding on course at speed when the board just went dead. No indication of any problems, no unusual readings from the navigational sensors."

She turned in her chair. "Mr. Kim?"

"Nothing out of the ordinary."

She looked around the bridge. It appeared much larger in the shadowy beam of Tuvok's hand-light. Several small hand tools and a padd were floating between her and the blank, gray main viewer. There was no indication of a live panel anywhere, no sound, no lighted indicators, nothing.

She tapped her communicator. "Janeway to engineering," she said, not really expecting a response. Why should the communicators work when the entire bridge, with its multiple-redundant backup systems, was inoperative?

She started when a voice answered. *"Ensign Vorik here, Captain. May I ask what is happening?"*

Janeway sighed. "I was hoping you could tell me. We seem to be experiencing a comprehensive systems failure."

"The situation here is the same," reported the Vulcan engineering officer. *"The lights went out and the warp core went into auto-shutdown. All of my systems appear to be nonfunctional, except for the emergency manual monitor for the engine core systems."*

"Was the warp core auto-shutdown complete?"

"Yes, Captain. At least it appears so. I'm still checking readings."

"See what you can find out, Mr. Vorik, and get back to me on the double. We've obviously got a big problem here."

Harry Kim had recovered a tricorder and flipped it open. It warbled comfortingly. Whatever it was that had disabled *Voyager*'s systems apparently didn't extend to handheld devices.

"Report, Mr. Kim."

Kim waved the tricorder around, staring intently at the display. "There doesn't seem to be any damage to the ship. I'm reading the crew lifesigns and, umm, what looks like three remaining power sources. Engineering, something in sickbay, and what looks like number three computer core."

"Captain," Tuvok interrupted. "Those systems—emergency manual monitor in engineering, the emergency medical holographic system in sickbay, and the backup navigational database in computer core three—are the only ship's systems not directly controlled by the bio-neural network."

"So you're suggesting that the bio-neural circuitry has failed?" asked Janeway.

"It is a distinct possibility," admitted Tuvok.

"How could that be?" responded Kim. "There was no warning . . . plus the bio-neural network isn't a monolithic whole—it's a bunch of independent subprocessors made up of individual gel packs. Everything has backups, especially bridge command and control systems. Nothing could bring the entire system down all at once."

"Nothing you are aware of," corrected Tuvok.

"Nothing *anybody's* aware of, Mr. Tuvok," shot back Kim.

Janeway's communicator beeped. *"Torres to bridge."*

"Janeway here. Go ahead, Lieutenant."

The chief engineer sounded peeved. *"What's happening? One minute I'm asleep, the next I wake up to find myself floating around my cabin."*

"Tuvok thinks we've had a massive failure of the bio-neural net. . . ."

"That's impossible," said Torres. Kim displayed a humorless grin, and Tuvok raised an eyebrow.

"I wouldn't be so sure, Lieutenant. Get to engineering. We need power up here. First priority is life support. If it is the bio-neural net, we need to repair it, or bypass it."

"Yes, ma'am. Torres out." Janeway frowned at the "ma'am," but didn't comment.

Janeway tapped her communicator yet again. "Janeway to all crew. As you are aware, we have experienced a major systems failure. I'm declaring a Red Alert, emergency status eleven. Report to your alert stations. Internal communications are down, so you'll have to use your communicators. Use them sparingly, as we'll need clear channels to coordinate the repair effort." She took a deep breath, then continued with a reassuring tone. "We should have life support systems back on-line soon. Please assist the engineering teams as necessary. Everyone remain calm, I'll keep you posted as the situation develops. Senior officers, report to . . ." She was about to say *report to the bridge,* but decided against it. With all systems down, there was nothing for them to do here. "Report to engineering. Janeway out."

She nodded toward the exit. "Gentlemen, crank that door open. Tom, you have the conn. Everyone else, with me."

Paris's eyebrows furrowed and he gestured around at the dead control panels. "What good can I do here, Captain?"

"We need someone here in case systems come back on-line, and also to secure the bridge," she said. Paris did not reply, but his expression showed he was not happy with the order.

Main Engineering

Janeway, Tuvok, and Kim reached engineering to find B'Elanna Torres deep in conversation with Ensign Vorik, her Vulcan assistant. Chakotay arrived soon after.

Everyone clustered around the sole light source. The emergency manual monitor station beamed cheerfully, even emitting a good-natured beep and warble every so often, as if to reassure the crew that something was still working.

Janeway turned to Torres. "What have you got, Lieutenant?"

"No good news, Captain. It looks like Tuvok was right—none of the systems controlled by the bio-neural network are functioning."

"Can we get life support back on line?"

"I don't know. We might be able to bypass parts of the bio-neural network and get at least partial life support in one or two sections, but without the network connections, there's no way we'll be able to sustain the entire crew."

"How long have we got?"

Torres ran the back of her hand across her knotted forehead. "Well, the breathable volume of ship's atmosphere will become poisoned by CO_2 within twenty or thirty hours. Also, without temperature regulation, it's going to get very cold, very fast, especially in those areas of the ship closest to the outer hull."

"Recommendations?"

"We should disperse the crew evenly throughout the ship. The less physical activity, the better. A body at rest consumes less oxygen," said Chakotay.

"Our first priority should be atmosphere regeneration," said Torres. "I'll try to get one space habitable, something large enough for the crew."

"The shuttlebay," suggested Kim.

Torres nodded. "Good idea. It's already got a self-contained atmosphere control system, so it shouldn't be impossible if we can restore power."

"If we cannot repair the problem quickly, there are also long-term concerns," added Chakotay. "Without replicators, our survival rations will only last a couple of weeks. Then there's the problem of waste disposal and hygiene."

"Let's get through the day," suggested Janeway, "before we start worrying about that. Concentrate your effort on the environmental systems, then . . ."

A series of shrill beeps from the emergency manual monitor console interrupted the captain. Ensign Vorik silenced the alarm. "Captain," he said, "it appears that we have an even more urgent problem." He pointed at a flashing display.

"Number one fusion reactor," he said. "It's overheating."

"What?" Torres examined the display. "You're right," she said. "The starboard impulse fusion reactor seems to have lost control systems power before auto-shutdown was complete. It's overheating. We're looking at a meltdown within four or five hours, if we can't stop it."

"Great," muttered Chakotay. "How *do* we stop it?"

Torres and Vorik exchanged glances. "Without power, I can't think of a way. As far as I know, in our current condition, we can't even eject it." Vorik raised an eyebrow and nodded in agreement.

"Wonderful," observed Chakotay grimly. "Will it explode?"

"Unlikely," said Vorik, "but not impossible."

"Doesn't matter," said Torres. "Even if it doesn't blow us up, a meltdown will breach the tritanium confinement bottle. The gamma radiation alone will be enough to kill us all."

"Great," said Kim sardonically. "What else can go wrong?"

"All these things are results of the system failure," said Chakotay, "but what about the cause? What caused the bioneural net to crash in the first place?"

They all looked at each other.

It was Tuvok who finally spoke. "I see four possibilities. First, it could be a sickness—we already know the gel packs are susceptible to biological infections. Second, it is possible that some external force is responsible, some sort of spatial anomaly or energy field undetectable to our sensors. Third, it could be just an extremely unlikely combination of random factors." He looked around at everyone. "Coincidence, or simply bad luck."

"I didn't think Vulcans believed in coincidence or luck," observed Chakotay.

Janeway waved Tuvok's response down. "And the fourth possibility?"

"A deliberate action by one or more members of the crew."

"Sabotage? That's impossible," said Janeway.

"About as impossible as a failure of the entire bio-neural network," said Chakotay.

"Yes, but to what end? What possible benefit could come from crashing the bio-neural net?" Janeway looked around at the assembled faces. No one answered.

It took several minutes for the remaining senior officers to assemble in engineering. When everyone was accounted for, Janeway took a deep breath and tapped her combadge.

"Captain to all hands. Stand down from Red Alert. Maintain alert condition eleven. All personnel not directly involved in the repair effort, report to your quarters and wait for further instruction. Keep your physical activity to a minimum. Janeway out."

"So, it looks like we're going to fry, suffocate, freeze, and then starve—let's concentrate on them in that order," said Chakotay. He anchored himself in the center of a circle of personnel. "Lieutenant Torres, you lead team one. Find a way to either shut down or eject the fusion reactor. This is our top priority; you are authorized to procure any resource or personnel you need to accomplish this task. Ensign Vorik, you will assist Lieutenant Torres. I think you both understand the importance of your assignment." Torres smiled grimly; the young Vulcan nodded once.

"Team two will report to Captain Janeway. You are responsible for getting life support back on-line—first in the hangar bay, next for the entire ship.

"I will lead team three. We will attempt to ascertain what happened to the bio-neural net and find a way to get it back on line.

"Tuvok, I want you to remain in engineering and coordinate the repair teams.

"Everybody understand their assignments?" The assembled

teams indicated that they understood. "Okay. Good luck to us all. Let's get to it!"

Fusion Reactor Bay 1

Chief Thompson put her palm to the bulkhead. "Damn," she said. "It's already hot to the touch. That's not good, not good at all. Help me with this access panel."

Ensign Vorik stepped up to assist Thompson, the engineering chief responsible for the maintenance of *Voyager*'s fusion reactors. Together they removed the panel from the bulkhead. A green glow emanated from the opening. Lieutenant Torres peered over their shoulders.

"The containment field is already starting to decay," noted Vorik.

"Mmm," agreed Thompson. She poked an instrument into the opening. "It's worse than I thought."

Torres tapped her combadge. "Torres to Tuvok."

"Tuvok here."

"The control circuitry in the reactor is fused beyond repair. There is no way we're going to be able to save the reactor." Torres wiped a bead of sweat from her nose. "And it gets worse: the containment field is failing much faster than anticipated."

"How much faster?"

Thompson handed the tricorder to Torres. "According to tricorder readings," said Torres, "it looks like we have about two hours before meltdown. However, we can expect a radiation release once the containment field degrades below twenty-five percent. That only gives us about ninety minutes to figure out how to eject the reactor."

"Unfortunate," said Tuvok. *"Any ideas?"*

Thompson and Vorik exchanged looks. "None come to mind," replied Torres.

Thompson shrugged. "I suppose we could cut the reactor out of its mounting, manually blow the ejection hatch, and shove the damn thing out with our bare hands."

There was a long silence. Finally, Torres responded. "We can probably separate the mounting braces; they're designed to detach. But the fused control circuits will keep us from blowing the ejection hatch."

"What about a plasma torch?" suggested Thompson. "We can cut the hatch open."

Torres shook her head. "Too slow. We'd never be able to cut through the hull with handheld tools in the time we have. It'd take a ship-mounted phaser to be able to do that. . . ."

It occurred to both Thompson and Vorik simultaneously. "The shuttlecraft," muttered Thompson.

Torres pondered the idea. "It might work," she said thoughtfully. "Tuvok, do we know if the shuttlecraft onboard systems were affected by whatever caused the bio-neural failure?"

"No," he responded, *"but since they do not use bio-neural technology, shuttlecraft systems should be functional."*

"How will you get the shuttle out of the hangar?" asked Vorik. "Without power, there's no way to open the hangar's space doors."

"We blast our way out," suggested Torres. "With the shuttlecraft phasers."

"That's a little tough on the space doors," commented Thompson. "That'll make it impossible to use the hangar as a life support station."

"True," said Tuvok. *"But it's better than imminent radiation poisoning. Begin freeing the reactor from its mountings. I'll contact the captain and arrange for the use of a shuttlecraft."*

"Aye aye," said Torres. She looked at Vorik. "Let's get on with it," she said. "It's gonna get awfully hot in here, real soon."

Shuttlecraft Hangar Deck

Janeway motioned for her crew's attention. "There is a change of plans," she said. "We're moving to cargo bay one. Take whatever equipment you need and get down there on the double." She turned to Harry Kim. "Mr. Kim, you're with me."

While the repair crew hastened to comply with the captain's orders, Janeway pulled Kim aside. "The reactor is failing faster than expected and cannot be shut down," she said quietly. "The reactor ejection systems are off-line, so we're going to use a shuttlecraft's phasers to remove the reactor ejection hatch and tow the reactor to a safe distance from the ship."

"How are we supposed to get a shuttle out of the shuttlebay?" asked Kim, indicating the massive hangar doors. "There's no way to open the space doors."

Janeway smiled bitterly. "There is always a way, Harry. You'll just have to blast your way out."

It took a moment before he understood what the captain had said. "Me? You want *me* to pilot the shuttle?"

Janeway nodded.

Kim looked stunned, and his voice rose an octave. "Captain, uh, wouldn't Tom, ah, Lieutenant Paris, be a better choice?"

Janeway's eyebrows rose. "Are you questioning my orders, Ensign?"

"Uh, no, Captain, it's just that I . . ."

"Harry, I want *you* on that shuttle. There's no time to get Tom down here, and you're fully qualified as a shuttle pilot. You're the best man for the job." She placed her hand on Kim's shoulder and smiled. "Don't worry, it'll be easier than any of the simulations at the academy. Plus . . ."—her smile became somewhat coy—"if you make a mistake and hit the fusion reactor, we'll never know it."

Kim swallowed hard. "I'll be careful, Captain."

Janeway nodded. "Coordinate your activity with Ensign Vorik's team. Give us a few minutes to clear the hangar, then move fast."

Sickbay

Chakotay placed the bio-neural gel pack against the padded diagnostic bed and removed his hands slowly to keep it from floating away in the zero-G. The Doctor and his Ocampan assistant, Kes, stepped forward and examined the lopsided object with much interest. The Doctor produced a scanner and waved it around the pack. Being a computer-generated holographic projection, the Doctor was not affected by the loss of gravity. He walked normally around the diagnostic bed.

Chakotay found it quite disconcerting. He grasped the scanner assembly next to the bed with white knuckles to keep from floating away. "Any ideas, Doc?" he said.

The Emergency Medical Hologram scratched his bald pate. "There doesn't appear to be any damage to the pack," he said, a trace of irritation in his computer-generated voice. "It should be working."

"Any trace of contaminants or infectious organisms?"

The Doctor shook his head. "Nothing. The electro-neural pathways are clear, the ODN interface microtendrils are all operating properly, and the . . ." The doctor suddenly opened his mouth wide, sucked in a deep breath, and then released it slowly and with apparent relish.

It was a moment before Chakotay realized the incongruity of the action. "Doctor, did you just . . . *yawn?*" he asked.

The Doctor looked slightly guilty. "Pardon me," he said. "I am not quite clear on the proper etiquette for such involuntary actions," he professed. "I will cover my mouth next time."

"No, that's okay," said Chakotay. "It's not the fact that you neglected to cover your mouth, it's the fact that you . . . *yawned.*"

"Ah, yes," said the Doctor. "You're wondering why a holographic simulation feels fatigue. It's an experiment I am running. I am attempting to better understand the effects of fatigue on the human body. It is a part of my ongoing research into humanoid physiological . . ."

"I suggest that you suspend your experiment for the duration of this emergency," interrupted Chakotay. "We need you operating at one hundred percent efficiency."

"Of course," said the Doctor. "I will cease at once." The Doctor paused for a moment and stared out into space. "Hmm, that's odd," he said. "I don't seem to be able to disengage the fatigue subroutine. How disconcerting!"

"Can you run an internal self-diagnostic of your systems?" asked Kes.

The Doctor looked worried. "Already under way," he said. "It'll take a few minutes."

Fusion Reactor Bay 1

Torres grunted at the strain, then backed away from the reactor mount. Sweat stained her uniform, and she breathed in short, shallow gasps. "It's not moving," she said. "Scan it again and see if there's a mount we missed."

Ensign Vorik punched at the face of his tricorder. Unlike Torres, the young Vulcan seemed impervious to the scorching heat. He nodded. "Yes, it appears as if there is one more on the underside. You should be able to get to it from the rear of the housing."

Torres nodded, too hot and tired to respond verbally. She pulled herself from underneath the spherical reactor housing and worked her way around the back. "Damn, it's hot," she muttered. The reactor casing itself was far too hot to touch, and had heated the stale air in the small compartment to a point where it was barely breathable. "One last mount," she muttered to herself. One final mount. She'd already disconnected the piping and wiring connections and severed the remaining mounts with her phaser. One more to go.

There was no way to reach it. "I can't get to it," she said. "There's no way to get to it without squeezing under the reactor shell. It's just too hot."

"Can you see the mount?" asked Chief Thompson, the third member of the team crowded into the tiny reactor compartment. "Maybe if you're careful you can phaser it from a distance."

Torres shook her head. "Can't see it," she replied. "It's too far underneath. And I don't think it's a very good idea to fire a phaser blindly at a thermonuclear reactor mount. If I missed . . ."

She didn't need to finish. They all knew what would happen if the phaser beam cut into the reactor housing—instant immolation in nuclear fire.

"Why don't you let me try?" suggested Thompson. "I'm a lot smaller than either of you, and I might be able to fit."

Torres eyed the reactor dubiously. "You can try, but I don't think it'll make any difference," she said. She moved carefully from behind the reactor to allow the diminutive Thompson to pass. Without gravity, it was difficult to operate in such closed quarters.

Thompson nodded to Vorik, who held the tricorder. "Guide me," she said.

Shuttlecraft Hangar Deck

Harry Kim powered up the shuttlecraft and considered the best course of action. Normally, the annular confinement field would allow him to leave the shuttlebay without depressurizing the hangar. Without power, there was no annular confinement beam. There was also no way to decompress the bay. When he blew the doors, hundreds of cubic meters of atmosphere would rush out into space with the force of a hurricane, carrying every loose object in the hangar with it. "Including the shuttle, if I'm not careful," he muttered to himself.

He activated the exterior speakers. "Preparing to fire phasers. Clear the shuttlebay."

He scanned the sensor panel to verify that the hangar was indeed empty, then reconfigured the panel for weapons fire.

"Warning," said the shuttlecraft computer. "Minimal safe distance from *U.S.S. Voyager* not achieved. Weapons fire at this range may result in damage to *U.S.S. Voyager.*"

Harry chuckled humorlessly. "You got that right," he said.

The clamshell hangar doors appeared in the targeting display. He plotted the beam path to cut away the portside space door, minimizing damage to the starboard door. Next, to avoid tumbling out into space, he activated the maneuvering thrusters and set them to station-keeping mode.

The computer didn't like that, either. "Warning," it said, "the use of reaction control thrusters in the shuttlebay is prohibited."

"Shut up," said Harry, and fired the phasers.

Fusion Reactor Bay 1

Torres looked over Vorik's shoulder as he punched up scanning mode on the tricorder and pointed the sensor array at the reactor housing. The EM interference from the collapsing containment field hindered the readings, but there was still a clear enough image of Thompson to help guide her to the recalcitrant mount. "Stop there," Vorik said. "You are right above it. Look underneath and you may be able to see the mount."

The tricorder screen traced her movements. "Can you see it?" Vorik asked. He spoke loudly to be heard over the rumble of the reactor. There was no answer. The figure on the tricorder screen moved lower. "Be careful," he warned. Again, there was no answer. Then they heard the warble of a phaser, and saw the heat imprint on the tricorder screen.

"Did you get it?" Torres called.

"Yeah, I got it. I'm coming out."

"Great job, Chief!" congratulated Torres. "I didn't think that . . ." A muffled explosion drowned out her praise. The entire compartment shuddered. Freed from its moorings, the reactor housing shifted slightly. There was a short, staccato scream. "Thompson?" she called. There was no answer.

Torres pushed her way behind the housing, burning her shoulder when she lost her handhold and floated into the casing. Thompson's boots were jutting from beneath the reactor. "Gina!" Torres cried, and tried to reach her, but there was no way; the heat was far too severe.

Then Vorik was behind her, pulling her away. He pushed the tricorder into her hands and squeezed behind the reactor.

Torres punched the tricorder's controls, changing from deep scan mode to lifescan. Thompson was not breathing, but she was still alive. Barely. "Vorik, can you get to her?" she cried.

Vorik did not answer. He was busy trying to reach the motionless form without touching the scorching reactor casing. If he could just get his hand on her boot, he might be able to pull her out, revive her.

The flesh on his chest seared painfully as it came into contact with the red-hot reactor housing. He recoiled from the unexpected intensity of the pain, a movement that sent him spinning back across the room. Hands flailing, he bounced off the ceiling before he managed to grab the edge of a control panel and stop his motion.

Torres stared at the tricorder. Thompson's lifesigns were

fading rapidly. "Help," Torres cried, pounding her communicator. "Medic! I need a medic in the fusion reactor compartment!"

Cargo Bay 1

There was a sound like thunder and the entire ship vibrated. Janeway clutched at the edge of the open ODN access panel and waited for Kim to report. She was about to call him when his exuberant voice came through her communicator. *"Whew, I made it,"* he said. *"I underestimated the force of the atmosphere evacuation. The power of the wind almost smashed me into the starboard space door."*

Janeway heard Tuvok's voice. *"Then I take it, Ensign Kim, that you have safely exited the ship?"*

"Yes, sir," came the response. *"I'm moving into position now. Let me know when the reactor chamber is clear so I can begin cutting away the reactor ejection hatch."*

Janeway smiled and let loose a small, private sigh of relief. Kim was young, inexperienced. *This will be a great confidence-building exercise,* she thought, *if only he manages to keep from blowing us up.*

Janeway turned back to her work, but only for a moment.

"Medic! I need a medic in the fusion reactor compartment!" Lieutenant Torres's shrill call came through all their communicators—an all-channels emergency broadcast.

"Stand by, Ensign Kim," came Tuvok's voice over the communicator. *"There appear to be injuries in the reactor compartment. I will signal you and let you know when it is safe to continue."*

The Bridge

Tom Paris tapped his fingers on the dead helm console, listened to the comm traffic, and tried to ignore the dark, silent bridge around him.

That should be me out there, not Harry, he thought anxiously. *The poor kid's probably breaking out in hives about now. I hope he can handle it.*

Something floated by in his peripheral vision. He jumped,

startled, and the combination of abrupt movement and zero-G almost sent him spinning away from the console.

It was a tricorder. He clutched at the edge of his chair to steady himself, then angrily snatched the floating tricorder from the air.

"What am I doing here?" he moaned, and waited for his heartbeat to return to normal.

The sudden jolt and thunderous noise did nothing to calm him. *Oh no,* thought Paris. Images of Kim's shuttle crashing into the hangar deck flashed through his mind. He was reaching for his combadge when Kim reported his successful egress from the hangar. He let his hand drop to his lap. "I knew you could do it, buddy," he said aloud.

Then came the frantic all-hands call from B'Elanna Torres. *"Medic! I need a medic . . ."*

Cargo Bay 1

Janeway furrowed her brow. Injuries? Damn! She tapped her combadge. "Janeway to Torres. What's the status in the reactor chamber?"

Torres's voice was frantic. *"Torres here, Captain. We freed the reactor from its mounts. There was some kind of explosion and the reactor housing broke away and . . ."* Her voice cracked and she paused. *". . . and Thompson was crushed. She's dead."* Her grief was evident, even through the distortion of the combadge. *"Vorik was also injured, burned. What happened, Captain? What was the blast?"*

"It was the shuttlecraft *Faraday* blowing the space doors open," she replied.

"Ah, damn it to hell," Torres replied. *"I should have thought of that, been prepared. If there had only been more time . . ."* Her voice crumbled into a shuddering sigh.

Janeway closed her eyes and took a deep breath. "Lieutenant," she said sternly, "I need you to clear the reactor chamber. Ensign Kim is prepared to remove the ejection hatch with the shuttle-craft phasers. I understand your grief at the loss of Chief Thompson, but remember that her actions probably saved us all. She will be remembered, but in the meantime, you've got to finish your job. Get that reactor ready to be jettisoned and clear the reactor chamber!"

"But, Captain, her body is trapped beneath the reactor. It'll take a few more minutes to free her and . . ."

"Negative, Lieutenant," Janeway said. "You will concentrate your actions on preparing the reactor for jettison and clearing the reactor chamber. Is that clear?"

"But, Captain . . ."

"That's an order," she said, hating her responsibility. She waited for the response.

"Aye, Captain," Torres replied quietly. *"Torres out."*

Janeway sighed heavily and tried to concentrate on her task at hand, bypassing the bio-neural life support controls for the cargo bay. *I must have a talk with Harry Kim once this is over,* she thought. *He's going to blame himself for Thompson's death.* The loss of Chief Thompson was a terrible tragedy, but they'd be lucky if any of them survived. She sighed again and reached inside the access panel to reroute an ODN junction.

Sickbay

Chakotay pulled the isolinear chip from the console and half-floated, half-dragged himself into the Doctor's office. The Doctor was seated at his desk, arms crossed, head down, snoring lightly. Chakotay frowned.

"Doctor!" he called, shaking the Doctor as vigorously as possible considering the lack of gravity and his lack of solid purchase. The Doctor looked up, dazed. "What happened?" he asked, his voice slurred.

"You fell asleep again," said Chakotay.

"Extraordinary," replied the Doctor, wiping the holographic drool from the side of his mouth with his uniform sleeve. "I was analyzing the data from the gel sample and I closed my eyes for a moment and . . ."

"And you fell asleep," finished Chakotay grimly. "Doctor, we need you. This conduct of yours is totally unacceptable. I could put you on report for sleeping while on duty."

"I know that," snapped the Doctor. "Believe me, Commander, I don't cherish being saddled with humanoid weaknesses like fatigue and . . . and . . ." His sentence was cut off by a tremendous yawn. He looked up guiltily. "Perhaps we should ask Kes to complete the cellular scan."

Chakotay nodded at the groggy hologram. The Doctor's eyes were already closing. "Yes, perhaps we should," said Chakotay.

Shuttlecraft *Faraday*

With her exterior and running lights extinguished, *Voyager* was visible only where she obscured the background stars, a ghostly shape against the blackness of interstellar space.

Harry Kim activated the forward spotlights of the shuttlecraft, illuminating the trailing edge of *Voyager*'s primary hull. Clearly visible in the circle of light, the emergency ejection hatch for the number-one fusion generator was a deceptively easy target. *My first chance at firing shipboard phasers at another vessel,* he thought wryly, *and it's my own ship.*

Kim carefully set up a firing solution that would remove the hatch without causing major collateral damage, or worse, hitting the already unstable fusion reactor.

How would Tom handle this? he wondered. He considered contacting his friend for advice. He raised his hand to tap the combadge on his chest, then slowly lowered it.

No, he thought. *No, I can do this myself.*

He talked to himself as he worked. "Narrow, millimeter-width beam, low power to the emitters. Watch out for the pyrotechnic bolts." He knew that the explosive bolts that were *supposed* to blow the hatch during an emergency reactor ejection were now nothing more than a dangerous nuisance. It might take a while to cut the hatch away, but better safe than sorry. Don't want to blow the ship up, and hitting an explosive bolt or burning through the reactor housing *will* do just that.

When he was ready, he thumbed the comm panel. "Kim to Torres. I'm in position. Let me know when the reactor bay is clear."

There were casualties, Tuvok had said. Chief Thompson dead,

Ensign Vorik injured. While he waited he double-checked the firing solution, his hands flitting nervously over the controls, thinking about all the ways he could screw this up. . . .

The comm panel sprang to life. *"Okay, Harry, the bay is clear,"* reported Torres. *"Uh, Harry, we were unable to retrieve Chief Thompson's body. She's still in the compartment. Once you move the reactor to a safe distance . . ."*

"You want me to recover the body," finished Kim.

There was a short silence before Torres responded. *"Yes."*

Kim nodded to himself, grimly. "Understood."

"I'm sorry, Harry," the half-Klingon Torres said. Then, *"Fire at will. We're all counting on you."*

Great. I could've gone without that last part, B'Elanna, he thought. *I'm* much *calmer now. . . .*

His index finger floated above the "execute" key while his eyes scanned the setting for a final time. He took a deep breath. *Well, here goes nothing. . . .*

He pressed the key and the phasers lanced out to the *Voyager.* Slowly, ever so slowly, the beam moved around the periphery of the ejection hatch. A cloud of sparkling crystals formed around the hatch as atmosphere escaped into the cold vacuum of space.

Seconds before the preprogrammed sequence was to end, the hatch tore loose and spun away from the ship. Harry quickly deactivated the phasers.

He realized he'd been holding his breath. He let it out sharply. "Well then, that wasn't so hard."

The reactor housing slowly drifted out of the hatch, propelled by the last vestiges of air escaping into space. Harry immediately captured it with the shuttle's tractor beam to help guide it out. Debris floated around the reactor housing like a halo, also caught in the tractor: pieces of bulkhead, clumps of torn ODN conduits, and the body of Chief Gina Thompson.

Sickbay

Someone was shaking him.

"Doctor! Doctor!"

He opened his eyes. It was Chakotay. He must have fallen

asleep again! "I'm awake, I'm awake," he said groggily. He wiped his eyes to clear his vision.

Chakotay was handing him a padd. He took it.

"These are Kes's results from the cellular scan. What do you make of it?"

The doctor squinted at the report. He had trouble focusing his eyes. He was tired, so tired. "How do you people function like this?" he asked grumpily.

Chakotay motioned impatiently at the padd. "The report, Doctor."

"Oh, yes. Well . . ." The Doctor stared intently at the report. "The level of cellular activity of the gel pack is far below normal. Electrolyte levels and the percentage of free . . . hold on, now, what's this?"

Chakotay leaned forward. "What is it?"

The Doctor pointed at a line on the report. "Look at this. Right there. Elevated synthotonin levels."

Chakotay waited for the Doctor to elucidate. No explanation seemed forthcoming. "Well?" Chakotay prompted.

"Oh, yes, excuse me." The Doctor rubbed his eyes. "The explanation is quite simple, really. This gel pack is asleep."

"What? You're kidding me!"

Chakotay turned to the examination table. The gel pack lay there, a brownish mass of goo in a clear, flexible pack, with a hard ODN connector running the length of one side. He turned back to the Doctor. "How can a gel pack be asleep?"

The Doctor's only response was a soft snore.

Cargo Bay 1

Janeway's team was making headway. Most of the bio-neural network controlling the environmental systems for the deck had been bypassed, leaving only a few finishing touches before life support could be restored to the cargo bay.

Janeway closed the panel where she'd been working. Her back hurt. She pushed a stray strand of hair from her face and turned to assess the activities of the other members of her team.

Her communicator warbled. *"Chakotay to Captain Janeway."*

"Janeway here. Go ahead, Commander."

"The Doctor has completed his preliminary biological analysis of the gel packs," he said. *"He's come to the conclusion that the gel packs are, well, that* Voyager *is, um, asleep, Captain."*

She started to reply, but no words came to mind. "Asleep?" she finally managed.

"Asleep," confirmed Chakotay.

Janeway felt her eyebrows climb to the top of her forehead. "Well now, that's . . . that's . . . extraordinary."

"And that's not all," continued Chakotay. *"The Doctor's asleep, too."*

Janeway reached out and steadied herself against the bulkhead. "I'm afraid I don't understand," she said.

"Me neither," said Chakotay. *"I've already contacted Lieutenant Torres. I think you'd better get up here, too."*

"On my way," she replied.

Sickbay

Chakotay and Kes were waiting. The Doctor, free from the awkwardness of zero-G, was nonetheless swaying slightly. Torres was also there, waving a tricorder at the Doctor.

"Okay, report," Janeway said.

Chakotay shook the woozy hologram. "Doctor?"

"Uh, yes, Captain. The, ah, gel packs we analyzed all exhibited decreased cellular activity and lowered operating temperature. It was the same in every gel pack we tested. Further scans indicated the presence of synthotonin, an artificial substance designed to depress the activity of the bio-neural circuitry for regenerative purposes."

"Regenerative purposes? Explain."

Torres cut in. "The biological components of the gel pack are based on living cellular material. Just like the cells that make up our bodies, the cells in each bio-neural circuit require periodic states of reduced activity in order to regenerate cellular energy levels."

The Doctor nodded, stifling another yawn. "These periods of reduced energy are achieved by introducing synthotonin into the organic media that make up the gel pack. This usually occurs about once a month for each gel pack, depending on its level of activity. The gel pack, in effect, takes a short nap."

"Bio-neural network downtime is avoided by staggering the regenerative cycles so that no two packs are inactive at the same time," said Torres. "At least, that's how it's supposed to work."

"So what you're saying is that the entire bio-neural network, all of the gel packs, decided to take a nap at the same time?"

The Doctor nodded. Janeway couldn't tell if he was signaling the affirmative or simply nodding off to sleep. Chakotay shook him. "Yes, yes," he replied.

Janeway looked at Torres. "Could the Doctor's . . . condition . . . be related to this problem?"

"I don't see how," said Torres. "The EMH environment operates independently from the main bio-neural network." She stared at the Doctor. "But it is too much of a coincidence to ignore."

"Agreed," said Janeway. "Let's assume that they are related, and figure out how to wake up the Doctor . . . and *Voyager*."

"Kim to sickbay." Harry Kim's voice sounded flat, and not just due to the audio filtering. Janeway nodded to Kes.

"Kes here."

"I've returned to the shuttlebay. I have . . . a casualty."

Janeway closed her eyes and tapped her combadge. *Thompson,* she thought. *Harry has her body.* "Harry, secure the shuttle-craft," she said gently. "When you're ready, use the shuttle's transporter to beam directly to sickbay."

"Aye, Captain."

No one spoke for a long moment. Janeway took a deep breath. "Let's get to work," she said.

Main Engineering

"Okay, let's put all the pieces together," said Torres to the group. "The Doctor activated his fatigue subroutine when?"

Most of the command crew, along with Kes and Neelix, were gathered around the emergency manual monitor in engineering.

"Yesterday," replied Kes.

"But the bio-neural network failed this morning," observed Chakotay. "Nearly eighteen hours later."

"You've also got to keep in mind that the Doctor's EMH program uses a dedicated subprocessor that has no ties to bio-neural circuits," said Torres. "None whatsoever. There's no way his fatigue subroutine could have contaminated the bio-neural network."

"But isn't the Doctor's program backed up daily to the main computer core?" asked Tuvok. "And isn't the main core part of the bio-neural network?"

"Yes, but that's simply an automated batch process that takes a static image of the EMH at the given time and downloads the image to the core storage," replied Torres. "There's no programmatic interaction between the two systems."

"When was the Doctor's last scheduled backup?" asked Janeway.

Torres flipped open her tricorder. "Oh eight hundred hours this morning." She looked up. "Three and a half minutes before the systems failure."

"It can't be a coincidence," said Chakotay.

"I agree," said Tuvok. "There must be some element of the Doctor's so-called fatigue subroutine that affected the entire bio-neural network, causing the system shutdown. I recommend that we go to the computer core, isolate the subroutine, and delete it. Doing so will likely restore the network to normal functionality."

Janeway nodded. "If this works, and I have every confidence that it will, I think I'll have a little talk with the Doctor about his sleeping habits."

Smiles spread through the group. Janeway started toward the open gangway. "Follow me," she said. "I think it's time we gave our ship a wake-up call."

The Bridge

Tom Paris watched as the bridge came to life, one station at a time. He tapped his combadge. "Whatever it is you guys are doing," he said, "it's working." Within minutes, Paris could feel his weight starting to return, as the artificial gravity generators began to operate. All systems were back on-line when he heard the turbolift doors open.

"Ah, Harry, glad to see you!" he said. "Actually, I'm glad to see *anybody*. I was getting lonely up here all by myself."

Kim nodded. "Good to see you too, Tom."

Tom stood up and stuck out his hand. Kim looked at it cautiously. "What's that for?" he asked.

"I just want to shake your hand," Paris replied. "I was monitoring the progress reports. You did a damn fine job piloting the shuttlecraft. Couldn't have done better myself. Saved us all, you did."

Kim looked down. "No, not all of us."

Paris cocked his head to one side. "Now Harry, you did what you had to do. So did Gina Thompson. She died saving the ship—doing her duty. Just like you were doing yours."

"I know, Tom, it's just that . . ."

"Just that what?"

The bridge doors opened, admitting Captain Janeway, Tuvok, and several relief crew members. Paris pulled Kim to one side, away from the others. "Just that what?" he prompted again.

Kim shook his head. "I could have warned them before I depressurized the hangar. Given them time to prepare . . ."

Paris stopped him. "How were you supposed to know what would happen?" he whispered. "As far as I know, no one's *ever* blasted their way out of a shuttlecraft hangar. What you did, Harry, was heroic."

"But . . ."

"But *what?* What could you have done differently? No, don't answer that. Hindsight can be unforgiving. Believe me, I know." Paris lowered his voice and put both hands on Kim's shoulders. "Remember, I got three officers killed because of sheer arrogance, thinking I was the greatest pilot that ever lived." Paris stared at Kim until Kim met his gaze. "Harry, today you saved your ship and everyone aboard. That's something to be proud of. I wish I could say the same."

Harry nodded slightly; the pain in his eyes lessened somewhat. "Thanks, Tom. Thanks for everything."

Paris nodded. He released Kim, stepped back, and stretched. "Now, if you don't mind," he said in a loud voice. "It's been a long day, and a long shift. I'm headed to my quarters for a little shut-eye."

Kim nodded, smiling. "Me too, as soon as I check out ops and my relief gets here."

"Goodnight, Harry."

"Goodnight, Tom."

Captain Janeway had watched the hushed interplay between the two junior officers out of the corner of her eye. After Paris left, she wandered back to Kim's station.

"Well, Harry, it's good to have the lights back on, isn't it?"

"It sure is," he replied fervently.

"By the way, that was great work you did today," she said. "I think a commendation is in order."

Kim was taken aback. "Uh, Captain, I don't think I deserve . . ."

"Mr. Kim," she said sternly, "are you questioning my judgment again? That's twice in one day!"

"No, Captain, of course I'm not!"

She smiled. "Good. I won't have my junior officers questioning my orders. Now, I have one more order. Get the hell out of here and get some sleep."

Kim grinned. "Yes, Captain."

She returned his smile and watched him leave before continuing a slow tour around the bridge. Each station was alive with light and sound, indications of a healthy starship.

And after her little "nap," a well-rested starship, she mused.

She stopped behind her command chair, rested her arms across its back, and watched as the relief bridge crew took their places around the bridge. "What a day," she murmured, and stifled a yawn.

Time for rest. "Officer of the Deck, you have the conn," she said, and turned for the turbolift. "Keep me posted if any more problems arise." She stepped into the lift.

"Goodnight, *Voyager,*" she said as the doors closed.

Ambassador at Large

J. A. Rosales

"Mr. Paris, get ready to make a run for it."

Like chess pieces hung above a star-washed board, the three silvery barbell-shaped assault ships faced the *U.S.S. Voyager* in a pattern of unmistakable menace. Between the Federation cruiser and the hostile trio of corsairs drifted a tiny ship, barely larger than a runabout and seemingly built of strange, pulsing orbs of red-orange light. The orbs pulsed only dimly now, and their dying light cast a russet pall across the hulls of the four vessels surrounding it. None of the ships moved.

"Still no response from the small ship," said Mr. Kim, manning the operations station on the bridge of the *Voyager.* "Just the same automated distress signal."

Captain Janeway turned away from the screen and faced her first officer. "One guess as to what those coded transmissions were."

"Calling for reinforcements," said Chakotay immediately. "It's exactly what I'd do."

"It would be inadvisable to be here when they arrive," said Tuvok, his speech as unhurried and thoughtfully composed as his Vulcan demeanor. "We are, roughly speaking, evenly matched with the Mondasian ships arrayed against us—even at a slight disadvantage. The arrival of even one more ship would considerably change the odds in their favor."

"And while they can call on reinforcements," finished Janeway, "we cannot. Time's not on our side." She turned to Lieutenant Torres at the engineering station. "But we still have a duty to respond to this distress call," she said pointedly, "and if at all possible, we have to get that pilot out of there alive."

"*If* he's still alive," said Torres irritably, stabbing away at the controls in front of her. She spun around to punch at the transporter controls and then back again to check the columns of sensor readings that rushed by in response, then looked up at the captain. "I'm still reading lifesigns, but I don't know why. According to these readings the inside of that ship must be awash with radiation from the engine damage." Her heavy half-Klingon brow knitted in consternation. "The radiation's making it hard to get decent readings, and it looks like there's some other kind of interference."

"Incoming message," said Kim.

"On-screen," said Janeway, turning back toward the huge viewer that covered the front quarter of the bridge.

The sight of the small globular ship and the three shiny assault vessels was replaced by the frozen silver mask that was the face of the Mondasian commander. Janeway gazed at the immobile metallic visage with outward calm and confidence, but inwardly the sight made her stomach turn. The Mondasians' speech and appearance had at first seemed to indicate some kind of machine-based intelligence, but this encounter was gradually bringing forth a kind of careless hatred and cruelty that Janeway suspected could come only from a living creature.

"Captain Janeway of *U.S.S. Voyager:* It has been affirmed that the small alien ship will be returned with us. Interference in this action will not be tolerated. You will now withdraw from Mondasian space." The Mondasian's voice was cold and passionless, and when he spoke the thin slit of his mouth did not move.

"I guess those reinforcements are closer than we thought," said Chakotay quietly.

"Our sensors show that the pilot is still alive," said Janeway, "and very probably in need of medical attention. We show that his environment is very like our own—"

"That is not your concern."

"You have not indicated that the pilot will be given the assistance he needs."

"That is not your concern."

The captain glared at the soulless silver mask that filled the screen. "The pilot of that ship requested our assistance," she said dangerously, "and we are here to render it. Removal of that ship without said assistance is unacceptable to us." The implied threat hung in the air for a moment, but if the Mondasian commander perceived it he gave no indication.

"The disposition of any alien beings aboard is not your concern," he replied tonelessly. "The ship will now be removed by us for analysis. Withdraw immediately or be destroyed." The masklike face disappeared, and on-screen the small ship began to move toward the Mondasian formation.

"They have the ship in a tractor beam," said Tuvok, "and are powering their weapons systems."

"Reading two more assault ships just entering sensor range," said Paris. "ETA, two minutes and closing."

"Got him!" said Torres. Janeway whipped around to face her chief engineer and watched as the half-Klingon's lip curled around a triumphant grin. "Transporter locked on, Captain."

"Good work, Lieutenant," said Janeway, feeling the infectious smile begin to creep across her own face. "Beam him directly to sickbay. Mr. Tuvok, auxiliary power to the shields." She sat down in the command chair and took a short, unsentimental last look at the three blunt silver ships, squatting possessively over their little prize. "Mr. Paris, get us out of here."

* * *

The Doctor's voice had taken on a decidedly cheery tone, one he used only when talking about his two favorite subjects: medical innovation and himself. At present he had managed to hit on both at once and was in high spirits as he chattered through his familiar patter.

"Originally, I was programmed to be proficient in over fifty specialties," he was saying, "but since I assumed the post of Chief Medical Officer, my expertise and knowledge have expanded considerably. Indeed, there are some fields in which I am now proficient that were not even conceived of at the time of my activation—fields which, in all modesty, I can be said to have invented." He seemed to inflate slightly, and was not in the least disturbed by the hand which was passing through his midsection.

Janeway knew she and Tuvok had walked in near the beginning of this monologue, and hard experience had taught her that the Doctor would spend as much time on his personal history as the listener would allow. She cleared her throat, and his attention snapped toward her.

"Ah, Captain Janeway," he said brightly. "I was just telling our visitor here about the Emergency Medical Hologram system. He seems quite interested."

Janeway looked over the man standing in sickbay, who a moment ago had been passing his hand through the Doctor's holographic form. He was dressed in a tight-fitting jumpsuit made of a white, metallic fabric, with a wide collar on which was set a metal device with a blue stone, and from which hung short robes cut in a vestlike pattern. He was thin with age and taller than Janeway despite his slight stoop, and had a full head of close-cropped white hair that may have once been blond. He grinned a toothy grin and ran a thin finger across his sharp chin, his face buckling into a tracery of tiny lines like finely aged leather.

"A hologram," said the man in a bemused and robust voice. "Hard to believe."

It took Janeway a moment to realize what was bothering her so much about the man's appearance, and a moment more to accept what she was seeing here on the distant edge of the galaxy, tens of thousands of light-years away from the nearest Federation outpost. She fixed the Doctor with a questioning gaze.

"He looks human," she said.

"He is," the Doctor replied cheerily, oblivious to the incongruity. "And in perfect health. And, I might add, in remarkable shape for someone over one hundred years of age."

"You must be Captain Janeway," the man said, and grasped her hand in a firm grip. "I can't tell you how happy I am to meet you." He looked at Tuvok, and his pale blue eyes glinted with wonder and recognition. "Say, you're a Vulcan, aren't you?"

"This is Mr. Tuvok, my chief of security," explained Janeway as the man pumped Tuvok's hand. "And you are . . . ?"

"Bailey," the man said, and grinned again. "I'm Bailey. Say, I don't mean to impose, but could we get a bite to eat somewhere?"

The mess hall of *Voyager* was awash with people, most of whom tried politely not to stare at the old man in the white metallic outfit as they rushed by. But Bailey was barely aware of their efforts, or even of any specific person or thing that he encountered for more than a few seconds before his unanchored attention was swept along to the next. He had seemed fascinated by the very corridors through which they'd passed to get there, mere gloss black and battleship gray conduits flowing with crew. Only once had Janeway managed to capture his undivided attention, by mentioning his now-lost ship.

"Don't worry about that," he'd said, suddenly serious. "I'll deal with that later. I don't think it's in any real danger."

Now, in *Voyager*'s mess, Bailey was submerged, temporarily overwhelmed by the swirling currents of the lunch rush. He stood in front of Janeway and Tuvok, just inside the doorway, swaying with the ebb and wash of moving bodies and the low murmuring din of the wide-windowed room, with his grin pasted foolishly across his face, his head oscillating to take in the multicolored lake of the crowd. Neelix spotted them from behind an island of serving trays stacked far too high for his unimpressive stature and darted out to greet them, his chef's hat jammed firmly down over his head like a large starched sock.

"Captain, I had no idea you'd be here for lunch," he said, wiping his hands excitedly on a towel, "but you couldn't have picked a better day! I'm serving a light salad of *horva* greens and *kanda* roots with vinaigrette—an old Talaxian recipe, and the perfect thing for the officer on the go." He nudged her and winked knowingly, and began to lead her over to the front of the serving line. "There's Gorandian pot pies, served piping hot and packed with fresh vegetables harvested just this morning from our hydroponics bay. And might I recommend with them some of the excellent *nalxak* soup, a traditional lunchtime standard in every Talaxian household. Why, I remember my mother calling us in for *nalxak* every day for an entire summer, and we never stopped running as fast as we could to get it! And if that weren't the perfect lunchtime menu already—"

"Could I get something from your, what do you call them—food slots?" asked Bailey.

Neelix stopped, puzzled, and then reeled as if a slow poison had suddenly taken effect. He staggered and slowly, dazedly turned toward the old man. The hand with which he'd been guiding Janeway now seemed more like the claw of some stricken seabird as it gripped her arm, digging into it with a desperate and fading strength.

"You mean the *replicator?*" Neelix's voice was almost too small to be heard, and his eyes seemed to have trouble focusing.

"No offense," said Bailey. "All that stuff sounds great. But I think I'd like something from the replicator."

For a moment Janeway thought she was going to have to grab Neelix by both arms to keep him from pitching to the floor face first. But the stalwart chef rallied, regained his composure in a frosty breath. He pulled himself up to his full height, only half a head shorter than Bailey, and stared icily into the old man's face. Bailey looked as though he were about to say something, but thought better of it.

Janeway put herself between the two of them and looked Neelix squarely in the eye. "I think a salad would be wonderful right now," she said, steering him back toward the serving line, "and that *nalxak* soup sounds like the perfect follow-up. Tuvok, you can show Mr. Bailey where the, ah . . . ." She hesitated to say the word in front of Neelix, who was still staring cold murder at Bailey over his shoulder as she pushed him back behind the counter.

"Of course, Captain," said Tuvok coolly. "This way, Mr. Bailey."

A bank of replicators lined the far wall of the mess hall, a fortunate distance from the serving line. Bailey watched the ensign ahead of him request a drink, then stepped up to the little alcove himself.

"I don't need any kind of . . ." He left the question unfinished and looked at Tuvok, indicating some sort of object with his hands. Tuvok raised his eyebrow and looked back at him without comprehension.

"Simply state the food or beverage you desire, along with any appropriate qualifying parameters," instructed the Vulcan. "If the template exists within the computer's memory banks, it will be replicated."

Bailey turned toward the machine. "Chicken-fried steak. Mashed potatoes with cream gravy. Green peas." The control panel beeped, and neon blue energy coalesced inside.

By the time Janeway made her way to the table with her salad and soup, Bailey was more than halfway through the steak and had made a sizable dent in the potatoes. As she sat down he stabbed another forkful of gravy-drenched meat into his mouth, and his eyes rolled back toward the ceiling.

"Sometimes you don't know what you're missing," he said after finally swallowing.

Janeway straightened the napkin on her lap and gazed purposefully across the table. "I'm glad you approve of our fare, Mr. Bailey. But now I believe there's the matter of some unanswered questions."

"I'll say there is," agreed the visitor, loading another fork and targeting it for launch. "How the deuce did a Starfleet vessel end up all the way out here, anyway?"

"He's a master, I'll admit that," said Janeway, her face clouded. She was sipping coffee in the briefing room while Tuvok stood stiffly across from her. Bailey was somewhere else in the ship, getting the visitors' tour from Commander Chakotay.

Janeway was attempting to analyze her conversation with the strange old man and making little progress. She had spent just over an hour in the mess hall chatting with Bailey, and it was only after they had left that she realized she still knew almost nothing about him. Her question-and-answer session had been just that—all questions for her, all answers for him. She sighed.

"An hour with the man, and all I can remember is finding out that he's from Kansas," she said. She sipped again and looked at Tuvok. "On the other hand, I believe I gave him a pretty thorough primer on the last eighty years of Federation history. I'd say we didn't get as much out of that as I had hoped."

"Do not sell yourself short," responded the Vulcan. "It was an excellent primer on Federation history. However, I did observe a pattern to Mr. Bailey's questions and responses, from which I believe we can deduce a greater body of information than that which he volunteered."

Thank heaven for his steel-trap mind, thought Janeway. "Please," she said aloud, and motioned for him to continue.

"First," he ticked off, "Mr. Bailey is obviously from human space. He did not ask for clarification of any terms you used or planets you indicated, and his questions showed an extensive knowledge of Earth and the various races and core worlds of the Federation, up to a point. His knowledge was not particularly current—his questions regarding the Klingon Empire show that to be true—but he shows every sign of having been raised in Federation space.

"Second, he is not particularly interested in this vessel as a military presence. He asked nothing about its armament and showed little interest in its propulsion system."

"Although I recall talking to him about it," said the captain dourly.

"About recent advancements in the physics, yes," confirmed Tuvok. "But he asked about that only after you revealed that warp physics was your preferred area of study. I suspect it was a ploy to keep you talking and off-guard—speaking about something you enjoy."

"It certainly worked. So he's not a military man."

"I did not say that," said Tuvok. "On the contrary, he showed a great deal of interest in *Voyager*'s personnel, mission, operating parameters, and contact protocols, and seemed to have an innate knowledge of how a vessel of this size is run and of the training and drills involved in maintaining readiness. And," he added meaningfully, "he referred specifically to Starfleet, before anyone else with whom he has had contact."

Janeway looked up. "Perhaps the Doctor . . . ?"

"I checked with him. The term was not mentioned. And I also confirmed that there was no trace of radiation upon him when he was initially beamed to sickbay."

The captain gazed thoughtfully at the reflection of her coffee mug in the glossy black surface of her desk. "I wonder if I've made some type of mistake," she said. "Given away too much. I feel as though he put me under some kind of a spell."

"Very unlikely," Tuvok reassured her. "Mr. Bailey is an extremely skilled conversationalist. His ability to direct a dialogue speaks of years of practice combined with innate skill." He raised his eyebrows puzzlingly. "I admit, I found myself quite caught up in the proceedings even as I observed him. I was tempted to join into the conversation also, to 'put in my two cents' worth,' so to speak. He is a very open, likable man."

The captain smiled. "About whom we still know almost nothing. Institute a search of the ship's database—if he grew up in Federation space, we should have some record of him."

"My thoughts exactly."

"Computer," she said to the console, "where is Mr. Bailey now?"

"Mr. Bailey is with Commander Chakotay in the mess hall," said the mechanical voice.

"I might have known," said Janeway, standing up and straightening her tunic. "Mr. Tuvok, you have the conn. Call me if you find anything."

"She ran her own little shop in this tiny corner, just off the central plaza near the Street of Menders," Neelix was saying. "The order the spices are put in is the secret. You see—"

"I hope I'm not interrupting anything," said Janeway, standing just behind the cook. Across the table Chakotay looked slightly startled. Neelix swiveled in his seat to look at her, an intense little smile cutting across his round face.

"Captain Janeway! Not at all, not at all," he said jovially. "I was just telling Mr. Bailey here about how I got the recipe for the Atekian apple pie."

"It really *is* excellent," said Bailey, happily severing another chunk from an exceptionally large slice on his plate. "You've sure done a lot of traveling, especially to get this much expertise."

Neelix shook his head with as much modesty as he could manage to scrape together. "Well, I don't like to brag," he offered, and the truth nearly snapped under the strain.

Bailey smiled admiringly around a mouthful of pie. "That place you were telling me about—the mining colony."

"Cetelvia," Neelix said, his voice growing low and dramatic. "Now there's a place you don't want to go without a plan. I was only there for four weeks, but let me tell you—"

"I'm afraid I'm going to have to commandeer our guest, Mr. Neelix," broke in Janeway. "We have some unfinished business to attend to."

"Oh," said Neelix, crestfallen. "Of course, Captain."

"I promise to get him back as soon as I can," she reassured.

"Maybe for dinner." Bailey grinned.

Neelix brightened immediately. "Oh, you wouldn't want to miss that! Tonight it's Karavian spun casserole made with real *sefa* noodles, and fresh-baked wheat bread! I learned to make it on board a Karavian mercenary cruiser—"

"I'm sure it'll be delicious," said Chakotay, hustling Bailey out of the room in front of him.

"Nice meeting you!" called Bailey over his shoulder, and then they were gone.

Janeway was sure that Bailey was at a disadvantage shut in the briefing room with her and Chakotay. She was astonished that she still didn't seem to be getting anywhere with him.

"The *point,*" she heard herself saying, "is that I'm beginning to feel you've taken advantage of our hospitality." How had she gotten so far off track? She had asked him about his ship, and he had said something about *Voyager,* and then—

"I didn't mean to take advantage of you," Bailey apologized. "It's just so nice to see some human faces for a change. A whole ship full of people like myself . . ."

"Exactly how long has it been since you were around other humans?" asked Chakotay, seizing on the statement.

Bailey grinned. "A long time. Longer than you've been out here."

"Exactly how long is that?" Janeway asked.

"You said it's been about two years," said Bailey. "Since Mr. Chakotay's ship was destroyed, and the Array that brought you here. You said there was another one out there somewhere?"

"Not how long *we've* been out here," said Janeway, "how long *you've* been out here."

"I just entered this sector of space a few days ago," said Bailey. "I haven't been in this area all that long at all. In fact, I could use some advice on where to stop off for supplies."

Janeway irritatedly tried to remember what her original question was, and found that she couldn't. She turned back toward their guest, who looked at her with rapt attention. She brushed her hand across her forehead and counted to five.

"Mr. Bailey, I believe you are the most evasive person I have ever met."

Bailey looked hurt. "Captain, I've tried to—"

"Save it. If it's not a straight answer, I don't want to hear it, and I haven't heard one yet." She dropped into the chair behind her desk and eyed their visitor. He sat quietly and did not appear the least bit nervous. He looked back at her with sharp blue eyes, pale and unreadable. A Mona Lisa smile graced his thin, wrinkled lips.

"Who are you, really?" she asked.

"I'm Bailey," he said. "Really." He ran his finger absently across the blue stone in the metallic ornament on his collar. "All right, so I may have been a little standoffish. But first things first. I need my ship back."

Janeway and Chakotay looked at each other.

"That may not be possible," Chakotay said. "It was heavily damaged when we found you, and was confiscated by the Mondasians just after we beamed you off. It's probably light-years from here by now, if it's still in one piece."

"Regardless," said Janeway, *"Voyager* is not going back into Mondasian space. I won't endanger my crew again for your convenience. I'm afraid you're stuck here with us, at least for the time being." The comm whistled, and she touched the panel. "Janeway here."

"Captain, there are a number of ships approaching," said Tuvok. "They are on an intercept course, and heading this way at upwards of warp 7."

"On my way," said Janeway and headed out the door and onto the bridge, followed closely by Chakotay and Bailey.

"I'm reading one small ship, followed by several larger vessels," Tuvok reported. "They are changing course to follow our movements. Just coming into visual range now."

"On-screen," said the captain.

A tiny dot appeared in the center of the starfield. It grew brighter with each passing second, but did not seem to get any larger.

"Can we outrun them?" asked Janeway.

"Negative," said Tuvok. "The small lead ship is moving at nearly warp 9. The pursuing ships . . ." He checked his sensor displays. "They are Mondasian assault ships. Seven in number."

The blunt front ends of the assault ships came into focus, their silvery hulls reflecting the white light of the rogue star they pursued. They were some distance behind it and seemed to be slowly losing the race, but a long way from giving up.

"Red Alert," commanded Janeway, and the klaxon hooted briefly to life around them.

"ETA to intercept by the lead ship, forty seconds," said Paris at the helm. "ETA for the Mondasian cruisers, three minutes."

On-screen the shining lead ship at last resolved itself into a cluster of brightly glowing orbs. The dazzling little soap bubble closed on *Voyager* and fell into place beside it, pacing the larger ship perfectly and dimming a bit to a neon red-orange glow. Janeway looked at the screen, and then looked accusingly at Bailey.

"Sorry," said Bailey sheepishly.

"Mondasian ships still closing," said Tuvok. "They are slowing and powering up weapons."

"Open a channel," said Chakotay.

"They are not responding to hails," said the Vulcan. "They are moving into an attack formation."

"I didn't mean to cause you any trouble," said Bailey, and Janeway tore herself away from the screen to look at him as he spoke. He looked at her plaintively.

"When you showed up in response to my signal . . . well, I figured the Mondasians could wait. But it looks like they're not real patient." He grinned again, the lines spreading out from the corners of his mouth like ripples from a pond. "Ah, to hell with them. They don't even drink coffee." He fingered the stone on his collar again.

"I'm in trouble," he said to the air, "and so are my friends here. Could you come and get me?"

On the screen the assault ships began to close, their stubby gun mounts softly leaking excess energy like saliva from a hungry dog's lips. They looked to attack in two waves, the first of which would surely shatter *Voyager*'s shields like a dome of glass. The second would leave only wreckage.

"Target the lead two ships inbound, and the aft of the outer two ships on the pass." The captain looked at Chakotay. "If you're right about their shield arrangement—"

"Captain, I'm reading another ship," interrupted Paris, his eyes widening. "Very strong reading. Captain . . ."

On-screen the view changed to forward, and an orange dot appeared and grew quickly into a spherical cluster of lights. It grew larger, the lights forming crisscrossing lines across its surface. A bright spot detached from the sphere and broke into seven spinning, multicolored cubes that Janeway caught a glimpse of as they shot past *Voyager* toward the Mondasian fleet.

Janeway glanced at Bailey, who was looking at the screen with a pleased expression. "Aft view, Mr. Paris. Show me the Mondasians."

The assault ships had slowed considerably, and their formation had drifted far out of true. In front of each ship now rotated a flashing, particolored cube, hanging like a Christmas ornament a few hundred meters from its bow, slowly spinning in the cosmic breeze.

"Composition of each cube . . . unknown, but possibly metallic," said Tuvok. "I am reading a solid cube, one hundred seven meters on each edge. I am not reading any type of internal components."

Chakotay stared at the screen, then turned to Bailey. "What are those things? Are they dangerous?"

His question was answered as one of the assault ships opened fire on the cube in front of it. There was a huge white flash, and *Voyager* bucked sideways as the shock wave hit.

Janeway blinked the spots out of her eyes. On the screen six assault ships remained, each with its own cube. All that remained of the seventh and its attendant was a shattered engine section, rapidly receding end over end.

"Reading a radiation surge," said Ensign Kim at the ops station. "Shields filtering most of it. Radiation count dropping."

The remaining assault ships had begun backing away from their cubes. Or at least attempting to—the multicolored gems stuck to the fronts of the ships as if glued there, maintaining their positions with perfect synchronization through the complex withdrawal pattern. In moments the assault ships were retreating at warp speed, along with their strange new, and potentially lethal, figureheads.

Janeway blinked. "Forward view," she ordered.

The massive alien sphere was larger than a dozen *Voyager*s now, and still growing. Its size surpassed that of a Federation starbase, and still it grew until it was a small moon, its surface covered with glowing orange orbs as big as starships. It ceased to increase when it finally took up all of the screen and most of the vast dark sky, and Janeway could clearly see the pulsing pattern of the giant globes on its skin like the arteries of a man-made star. Bailey stepped to one side of the screen, inserting himself into the stunned silence.

"I'm sorry I didn't introduce myself properly in the beginning," he said, "but you can't be too careful. That's one thing I've learned over the years. This is a dangerous section of space, and I had no idea what had happened to the human race after all this time. I'd especially like to apologize to you, Captain Janeway, for not giving you the courtesy due another officer in answering some of your questions."

"I think we may be getting some of those straight answers you were looking for," said Chakotay.

"I think, under the circumstances, we might be able to forgive some rudeness," said Janeway, "especially if it explains what's going on here. Who exactly are you?"

The man snapped to attention. "Lieutenant David Bailey of the *U.S.S. Enterprise,* formerly under the command of Captain James Kirk," he rapped, and then grinned again, his best expression. "Now on temporary assignment. A kind of ambassador at large, you might say. And I'm sure my current commander would love to have you as guests on his ship. Would you do us the honor?"

Janeway gaped at him like a fish. Next to her Chakotay flicked his eyes between the man and the screen, unable to decide which of them to disbelieve first. Janeway stood slowly, buying time for her mind to try and get around what she was seeing and hearing. She blinked deliberately and pointed at the glowing, pulsing mass that filled the screen. "Your ship?"

Bailey nodded.

"I don't see how we can refuse," she said.

"You could just say 'no thanks,'" said Bailey.

"No I can't," said Janeway. "And you know it. If I let this go, I wouldn't be able to sleep at night. I accept."

"Great!" said Bailey, and he, Janeway, and Chakotay disappeared from *Voyager's* bridge.

Janeway took a moment to check herself. She'd been through too many transports to find them disorienting, but this one had been more abrupt and unexpected than most. Chakotay was next to her, and Bailey just in front. She glanced around. The room was more cramped than she had expected; from the size of the ship she'd have thought it would have rooms the size of playing fields. The walls were partly hung with varying colors of the same metallic fabric Bailey was wearing, and a smell rather like fresh fruit blew softly through the air.

"Welcome," came a strange voice from behind them, and Bailey held out a hand indicating the direction. Janeway turned and was confronted by a small man—Janeway would have called him a child, except for his voice—dressed in a metallic jumpsuit much like Bailey's, but made of pure silver weave. He had a silver band wrapped around his bald head and was lying on a couch of the same fabric. He did not rise to greet them, but extended his hands.

"I bid you welcome," he said in his strange, tinny voice. "I am Balok. This is my ship," he swept his arms wide and looked around, "the *Fesarius*. Welcome aboard, Captain."

Years of top-notch Starfleet diplomatic training kicked in and somehow, against all odds, Janeway managed to keep from staring like a statue at the little man. She smiled sincerely and automatically, stepped forward and extended her hand. "I'm Captain Janeway of the—"

"Yes, yes, I know," he said in his slow, oddly deliberate cadence. "Captain Janeway, and Commander Chakotay. Come! Sit. Be comfortable. We will drink." They sat, and Janeway noticed Bailey glancing back and forth between them and the alien. It was the first time he had shown anything resembling nervousness.

Bailey saw her look, and smiled a little crookedly. "We don't get many visitors," he said.

"More the pity," said Balok, leaning over to a small drink service that had appeared at his elbow. "This is *tranya*," he explained, picking up two glasses full of orange liquid and offering them to the *Voyager* officers. "I hope you relish it as much as I."

Janeway took the little glass, which she could just hold between two fingers and a thumb. "Balok, this ship—"

"I know, I know," he interrupted again. "A thousand questions. But first, the *tranya.*"

"He won't do anything until you drink it," said Bailey, eyeing his own glass distastefully. He closed his eyes and downed half of his share, then put it down.

Janeway sniffed the liquid, which smelled rather like strong fruit punch. Chakotay took a sip and nodded appreciatively, and Janeway did the same. It had more taste than she'd imagined, and a strong aftertaste that faded through flavors like colors through a rainbow. Balok smiled and sipped his with gradual pleasure. Bailey shook his head in amazement.

"After all these years, he never gets tired of the stuff," Bailey said. "Somewhere down belowdecks there must be a *lake* of it."

"Balok—Mr. Bailey—" Janeway hardly knew where to start. The alien and the old man smiled blankly at her and said nothing.

"The ship," prompted Chakotay.

"Ah, yes," said Balok. "Provided by me, for Mr. Bailey's use. With it, he tests the races we encounter on my behalf."

"This was some kind of a *test?*" asked Janeway, her voice wary with anger. In her mind seven fully armed attack cruisers bore down on *Voyager* once again, and Mr. Bailey stood to the side taking notes.

"Not exactly," said Bailey hastily. "I really had no idea that you were going to show up. A Starfleet ship, after all these years." A dreamy look crossed his weathered face, and he glanced at Balok to see if the little man would interrupt. Balok settled back into his cushions and eyed the old man with quiet interest over the rim of his glass.

When Bailey spoke again, his voice traveled back through the years to a distant corner of the Alpha Quadrant, where a young lieutenant had just been promoted to helmsman aboard an intrepid flagship named *Enterprise*. Its captain, James Kirk, had encountered the *Fesarius* at the edge of known space and been tested by its commander to reveal the true nature of the human species. Balok had been amazed at the brashness and innovation of the legendary captain, who took the game of testing farther than anyone before him with a complicated bluff and a mythical substance known as *corbomite*. That anyone would produce such a fantastic lie, let alone deliver it with such conviction, was a wonder to behold, and when Kirk demonstrated the truth of the Federation's high-sounding words with a mission of mercy to Balok's "damaged" ship, he had been greeted by its sole occupant with open arms and the traditional drink.

When the *Enterprise* had departed, Bailey had stayed behind as both observer and ambassador. Balok, as it happened, was also an explorer of sorts, traveling through the cosmos on an interminable journey and testing those races he encountered for their intelligence and capacity. With his vast ship and almost incomprehensible technology—"We can scan through a starship's entire database in seconds," explained Bailey—he was all but invulnerable to attack, and spent his time inventing various threats to force his subjects into revealing situations. But his perspective was severely lacking, as Bailey soon discovered: Balok, as ancient and powerful as he was, had passed almost beyond the comprehension of lesser species.

That was where Bailey came in. Provided with a small ship, he went where Balok would never have gone. He boarded strange vessels built by unheard-of races, stepped into the exotic atmosphere of alien space stations, and tasted the air of a thousand planets unseen before by human eyes. Balok never left the *Fesarius;* he lived every experience vicariously through the eyes of his human proxy, spending long hours sipping *tranya* in rapt silence while Bailey talked himself hoarse. Sometimes the excursions lasted a few hours; other times Bailey was gone for weeks, or months, or more. Time slipped away, and the little collection of worlds known as the Federation fell behind them until they were a pleasant, distant memory, the mere first of many. Bailey had become a wanderer too.

Janeway looked into the old man's pale blue eyes and tried to comprehend the life he had chosen. "You left human space behind forever. Surely you must feel homesick sometimes, Mr. Bailey—how do you deal with it? With the loneliness, the separation?"

Bailey's eyes smoldered with an old flame, the spark of a fresh young lieutenant kept fueled for eighty years. "This is the best life I could ever have possibly chosen, Captain. This is what I joined Starfleet for—to see the galaxy, to go where no one's gone before. I've tasted the fruits of planets I couldn't have even dreamed of, seen places and people no human may ever see again. Sure, I've thought about returning sometimes." He leaned forward. "But why backtrack through worlds I've already seen, races I already know? Every day is a new experience out here, every week a new adventure. Every planet shows a new horizon, ripe with the promise of a million new sensations. Tell me, Captain: If someone gave you a ship like this and said, 'Go out and see the universe, and come back whenever you feel like it,' would you pass it up? How far would you wander, before you'd never come back?"

Janeway stared at Bailey, momentarily taken aback. Gone was the gregarious old man she had seen aboard *Voyager,* replaced now with a swashbuckling frontier officer from the golden age of Starfleet's space exploration. His eyes burned with daring and intelligence like two blue diamonds set in leather; and Janeway thought, *If this is the kind of man who served under him, what must Kirk have been like?*

"I can certainly see the appeal of it," said Chakotay, exhaling for the first time in what seemed like minutes.

"I thought you might," said Bailey, shrugging back into his former jovial composure like an old shirt that fit perfectly. "And after all, I'm out here because I wanted to be."

"Yes," said Janeway. The captain turned carefully toward Balok. "I hope I'm not being too forward, but I would like to ask—"

"You wish to know if I can assist you in returning home," he said, and a look of sincerest apology crossed the face of the little alien. "I am sorry, but this ship cannot perform that kind of magic. And we must continue with our journey—that is, if I can still speak for Mr. Bailey as my traveling companion."

"Wouldn't miss it for the universe," responded Bailey.

"Are you sure?" asked Chakotay. "That sounds like a better offer."

"You're right," said Bailey after a second. "Right now I only get the galaxy."

Balok laughed an infectious laugh, amused beyond his years. "What wonderful guests you are! I must give you a tour of my ship." He started to rise from the silvery couch.

"One more thing, Balok," said Bailey, jumping to his feet. "I have something I want to give the captain." He scuttled off through a nearby door to an adjoining room of the ship.

"Ah, yes," said Balok. "A most appropriate gift. You should be quite grateful to receive it, Captain."

Bailey returned with a small input tablet, gripping it with both hands. He gazed at it for a moment, then handed it to Janeway with an eager look in his eyes.

"It's a copy of my journal," he said. "The planets, races, and species I encountered, and what little I was able to learn about them. I don't know that it'll be very useful to you on your journey—we took the scenic route getting here—but I would like it to get back to Starfleet." He smiled sheepishly. "Technically, I'm still on duty. I hope this'll convince them I haven't spent the entire time stargazing and drinking *tranya.*"

Janeway scrolled through the entry titles, each neatly dated and indexed. "This is almost beyond value," she said. "Mr. Bailey, I don't know how to thank you for this. I wish we had something to give you in return."

"I have some of my own thoughts on that," said Bailey coyly. He smiled, and Janeway noticed a particular listing near the bottom of the entries.

"You've encountered the Borg?" she asked with trepidation.

Bailey curled his lip in disgust. "If you can say that. We didn't have much contact with them—no reason to hang around in their space. All of their planets are essentially the same."

"Not to mention dangerous," said Janeway.

"Not really, to us," said Bailey. "Actually, they're afraid of this ship."

"I can believe that," said Chakotay.

"And they are very poor guests," said Balok, shaking his hand in disapproval. "They talk only of 'assimilation' and 'resistance.'

And they did not like *tranya."* He shook his small head in shocked disbelief.

"I told you not to invite them over," said Bailey.

The *Fesarius* dropped away in *Voyager's* rear viewer as the rogue planet and the Federation starship parted company, never to meet again. Janeway sat in the command chair and paged through her copy of Bailey's journal, scanning slowly through a lifetime of experience dropped suddenly into her hands. Much of his journey was off their planned path and would probably be useless to them in the short term, but the small points of intersection offered tantalizing clues as to what they would encounter. It was an astonishing thing, Janeway realized—a chance encounter on the edge of nowhere had taken a single man on what was probably one of the great epic journeys of human history, and another had brought her and her crew to this place to bear witness to it. *If God doesn't exist,* she thought, *synchronicity is doing a darn good imitation.*

Tuvok tapped her on the shoulder and motioned toward the ready room. She went, and he followed.

"I hope my records look this good when I report back to Starfleet," said Janeway when the door had closed. "This is better than a holonovel."

"You had expressed some interest in preparing excerpts for the crew," prompted Tuvok.

"I think it might be good for morale," said the captain. "Besides, you've got to admit this is pretty exciting stuff."

"I consider that it may have some appeal on that basis to certain members of the crew," he said carefully. "Nevertheless, as the ranking member of Starfleet security forces, I would like the opportunity to review any sections prior to their general release."

"I think I can trust your judgment." She glanced at him curiously. "I take it you've already begun to review the material, then?"

Tuvok shifted uncomfortably. "Purely for security purposes. It is indeed a wealth of information, almost beyond compare in my estimation. I can hardly believe," he said, and his eyebrow raised conspicuously, "that Mr. Bailey would trade it for a complete set of our replicator ration patterns. Perhaps he finds food in the Delta Quadrant too flavorful and interesting."

"He said he'd spent two years trying to program in chicken-fried steak on his own," said Janeway, "with no luck. Besides, it wasn't just the journal." She smiled, plucked a glass from the little tray on her desk, and handed Tuvok a small goblet full of thick orange liquid. "We also got twelve barrels of *tranya.*"

Fiction

jaQ Andrews

The stars were out again.

That was three nights in a row now; Renaii hadn't seen such a long streak of clear skies for years. The light film of volcanic ash, almost constantly spewing from countless mountains across the surface of Draanis IV, usually obscured any hope of viewing the tiny points of light that evidenced any existence outside the thick, soupy atmosphere of the planet. The same ash also usually prevented anyone from staying outside for extended periods of time, clogging up the nasal passages, the throat, the lungs. But tonight was an exception.

Renaii closed her violet eyes, sacrificing for a moment her view of the stars, and took a deep breath of the air around her. She stood perfectly still, her dark skin and hair making her nearly invisible in the night, as her chest expanded and contracted with her respiration. It was still dirtier, dustier than the air recycled by the plant life her people had cultivated in the vast network of underground caverns in the past three hundred years, but she swore what she breathed now was the freshest she'd ever inhaled.

Her eyelids opened, almost of their own volition—the sight of stars was too precious to be wasted. She could breathe just as deeply with her eyes open and toward the sky as she could blind and standing neutral. Even the normal sting of ash in the air was virtually unnoticeable tonight; three days had allowed a great deal of ash to dissipate. The experience was something she relished. It was also something she did not wish to keep to herself.

"You really should come out here," she called to the man through the door she'd left open in the side of the rock face. He was tall, the tiny patch of gray hair at his temple having grown slowly but steadily over the last few years. "It's so clean, and beautiful. It hasn't been this clean since we were married."

The man looked up from the rock he was engraving. It was a picture of a creature from his native planet, a mighty beast with thick fur and a noble snout, posing in an almost humanoid stance. The carver had no supplies to color the animal its proper deep brown, but it looked majestic enough in the subtle shades of gray of the stone.

He purposely did not put down his fine carving knife. "Stargazing again, Renaii?"

Her smile was tempered slightly, but at the same time turned up as well by her husband's subtle teasing. "It's not as if we often get the chance."

The man had returned to slowly chipping away at a section of his stone. "You mean you don't often get the chance."

Renaii turned back toward the door. "It's rare. It's beautiful."

"It's out of reach." The carver carved, more vigorously now, keeping all but a fraction of his attention firmly focused on the stone in his hands. "It's the past—it's *my* past. I can't go back to that—no one can."

Renaii strode into their home, took the stone from her husband's hands, and placed it on the table with her own hand over it, to prevent him from retrieving it. "Looking at the stars won't hurt you. You can't hide out in this cave all the time, not when the chance to stand outside is so uncommon."

"Staying here is exactly what I have to do," he said, but Renaii had already pulled him out of doors. "The stars aren't part of me anymore, I've accepted that. I enjoy that, in fact."

"That doesn't mean you can't look at them."

The pair stood on the surface of the planet, unprotected by any heavy clothing or gear, a rare opportunity. They gazed, unspeaking, into the dark—but brighter than many—night. Despite the relatively clear conditions, there was still a fair amount of dust in the air, and there would always be the normal distortion of the atmosphere to muffle the intensity of the stars' luminosity. But Renaii, the man knew, had no way of knowing that, or at least of fully appreciating that. She had never seen the stars unfiltered, unobstructed, bare.

He raised his arm, pointing to the heavens. "Those points of light out there—they aren't truly right *there,* where we see them, at all. The light has been bent, refracted, through the atmosphere of this planet, so that what seems to be directly that way really just bounced there through layers of gases. Even if we escaped that, though, we still wouldn't get an accurate picture. The closest of those stars is billions of kilometers away; its light has traveled for years to get here, and by now, that star isn't in that place anymore. The effect is amplified for every other star. Some of them, we're looking at them as they were thousands of years ago." His eyes became farther away than that. "Looking at that sky . . . it's looking at the past." He lowered his face, glowered at the ground.

Renaii had the faintest hint of a smile on her lips. "I know my astrophysics," she said. "My ancestors were spacefaring, just like you were." She found no reflection of her own amusement in her partner's face. "I'm sorry. I shouldn't have made you come out here. I'm sure it's hard enough to let go of the stars."

The man quickly brought his head up. "I've let go. This is my home now," he assured her, holding her shoulders. "I'm content. I'm living with the woman I love. What more could a man ask?"

Renaii's smile returned, with much greater intensity this time. "Everyone else has gone to bed. We probably should too."

"I tried," the man answered, his mood lightening, "but it's kind of difficult when your wife is pacing in and out of the house."

"Well, I promise I'll go to sleep this time," she replied, grinning. "Or at least I'll stay in bed. What happens from there is up to you."

"I'll keep that in mind."

They started to head back inside, and Renaii was suddenly picked up by her husband and carried across the doorway. She giggled and hugged the man close. "Oh, I love you, Chakotay."

Her husband just smiled and kissed her.

Another woman had also been standing outside, gazing at the stars; she had been entirely motionless for several minutes, letting the tiny (in appearance) specks of light occupy her whole consciousness. Perhaps "letting" is the wrong word; there was little she could do to stop herself from becoming lost in the bright white pinholes above her, for a short time at least. They called to her, as they always had, even when she couldn't see them. But tonight was the most vivid reminder of that calling she had experienced in four years. It was not something she was able to ignore.

But she had come back into the tunnels since then. It would not help to stare at the stars, especially these stars. She had seen them from countless angles, at countless distances, and the picture she'd seen above her was no more than a dim duplicate of what she knew the stars could really be. She had resumed walking toward Nelistrom, one of the many underground villages scattered across this continent of the planet. It was the third day of her journey, and she wanted to be able to sleep in Nelistrom before visiting the small residence, just beyond the outskirts of the village, that was her goal in the morning.

Kathryn Janeway sighed. It would have been so much easier had Chakotay decided to keep his combadge like most of the rest of the crew; but after the crash, he had been one of the people most willing to adapt to a new life here. He'd seemed almost scared to retain anything at all from his life on *Voyager;* he had instantly immersed himself in the local culture of the first village the crew lived in together; he'd given away his uniform and all his instruments; and these days, he never kept in touch with any of his shipmates.

Not that Janeway could completely absolve herself of that last crime; it had become increasingly more difficult to maintain contact with people she no longer could officially command, as the years went by and she became more and more attached to the Trevin who lived in her home village. Her lip turned upward at that thought. Her village. It was only recently that she had even begun to think of it as home. Four years ago, her only intent was to spend a few nights there while brainstorming ideas with her crew on how to get themselves off Draanis IV. It had been considerably more than a few nights before she could bring herself to accept that there was no way to leave, as badly damaged as their starship was, as restrictive as the planet's abnormal gravity well was.

She laughed openly at that thought. The planet. She was glad, now, to have never given up hope. True, the solution was not anything like she had expected, but nevertheless, it was a solution. As it happened, getting off the planet was unnecessary.

For they were not on a planet.

Chakotay picked at his breakfast, stringy green vegetables grown with difficulty in the low light of the caverns. *Grown,* he told himself. *Not replicated. Not even stored from whatever we could find on alien worlds and packed into our cargo holds. This is fresh—this is the real thing.* The vegetables were actually not all that unpleasant, but it was all that had been available for a while now; for some reason, little else was growing. He swallowed them down, slowly, but without complaint. He wouldn't want to upset Renaii.

She couldn't help noticing his forlorn expression, though. "I know, *verethi* again, but it's all we lowly farmers have been able to harvest so far. The other plants are just taking longer to ripen than usual."

"It's fine. Just a bit odd that the only thing that's growing is the vegetable with the most questionable reputation for appeal. I think it's a farmer conspiracy."

She took a hefty bite of her own, making sure to show that she was enjoying it. "Hey—the soil pH is way off this year, and that's screwing up all the crops. I know you artists of the community don't like to worry about those kinds of things, but we deal with reality down there, unlike you. Admit it—you depend on us."

Chakotay grinned. "After you admit living wouldn't be worth it if it weren't for us useless artists."

Renaii returned the smile. It was hardly the first time they'd had this mock argument. "You can think that if you like," she hedged without any conviction, admiring another of her husband's carvings.

"I'll think that," Chakotay returned confidently, "and I'll be right."

They were interrupted by four quick raps on the door leading further into the caverns, toward the village proper. They turned at the sound.

Chakotay stood up first. "I'll get it," he said, walking to the door.

"Careful," Renaii teased, "it might be the farmer secret police coming to arrest you."

"I'll take my chances," he replied, hand on the doorknob. He opened the wooden door, expecting one of the townspeople; they often stopped by in the morning, curious to see what the "new" artist was up to now.

His expectations were not met.

"Hello, Chakotay," said a voice from a face he had not seen in four years.

Chakotay, usually an eloquent man, stared dumbly at Kathryn Janeway for several seconds, his mouth stuck slightly open. He stuttered, neither smiling nor frowning, still registering the sight of her. She took the weight from his shoulders momentarily.

"A 'hi' would be sufficient," she said with a twinkle.

"Hi," Chakotay quickly returned, exhaling heavily.

"It's good to see you."

"It's good to see you." He was still deciding if he meant it.

"You didn't have to repeat that." Janeway smiled. "May I come in?"

Chakotay stepped out of the door frame. "Yes, of course . . . please. I'm sorry . . . this is kind of unexpected."

"Sorry to drop in unannounced," she replied, striding in slowly, glancing around, "but I had no method of contacting you directly, and sending a message through one of the villagers seemed awkward."

"Dropping in on a married man and getting that reaction certainly qualifies as awkward, in my book," Renaii said coyly from her seat at the table. "You cheating on me again, Chakotay?"

Janeway flinched a millimeter. "Seems I've missed a bit here," she said.

"Long story," Chakotay interjected quickly, "a running joke." He turned to his wife. "Renaii, this is Kathryn Janeway, the woman who commanded *Voyager* before—and slightly after—the crash. Kathryn, my wife, Renaii."

The two women touched the tips of all their fingers in the customary Trevin greeting. "A pleasure," Janeway said.

Renaii nodded. "Likewise. I've heard a lot about you."

"Well, I wish I could say the same," Janeway said flippantly, casting a sidelong glance at Chakotay. "Your husband here hasn't kept in contact since we arrived here."

"Yes, he's always been rather hermitty. He loves everyone; he just doesn't talk to them that much."

"I wanted to fully embrace our new life, Kathryn," Chakotay said. "I know I haven't sought out my former shipmates, but that's just because they're not my shipmates anymore. *Voyager* is gone. I told you four years ago—if we're going to live here, I might as well make it my home."

Janeway looked over at Renaii for a second before turning back to Chakotay. "Actually," she began slowly, "that's what I came to talk to you about." She stopped and glanced at Renaii again, fleetingly.

She got the message. "Um, you two can talk alone for a

minute, if you like," she said, turning around the table and heading into the next room.

Chakotay never took his eyes off Janeway. "You still haven't given up, have you?"

"I'm glad I never did, Chakotay." Janeway had excitement in her eyes. "I've made a remarkable discovery. We are not on Draanis IV. We're not on any planet at all."

Chakotay dropped his eyes to the floor. "Kathryn, you know I respect you. I always have. You're one of the strongest people I've ever met." He grasped her shoulders. "No one was hit with this harder than you. You had the most difficult time making the adjustment to living here after *Voyager* was caught in this planet's gravity well. We are here. You have to accept that."

"No I don't," she insisted, "because it's not true. We are not marooned on a volcanic planet with a subspace-warped gravity well. We are on a holodeck."

Chakotay couldn't help chuckling. "A holodeck. Kathryn, it's been four years. The ship couldn't possibly run itself for that long while its entire crew is cooped up in one room. Come to think of it, you couldn't even get the whole crew into one holodeck, even with its artificial distance mapping."

"The whole crew isn't here. Most of them died in the crash— at least, that's what this simulation has as its scenario. Hear me out." Her last statement was a command, something Chakotay was used to seeing in her—but wished he didn't see now.

"All right," he said after a moment. "I'm listening."

She took a seat at the table, and gestured for him to do the same. "A few days ago, I was climbing a rock face in one of the less-explored caves outside of my village. I got a little reckless, and I wasn't careful about some of my steps. As a result of one of my more adventurous and creative leaps, my foot missed the crevice I was aiming for. I fell several hundred meters."

"And you survived?" Chakotay was incredulous.

"Not only did I survive," Janeway emphasized, "but I didn't have a scratch. I was hardly even sore. Don't you see? No one could come out of a fall like that completely unharmed. The holodeck safeties must have recently been reactivated."

"I hate to be a doubting Thomas," Chakotay responded, "but

there have been documented cases where people have survived falls from great heights. It's uncommon, and amazing, but it does happen." He rose and walked to her side of the table. "I don't think you can base an entire theory on this one bit of evidence. You're holding on too tightly to the past, Kathryn." He caught notice of a gray shape around her waist. "Look at you. You're still carrying your phaser and your tricorder. That's not our life anymore."

Janeway rose as well. "I can see it's not going to be easy to convince you."

She drew her phaser, pressing the right-hand button repeatedly to maximize the device's power setting. She pointed it at a corner and fired, vaporizing a large metal pot with a violent sizzle and a swirl of red. She then reversed the weapon, pointing it directly at her own stomach.

"Kathryn, what are you—"

She fired.

The churning red beam slammed into her body, and a portion of her clothes glowed hotly red. But she remained standing, her expression unchanged. After a few seconds, she lowered the phaser. The glowing spot disappeared.

Renaii rushed into the room, spurred by the loud noise moments before. "Chakotay, what's—"

"A few more minutes, Renaii," Chakotay interrupted, never moving his intent stare from his former captain. He tore his eyes away to look into Renaii's. "Please."

She returned the gaze, but said nothing. She slowly walked out of the room again.

Chakotay took a long time to start thinking again. He let his mind go blank first, to prevent his conflicting thoughts from slugging each other out and totally robbing him of his rationality. He turned to Janeway. "That could have been arranged as well."

"But you know it wasn't. I'd have no reason to." She placed the phaser on the table. "You can try it yourself, if you like. I can guarantee it won't hurt you. I salvaged it from the wreck of *Voyager* after my fall, and after I'd done several other things to myself I never would have under normal circumstances, to make sure I wasn't crazy. I wasn't."

Chakotay picked up the weapon, but did nothing other than look at it with confusion.

"This life we've been leading for the past four years is a lie, Chakotay. If it were real, I'd be dead right now. There's someone outside the holodeck, someone who reactivated the safety protocols."

Chakotay glared at her. "So why not just end the program?" he asked angrily. "You've gotten everything perfectly figured out, Kathryn. Just end everything."

"I can't." Janeway was stolid. "Whoever is out there hasn't been able to restore voice control or open the doors. It's possible they can't. We have to find a way out from in here. And I'd like your help."

"So you're just going to destroy everything that we've been through? We've built lives here. And I think it's damn arrogant of you to come into my home and tell me it's not real, just because you don't want to accept that we have to stay here."

"You don't really believe that." Janeway came around the table. "I know this is a shock, but you just saw the proof. Draanis IV, Nelistrom, Renaii—they're all just parts of this program. You let go four years ago, Chakotay. You have to let go now."

Tears were forming in Chakotay's eyes. "I didn't want to let go then. It wasn't as easy as I made it look." He glared straight at her. "I worked a long time to accept this new life. I'd accomplished that. Now . . . you want me to abandon it without a second thought. I can't do that."

Janeway was incredulous. "It's an illusion!"

"Maybe so. But it's been real for four years for me. I can't ship myself off to somewhere else we don't even know how to get to. Who knows—maybe that's just some program, too, 'Captain.'" He turned away.

"All right," Janeway said quietly. "It's sudden. I understand. You need some time to think." She produced a combadge from her pocket and handed it to him. "When you're ready."

He took it from her reluctantly and tossed it on the table.

Janeway withdrew from the room, shutting the door quietly behind her.

Renaii wasn't sure she heard the other woman leave, but she couldn't keep up what amounted to hiding in another room. She'd heard everything that had happened—though admittedly not entirely by accident—and she was shocked by what was put forth that morning. She walked out of her bedroom to find Chakotay indeed alone, staring at the device Janeway had given him, unmoving, solemn. He must have been turning over his life in his mind, trying to make sense of what he remembered for the past four years. The silver and gold delta shield seemed to stare right back at him, even more stolid than he was, and with considerably less emotion.

Chakotay picked it up. Even though it was replicated, a hologram, like everything else he could see, it pierced through the reality barrier and spoke to him as a relic of the true world. It was truth.

"It's beautiful," Renaii said as she approached her husband.

"It's a combadge," Chakotay replied, void of expression. "I can contact Captain Janeway with it if I want to."

Renaii hesitated. "I know what it is."

Chakotay turned to her. "You heard us talking, then?"

"I didn't need to." She took a deep breath and let the words spill by themselves from her mouth. "Chakotay, I'm sorry I never told you earlier."

He narrowed his eyes. "Told me what?"

"About this place. About the illusion."

For the second time that morning, Chakotay was stricken speechless. You *knew!?* There was nothing he could say to an admission like that. A part of the program knowing it was a program—

—unless she wasn't part of the program.

He backed away from her. "Who are you?" he asked quickly.

She stepped toward him, but more slowly than he was backing away. "I am Renaii," she said, explaining as if to a child in doubt, "and I am your wife. And I do love you, Chakotay, please don't think that I don't."

274

"You'll excuse me if I'm not quite sure what to think at the moment."

She ceased her advance. "But I'm also an operative for the Trevin Resistance Movement. I had a mission to carry out here."

Chakotay felt his former—real—and present—illusory—lives collide again. She wasn't a program, she was flesh and blood. "Real" was a different question. He checked his previous thought—she was a part of the program, just not a holographic part.

"Can we talk about this?" she was saying.

Chakotay almost looked as if he were going to respond directly. As it was, he responded the only way he could. He fingered the combadge.

"Chakotay to Captain Janeway."

"I didn't expect to be back so soon," Janeway said as she walked in Chakotay's door.

"I didn't expect my life to collapse this morning," he replied. "But things turn up."

Renaii was seated at the table. "I haven't asked her anything else," Chakotay whispered to his captain. "Quite frankly, I don't trust myself talking alone to her right now. And I have the feeling you're going to need to hear this."

"Your feelings are understandable," she whispered back. "And from what you've told me already, I definitely want to hear what she has to say."

The two *Voyager* crew members joined Renaii, Janeway across from her, Chakotay as far away from her as the table allowed. She tried to meet eyes with him, but he dodged them.

Janeway was all business. "Renaii," she said. The dark woman darted her head around to face her. "It was a pleasure to meet you this morning. I can only hope that we can continue having a pleasurable relationship."

"You're easing into the interrogation, Captain," Renaii replied. "I know you want answers from me, answers that, ideally, I could have given to you a while ago, but it wasn't deemed wise at the time."

"Let's start at the beginning; Chakotay told me you're part of something called the Trevin Resistance Movement. Are you saying that there is actually a Trevin people?"

"This program didn't come totally out of our imaginations," Renaii responded. "A Trevin ship did crash on Draanis IV three hundred years ago, and the planet, including the gravity well, is pretty much as it is in this program. But of course you didn't really crash there. And in the past century, there have been some pretty vast political changes there. Ships from a planet called Dernovin made contact with us about a hundred years ago—their ships could pass through the gravity well without much problem, because of some special technology they had. But they didn't offer us passage home, even for a price. Dernovin annexed Draanis IV and used my people as slaves in developing computer technology. They stole what we had developed on our own and forced us to work on their projects, separated from each other, of course. But they couldn't keep us apart all the time, or from learning a few things along the way."

She paused, and tried to gauge Chakotay's response with a look. "Keep talking," he said, steel-faced. "I assume there's a bit more story before you get to the present day."

She gave up trying to look at him. "Three months ago, the Trevin Resistance Movement was able to gain control of one of the Dernovinian ships that landed on Draanis IV; we connected to its main computer through a remote link. A small group of us escaped from that planet, and we vowed that we would liberate the others, by any means necessary. It was decided that we needed to stage some kind of attack on Dernovin. But we knew we couldn't do it with the ship we hijacked; we needed something more powerful."

"And *Voyager* just happened on by," Janeway said sardonically.

"It wasn't an accident that we picked your ship. It's quite famous, you know. We'd heard stories, almost legends, about your ship, about all the battles you'd been through, how powerful it was. And since you would be heading close to us, we decided we'd take it. All we had to do was be sure we could figure out the computer so we could set up the same kind of remote link we did with the Dernovinian ship. That wasn't a problem; your systems are remarkably . . . I believe your culture's term for it is 'user-friendly.'"

"We aim to please."

"After we'd taken control," Renaii continued, "we wiped your short-term memories and implanted approximately four years' worth of new engrams in your long-term, so we could hold you, all of your crew in various holodecks, in this program while we used the ship. It hasn't really been that long, Captain—most of your memories since the crash were artificially implanted. The program has only been running six weeks."

"Six weeks?" Janeway leaned forward. "I have quite vivid memories of watching my starship and my crew die. Are you telling me that didn't happen even on the holodeck? That those are just implanted memories?"

"That's exactly what I mean. With a ship full of programmers and scientists, it wasn't hard to figure out your holodeck or your brains. They're basically just very intricate computers. I have four years of false memories, too, to make sure I could play my role, keeping the world in here and the other holodecks running with none of you suspecting anything, accurately. But no one expected I would have to keep it up this long."

Janeway rose and paced away, around the room, back to the table. "All right. You commandeered my ship. Why put us in here? It would have been much easier to kill us."

"We didn't want to hurt anyone."

"You stole my ship to attack a planet!"

"We didn't use direct force!" Renaii calmed herself, and hoped Janeway would keep calm as well. "This was less work-intensive than keeping you all unconscious for long periods of time. Our plan was to use *Voyager*'s deflector dish to create a powerful, directed solar flare that would knock out power systems in the settlements on the bright side of Dernovin's moon. It was intended as a demonstration, a protest, rather than a violent attack."

"You sound as if it didn't work."

Renaii glanced down. "I don't know. They put me in here completely independently. They would find some way to contact me if they needed to, but they didn't want to risk having any links to the outside, other than holodecks, in here. I haven't heard from them at all."

"How long was this attac—mission supposed to take?" Janeway made a point of not catching her misnomer in time.

"A week, maybe two."

"Sounds like we've been hung out to dry."

"They probably just ran into some unexpected contingencies," Renaii insisted.

"I have a hunch those unexpected contingencies were a trained Starfleet crew taking advantage of some tiny mistake they noticed with your plan," Janeway said confidently. "Someone out there reinstated the safety protocols in this holodeck, and somehow I don't think it will be long before that same person finds a way to get us all out."

The air crackled.

As if on cue, Chakotay's cave house disappeared, replaced by a large black, silver, and yellow room with two dozen confused Starfleet personnel scattered throughout. The main door slid open, with a much-missed mechanical thunder, and a figure appeared just in front of it.

"Welcome home," the Doctor chimed.

Janeway stepped slowly out the door, taking in the lighting, the contours of the starship's gray paneled corridor. There was no debris; everything was intact; her ship was healthy, whole. She wasn't quite sure what she'd expected, but four years of false life had resigned her to the sight of a dead, broken hulk. This ship was definitely not dead or broken. Although—it wasn't exactly brimming with life either.

She snapped out of her amazement and turned to the Doctor, still standing just inside the holodeck. "Doctor—good work. I can't tell you how good it is to be back."

"I can sympathize," the man of light responded. "I've only just been able to reactivate my holographic matrix. I've been stuck inside a data loop between my own systems and the holodecks' for six weeks now."

Janeway became disappointed. "So you can't give us a status report."

"Sadly, no. I've only had access to systems directly related to my functions, and that would be only the sickbay holoemitters and the holodeck. But that is how I was able to punch through the Trevins' programming and rescue you—and, soon, the entire crew—in, I must say, a brilliant bit of virtual negotiations."

She cut him off. "I'd love to hear about it, but I'm afraid we have a ship to retake. Do whatever you did with the other holodecks, get the rest of our people out, but warn them not to use the main computer. We have to act quickly if we're going to take the Trevin by surprise." Her captain's instinct was screaming at her; she could tell the starship was adrift, moving just enough to have been not completely stopped, or perhaps jarred from a stop. Either way, it was not what she would have expected from a ship being used to launch an assault on a moon, but the fact remained: *Voyager* was not hers. And she needed it back.

After she'd filled everyone in on what they needed to know in order to function once again as Starfleet officers, she led them to the nearest storage locker and keyed it open to reveal phaser rifles for her and several others. "Torson," she called to the only crew member she could identify as security personnel, "keep an eye on our friend Renaii here. I don't want her giving her comrades any warnings. Get her to the brig if you can."

He took a phaser and grabbed Renaii's arm. She tried again to make contact with Chakotay, but he was already in conference with his captain. "We should assault the bridge first," he was saying, vehemently ignoring the woman he'd called his wife as she was led away. "We don't have enough people to split up effectively if they've fortified Deck 1. We'll have to take them out one room at a time."

"We will split up," Janeway said, "but only to get on different turbolifts to the bridge. I'll signal all the teams and we'll simply burst out and attack."

"Clean and simple. Always seems to work best."

"Let's go."

Chakotay found himself wishing there were more complexity to their plan on the lift up. There was nothing he could say to the crew members in the small compartment with him, so his thoughts naturally turned to Renaii. *We were incredibly happy together,* he thought. *Almost perfect, even on that hell of a planet. Too bad you were lying the whole time.*

The lift stopped. No one moved for a few minutes; Janeway was making sure all the turbolifts made it to the bridge before she gave the word to invade. It was a tense silence. *But I suppose I'm used to it by now, being betrayed by women I love. Seska, you—not a big deal anymore.* He gripped his phaser rifle tightly, eager to get on with their takeover.

He swore it was an hour before the almost inaudible click of combadge activation preceded by a millisecond Captain Janeway's signal. "Now!" called every Starfleet insignia in the chamber at once.

Chakotay surged toward the door, and as it parted, the other crew members leaped into action as well. They had taken the rear center lift; Jules and Tarrine swung around to cover the security station usually occupied by Tuvok; Kardesh, Hume, and Y'Lanni concentrated on the aft stations; all of this happened nearly instantaneously, automatically, with no conscious thought necessary.

"No one move!" yelled Janeway from across the room.

No one moved.

When the crew took the concentration to examine their targets, they discovered why.

"They've all been dead for weeks," Chakotay whispered incredulously.

The captain's chair, ops, the conn—every chair on the bridge held a decaying, rancid body of what he could only assume was a member of the Trevin Resistance Movement. Their clothes were all perfectly intact, but their skin was literally hanging off their bones, their skeletons slumped in their seats.

"I have the feeling," Janeway said, "this wasn't in their mission plan."

"Relax, everybody," Chakotay recommended. "Doesn't look like there'll be any firefight here today."

"Computer," Janeway called, looking up, "are there any humanoid life-forms on this vessel other than those in holodecks and on the bridge?"

"Two," came the electronic reply, *"one human, brig; one unidentified humanoid, brig."*

"Renaii and Torson." Janeway moved gingerly between the bodies, giving a particularly nasty look to the one in her chair. "Something killed everyone on this ship," she said, addressing everyone in the room. "Get into all the automatic logs, and the Trevins' logs if they kept any. I want to know what did this."

"They did this to themselves."

Chakotay was hunched over an engineering station on the bridge, decoding in his mind scattered bits of sensor readings and internal recorders into a logical narrative. Reports of various information that might be somehow useful had filtered in from officers all around the bridge over the past few minutes. The final piece had just clicked into place, and Chakotay had immediately called Captain Janeway over to the station.

"Are you saying they all committed suicide? Like some kind of cult?"

Chakotay clarified himself. "No—it looks like an accident. They didn't know how to use Federation equipment properly. Remember the plan they were going to use?"

"Focus the deflector beam on the sun," Janeway recited, "and create a solar flare to knock out power on Dernovin's moon."

"Right." He brought up a series of graphs and diagrams. "They definitely fooled with the attenuation of the deflector dish. This frequency and power curve are nothing like what's normally used for displacing interstellar matter."

"I'll say. They channeled nearly everything *Voyager* has into a beam the thickness of a pencil. That's probably dozens of times more powerful than even what the *Enterprise* tried to use against the Borg just before Wolf 359."

"It was—that was the problem." Chakotay turned away from the console. "That much raw energy slamming into a tiny point on the surface of a ball of pure nuclear fusion created a hell of a reaction. Now, that's what the Trevin were hoping for, but they didn't get their calculations quite in sync with the technology they had to work with. They couldn't focus the flare, and a part—a big part—of the flare's energy traveled straight back through the deflector beam."

Janeway gasped. "We're lucky the entire ship wasn't vaporized!"

"Lucky, maybe—that the Trevin were at least smart enough to shut off the beam once they saw what was happening at the other end. A good portion of the flare still made its way directly into our systems, knocking everything around horrendously. Some of the secondary hull was vaporized. It's nothing we can't repair, but duranium vapor, when mixed with phaser coolant and a host of other materials also released by the explosion, is highly poisonous. It was only a matter of minutes before the whole interior of the ship was gassed to death."

Janeway turned aside and sat down heavily on the side stairs. "Only the holodecks, with their independent life support systems, weren't affected," Chakotay elaborated. "Sometimes being a prisoner isn't so bad, I suppose."

Janeway still said nothing, only held her head in her hands. "It was their own fault," Chakotay said again. "They were so eager to advance their cause, they didn't take the time to learn what they were dealing with."

"There's an old saying on Earth," Janeway mused. "'Education is paramount.' Appears that's true." Her eyes became distant for a second. "Chakotay," she began slowly, "you said that the flare they created was unfocused."

"Right. And huge. They couldn't—" He stopped and breathed deeply, quickly. "Captain, a flare that powerful—"

"Get us to Dernovin. Fast."

Voyager had been drifting for over four weeks, but a powered starship can make much better time than one floating free. It was only minutes before the vessel's crew had determined their position and rushed toward Dernovin.

What they found was not an ideal situation.

The moon was completely unharmed. The failure of the Trevins to focus the solar flare properly caused it to miss the tiny world cleanly. Dernovin itself was not so lucky. The flare was not so misaimed that it avoided any contact at all; in fact, the unfocused flare's radiation ripped into a city on the planet's northern continent. Power had not been shut down, as had been planned for the moon; it had been disrupted, and released. Every conduit for miles around had surged with energy, and simultaneous explosions had engulfed the entire city.

"We don't expect to find anyone alive in Gortella."

Dernovin's Grand Minister sat somberly in front of a viewscreen, his image transmitted instantaneously to the starship *Voyager* in orbit. Gortella was now a smoldering ash pile, though rescue teams were still combing through wreckage in distant hopes of saving at least one life. They hadn't yet succeeded.

"I'm so sorry, Minister," Janeway effused, still horrified by the destruction of which she'd learned just moments ago. "I assure you, this was not an act of the Federation or this vessel's rightful crew. We had no idea—"

"I know it's not your fault, Captain Janeway," the Minister assured her, with almost as much displaced anger as reassurance. "The Trevin were more than happy to take credit for this atrocity. They've been a dubious resource ever since they were annexed a century ago. I always thought they were more dangerous than they let on—more trouble than they were worth, frankly. Well, I was proved right thirty-one days ago. They are trouble."

"Minister, we have a strict policy of noninterference in the affairs of other societies or governments," Janeway said, "but I must say, the Trevin do have legitimate issues to take up with Dernovin, and they've shown they're willing to fight you. A peaceful settlement would be in everyone's best interests. I would be happy to mediate—"

"That won't be necessary," the Minister interrupted. "The Trevin problem has been eliminated."

Janeway hesitated. "Eliminated?"

"After this incident, the Council was easily convinced to let me do what I've wanted for years. The Trevin colony on Draanis IV was a den of violent individuals. Their deaths were a victory for peace and justice."

The bridge was in shock. Chakotay shot up from his seat and tried to speak, but it came out a wheeze: "You executed—"

Janeway gave him a sharp glance, a warning: It's not our affair. We've been dragged in too much already. Chakotay reluctantly held his tongue. The captain turned back to the Minister. She could not find words immediately, but the Minister had no such difficulties.

"Now, Captain, I believe you mentioned there was one survivor of the attack on our world on your ship?"

Janeway recovered her composure. "Ye—yes. Renaii. She didn't play a direct part in the attack; she oversaw the computer program in which my crew was confined."

"I would like to extradite her from your detention facility, for trial and punishment here."

Janeway looked back at Chakotay. His eyes had become glazed over. She turned back, trying to think of ways to keep Renaii from certain execution. "She was more directly involved with crimes against my own crew. I want to keep her on board and—"

"Captain, she was part of an operation that destroyed an entire city and everyone in it, on my planet," the Minister said harshly. "I demand her extradition."

His case was compelling. "I can't, in good conscience, keep her from . . . justice," Janeway replied, blank.

"Very good," the Minister responded. "I'm glad we could work together smoothly."

"Glad we could work together."

She wasn't.

The security officer had been dismissed, leaving only the transporter technician behind his chamber of transparent aluminum, which blocked enough sound to allow him to hear only the one word he needed to perform his duty. Chakotay and Renaii's conversation would not be intruded upon.

"So this is it?" Renaii stood on the transporter pad, her face pleading. "My whole culture is dead, and you're sending me down to the people that killed it?"

"You're being tried for your crimes," Chakotay answered, as stolidly as he could.

"Come on, Chakotay," she said. "We both know they're just

going to execute me. There's no such thing as a fair trial for a Trevin on Dernovin."

"We're obligated by our own laws to turn you over to their government."

"You're obligated to send me to my death for fighting for freedom?"

Chakotay let his anger loose then. "You imprisoned me. You imprisoned everyone I hold dear. You didn't even tell anyone they were imprisoned! And to top it off, you used the closest thing we have to a home as a weapon of war."

"And I betrayed you."

Chakotay was stung with his own emotions thrown in front of him. "And you betrayed me."

"I was doing my job. I never wanted to hurt you."

"You led me to believe you were in love with me," he spat. "And your scientists implanted memories of love in me so I would be duped by you. Call me crazy, but I don't exactly call that playing fair."

"I had implanted memories too, Chakotay. And even though I knew they were false, they contained love for you as well. I did love you."

"And yet you kept right on lying to me."

She threw her arms in the air. "I had no choice! I couldn't sacrifice the mission for my own personal reasons!"

"And I can't shirk my duty to save someone I've been convinced I love."

She gazed at him. "'Convinced,'" she said. "All right. If that makes you feel better. All your feelings toward me were manufactured. You don't have to worry about your love for me—it wasn't real."

Chakotay glared straight into her eyes. "Just like yours."

She never got to open her mouth.

"Energize," came the key word from Chakotay's lips. The technician pressed a memorized series of touchpads, and Renaii disappeared in a silver shimmer.

I, *Voyager*

Jackee C.

[From the memory records of Awnedre]

Warmth of sunshine fell gently on my newly taken form. I thrilled at the delicate wings at my back, flitting, twitching, allowing me to spring forth to a lovely red blossom. The inviting softness of its petals encompassed this form's limited visual perception; but I didn't mind. This outing was for exploration, my final steps toward adulthood.

Something clicked on the edge of my mental perception . . . something decidedly different, infinitely more interesting than crystal tending. I turned at the speed of thought and saw . . . reached . . . and touched a mind . . . Hers. She. Captain Kathryn Janeway is how she thought herself. That's her designation.

She was turned toward another, laughing. The other was very dark, and stiff. He thought himself Tuvok. His mind was very ordered, at sharp angles and not very inviting. I was so caught up in my Immersing with these beings that I didn't watch where I was going. I flew right into the dark material of Captain Kathryn Janeway's uniform.

I was surprised at the way her mind focused so directly onto me. The sense of awe and wonder I perceived was unlike anything I'd felt from the other minor beings on this world; it was mesmerizing. I turned in my flight for a deeper look.

She held out a hand toward me. Unable to resist, I settled softly upon it.

"Tuvok," she spoke physically, a whisper. Her voice was very interesting. I could feel the sound waves wash over me in gentle pulses. "Look at this beautiful creature."

Tuvok eyed me with obvious disinterest, his darker eyes and features dispassionate. "That appears to be a rather *large* butterfly, not unlike the *canias* found on Hypras 7." His voice was not so soft as Captain Kathryn Janeway's.

"Yes." She smiled indulgently. "But look at the way the light plays against its wings. It's beautiful." Her eyes returned to my form as she continued to gaze in wonder. Then gently lifting her hand skyward, she continued to speak, but directed her words toward me.

"Fly away, little fellow," she said. I lifted into the air and dropped the physical persona. I wanted to know more about this one. And to do that I'd have to leave this limited form behind.

She gasped. "Did you see that?!"

"Indeed," Tuvok replied, removing an instrument, a tricorder, from a clip at his waist. "There is nothing here, Captain," he concluded after making several sweeps with the device. I expanded so as to avoid the gentle energy particles that fanned the area.

"I have a difficult time believing *that* was a natural phenomenon," she murmured, casting her Vulcan friend a look before tapping an instrument on her chest. I moved in for a closer look at the obviously mechanical device. I saw the inner machinery communicating on a very simple principle but in complex patterns at her tap.

"Janeway to *Voyager.*"

"*Voyager* here," a male voice sounded. At the sound, a myriad conflicting emotions washed over and nearly overwhelmed me. I pulled away from the device and limited my perceptions to her. She was clear and determined; it burned in her features.

"Commander, run a level-1 scan within a hundred-kilometer radius of my signal."

"Acknowledged. Is there something the matter, Captain?" the voice returned.

Ready now for the contact, I reached along the link toward the other mind. Through the carrier wave of the combadge, at the speed of thought, I found him. The initial rush of emotion that I'd perceived had abated. This mind . . . Chakotay he thought himself . . . was now curious, seeking an answer as well. Something vague and obscure, though, hovered in the distant recesses. I could not touch them easily unless he brought them to the fore.

"Perhaps," Captain Kathryn Janeway replied, her voice interrupting my curiosity. But Chakotay's mind called her "Kathryn" in the most compelling way. His perception of her as such was so sharp that I immediately chose to do the same. She continued.

"A life-form, very similar to a butterfly, just landed on my hand. . . ."

A smile. A mental picture so strikingly accurate as to be shocking assailed me. Even her expression of awe was present. These creatures were definitely more than I'd initially thought.

Kathryn continued to speak. "I told it to fly away, and it did. And then it shimmered right out of existence. We can find no evidence of it with the tricorder."

A frown now covered Chakotay's features as he struggled with some memory. Something very old and trapped beneath another, but he could not bring it forward. I moved in closer, curious. I caught only a hint of blue sky and barren ground before he gave up, obscuring it again.

"That's . . . strange," he replied aloud, a slight catch of confusion evident in his voice.

"What is it, Chakotay?" she asked, not missing the slight nuance in his voice.

"Uh, nothing, Captain," he replied, gathering himself, fighting some small embarrassment.

"All right. Janeway out." She hadn't really believed him, and she was right. I waited. It wasn't long before his mind turned to the memory records that would reveal more.

He began by trying to recapture the buried memory, toying with the spot, *déjà vu,* his mind called it. Very interesting, these creatures. I thought of opening myself to another of the minds in this place, but a small jolt hit me.

A familiar pattern on the console had broken into Chakotay's mental meandering, dragging me along. The storm was coming. It looked so beautiful from here, on this ship's instruments. My family would be there; I could hear them calling to me already. But how would I return to the surface?

"Voyager to Janeway," Chakotay'd provided the way for me. I leapt on the carrier and trailed it home. I could hear his thoughts and words along the beam. "There's one heck of a storm brewing, Captain. Suggest you and the away team return to *Voyager.* The ionic radiation is nearly off . . . sc. . . ."

"Understood, Commander," Kathryn answered, looking toward the rapidly graying sky. It was strange but the clouds were lined with some sort of shimmery silver effect. The winds were picking up even as she spoke. "The levels seem to be affecting communications as well. Have the transporter room standing by."

"U . . . . d, C . . . tain."

"Tuvok." Kathryn turned toward her Vulcan just as large pellets of rain began to fall. "You bring the rest of the team into the meadow. I'll go get the sample cases!" The winds were gusting strongly enough to nearly knock her over.

"Aye!" Tuvok replied, and moved toward the cluster of people several hundred yards away.

Kathryn moved in the opposite direction, toward a small ravine. I saw a case that must have been hers perched atop a rock in the vicinity. It had fallen over and the contents were beginning to spill out. Clear blue crystals peeked from within.

I could hear the "voices" of my people crying out on the winds, in the storms in telepathic fury. *No! No! It must not take what is sacred!*

By the time she'd collected the blue orbs into the case, Tuvok and the rest were on their way toward her position. She leaned her back up against the rock and dug her heels in. Removing her combadge, she proceeded to adjust the strength so as to boost the signal on her end.

As the group gathered near, she wrapped one arm around the case and yelled into the combadge. *"Voyager,* six to beam up!" The crew stood as closely together as possible, then a spire of cohesive energy began to separate their atoms. They were being transferred . . . transported.

NO!!

One of the beams was broken off as a burst of angry lightning fell from among my kin. I looked on in shocked horror as Kathryn reeled back semicohesive, and fell over the drop-off into the ravine. The blue orbs returned to their home within the ground, and the crew returned to the ship. I returned with them.

The tingle was odd. A very different way to travel indeed. All of the minds were one with my mind, all their physiology, *all of them,* was me for several seconds. As everyone coalesced, they immediately slumped on the platform. I could feel the nausea that washed over the group. Immediately grasping that something was wrong, I determined not to ride in that device again.

While other members of the team continued in their illness, Tuvok rose to his feet and looked about himself. "Where is Captain Janeway?"

"I'm trying to get a lock on her now," the technician responded. "I've got something; the phase variation that was present with the first transport is no longer present. Resetting parameters and energizing . . . now."

Tuvok's clinical mind followed a precise set of guidelines as he considered ordering the ill crew members to sickbay. But he thought better of it as they were humans and would no doubt want to wait for assurance of their captain's safety.

A small device shimmered into existence on the transporter pad. Kathryn's combadge.

I searched for and found Chakotay. His mind was relieved, it emanated from every pore. He'd checked the sensor logs and found that the comm signals of all the away team members were aboard. I had to change that. It took a bit of doing, but I slipped my memory of Kathryn's beam being separated from the others over his active thoughts.

He squeezed his eyes shut as the image of Kathryn's beam-out played on. I felt the shock that ran through him as the lightning separated her, knocked her over the rise into the ravine.

His eyes flew open in sudden anxiety and latched onto the level-1 scanning output that ran in the corner of his console's screen. There was something odd about the storm, some sort of electromagnetic disturbances that were growing exponentially, making transport impossible. He lamented his inability to get a decent scan through the "soup."

The turbolift door slid open, revealing Tuvok. Nothing in his manner indicated the deep unrest within over the location and condition of his friend and captain, nor the nausea that still plagued him.

"Report," Chakotay ordered, even as he tried to come to terms with the vision he'd seen. I was amazed and disappointed at the way he'd shoved the anxiety away from the fore.

Tuvok reported the problems with the transport out and the fact that they were only able to get the captain's combadge. Chakotay calmly asked for Tuvok's suggestions on how the captain's combadge might have been separated from its owner. It was obvious from Tuvok's and the crew's manner that no one detected the inner horror that'd speared through Chakotay when he'd learned that bit of information; his concentration had slipped for a second.

"She was holding the device in her hand during beam-out," Tuvok replied to the question. "It may simply be that she dropped it, and did not find it before it was beamed aboard."

Chakotay nodded. It was logical, and the facts fit. It also fit with the vision of her beam being separated from the others. But what of the ravine? I sensed the statement he would make before he said it. "Estimated time until the storm is over?"

"Two hours and forty-two minutes," the answer came from the helm.

"There were very high winds, and a great deal of precipitation, but as the temperature was rather warm I do not believe that two hours and forty-two minutes would constitute a life-threatening situation for a Starfleet officer." Tuvok's words were clear and logical. No one but me could sense his worry and desire to do something. It was odd; his expressions and words were currently at odds with his inner thoughts.

The stray thought of taking a shuttle down to the planet and getting the captain shot through Chakotay's mind, but then it tottered in favor of another: accepting Tuvok's suggestion, albeit reluctantly. I could not let that happen! Kathryn had fallen into the ravine; in forty of their minutes it would be flooded.

I considered both Chakotay and Tuvok; my options were slim. My people were not allowed to reveal ourselves to outside beings—lower creatures, physical only. But the vision had not helped. I knew suddenly without a doubt that if anything happened to Kathryn that Chakotay or Tuvok could have prevented they might have difficulties in the aftermath. And it would be all my fault.

In determination I made True contact with Chakotay's mind. I felt my processes sear across his consciousness even as he stumbled away from Tuvok. The melding of minds was . . . uncomfortable. I simultaneously felt myself limited as human minds are, and Chakotay's mind stretched to the edges of the infinite. The entire procedure was claustrophobic for me, overwhelming for him. I spoke quickly mind to mind: He *must* find Kathryn. She needs him.

Moments later I could sense the bridge around me again. Tuvok was holding Chakotay's arm, asking if he was okay. Chakotay was flat on his back before the command area. He opened his eyes in understanding.

"Tuvok, you have the bridge. Kathryn is in danger; I'm going to take a shuttle to the planet to find her."

"Commander," Tuvok spoke dryly. "You have just very nearly lost consciousness. I do not think it is a good idea for you to take a shuttlecraft to the planet."

"Someone . . . something, is trying to communicate with me, Tuvok. It told me that Captain Janeway is in trouble. I have to go to help her."

I touched the memory record of Chakotay's experience to

Tuvok's mind; there was no time for arguments. He latched immediately on to my mind for a second, then released.

"Very well," he said.

"Are you there?" Chakotay spoke aloud when he reached the shuttle. "You knew about Kathryn. Can you tell me if she's okay? Is she hurt?" His anguish was visible as his hands worked at the shuttle's controls. He glanced around behind himself as if he might see me. I remained silent, unable to take on a physical form away from my planet and reluctant to further trespass the laws of my people.

After a minute he gave up and concentrated on flying the shuttle. It had penetrated the outer atmosphere and was headed directly for the storm. I could hear the protests, the angry accusations that were shot toward me. They buffeted the little craft, causing several systems to blink. Chakotay had his hands full just keeping the thing airborne until he could find the beam-out location; no easy trick that, without reliable instrumentation.

I met with my family in the debate of the mind:

*Let him pass unharmed. He has an important mission, and is worthy of the passing. He is *intelligent*, thoughtful. . . .*

How can this be? All life-forms on this planet are Basics, aside from the Family. They live, but not Truly.

They have a vessel outside this planet; they've visited other worlds, other people. If you only open your minds fully you will see. If only you don't blind yourselves to them!

They are of limited mind, limited accomplishment. They are limited and therefore unimportant. You will disentangle yourself from them at once!

They are not so limited as us! As you! I will not let you harm him!

I expanded toward the console and showed Chakotay the way. My family moved away in shock, stunned that I'd chosen apart from them.

The little shuttle still rocked until it exited the cloud mass— and entered a torrent. Rain poured from the sky in great giant sheets, obscuring the shuttle's view. In close vicinity to the clouds, the sensors still did not come back on-line, but with the diagram I'd placed on the console Chakotay was easily able to find the beam-out spot. With the shuttle pointing in the correct direction, the vessel's forward motion aided in removing the rain from the viewscreen. Chakotay let out a breath.

He set the shuttle down near the large rock where the beam-out had occurred. He was out the door almost immediately after, examining the soggy terrain. I flashed the vision again in his mind; he didn't even close his eyes this time, but let it happen. When it was over, he ran toward the ravine calling her name.

There was a soft sound from over the edge. I moved and found Kathryn; she hung, with flagging strength, on to a root that jutted out of the side of the ravine. Little pieces of organic debris clung to her face and upper body as the waters rushed beneath her, pulling her legs in their wake. I knew a broken leg when I saw one.

"Kathryn!" Chakotay cried from above, leaning over the edge, the downpour having plastered his hair to his face.

Chakotay reached an arm over the edge and was able to touch Kathryn's arm where it was clinched to the root. "I'll be right back," he said reassuringly. With that he was up and running toward a large tree. Quickly tying a rope around the tree, and then attaching it to his waist, he hurried back to the edge. He eased swiftly into the waters beside Kathryn, standing between her and the rushing waters. He then dropped beneath the waters and tied a safety line around her waist before resurfacing.

Kathryn didn't need to be told what to do next; she grabbed on to him and clung. It took several minutes, but Chakotay pulled them both slipping and sliding up the muddy wall.

"My leg is broken," Kathryn murmured unsteadily when they'd reached the top. Her hair had completely washed out of the ponytail she'd worn it in; it now lay matted against her face and back.

Chakotay nodded his understanding and leaned her against a near rock as he undid their ropes. The jagged scar along her leg was frightening now that he had a better look, and the dazed look in her eyes did little to reassure him. Throwing the coiled rope over a shoulder, he brushed the hair away from her face.

"Kathryn," he said, worry evident in his voice. "You're going into shock. I'm going to pick you up and carry you to the shuttle. In just a few minutes we're going to be back on *Voyager.*"

Kathryn didn't respond. I was worried, too. I'd never experienced this state before. Shock, Chakotay had called it. It was strange, distant, removed.

When the shuttle took off this time, my people did not interfere. But they did not welcome me into the cloud either. I had made my choice, committed the unforgivable. I took some of the blue stones with me.

I have come to learn the meaning of the name of their vessel, and of their coming to this place. They are brave and True. Proudly I would call them my people. And I, *Voyager.*

Monthuglu

Craig D. B. Patton

Captain Janeway's log—"Captain's Log, Stardate 50714.2. We are navigating around a region of space which the Travellers have told us is occupied by the Tarkans. According to the Travellers, the Tarkans are an extremely hostile race. The detour will add a month to our journey, but I feel it is a worthwhile price to pay. Nevertheless, we are making every effort to take the shortest route possible around their territory."

Ensign Kim's log—"Operations Officer's Log, Stardate 50716.5. *Voyager* has picked up what appears to be a nebula on long-range scans. For some reason, I am unable to classify it at this time. Either the readings are distorted or this is a never-before-encountered phenomenon. Background radiation and other known forms of interference are at standard Delta Quadrant levels. We are proceeding toward it. I will try to resolve the data on route."

Commander Chakotay's log—"First Officer's Log, Stardate

50717.1. We have arrived at the edge of the huge gaseous anomaly. Mr. Kim originally termed it a nebula but has since retracted his assessment since the computer cannot classify it. About the only thing we have determined with any certainty is that it completely fills the region of space before us. With Tarkan space still blocking our direct progress toward Alpha Quadrant, we are now stuck in a corner. Another detour will cost us an unknown amount of time. The alternative is to pass through this anomaly. We are in the process of analyzing it further."

Ensign Kim's log—"Operations Officer's Log, Stardate 50717.2. I completed my analysis of the anomaly and have concluded that it is, in fact, a new type of nebula. I have therefore designated it a Class 12 nebula. In addition to being unusually large, it is far darker than any nebula previously recorded. As we are nowhere near any stars, I originally classified it as a standard dark nebula. I also explored the hypothesis that this was simply an ancient planetary nebula whose originating supernova had burned out long ago. However, this nebula did not ultimately correspond to the profile of either type. It appears to remain stable in size, rather than expanding as do planetary nebulae. It also contains stronger energy currents than any recorded nebulae of either type and is full of extremely dense dust nodules. We are unable to scan further than two light-years beyond its perimeter."

Captain Janeway's log—"Captain's Log, Stardate 50717.4. I have met with the senior officers and decided to take *Voyager* through the nebula rather than add even more time to our journey. In addition to keeping us on our revised schedule, it will allow us a unique opportunity to more closely study this new class of nebula. We are making preparations for the traverse and will begin at 0800 tomorrow morning."

Lieutenant Commander Tuvok's log—"Tactical Officer's Log, Stardate 50717.4. I am making an official entry in this log to note that Captain Janeway has chosen to enter this nebula against my advice. Our discussions with the Travellers included no mention of this anomaly, and we are unable to scan the path ahead effectively. We do know that we are in close proximity to a hostile race. I believe it unwise to enter a never-before-encountered phenomenon under these conditions. However, mine was the only dissenting voice on this subject. The captain has made her decision, and I am now taking every precaution to make ready for the traverse."

Ensign Kim's personal log—"Stardate 50718.1. I can't sleep, so I thought I would make a log entry. I'm pretty wound up right now. I guess I'm still amazed that we've discovered a new class of nebula. It's been over two hundred years since that last happened. This is the most exceptional part of our journey: the chance to discover people and things that have never been seen before. Even the Federation's deep-space probes haven't located anything like this nebula. It's only because *Voyager* passed this way that we know about it now. When we get back, it will take years for Federation scientists to catch up to what this crew will have learned. Maybe we can all just retire and become professors."

Neelix's "Good Morning, *Voyager*" show—"Hello again, shipmates. Today, as you know, is a historic day for us all as we begin our journey through the Harry Kim Nebula. I've received special permission from Captain Janeway to carry the show live as we enter the nebula, so that those of you who are off duty can see and hear what is happening. I'm here in the Mess Hall with several dozen of your crewmates, watching out the window as we begin to enter this dark, almost midnight blue cloud of gas and dust. Let's see what's on people's minds, shall we? Ah, Ensign Oliver of biosciences, what do you think of getting the chance to travel through this nebula?"

"I think it's great, Neelix. It's a rare opportunity to get to explore a completely new space phenomenon. I joined Starfleet so I could have experiences like this one."

"That's wonderful, Ensign, thanks. Now I hate to interrupt, but the big moment is here. As you can see, *Voyager* has reached the perimeter of the cloud. The nebula fills the view above and below us now; we can't see any stars at all. Looking forward, we can see the edge of the nebula, like a huge curtain that the ship is cutting through. I must say, it's a very strange feeling. Almost like we're being swallowed by the dust and gas. Oh, now that's interesting, we can see the edge of the cloud actually moving across the windows here in the Mess Hall now. All the swirling dust and gas make it look just like a puffy cloud. Of course, those are usually white—but other than that, the effect is the same. And now the edge of the cloud has passed us by here in the Mess Hall. In only a few more moments, the nebula will engulf the entire ship. Everyone here is chattering away excitedly about the view. We can't see much outside anymore. It's just one sea of . . . What's this? The lights are flickering a bit now. We seem to be having some sort of . . ."

Commander Chakotay's log—"First Officer's Log, Stardate 50718.4. As soon as *Voyager* entered the nebula, we lost main power and had to switch to the auxiliary. Lieutenant Torres reports there is no damage to the warp drive but is at a loss to explain the outage. Since we would not go to warp inside a nebula anyway, the captain and I feel we should proceed while we get the mains back on line."

Lieutenant Torres's log—"Chief Engineer's Log, Stardate 50718.4. I have traced the problem with main power to an irregular flow in the plasma conduits on Deck 10 and have assigned Ensign Bolya to perform the repairs. I expect to have main power restored in less than an hour."

Emergency Medical Holographic Program's log—"Chief Medical Officer's Log, Stardate 50718.5. I have just completed treatment on Ensign Bolya for a mild case of frostbite to his extremities. Apparently, the life support system in one of the Jefferies tubes failed while he was performing repairs on a plasma conduit. There appeared to be no lasting effects, so I have released the patient."

Ensign Bolya's personal log—"Personal log, Stardate 50718.6. I wound up in Sickbay today after a bizarre experience. Lieutenant Torres assigned me to repair the plasma flow regulator on Deck 10. I was working on the unit when I noticed that I had started shivering. I assumed it was because I was lying on the metal floor of the Jefferies tube and I tend to get cold so easily. The air was fine. I worked a little bit more. But then I felt the hairs on my back start to stand on end, like they do back on Ilyara in winter when I'm outside too long. I started to shake uncontrollably and dropped the tool I was holding. The climate control in the tube must have malfunctioned. Anyway, I called for an immediate beam-out to Engineering. Lieutenant Torres took one look at me and sent me to Sickbay. Turns out I had frostbitten my hands and part of my face just in that short period. Guess I'm glad I decided to leave when I did."

Lieutenant Torres's log—"Chief Engineer's Log, Stardate 50718.6. We have completed repairs and restored main power. However, we now have a new mystery to solve. Ensign Bolya suffered frostbite while attempting to make the repairs. He reported that the environmental controls failed. However, I can find no evidence in the ship's logs or the Jefferies tube itself to support his statement."

Captain Janeway's log—"Captain's Log, Stardate 50718.7. We've experienced a twenty percent increase in the velocity of the nebula's natural energy currents. I expected this kind of turbulence to be part of the traverse and have recalled Lieutenant Paris to the bridge to take the helm until we reach a calmer section. The ship is in no serious danger."

Ensign Harry Kim's personal log—"Personal log, Stardate 50718.8. Something strange just happened. I was practicing oboe. About fifteen minutes ago, I noticed a background noise as I played. I thought it was just the ship's engines until I realized it actually followed along, accompanying me. So I stopped playing. But when I listened, I couldn't hear it anymore. I started playing and it started right up again. I stopped again and so did it. So then I assumed something was wrong with the oboe and cleaned it. It seemed fine, but when I started playing, the sound resumed. Kind of a really low, faint humming. So then I figured it must be Tom Paris playing some prank, and I called his name. No answer. It turns out he's on the bridge and has been for the last three hours. I just played a little bit more. The sound is gone now."

Ship's log—"Ship's Log, Stardate 50719.2, Lieutenant Commander Tuvok in command of Gamma shift. Energy currents remain steady; however, ambient density has increased by thirty percent. Lieutenant Paris has been relieved at helm as it appears we are holding steady on our course. Sickbay reports that Transporter Chief Xiu has been admitted with a broken nose resulting from a fall while sleepwalking. Nothing else worthy of note at this time."

Lieutenant Commander Tuvok's personal log—"Personal log, Stardate 50719.4. I have just completed meditation in an attempt to refocus my senses. While on duty last night with Gamma watch, I experienced a mild hallucination on two separate occasions. Each time, I perceived motion at the extreme left of my visual field. However, when I turned to look, I saw nothing. I have no rational explanation for this, but it is not interfering with my duties enough to warrant significant concern. I will, of course, bring it to the captain's attention if it begins to do so."

Captain Janeway's log—"Captain's Log, supplemental. In all my years of space travel I have never seen a nebula quite like this one. We have had to compensate for dramatic fluctuations in both the density of the cloud and the velocity of its currents. At times, turbulence actually buffets the ship. Lieutenant Torres and Ensign Kim have both been collecting as much data as possible but have little to offer in the way of explanation concerning the nature of this unusual nebula. Despite the somewhat bumpy road, the crew still seems to be enjoying the adventure of discovery."

Ensign Kim's log—"Operations Officer's Log, Stardate 50719.7. Energy currents have dramatically increased again. We are at full power just to keep the ship going in a straight line. Cloud density is up by forty-seven percent since the last reading I took just twenty minutes ago. At times the sensors show the cloud to be practically a solid mass of . . . something is ahead . . ."

Commander Chakotay's log—"First Officer's Log, Stardate 50719.7. We have encountered several ships that appear to be heavily damaged and adrift in a strangely quiet region. We were battling the strongest currents yet when *Voyager* passed through an almost physical wall into something like the eye of a storm. We are surveying the ships in an effort to determine what happened to them. Preliminary scans reveal no lifesigns or energy signatures. The ships do not correspond to any known Gamma Quadrant cultures."

Ensign Kim's log—"Operations Officer's Log, Stardate

50719.7. I have picked up a faint lifesign on one of the ships. Sensors are having difficulty penetrating the area directly around the survivor, but readings indicate one humanoid life-form."

Captain Janeway's log—"Captain's Log, Stardate 50719.8. Mr. Kim has determined that it is safe to transport an away team into the ship containing what we assume to be a survivor of whatever has taken place here. Commander Chakotay has assigned Lieutenant Commander Tuvok and Lieutenant Torres to his team."

Lieutenant Torres's mission report—"We just returned from the alien vessel. It is in extremely rough shape, though I am not sure yet what caused the damage. We detected no signs of energy-weapon scarring but the hull is ruptured in several places. Emergency doors isolated some of the breaches, preventing access to several areas of the ship. The computer system is down, as is main power. The ship is running on what I assume to be their emergency backup, but even that is almost drained. The ship may have been adrift here for some time. My first assessment indicates that their technology lags well behind our own. There won't be much to salvage from the bridge. A breach in the engine room makes access to that section impossible, so I doubt we'll gain much in raw materials either."

Lieutenant Tuvok's mission report—"We have returned to *Voyager* with the survivor that was detected by the ship's sensors. We found him unconscious in the command chair on the bridge, which implies he is the vessel's captain. He is currently undergoing treatment in Sickbay. He appears to be the only survivor. We found no bodies, even though the bridge layout clearly suggests that it is normally staffed by a dozen crew members. Given that we have found no signs of energy-weapon discharge, I don't believe this is the site of a battle. My initial hypothesis is that the ship experienced some sort of natural catastrophe and that the captain ordered the crew to abandon ship. The captain remained behind with the vessel to await the end. However, it apparently never came. This explanation is supported by the fact that the other vessels present here are significantly different from each other, suggesting they may come from a variety of races. Lieutenant Torres and Ensign Kim are analyzing the damage to the ship's hull in an effort to determine what caused it to rupture."

Commander Chakotay's mission report—"We successfully located the only survivor and transported him aboard. He appears to be the ship's captain. He is currently undergoing treatment in Sickbay. We found no sign of the other crew members' bodies. The ship is an eerie place. It is torn to pieces and running on emergency power. The bridge was very dimly lit. Smoke filled the air. There was a moment while I was exploring a passage alone when I thought I heard someone calling out. I couldn't make out the words. I went toward the sound and yelled back. No one answered me. My tricorder did not indicate any life-forms were present. I assume I heard metal creaking somewhere and imagined it was a voice. The whole environment is pretty unsettling. I think we're all glad to be back aboard *Voyager*."

Emergency Medical Holographic Program's log—"Chief Medical Officer's Log, Stardate 50719.9. I have completed the initial examination and treatment of our new guest. The patient remains unconscious. He belongs to a species we have not previously encountered, making it difficult to assess him in any great depth or to prescribe treatment. I do not want to risk giving him standard humanoid stimulants until I learn more about him. The patient seems to be in relatively good physical condition, particularly considering the fact that he had been adrift in a shipwreck and unconscious for an unknown period of time. I am continuing my analysis."

Captain Janeway's log—"Captain's Log, Stardate 50720.3. Having met with the senior staff, I have decided to continue on our current course through the nebula toward the Alpha Quadrant. Our theory is that the nebula's energy currents may vary considerably in intensity. While we have not encountered any turbulence severe enough to rip a ship apart, the phenomenon may simply be in a quieter phase. I believe we should continue on our path quickly, before the currents change. Lieutenant Torres and Ensign Kim report that the hulls of most of the shipwrecks are constructed with materials inferior to those found in *Voyager*'s hull. It is our hope that, should we encounter more severe turbulence, we will be able to survive the pounding better than they did."

Ensign Kim's log—"Operations Officer's Log, Stardate 50720.3. We have just reentered the distinctive wall of dust and gas that envelops the core of this nebula. Conditions are roughly equivalent to those we found on the way into the core. Currents and density are at the same peak levels recorded earlier."

Emergency Medical Holographic Program's log—"Chief Medical Officer's Log, Stardate 50720.3. The patient has regained consciousness on his own and is alert. I administered no treatment. He seems quite startled to find himself aboard *Voyager* and asked me if he was dead. I assured him he is very much alive and have asked Captain Janeway to come down to meet our guest, who calls himself Captain Uthlow."

Lieutenant Torres's log—"Chief Engineer's Log, Stardate 50720.3. We appear to be having some sort of malfunction that is limited to the doors on Deck 10. I was on my way here from the bridge when I discovered it. As I walked down the corridor from the turbolift, I realized that the door hadn't closed behind me. It did a moment later, but a few steps further down the corridor I saw the door to Storage Locker 12 slide open. No one came out, and when I walked up to look in, no one was inside. I closed the door with the manual release. Then I found the door to one of the Jefferies Tubes open. Again, no one was inside and I was able to close the hatch. I have assigned a repair crew to investigate."

Captain Janeway's log—"Captain's Log, Stardate 50720.4. I had a brief but disturbing conversation in Sickbay with Captain Uthlow, the alien brought on board by the away team. He is quite amazed that *Voyager* has been able to remain intact so far. Uthlow's ship was exploring this nebula, which his people call the Tenebrous Cluster due to its dark appearance. While they mapped the cluster and gathered data on its composition, they encountered more than just the strong currents we've observed. Uthlow claims the cluster is inhabited by what he calls 'Monthuglu,' a group of entities he says are responsible for the damage to these ships and the disappearance of their crews. I pressed him for more information, but he grew increasingly upset by my skepticism regarding some of the more incredible parts of his story. I need to keep in mind that he lost his ship and his entire crew on that mission. He certainly has no obvious reason to deceive us, and we saw a dozen destroyed ships with no definite cause. I have ordered the ship put on Yellow Alert and asked Lieutenant Tuvok to meet with Captain Uthlow and me in my ready room for a more formal discussion."

Emergency Medical Holographic Program's log—"Chief Medical Officer's Log, Stardate 50720.5. I have treated and released Crewman Okira for minor injuries he sustained in a fall while working in Engineering. He apparently was not paying close enough attention to his work environment and thought that an open hatch was closed. He sustained a severe cut to the upper scalp. Crewman Okira insisted that he looked at the hatch and that it was closed just before the accident, but since I can find no indication that he might have been hallucinating, I must assume he is simply mistaken."

Lieutenant Commander Tuvok's log—"Tactical Officer's Log, Stardate 50720.5. I have met with Captain Janeway and Captain Uthlow. According to Captain Uthlow, we are in grave danger. He calls the race that inhabits this nebula 'Monthuglu,' but I do not think that is a formal species name. Instead, the word appears to originate in his culture's mythology. In their stories, Monthuglu are evil spirits that have no physical form. They are an invisible force that kills and carries people away. The entities in this nebula never showed themselves to Captain Uthlow and his crew. None of their sensor data could explain what was happening. I suspect that is why they branded the species with a popular myth out of their folktales.

"He says that the Monthuglu have the ability to gain control of physical matter, including machines, and that once they determined how his ship worked, they caused severe malfunctions that led to multiple hull breaches. These ruptures apparently allowed the creatures to enter the ship, and they began to kill off his crew. As the ship fled, the Monthuglu invaded the bridge. Captain Uthlow saw his senior officers killed before his eyes. He states that they were absorbed by an enemy he could not see or fight. For whatever reason, they left him for last. He remembers hearing a loud screeching in his ears and what he describes as an icy pain enveloped him. The last thing he recalls is catching a glimpse of the nebula cloud parting and the core emerging beyond. Then nothing. Given that Uthlow was not killed and we found no invading force on his vessel, I hypothesize that the attackers abruptly left the ship. It is possible that their species is unable to exist in the core of the nebula and they were forced to retreat. Ensign Kim is examining the possibilities in order to provide us with a report on defensive tactics we can use should we encounter this race. The ship remains at Yellow Alert."

Ensign Kim's log—"Operations Officer's Log, Stardate 50720.6. I have completed my analysis of the nebula cloud, its core, and the readings we took aboard Captain Uthlow's ship. I find no indication of sentient life anywhere. The core of the cloud is largely free of most of the gases that make up the main body: nitrogen, parmacon, and helium. It is possible that the alien species requires the presence of one or more of these gases in order to exist or move, but that is just a wild guess based on what Captain Uthlow has told us."

Captain Janeway's log—"Captain's Log, Stardate 50720.6. I have met with the senior staff to review our situation. Unfortunately, even with the few facts that we have and Captain Uthlow's knowledge of the nebula, there are no real options to consider. We must continue through the Tenebrous Cluster to reach normal space again. According to the explorations that Captain Uthlow and his crew made prior to being attacked, the cluster is relatively symmetrical. Thus, we must travel roughly the same distance no matter what course we set. I have decided to continue on our original heading, toward Federation space. We simply have no way of predicting the behavior of these aliens. Therefore, I believe it is in our best interests to continue on our way and hope for the best."

Commander Chakotay's log—"First Officer's Log, Stardate 50721.0. *Voyager* continues to travel through the severe currents of this nebula. The conditions are very unsettling. The ship is being tossed about, pushed by the energy currents and colliding with highly concentrated dust nodules. Not much can be seen with the visual scanners and even less out the windows. I imagine ancient sailors on Earth felt like this while struggling through ocean storms: holding on, bracing against the next blow, wishing it would end. It would feel more like a romantic adventure if we didn't know that hundreds, if not thousands, of space travelers have lost their lives here to an enemy we haven't seen yet. At Captain Janeway's request, Captain Uthlow has remained on the bridge with us. He has pretty much kept to himself. I think he feels frustrated by the fact that we have been unwilling to accept his supernatural interpretation of events."

Captain Janeway's personal log—"Personal log, Stardate 50721.1. I'm having a little trouble sleeping tonight. I went to the holodeck and spent some time walking under the stars in Neelix's resort program. The quiet of the night with only the torches and moon for light is very relaxing. It helped to take my mind off things for a while, until I came across Neelix himself. He was on a walk, too. He is concerned about the general morale of the crew. The Mess Hall was very quiet during dinner this evening. I told him not to worry. I think everyone is just focused on the task at hand. We face a threat of unknown proportions and can't expect the crew to just shrug it off. He seemed to accept that and feel better. We talked for a while about the joy and fear that both come with exploring new areas of space and then went our separate ways. I'm going to catch a few hours of sleep and then relieve Chakotay on the bridge."

Commander Chakotay's log—"First Officer's Log, Stardate 50721.2. I spoke with Captain Uthlow for some time about his people and his experiences here in the Tenebrous Cluster. I find him to be a sensible and thoughtful man. What happened to him and his crew has deeply scared him. He was responsible for the safety of a hundred crew members and is the only one left. Despite his obvious pain, he is very focused on assisting us in our journey out of the nebula, particularly since he thinks we are a bit naïve. Uthlow believes our reliance on technology to be a weakness as well as a strength. While he is impressed by what we have, he told me he fears we may be blinded by it. His people readily believe that there are things which are beyond explanation, forces which can't ever be dismissed by science. At his urging, I rechecked the most recent departmental reports. The results are rather dramatic. I will make a full report to the captain when she comes on duty in half an hour."

Captain Janeway's log—"Captain's Log, Stardate 50721.3. Commander Chakotay has provided me with a report that shows no fewer than a dozen unexplained mechanical or computer failures since we entered the Tenebrous Cluster. They are all minor, but that's an alarming number. I also received a report from the Doctor, who informs me that he has treated numerous people for injuries resulting from 'careless behavior' in the last few days. He suggests that the crew may be in need of shore leave, since the frequency of these types of incidents has increased dramatically of late. One could almost say that the crew are experiencing unexplained malfunctions as well. None of these incidents indicates that we are in any jeopardy, of course, but taken together, it does seem that there is a pattern of problems which began when we entered the nebula."

Captain Janeway's log—"Captain's Log, supplemental. I am greatly troubled by what is taking place here. We are unable to identify a cause for any of the ship malfunctions, and it is difficult to write them off as coincidence. Captain Uthlow's concern is increasing. He continues to insist that these are not random phenomena at all, but actually the initial attacks by Monthuglu. I am beginning to understand how the Monthuglu myth gained such life with his people."

Ensign Kim's personal log—"Personal log, Stardate 50721.3. I just woke from a horrible dream. . . . My heart is pounding. . . . I'm really thirsty. I dreamt that I was in a pitch-dark cave. Alone. But I had the feeling I was lost or looking for someone, as though I wasn't supposed to be alone. I edged my way through the cave slowly, because I had no lamp. The floor and walls were jagged, but the passage went fairly straight for a while. I only stumbled once or twice, tripping over boulders on the floor. I kept one hand on the wall, so I could backtrack if necessary, and waved the other hand in front of me. That worked well because I didn't bang my head when I came to what seemed like a dead end. I felt around the walls with my hands and found a narrow crack near the floor. It was even blacker inside it, but I could feel a slight breeze coming through, so I knew there was more passage beyond. I knelt down and pushed myself inside. It wasn't tall enough for me to crawl through, so I had to slither forward and push with my feet. The walls pressed against me. Sharp edges of rock snagged my clothes and scratched at my face. It was hard work to move. I had just found the other end of the crack with my hand when my left leg got pinched in a tight spot. I turned my leg a bit to try to slide it through and made it a lot worse.

"Pain seared through me, and I realized that I was now truly jammed. I tried to push myself backwards with my hands but couldn't move. I was stuck in the crack. Then I heard sounds ahead of me in the open passage, faint at first, but getting nearer. They were like voices, but distorted. Kind of a screeching. They got louder and louder, building into a terrible noise of overlapping voices. Then I saw something coming. It looked like a cloud of mist. My mind screamed at me to get away but I was trapped. The mist advanced toward me. It drew up to the crack, just a few feet from my face, and started to reshape itself. It became a face. My face. I was staring at an image of myself. The screams and cries built and then, slowly, the image of my face contorted in pain. The skin peeled back until I was staring at a huge skull. All the voices stopped except one. I realized that it was my own voice screaming and woke up. . . .

"It took me a moment to realize I had been dreaming. I opened my eyes and it was still dark. Maybe it's just all this talk about the Monthuglu. I'm keyed up, waiting for something to happen. When I'm on duty at least I keep busy. Having the ship run at a standing Yellow Alert gets unnerving after a while. I wish I didn't have to sleep. Tuvok has stayed at his post. I wanted to as well, but Commander Chakotay ordered me to take a break. I should tell him that being on duty is less stressful."

Lieutenant Commander Tuvok's log—"Tactical Officer's Log, Stardate 50721.4. The ship is at Red Alert due to the possible presence of the Monthuglu. We have had a major power disruption here on the bridge. The main and battle lights have both failed, leaving us with nothing but the glow from the consoles.

There is no immediately apparent cause. Short-range scans detect nothing unusual. Long-range scans are still inoperative as a result of interference from the cluster. We continue our scans. Captain Janeway has called a conference."

Captain Janeway's log—"Captain's Log, Stardate 50721.4. It appears that we are in fact experiencing some sort of unusual phenomenon. For lack of any other data, I have been forced to turn to Captain Uthlow for some kind of insight into what is happening and how to combat it. Captain Uthlow believes that the Monthuglu are beginning to gain an understanding of our key systems. His bridge experienced malfunctions just prior to the final wave of attack when the ship's hull breached. He has urged us to make a run for it in the hope of reaching the edge of the nebula before things get worse. I am keeping the ship at Red Alert and have ordered Lieutenant Paris to increase speed on our course. The ride may get a little rougher, but I want to be clear of the nebula as soon as possible. I have taken the next watch and ordered Commander Chakotay to get some rest. He has been on duty for eighteen hours straight."

Commander Chakotay's personal log—"Personal log, Stardate 50721.7. This region of space is truly a malevolent place. I just had a horrible encounter while attempting to contact my animal guide. I initiated the vision state without difficulty, entered my centering space and looked for my guide. But I did not see her. I waited, breathed, and tried to be at peace. After a short period, I became aware of another presence, looked and saw a murky shape moving toward me. It approached the way that she always does, but as she came near, she suddenly grew several times in size. In that same instant, the sky turned dark and stormy. Lightning slashed across the landscape and a wind roared from out of nowhere. I had only a moment to absorb it all before she was right on top of me. She towered over me, opened her mouth, and screamed with a sound I hope to never hear again. It was agony—nothing like an animal. More like a disembodied voice out of hell. I tried to end the vision but could not break free. She lunged at me with her mouth gaping. I started to run, but she moved too quickly and seized me with her jaws in an instant. I heard myself scream as her teeth pierced my body. I thought I could actually feel the pain but suddenly awoke from the trance. I have never heard of such a thing happening. All I can think of is Captain Uthlow and his Monthuglu stories. I'm going to talk to the captain right now. I'm starting to believe in them."

Captain Janeway's log—"Captain's Log, Stardate 50721.7. Commander Chakotay has suffered an attack in his quarters. Having learned of the encounter, Ensign Kim has described a vivid nightmare he had before coming on duty. It appears that the Monthuglu possess the ability not only to manipulate matter, but also to invade our very minds. If that is so, a major attack may be imminent."

Lieutenant Tuvok's log—"Tactical Officer's Log, Stardate 50721.8. We are urgently seeking some means of defense against a race that is apparently out of phase with our normal space or time. These creatures also appear to possess acute mental powers that can be used against a subject who is asleep or in a meditative state. As a result, the captain has ordered the crew to remain awake as much as possible and not to engage in any kind of mental exercises. We have increased speed as much as Lieutenant Paris considers safe, but the severe shearing action of the currents continues to hinder our progress. I am randomly rotating the shield harmonics and have electrified the hull in an attempt to prevent further assaults."

Ensign Kim's log—"Operations Officer's Log, Stardate 50721.9. We are experiencing heavy buffeting from the worst currents we have seen yet. EM hull pressure has risen to dangerous levels. Lieutenant Paris has reduced speed, but we have suffered minor structural damage to the outer hull, and internal power is fluctuating. . . . I have just received word of a plasma leak in Engineering. Repair teams responding."

Lieutenant Torres's log—"Chief Engineer's Log, Stardate 50721.9. The plasma leak is contained, but my people are very shaken. We were trying to compensate for a severe power brownout on Deck 5 when one of the plasma injectors in the warp core pit ruptured. Everyone started to dive for oxygen masks and erect a containment field at the same time. The field was quickly in place, but a cloud of plasma built up within it. As it grew, shapes began to appear. At first it just looked like swirling shadows. But then we saw faces start to emerge. They were gruesome, with hideous, bestial heads and features. Some with horns. Some with long, jagged fangs. Humanoid arms with what looked like claws and hooves flailed out and kicked at the force field. The faces roared in frustration but made no sound. Only the ship's alarms and the screams of my staff filled the room. I finally came to my senses and shut off the plasma flow. The cloud dissipated quickly, the creatures seeming to howl in frustration as they vanished. I don't know what we just saw and I don't want to see anything like it again."

Lieutenant Tuvok's log—"Tactical Officer's Log, Stardate 50722.0. We have just had an intruder physically appear before every crew member in Engineering, but we have no data on it. Internal sensors show no one but the crew. Moreover, video playback shows nothing of note in the cloud of plasma, despite the reactions of the crew. I have no explanation for what has occurred. Even if this race possesses the ability to alter what humanoids perceive, they themselves should be visible. I am obviously at a complete loss to understand and combat these creatures."

Captain Janeway's log—"Captain's Log, supplemental. We have emerged from the Tenebrous Cluster. As we ran for the boundary of the nebula, systems continued to fail intermittently and the ship rattled around us. I had just asked Mr. Paris if he detected the edge of the cluster when I began to hear a low noise. I ignored it at first. But the sound intensified and everyone on the bridge began to look at each other. I realized that we all heard it. It was a deep, guttural howl. Then Ensign Kim cried out and pointed above our heads. A dense fog emanated from the ceiling. Captain Uthlow started to scream. Tuvok immediately erected a containment field between us and the ceiling. But it didn't hold them. The cloud condensed into a group of shapes. It appears that we each saw something different in the cloud. I saw several young women with their arms extended toward us. But Ensign Kim says he saw seven ancient warriors with swords drawn. Lieutenant Paris saw monstrous, skeletal creatures with fire where their eyes should be. Only Tuvok seems to have seen just a cloud. But all of us saw the same thing next.

"The shapes lunged downward around the screaming Captain Uthlow. They dissolved into an unrecognizable mass swirling around him. Several bridge officers tried to intervene in that instant but found they could not move. On the viewscreen, I noticed the gases starting to part and stars emerging in the distance. We had reached the edge of the nebula. The screams of the captain and the howls of his tormentor brought my attention back to what was happening on the bridge. Captain Uthlow started to disappear before our eyes. He reached out to me at the last moment, pleading. Then he faded away before our eyes within the cloud. Moments later, the cloud resumed the shape of the women and lunged toward me. My ears rang with their high-pitched screech of anger—then of frustration—as the cloud suddenly dissipated. *Voyager* had cleared the nebula and reentered normal space. . . .

"We continue on course for the Alpha Quadrant, but there are more questions than answers regarding the Tenebrous Cluster's terrifying inhabitants and the fate of Captain Uthlow. Since we have no intention of reentering the cluster, I am quite confident that we will never fully explain the events of the last few days. But I am equally sure we will not forget them."

Because We Can*

*We've been asked a number of times why we decided to publish a fan-written anthology. Here's part of the reason: so that the two of us could publish our own fan stories in a real honest-to-Betsy book. Obviously, just kidding. And we'd like to make it clear that these stories were not part of the contest (and, in fact, they break several of the rules we held you folks to) and that no fan-written stories were bumped to make room for "The Man Who Sold the Sky" or "The Girl Who Controlled Gene Kelly's Feet."

The Man Who Sold the Sky

John J. Ordover

It's not fair, the seventy-year-old man thought as he lay dying in a Los Angeles hospital. *There was so much of the future I wanted to see.*

There was no doubt in his mind that he was dying; things were just not right inside him, and each time the heart monitor on his bedside beeped he could feel more of himself drifting away. When he was a child, his chronic asthma had sometimes brought him close to death, but that was a different feeling, a fearful one, not this quiet frustration that he would never know what happened next.

Not that I have done so little in my life, he thought. *Many people have dreams, but very few have those dreams come true as well as mine have, and even fewer see their creations bring pleasure and hope to so many around the world. I may not have lived as long as some others, but I have prospered.*

A high-pitched humming sound filled the room, and he

opened his eyes. His fading eyesight took a moment to register the six figures who had appeared around his bed. He could not see them clearly, just as outlines of colored shapes, and he wondered if they were truly there or just creatures of the drugs he had been given. He tried to greet them, but he was too weak and his words came out as a choking cough.

"Goddamn primitive medicine!" a blue-clad figure to his left exclaimed. The figure moved toward him, followed by another blue figure, this one topped in red.

The old man heard an electronic whine. "We got here just in time," the red-topped figure said in a deep but feminine voice.

"Damn right," the blue man said. "You stabilize him, I'll get the homeostasis booster ready."

The old man felt a moment of fear as the figures moved toward him, but there was something about them that made him certain they meant him no harm. There was a feather touch on his arm, so light he could not be sure he really felt it. Almost at once he felt much better, as if there was no longer any need to fight for life. Am I dying now? he thought. Is this death? He lay back and listened calmly to the oh-so-familiar voices around him.

"Sir," a new voice, a high-pitched monotone, said from the right side of his bed, "I must remind you that what we are attempting is extremely dangerous."

"I understand the risks," a cultured British accent responded, "but for him it is worth the chances we must take. There is no limit to what we owe this man."

"Besides," said a voice more playful than the last—but, the old man thought, having the same air of command. "The odds are on our side for once—"

"Yes, Captain," put in a sharp, intelligent voice from his left side, "I would calculate them to be—"

"Don't!" snapped the blue-clad man by his bedside. "Jim, I'm giving him the booster." The old man felt another phantom touch on his arm. "Give me five minutes and he'll be ready to transport." Well, the old man thought, if this is the end, it's entertaining at least.

"Sir," he heard the monotone voice ask, "whatever the odds,

should we risk what could be many lives for the sake of any one man?"

"Sometimes," the sharp voice from the left of the bed replied, "the needs of the many are outweighed by the needs of the few, or the one."

"I do not understand," the monotone replied.

"It took me many years to learn it," the sharp voice said. "It is a very human thing."

At last it came to the old man who these people were. Now I'm certain of it, the old man thought; it's the drugs, or I'm dreaming.

"Jim," the blue man said, "he's ready for transport. Better make it fast."

"Right." There was a beeping sound, and a muffled voice from somewhere that the old man could not hear clearly. "Seven to beam up," he heard the playful commander say.

The old man felt the blue man step away and a yellow-clad figure move toward him. When the figure bent down the old man saw a man's face, a face he recognized and that made him doubt his sanity again. He knew this man, these people, as well as he knew anyone, as well as he knew himself, knew how impossible it was that they were here. "We're taking you away," the commander said. "Do you understand?"

The old man nodded, then tried his voice. It was hard to talk but he tried his best. "Where are you taking me?" he asked calmly, not certain he really spoke aloud.

The commander seemed to hear him and flashed him a boyish smile. "To where you've always been," he said. "To the future."

The old man smiled. That's okay by me, he thought, that's okay by me. Before he could ask more, the high-pitched humming came again and the room dissolved and he could no longer see.

The Girl Who Controlled Gene Kelly's Feet

Paula M. Block

There aren't any vocational counselors on the *U.S.S. Enterprise.* The fact is, there isn't even a chaplain, although there are numerous ecclesiastical tapes for those who require their comforting drone. And there's a universal-denominational chapel for those who like a little atmosphere with their drone. And there's a perfectly adequate psychiatric section, of which I happen to be a functional component, for those crewpersons with really overt adjustment problems. And that's not even mentioning kindly Doctor McCoy, who's always on call for those who merely need a shoulder to cry on that's fully equipped with a shrink's degree.

Of course, hypothetically, all of the messy problems which might have inspired a need for the services of the aforementioned persons, places or things should have been caught at the academy, during the initial matriculation procedure for Starfleet. But sometimes they're not, and they get covered up, or sometimes they occur due to the pressures of the job, and sometimes people go nuts for no reason at all. Hence the need for the annual psych workup that Starfleet imposes on all personnel, and hence my introduction to the inner workings of the mind of one Minnie Moskowitz, yeoman third class on the *U.S.S. Enterprise.*

She was one of the dozens I was assigned to check out that month, initially indistinguishable from all of the others, at least in terms of appearance (average), mannerisms (normal), or intelligence (slightly above normal), and all of the general items on the standard checklist. Even what originally caused me to take a personal interest in her, the casual revelation of what seemed to be a somewhat richer than average fantasy life, was not particularly unusual in her situation, considering the mundane chores of the yeoman-any-class. People who are bored, people who are dissatisfied, people who are depressed—they all have the tendency to fantasize a bit—and they're all in Starfleet, too. I've come to expect that sort of thing, and the only thing I normally check out in evaluating cases like that is whether the subject has the ability to comprehend that his/her fantasies are only an escape vehicle. And Minnie seemed to understand that perfectly.

"After all," she told me, "what else *is* there to do, stationed in a little room all by my lonesome, editing endless stacks of tapes. And then re-editing those same tapes. And recycling them. Why would *any*one in her right mind want to restrict her thoughts to reality with a career like that? Why shouldn't I want to dump all those tapes into a disposal chute every now and then. Don't you ever feel that way, Doc?"

"Probably twice a day, on average," I admitted with a small smile. "But tell me—what would you do if you weren't in Starfleet? What would you like to do?"

"What would you do?" she retorted.

"Me?" I thought for a moment. "Oh, I might become an exotic dancer on Argelius II. I always heard that I had excellent potential for a navel career." Yuk, yuk, yuk. "But, as the phrase goes, I asked you first."

Minnie leaned back in her chair. "I'm not sure," she said

thoughtfully. "I'm not programmed to do anything but this at the moment."

"Yes, but there must be something you'd really *like* to be," I urged. "Someplace you'd like to go."

She was silent for a moment; then a smile lit her face as she said, "I was a dragon once. I enjoyed that quite a bit."

"A dragon?" I echoed bemusedly.

"Yeah. Oh, in one of my fantasies," she added quickly.

"Of course," I said. "But there aren't too many openings for dragons these days anyway."

"That's the truth," Minnie agreed.

"Tell me about some of your childhood ambitions," I prodded.

"*My* childhood?" she said with a laugh. "Okay, here's Minnie Moskowitz's childhood ambition. The big dream was always to grow up to be the creative genius who figures out how to isolate the universal kitsch factor."

"The what?"

"All that's wistful in humankind. See, first you isolate it and then you learn to distill it into a good strong fix of altruistic nonreality and then you hype it. Not a bad ambition. If *I* could achieve that, maybe I'd be able to pull myself free from this damn body and soar."

"Soar," I repeated densely.

"Soar," she confirmed. "You know what it's like on a sunny day in the country when this nice warm breeze comes along and blows through your hair?"

"I'm afraid I spent most of my childhood in big cities and envirodomes. Is it anything like standing in the wind tunnel at the Academy?"

"Not really. It's like . . . it gets inside of me no matter what I am . . . where, I mean, and it fills me with this restless soaring energy. Not like a bird or anything with a body. It's this need to be nothing and everything at the same time. I always thought that if *I* had the choice of what I got made into, that I'd be the wind that moves the leaves on trees. Always moving and commingling and soaring . . ." She paused and glanced down distastefully. "In this body, though, I'm tied to the ground. Even flying around in this mindless flying robot ship. I can't soar."

I thought I understood what she was getting at, although I'd never put it quite that way. I often felt something like it myself. I felt an unprofessional wave of empathy for her. "But nobody can soar . . . not like that. Except in a fantasy, and you can't just exist on a hype."

"Yeah, but what if there *was* a way to hype into something so powerful that you could cut loose from your body completely and soar away from it . . . forever?"

I was at a loss for a reply. "Well . . . don't you think, uh, that you'd miss your body?"

She smiled at me just the way my grandmother used to when she thought I'd said something dumb. "It's just a body," she said.

"Oh, sure," I laughed. "Plenty more where that came from."

"Exactly," she said.

"Uh, yeah," I said, chalking it up to a belief in reincarnation.

"I suppose I've been talking too much," Minnie said suddenly. "You'll probably log me as a loon."

I shrugged. "A certain amount of craziness is necessary for survival on this ship. There's probably a certain number of cards missing from my deck, too."

Minnie grinned conspiratorially. "Ah, so you agree it's better to be nuts than earthbound mundane?"

"Well, to a certain extent," I said hesitantly. "But you know in this life, sooner or later some killjoy insists on putting crazy people in high-security cells and switching on the force field behind them."

"On the other hand, though, if you really *are* crazy, you probably won't realize you're being put in a high-security cell, and you certainly wouldn't hear the field being switched on. For all intents and purposes, you wouldn't be there at all. Me, I'd be flying off somewhere, *without* my body."

I scratched my nose absently. "Logical," I quoted the first officer. She was right. The nice thing about being crazy was not being cognizant of the fact that you were crazy. Well, one of the nice things, anyway.

"So what'll it be, Doc?" She held out her arms as if she were waiting for me to put her into an old-fashioned straitjacket. "Is it the padded cell for old Minnie?"

"Hell, I'd have to lock myself up if you were my criterion for judging nutsy people. Besides, you're already locked up in a little padded cell, editing irrelevant but vital tapes."

"That's for sure," she sighed.

I liked Minnie Moskowitz. Besides being the most interesting person I'd met since I'd completed my internship on Tantalus, she was also the most open person I'd encountered on the ship in the two months I'd been there, aside from a few male crewpersons who'd expressed an interest in "private sessions on my couch." "Listen," I said, "you're my last appointment of the day. Want to join me down in the rec room for a drink?"

"Don't drink," she said. "But if you're looking for a way to pass the time, I'll show you where I usually end up when I'm not on duty."

"Fair enough," I said, turning off the tape I'd been making of the session for my records.

Minnie Moskowitz mainlined on more than her own creative fantasies. She had also tapped into someone named Gene Kelly, who, I found out, was not one of the few members of the crew I had left to do a psych workup on. For one thing, he'd been dead for well over two hundred years—although apparently not for Minnie.

She'd discovered old Gene in a secluded corner of the ship's library, buried amongst the 20th-century musical extravaganza tapes—the same corner she led me to that afternoon, as a matter of fact. Apparently, the tape she wanted was right where she'd left it, for she found it almost immediately. She tripped lightly over to the nearest viewer and inserted it.

The image of a large Terran undomesticated feline appeared on the screen and roared at us, then faded away as three people in yellow overcoats replaced it. They were being rained upon—in fact, they were being *poured* upon—but strangely, they didn't seem to mind in the least. In fact, they were singing. At this point, appropriately enough, the words "Singin' in the Rain" were superimposed over the yellow-slickered singers.

"The one on the right," said Minnie, "is Gene Kelly."

"Oh," I replied. I was unimpressed at this point. Gene Kelly was only a grinning humanoid who didn't possess the common sense to come in out of the rain. Possible masochistic tendencies. And as for his two friends out there with him, well, lord only knew what *their* trip was.

Minnie tapped a button on the viewer and the tape sped ahead at fast forward. I glanced at her puzzledly and she explained, "The rest is okay, but this one particular sequence is the only important thing. The whole meaning of life in a raindrop. The reason for existence, there in a puddle."

"All that in a 20th-century movie?" I said in mock astonishment.

"Just watch," she demanded. "This is what makes Minnie Moskowitz tick."

So I watched. In this scene, Gene still didn't have the sense to come in out of the rain—and now he didn't even have his slicker on. He did have one of those antiquated rain-deflecting devices—umbrella, I believe the nomenclature was—but of course he wasn't using it. Instead, he was singing in the rain. Ah, logical, I thought, recalling the title of this epic. Gene was also dancing up a storm, if you'll forgive the pun. And getting frightfully wet. He didn't seem to mind. He said he didn't, anyway, and he was smiling very broadly as the rainwater streamed down his face and fell into his mouth.

I found that I had begun smiling myself. It was very incongruous, this silly man singing and dancing in horrible meteorological conditions, not even using his little umbrella for its man-made intention. He was cavorting with Nature instead of fighting it. And he was having a hell of a good time in those puddles. And then I realized what Minnie meant. Gene Kelly was soaring. There he was, smack dab in the midst of reality, soaked to the skin, feet firmly planted on the ground—and yet he was as far removed from reality and mundanity as you can get.

The stuff dreams are made of, I mused. That's what old Gene is. Pure kitsch. No wonder she's hooked on him.

"Not a bad ambition at all," Minnie muttered. "Think of it—distilling what he's got in his feet. What a rush. *I'd* like to control Gene Kelly's feet myself."

"Well, I suppose you can as long as no one else wants to use the tape."

"You don't really understand, do you?" she said. "That's still being tied to reality, to a body, having to play a tape over and over again."

"But that's all you can do," I said gently. "At least that's something. At least you can get the feeling for a few minutes at a time, watching this, or feeling the wind in your face. Some people never feel it. *Most* people never feel it."

"It's not enough, Doc," she said solemnly.

"Well," I began with an appeasing smile, "maybe we'll make it to the amusement park planet for shore leave. I bet it'd be just what the doctor ordered for you."

"The what?"

"The amusement park planet. I hear it's a terrific place, probably just what I need at this point, too. We're in the Omicron Delta region now anyway. If some emergency doesn't tear us away, that's where we'll probably end up. You ever been there for a leave?"

She shrugged nonchalantly, but there was something strangely coy about her expression. "Can't remember," she said. Then she rewound *Singin' in the Rain* and carefully put it back on the shelf.

There aren't any clues as to the passage of time on the *U.S.S. Enterprise.* Sometimes you have breakfast at midnight and sometimes you have dinner at dawn. It makes no difference on a starship. No antique grandfather clock ever sounds the witching hour, nor does the sun ever burst through a veranda window at cock's crow. The words "day" and "night" are irrelevant, and so are terms like "weeks" and "months" and "years." Birthdays often pass unnoticed and holidays are all but forgotten, with the exception of one or two. Time marches on, but we stay the same up here, floating around in our glorious relativity condenser. So it goes.

And so it went. I finished the interview portion of my workup and moved on to the more tedious task of entering the numerous tapes into their individual files. A is for Agbadudu, B is for Bartholomew, C is for Castanuela. And so on. G is for Garvey, H is for Harrison, I is for Ix. And so on into tedium. It was a well-known drag, and I found myself nodding off at my desk more than once. But onward—so on and so on and so forth all the way up through the M's, where I gave myself pause. Moskowitz, Minnie. I hadn't thought about her in any number of irrelevant weeks. I hadn't seen hide nor hair of her in that period of time, either, not that I had made any special effort to find her. It did seem somewhat unusual that with all the overlapping shifts I tended to work, Minnie never seemed to take her meals in the rec area when I did. Perhaps she ate in her quarters, or down in the film library with Gene Kelly.

Whatever, here in the midst of the clutter on my desk, was Minnie Moskowitz. Here in the midst of an advanced case of boredom, a mild case of loneliness, and just a touch of down in the mouth, was Minnie Moskowitz. Here in the midst of an empty, quiet office was a desk monitor and plop, into the tape slot went the Moskowitz tape, instead of into the Moskowitz file.

Should have programmed up a bowl of popcorn while I was at it, I decided, for even on tape Minnie was as entertaining as one of her 20th-century extravaganza films. She brightened up my evening more than an extended coffee break. And just think—now I could play her whenever I needed a lift. I could play her over and over again for myself, just like she played old Gene Kelly. An ironic and slightly disturbing parallel. As much as I personally delighted in Minnie's method of coping with "mundanity," I did not particularly relish the prospect of finding myself falling victim to the same habits. It was not . . . well . . . professional.

But then again, after studying under people like Leonard McCoy, one might get the impression that professionalism is not one of the chief prerequisites to becoming a good doctor in Starfleet.

And speaking of extended coffee breaks, there was also that holy old adage about all work and no play making for a worn-out lady shrink. Bless them words of wisdom. I suddenly found myself inspired to close up shop, put on my boots, and go for a walk down to the library.

"You're a very bad man!"

This, in the voice of a young girl.

"No, my dear. I'm a very good man. I'm just a very bad wizard."

That, in the unwizardly voice of an old man.

I approached the voices, weaving my way around numerous shelves and tape stacks. The sounds, I discovered, were being emitted by an activated viewer. Portrayed on its screen was a man of straw, a man of tin, and a man of lion-hide, in addition, of course, to the young girl and the unwizardly wizard.

"Aha—*Wizard of Oz,*" I guessed with keen insight. "I've seen that one."

Minnie glanced up at me and smiled. "You're a true patron of the arts, Doc."

"Well, I don't know about that, but we did have a copy of this at home when I was a kid." I sat down next to her and added in a confessional tone, "I always had a thing for the Scarecrow."

"'S nice," she said, turning back toward the screen.

"I take it that this is another of your favorites?"

Minnie scratched her head. "Not really. I had this compulsion to watch it, but it's not what I was looking for. It's too earthbound."

"Earthbound?" I echoed in disbelief. "But it's pure fantasy."

She shook her head. "Not pure. It's hopelessly tied down by emotional bonds. That cluck has the chance of a lifetime handed to her on a silver platter . . . or tornado, if you will, the opportunity to fulfill every daydream she's ever had. And she chucks it!" Her voice rose in disgust. "And for what? For *Kansas,* for crying out loud. Mundane old Kansas!"

"Well, yes, but . . ." But what? She was right. Why did I feel such a need to defend Dorothy's actions? Why did I feel so personally wounded? Why had I always identified so much with that dumb little cluck? "But she soared for a while. She didn't really want to soar forever. She just needed to get away for a little while, to avoid the bad things about reality."

"Yeah, I know somebody just like that," Minnie muttered to herself. "Me, though, I'd take a good pair of flying feet over that any day. You wouldn't catch me anywhere near Kansas if I didn't have to be there."

"You mean you don't need that sense of security that home will always be waiting for you? Or that you belong? Or that Auntie Em loves you no matter what?"

"Not me. That isn't in *my* backyard."

I hesitated before I commented, "But there's no place like home."

Minnie shrugged. "If you say so, Doc. Dorothy can go home, and you can go home, and I'll dance all night and still beg for more. That's my function."

And she pulled out the tape just as Dorothy was saying, "I think I'll miss you most of all," to the Scarecrow, who could say nothing at all, only look at her with fond tears in his painted eyes.

I stared at Minnie for a moment, thinking. It wasn't that she was unemotional. No one who wanted to soar that badly could be unemotional. Yet there was definitely something lacking in that girl's soul that I couldn't quite pin down.

Her clear gray eyes met mine and she said, "I must admit that I'm getting awfully tired of this game. I'm fed up with this girl's army." She chuckled. "I think my battery's wearing down. Maybe it's time for this one to go home after all."

She leaned forward until her head rested on her forearms and she sighed. I found my hand instinctively reaching out toward her shoulder in a gesture of comfort that I suddenly realized would not give her anything that she needed. The hand fell back to my side. I cleared my throat and said, "Don't supposed it's made the complete circuit through the grapevine yet, but the word came through this morning. About R and R."

"What about it?" she said softly.

"We're going to the amusement park planet. We'll be there the day after tomorrow."

Just what the doctor ordered, I told myself again. I was sure that it would be just what she needed. She looked more cheerful already. "Well," she smiled, "how nice. I guess now we'll see one way or the other."

"See what?" I asked.

"Whether there really is no place like it."

Like the amusement park planet, I assumed. Nothing else would have made much sense.

"Well, I wouldn't exactly call your life *boring,*" I said, chewing absently on a dandelion stem. "What was your childhood like?"

"Childhood?" the Scarecrow replied. "What childhood?"

I stared at him for a moment, embarrassingly slow on the uptake, then chuckled. "Oh, yeah, right! Silly of me. Should learn to leave the couch up at the office." I tossed the weed off to one side. "Pass me the potato salad."

He glanced into the picnic basket and noted, "There's an ant in the potato salad."

"Without the ant, if you don't mind."

He carefully picked up the (most-likely) computer-created insect between two gloved fingers and placed it onto a blade of grass. "There you go, fella," he addressed it kindly. "And don't bring back your pals." He handed me the container of potato salad and a fork.

"Thank you," I said.

"Oh, you're very welcome," he replied graciously.

"Listen," I said between mouthfuls of food, "are you sure you don't want something to eat? There's plenty here."

"Oh, no. I never eat. But I'll take some spare straw if you have it. That's how *I* fill up."

I checked the wicker basket briefly, and sure enough, there, neatly wrapped in a square of red and white gingham, was a small bundle of straw.

"Boy, they think of everything," I said, handing him the parcel.

"A most competent planet," agreed the Scarecrow, stuffing a handful of straw up either sleeve. "There now. That's much better, don't you think?"

He really didn't look any different to me, but his freshly-harvested appearance seemed so important to him that I commented, "Oh, undoubtedly. Indubitably, even." I finished off a leg of fried chicken and wiped my fingers on the discarded gingham. "What would you say to a little promenade?" I asked him.

A glimmer of mischief appeared in his dark shiny eyes. "Why, I'd say, 'Hello, little promenade!'"

I gave him a disapproving glance as he smiled at his own wit, which, unfortunately, had not come with the same money-back guarantee as his degree in thinkology.

The Scarecrow sprang lightly to his feet, then extended his arm to me. I grasped the gloved hand and pulled myself up. In spite of his cornfield sense of humor, I had to admit that he was excellent company to explore the amusement park planet with. Polite, cheerful, brave, devoted—who could ask for anything more? Not me, certainly. Not even subconsciously. I'd barely begun to look around this wonderland when I'd discovered him, pole stuck up his back and everything, smack dab in the middle of a previously unoccupied field. Helping him down was obviously the only proper thing to do, an action which immediately made us fast friends. I'd always needed a friend like him. I'd always known that he'd care for me as much as he cared for Dorothy, if we just had the chance to get acquainted.

We promenaded for a while, arm in arm, with me helping him to his feet whenever he stumbled, which was often. It was a fine, fine day, bright and sunny and filled with the scent of blossoms from untold galaxies. Here and there we'd run into a crew member, blissfully engrossed in some personally entertaining fantasy, from wine, women, and song to lightsabers at twenty paces. Everywhere I looked, a lifetime of carefully constructed and even more carefully guarded castles in the air had become, at least temporarily, tangible reality.

"I don't want to sound bossy or anything," said the Scarecrow suddenly, "but I would suggest that we avoid that area up ahead. Now, we could go to the right—some people say that it's very nice over there. Or we could . . ."

"What's wrong with straight ahead?" I was compelled to ask.

"Well," he said apologetically, "nothing really. If you like getting wet, I mean. I just noticed that it's raining up ahead."

"Raining?"

"Not that there's anything wrong with rain. It makes the corn grow and all that. But whenever I get caught in the rain I come down with the worst case of mildew . . ."

"Raining?" I repeated. Now, that was very interesting. One little cloud sitting up ahead, pouring its little gray heart out over an area about the size of one city block. And, come to think of it, now that I got a closer look at it, the area *was* a city block, an old, circa mid-20th-century Earth-style concrete city block.

Now, there was only one person I knew of whose dream-come-true consisted of getting miserably sopping wet in the dirty urban streets of wherever the hell that damn movie was supposed to take place, and I was more than mildly interested in seeing just what she'd cooked up to entertain herself down here.

I turned to the Scarecrow. "Would you mind if I went on by myself?"

He smiled at me with infinite fondness and understanding in his sad eyes, and I felt a pang of irrational guilt at the imminent prospect of abandoning him. You can't abandon a figment of the imagination, can you?

"It's all right," he assured me. "I'll be around." He winked at me. "If you want me, just whistle."

"Wrong movie," I murmured vaguely, watching him stumble off cheerfully toward a nearby field.

The street before me was night-dark, a most interesting contrast to the sunny day surrounding the city block on all sides. I stood at the very edge of an invisible boundary, feeling the sun on my back while inhaling the damp, cool richness of the tableau before me. As my eyes became accustomed to the shift in lighting, I found that the setting was exactly what I'd expected. Black asphalt gleaming under archaic streetlamps, pocked here and there with viscous-looking puddles that rippled under the continuous patter of rain. And, of course, the inevitable figure on the lamppost, authentically bedecked in wide-legged trousers, soggy trench coat and snap-brimmed hat—except this time, it was an unmistakably feminine figure.

It was Minnie Moskowitz, all right, cloaked by the shower, thick and fluid, a living sheet of energy, a companion to loneliness, a partner to dance with. Minnie danced with Gene Kelly's feet. I was positive that every terpsichorean movement she was performing had been originally choreographed by old Gene for that movie she'd shown me. Even though I'd only seen it once, I knew. I knew that she had every damn step memorized. I knew that she had practiced for ages.

I watched her, and I found that I was beginning to feel monumentally depressed. It wasn't quite fair, I thought enviously. Who gave her all the kitsch and the energy and the inspiration and left me with the drips and drabs of reality? Why wasn't I a doer and a dancer, instead of a passive observer? Oh, woe is the lot of the lowly shrink, who participates in life by sitting back and watching other people perform, who looks at raindrops but never plays with them.

I watched her, up and down the curb, in and out of the huge puddles, swinging the big black umbrella around in a wide arch. She was perfect, perfect, perfect. She was "Singin' in the Rain"; she was Gene Kelly's feet. And I was plain old Minnie Moskowitz, entranced, yearning to capture the essence before me. It was the damndest case of patient-therapist transference I'd ever encountered, and I was hating/loving every moment of it.

Then, as if awaiting his cue, out came the policeman (recognizable by the traditional accoutrements). He appeared from out of nowhere, swaddled in his slicker, officiously staring at the loony dancer in the rain.

End of the number, thought I, watching Minnie freeze in her tracks, just as Gene had frozen in his tracks. But the expression on her face wasn't quite right; it didn't match that of the original loony. And she didn't blithely close her umbrella, hand it to a grateful mundane passerby (which would have been me, I suppose), and trot unconcernedly into the humid horizon.

It wasn't quite right. Minnie/Gene slowly turned to face the copper and she/he said, "What the hell are you doing here?"

Abruptly the rain ceased. It didn't taper to a drizzle. It just . . . stopped. Totally.

The copper said, "I've come home. There's no place like home, y'know." And he pushed back his rain hood and . . .

. . . he . . . she . . . had the same face as Minnie's.

Minnie stared at Minnie and I stared at Minnie, and the backdrop, the rainy city street, the whole movie set, unobtrusively receded into the surrounding foliage. Minnie removed her raincoat and tossed it to the ground and the sun came out from behind that cloud which was no longer there and all the fantasy was gone. Except that Minnie was still standing there staring at Minnie, and I was still standing there staring at Minnie . . . and Minnie.

The Minnie I'd been watching dance was extremely perturbed. "But you can't. You can't just . . ."

"Can't what?" interrupted the other. "Can't come home? Not even for a five-hundred-parsec tune-up?"

"You can't just pop up like *this*. It's barely been a year. We had an understanding. You're not supposed to be here yet."

"Oh, don't get your raindrops in an uproar. The ship came here so I came here. I didn't have much of a choice."

"What if somebody sees us together? It could blow everything. If I'd known you were coming, I'd have gone underground."

"So what did you expect—a postcard? Besides, it doesn't matter anymore."

I had the peculiar feeling that I was invisible. Here I was, standing right out in the open, not ten feet away from the two of them, sunshine on my shoulders, a piece of straw or two in my hair, a clearly tangible entity, being totally ignored. It couldn't be that my blue uniform blended so perfectly into the sky that I was camouflaged, could it? Or that they both assumed that I was a figment of their imagination?

I decided to clear up any confusion about the matter by traversing the ten feet that separated the Minnies and me.

"Uh," I said, solid intelligence resounding in that monosyllable. I had, at that moment, realized that I couldn't just introduce my presence by bursting forth with, "Hi there—what a marvelous job of cellular casting one of you is—by the way, what the

334

hell is going on?" and I was searching fruitlessly for something more meaningful to say. As Gene Kelly–Minnie turned around to stare at me, I noted that her expression was one of alarm. The other Minnie, however, didn't seem terribly surprised to see me, and she greeted me with a friendly smile. "Hiya, Doc. Fancy meeting you here."

"Who is she?" Minnie (Gene) asked her look-alike.

"This is the Doc. She's one of the ship's shrinks. She's very understanding."

"Part of my job," I mumbled humbly.

"Yeah?" said Minnie (Gene). She chuckled nervously. "I suppose you feel entitled to an explanation about this."

"That'd be nice," I said. "I'm not about to force you into it, though."

The Minnie who knew me commented, "You might as well explain it. You'll probably have to to someone sooner or later. Besides, the Doc is a professional confidant."

Minnie (Gene)—whom I'd decided to think of as Minnie-1— eyed me suspiciously, then shrugged. "Okay, Doc. You're so professionally understanding, let's see if you can understand this. I'm Minnie Moskowitz." She paused to jerk a thumb at her twin. "She's not."

"I think I've got that much," I replied. "It follows, uh, that it's been 'not you' on the ship for the last . . . well, since I've been there."

"And I suppose you'd like to hear about 'why'?" Minnie-1 said.

Before I could reply, Minnie . . . 2 said, "She knows already. She's probably already diagnosed all your neuroses. After all, I was programmed with them. She's got them all on tape."

"Actually," I said, "I'm more interested in 'how.' How did you manage the substitution? The caretaker of this place, from what I was led to believe, would never have allowed anything like this to happen. Would he?"

"Caretaker's dead," Minnie-1 commented matter-of-factly. "Big Computer's in charge now. Don't you read the R and R updates?"

"After the Caretaker died, the Computer went through this

weird phase where it decided that it resented its role here," explained Minnie-2. "It got kind of hostile to visitors, and Captain Kirk was unlucky enough to be one of those visitors right around that time. Guess that was before your time on the ship."

"What happened?" I asked.

"He and Spock talked to it," said Minnie-2. "Convinced it that it was more blessed to be benevolent and subservient than to hijack starships. It wanted to learn about other worlds and other life-forms, but Kirk got it to go back to its creator's original program for gaining that information."

"By playing genie-in-the-lamp to whatever life-form traipses through here and picking up the knowledge subliminally," I said.

"That, and through the more direct method of communication that Kirk and Spock inadvertently set a precedent for: actually speaking to the Computer," 2 said. "The Big C got a real charge out of that."

"So when I came down for shore leave, with all my melancholy thoughts about my lot in life in Starfleet, I found out that the Computer didn't consider itself quite as bound by ethics as the Caretaker was, particularly not Federation ethics," continued Minnie-1. "It made me an offer I couldn't refuse."

"With my help," interrupted Minnie-2 with a small bow. "I acted as liaison and brought her down to see the Boss." She smiled at the reminiscence. "You should have seen her—she was so scared! I was a dragon that day."

"So Minnie talked to the Computer, and the Computer offered to let her stay and be Gene Kelly all the time," I realized. "But somebody had to go back to the ship after shore leave ended—"

"That would be me," said 2.

"So you were programmed to look just like her and act just like her."

"And feel just like her," 2 added. "And get crazy cravings just like her. And be bored out of my mind in Starfleet just like her. I was beginning to need a shrink myself!"

"You knew the job was dangerous when you took it," the original remarked dryly.

"I *didn't* take it," the other replied. "I was *sent* on it. I'm just a trans-droid. I don't get any choice as to what I'm cast as today or tomorrow. Or where I go."

"You sound a bit discontent with *your* lot," I noted.

"Mine is not to reason why," she replied, "nor to feel content or discontent. My function is to live out real people's fantasies for them. I've lived through a lot of them."

"But you seem to have a continuous flow of consciousness. What do you do between fantasies?" I inquired curiously.

"She's just a pile of cellular components," said Minnie-1. "You should see the factory down there. Remarkable."

"There's only a certain amount of resource material for the trans-droids, though," said the pile of components, "so we all get recycled. And there's a certain amount of memory retention from creation to creation, depending on how strong the emotional factor involved in the fantasy was."

I suspected there was a certain amount of emotional retention from creation to creation, as well as intellectual. While I had no doubts that the real Minnie Moskowitz wanted to control Gene Kelly's feet and distill the essence of kitsch from the universe, I had a hunch that it was this pile of cellular components that wanted to get out of its body and make trees dance. They probably had more in common than they thought.

"And what happens now?" I asked. "Whose shore leave is over in a couple of days?"

"The arrangement was that we'd switch back when the *Enterprise* returned for another R and R, presumably in about a year," Minnie-2 explained. "By then Yeoman Moskowitz would have been able to tell Big C everything it could possibly want to know, and I'd return filled with all sorts of new trivia to relate and amuse. Which I have."

"But it hasn't been a year," Yeoman Moskowitz said petulantly. "I'm not ready to go back."

"You'd *never* be ready to go back if you didn't have to," the trans-droid commented.

"Maybe I *don't* have to," Minnie replied.

"Of course you do," said Minnie-2. "There'd be an investigation if *no* Minnie Moskowitz went back to the ship. And C is very economically inclined. Recyclable cellular components are more valuable to it than some freeloading flesh-and-blood creature who needs to be fed and clothed and entertained to boot."

"I don't think C minds that. In fact, I think it's actually come to enjoy the pleasure of my company."

Minnie-2 laughed. "Don't be ridiculous. C doesn't enjoy anything. It's a computer."

"You haven't seen C lately. It's developed quite a sense of humor."

The trans-droid wasn't swallowing a word of it. "That complex has less potential for developing a sense of humor than a Vulcan proctologist."

"But you have a sense of humor," I pointed out.

"That's because *she* does." She pointed at Minnie-1. "C programmed me to be as much like her as possible. But nobody has programmed C."

The sky was such a brilliant azure, so crystal clear and empty of contaminating clouds, that the large raindrops that suddenly fell upon Minnie-2's head seemed to materialize from out of thin air. Perhaps they were just collected droplets shaken loose by the wind from the undersides of overhanging leaves. Perhaps, although I was under the same tree, and so was Minnie-1, and the wind was practically nonexistent at the moment. Anyway, the trans-droid was the only one of us who got doused.

"Nobody?" Minnie Moskowitz smiled sweetly at her double.

The Scarecrow and I sat back to back under the stars, listening to the summer breeze slowly moving the branches of the trees. The air was cool and dry, and visually enhanced by intermittent golden flashes from fireflies. In short, it was a lovely night. I was finding that it was quite easy to get hooked on the feel of the wind in my hair. Minnie had been right; it was absolutely *nothing* like standing in the wind tunnel at the Academy. There was nothing in my antiseptic backlog of experiences to match the scent and the texture of this zephyr. I didn't particularly relish the idea of leaving this place, so I could begin to appreciate both the Minnies' points of view.

Speaking of whom, the Minnies had gone off together, presumably to discuss their fate with the Wizard—Big Computer, that is. No one had consulted me as to my opinion about the situation. I wasn't invisible; I simply didn't matter. Although I hadn't voiced the sentiment that no matter what the outcome I would not report it to Starfleet, this fact was apparently understood. I would go back to the *Enterprise* in a few days with a Minnie Moskowitz and no one would know that anything had ever been amiss. Hopefully. I felt no sense of guilt about my complicity in this plan. My loyalty was to my patient, not my employer. That's not exactly the Starfleet way, of course, but in the past few days I'd come a long way from thinking of myself as one hundred percent Starfleet.

I turned as I caught a glimpse of a moonlit Minnie Moskowitz approaching us from behind some trees. "Greetings," I greeted pleasantly.

She sat down next to us without returning the salutation. "C says I have to go back to the ship. Tomorrow."

I was not sure which Minnie was speaking to me. I asked, "How do you feel about that?"

Minnie shrugged. "Well, that's the way it goes."

Very stoic. "Listen, it won't be that bad," I tried to assuage whoever this was.

"Oh, I know that," Minnie said. "I'm sure I can cope with the day-to-day reality, and being the same humdrum thing for the rest of my existence."

"I quite understand how you feel," said the Scarecrow. "I often feel that way myself, hanging all alone out there in the cornfield with those wretched crows. I'm not exactly happy but I manage to cope and—"

"I think she's employing sarcasm," I told the Scarecrow.

"Oh," he replied, pondering.

"No, I'm not," said Minnie. "I really *don't* mind. I can be as mundane as they come. It doesn't bother me anymore."

"Oh?" I said, pondering that one myself. Was this overcompensation in the wake of depression?

The Scarecrow had his own theory. "I think she's gotten a new brain. You'd be surprised what an improved outlook on life a new brain provides."

"Well, professionally speaking, I'd have to agree, but I don't think she's gotten a new brain." I stared at her. "Have you?"

Minnie smiled. "Of course not. I have a whole new essence. I'm no longer dysfunctional in the universe of humankind."

"Very impressive," commented the Scarecrow dryly. "But can you quote the Pythagorean theorem?"

"What are you talking about?" I pressed her. "Which Minnie are you, anyway?"

"Does it matter? One of us had to be sentenced to a lifetime of nonsoaring. It was only logical that C would choose me."

"You really *don't* mind?"

"I really don't."

"But what about dancing?"

"I've got two left feet anyway."

"What about rainbows?" asked the straw man.

"And singin' in the rain?" I added.

"The stuff of dreams. Pure kitsch. Unnecessary to a yeoman third class. I've enjoyed my shore leave, but now I'm looking forward to getting back to work."

There were only two possibilities, as I saw it. Either C's decision to send her back had snapped something in the real Minnie Moskowitz's head, or the Scarecrow was right: She'd gotten a new brain. A reprogramming from the Computer, that is. Which would mean this was Minnie-2.

"I can hardly wait," she went on cheerfully. "There's just hundreds of tapes waiting up there for me to re-edit. It's so nice to feel wanted."

"Uh, right," I said uneasily. "Listen, why don't you just relax for now and have some dinner. The Scarecrow has another picnic basket around somewhere."

"Oh, no," she said. "I couldn't possibly eat a thing."

"Not even a Saltine cracker?" asked the Scarecrow.

"Not even that. I'm much too excited. Do you know that before I left, my superior suggested that I might be taking on even more duties when I return? I might even get to program our section's coffee breaks. Wouldn't that be something?"

"That'd be something, all right," I replied softly, unable to accept what I was hearing. The Scarecrow brought me a picnic basket and I had a solemn last supper under the stars. Minnie didn't eat, not even a Saltine; the Scarecrow, naturally, did not eat. For some reason I felt guilty, so I didn't eat much myself. I kept thinking that there must be something that I could have done to help Minnie, despite the fact that she didn't appear to need any help whatsoever. And I continued to wonder which Minnie this was. I thought it was probably the trans-droid, considering her lack of interest in food, but the thought did not appease my sense of concern over the outcome of the whole matter. I was afraid to question her any further; she might have spouted some epitaph at me, like, "I don't need to go looking for my heart's desire down here anymore. It's been in my own little padded cell on the *Enterprise* all along," and I just couldn't have stomached that at the moment. Her whole sudden "there's no place like home" attitude was bad enough. She probably had a pair of ruby slippers on under her boots.

Minnie wanted to beam up to the ship immediately after dessert, as she was unable to resist the rewarding call of space stenography for another minute. I wasn't quite ready to accompany her, so I sent her on ahead.

"All right," I said to the Scarecrow after she had twinkled away. "What do you think? About her, I mean."

He scratched his thatched skull. "I'm not thinking, in this case. I don't think you should either. It might strain your brain."

"It's already been strained and sprained. But I still need to know."

"Well, you heard her yourself," the Scarecrow said. "Someone had to go back to the ship. C simply picked the best-suited Minnie Moskowitz."

"But which one was it?"

"Does it matter? That one is happy to go back to your ship and the other one is happy to dance under a streetlamp. Everybody's happy."

"I'm not," I said, frowning. "Everything's all copacetic for everyone—except me. I feel rotten. I don't understand what's going on and my once-in-a-blue-moon shore leave is almost over and I've got an awful headache."

"That's terrible. You shouldn't leave here in that condition. There must be something we can do for you here that will cheer you up."

"I doubt it," I sighed. "I don't know *what* I want anymore. I wish I didn't have to go back right away. I don't feel R and R'd up enough for life on the Big E just yet."

"Then stay here with us. We'd be honored with your presence."

I smiled faintly. "Well, it's nice to know that. Thanks, but that's not for me."

"Why not? It could be anything you want it to be. *You* could be anything you want to be."

I indulged him by letting my mind explore the possibilities for a moment, then laughed. "No, that's ridiculous. There couldn't be more than one Gene Kelly in the universe." I hesitated. "Could there?"

"Well, I really don't know," said the Scarecrow.

"Maybe Fred Astaire, though," I mused. "He's got a good pair of feet on him, too." I placed an imaginary top hat on my head and struck a pose. "What do you think?"

"Gosh, I think you'd be swell. Why don't you stay and be Fred?"

I laughed again. "I'm not really serious. I couldn't stay here forever."

"It wouldn't have to be forever. Just until the next time your ship comes back for shore leave. We really enjoy having company down here."

It was a tempting proposition. After all, what was a year or so out of my life? Time enough to decide whether it was more fulfilling to live around insensitive humans or compassionate androids. Time enough to decide whether I preferred thinking rationally or not at all.

"I don't know," I said slowly. "Do you really think—?"

"Oh, yes, yes!" The Scarecrow clapped his gloved hands together in glee. "Come on—let's go talk to C right away."

"C?" I repeated nervously. I wasn't certain that I was ready to meet face to face with Oz, the great and terrible.

"Of course. How else can you work out all the details?"

"What details? I wouldn't have to sign my name in blood or anything, would I? Or have to steal Mister Spock's broom?"

"Of course not," he reassured me. "Everything will be just hunky-dory!"

He led me to a dark narrow passageway set within a stony ridge. I couldn't recall having seen it there before. "Through here?" I queried.

"Through here," he confirmed.

"I'm really not too crazy about dark, confining passage-ways—" I began.

My words echoed hollowly against the dark, confining walls and I closed my mouth in order to better concentrate on not stubbing my toes.

"So you're the Big C," I addressed the console with what I hoped was a convincing show of nonchalance.

If it hadn't been a computer, I'd have sworn that it made a sound like a sigh. "That is the nomenclature that Yeoman Moskowitz prefers to use in addressing me. It is adequate, if uninspired. I am the custodian of this convenience. It is my understanding from your recent dialogue with one of my units that you wish to make arrangements for an extended stay on this planet."

"Well, you see, I'm not exactly sure. It isn't every day that you willingly sell your soul, you know."

"I do not wish your 'soul.' The Caretaker informed me that the souls of humans are unalterable by temptation. It is also my understanding that they are not a marketable commodity. The arrangement that I made with Yeoman Moskowitz was a much more reasonable exchange: information for temporary asylum."

"Not so temporary, it would seem."

"My programming will not permit me to reject her desire."

"Or mine?"

"Or yours."

That easy. How interesting. I wondered vaguely how many different patrons of this big amusement park had failed to return to their respective ships in the past year or so. It was a little spooky to consider.

"If you are ready, I can begin to program a replacement for you."

"Replacement?"

"To return to your ship in your place."

"Oh. Like that Minnie Moskowitz that went back a while ago."

"That is correct."

"What did you do to her, anyway? She's . . . she's different."

"A minor but necessary adjustment. It had originally been programmed to be exactly like the original, which made it as dysfunctional in its environment as the human one is. It will now be precisely what a well-adjusted human in Yeoman Mosko-witz's situation should be."

"Seems like a nasty trick to play on one of your units."

" 'Nasty' is an inappropriate modifier. My units function as they are programmed to function."

Yeah, but did they resent it? I doubted that C would know, so I decided not to ask. "What do you need from me," I asked instead, "in order to make . . . uh . . . me?"

"Very little. Your cooperation in a minor procedure. I believe you are familiar with psych-scans?"

"I've never been particularly fond of being on the receiving end of them, but I know all about them." I allowed C to draw the background material it needed and made a few professional suggestions as to which personality traits to underemphasize so that the trans-droid would fit into my mundane lifestyle. I asked how long the whole duplication procedure would take and was informed that the replacement would be ready by the time my leave was over.

"The work on the physical construct is almost complete," C concluded.

"Really? Where is it? Can I see it?"

"If you wish. It will be ready in approximately one of your hours. You may return at that time to view it. In the meantime, you may do whatever you desire. That is the purpose of this world."

I desired a walk outside. I needed some fresh air. It was all kind of intoxicating, knowing that everything around me belonged to me, in the sense that I could shape it and change it and control it, for however long I wanted. I could walk through the forests of Michigan's Upper Peninsula, or the crystal plains of Renan VII, or the red sands of Vulcan, all within the space of a mile. I could reencounter old flames, spark relationships with new flames, have an orgy. The possibilities were endless!

At the moment, though, I couldn't really think of much I'd rather do than walk quietly through this beautiful habitat that seemed to be the amusement park planet's natural unfantasized condition. I came to a clearing in the midst of some catalpa-like trees and paused to take a deep breath of the cool, clean air.

Okay, Doc, said the Jiminy Cricket of my soul, *what are you going to do with the rest of your life?*

I shrugged and mumbled a reply to myself aloud. " 'S not the rest of my life. Just a year or so. And by then I will be a much more fulfilled, self-confident person. Calm, cool, totally relaxed, capable of functioning in any and all surroundings—"

Able to leap tall buildings in a single bound—

"—content with all manner of mundanity, as witty and urbane and debonair as Fred Astaire on his best day."

Sure.

I caught sight of something at that point, something which popped up behind a rock, presumably from one of C's inconspicuous little trapdoors. Upon approaching the objects, I began to smile in recognition.

Top hat. And cane.

"Hey," I addressed the planet. "Thanks, but I'm really not much of a dancer." The Astaire accoutrements remained before me, and I picked them up out of curiosity. The hat was genuine imitation beaver fur—very fancy. The cane, well, I'd never really thought about what the original might have been made of, and C had guessed at a nice, durable lightweight polymer blend. It felt comfortable in my hand, familiar and well balanced. The hat was another matter. It fit my head just fine, but it was predictably weighty across the crown, and I knew that it was bound to give me a headache if I wore it for very long.

But it *was* a very cool hat, and I couldn't resist putting it on. And no sooner had I done so than I actually began to believe that perhaps I *was* something of a dancer, after all. I took a few tentative steps forward, pleased with the newfound spring in my step, and twirled my cane, glancing anxiously to the left and the right.

Ah, what the hell. There was nobody watching anyway.

"Eine kleine mood music, maestro," I requested, and somewhere I heard this marvelous orchestra strike up. I tried a few practice steps, and I must admit that my feet really seemed to know what they were doing. Of course, I had no partner to dance with, but as I recalled, that had never stopped Fred. I'd seen him dance with hat stands and chairs and even an empty room in his films. I didn't have anything like that around, but I'd gotten a better idea anyway. It topped any of Fred's classic numbers and maybe even matched Gene's rain dance. What I needed was a good strong breeze.

The catalpa branches above began to sway slightly, in response to a zephyr that had been nonexistent a moment earlier. "Very good," I murmured as the music again began to swell.

The trees were ripe with the white popcorn-shaped blossoms that grow in early summer, and the air became filled with them as the wind picked up.

I danced.

And God, I was good. I tripped the breeze fantastically. I was almost as light as the air. I didn't crush a single flower. They swirled gracefully around my ankles as I moved to the tempo of the swaying branches. I venture to say that I was poetry in motion for those blissful moments. I was sure right then that there was nothing better in life to be and nowhere better in the galaxy to live. I think I actually caught a glimmer of what it was like to soar.

Then somehow the glimmer faded, and it wasn't quite heaven

anymore. The wind was beginning to give me an earache and the hat was pressing heavily on my skull and natural clumsiness was suddenly betraying me, tripping me ungracefully over my white-tipped cane.

"Shit," I commented as I fell toward the leaves. It was definitely the wrong thing to say. I hadn't noticed any cows in the clearing, but I suddenly discovered that I had landed in a heap of unprocessed bovine fertilizer. Or perhaps "commingled with" would be a more accurate phrase. "Oh . . ."

Fortunately, I stopped the curse before I inflicted myself with some new catastrophe. I bit my lip, got up, found the nearest stream (and a wonderfully convenient bar of soap), and scrubbed myself off.

Just lovely. I wondered again if soaring was really my long suit. Or tuxedo. Or whatever.

The construction room was at the end of Corridor B. I don't know what I expected to see in there. Perhaps a bunch of hunchbacked dwarves dragging in stolen corpses in large duffel bags. What I actually found was a very neat workroom, filled with several small banks of computers, each equipped with several sets of waldoes, easily able to reach the long stainless steel tables before them. Almost all of the tables were unoccupied, I suppose because the majority of vacationing crew members had already returned to the *Enterprise*. At the far end of the room, I spotted one supine body in a blue Starfleet uniform, and I approached it somewhat apprehensively. She . . . "I" . . . hadn't been activated yet and was just lying there, staring glassily up at the ceiling. I'd prepared myself for a mild jolt of cultural shock, or whatever one experiences upon being faced with a doppelganger, but it didn't come. Either that or I was doing one terrific job of repressing it. I whistled softly through my teeth. The hair was the right color, the mole was in the right spot, the fingernails were uneven, the bust was a little saggy. "That's me all over," I murmured.

"That's *my* line," said a voice from the next table. "At least *you're* all put together."

I spun around in surprise and found myself staring at the

Scarecrow—or what was left of him, anyway. His legs had already been neatly detached by the mechanical hands, and they were presently working on removing an arm.

"What are *you* doing here?"

"Being recycled," he said calmly.

"Recycled? Why?"

"Why not? That's my function."

"But why are they taking you apart now? What if I want to talk to you later?"

"The component bin is a little low. Not all of your crewmates' fantasies have come home yet and C needed someone's raw material for a new construct. I volunteered."

His other arm was carefully detached, and I watched in growing discomfort. "For what construct?"

He smiled warmly. "Why, yours, of course. I wouldn't have it any other way. I'm happy to be you. We're very . . ." he searched for the right word, "uh, copacetic?"

I winced. "But my construct's already made."

"Oh, no—all the internals still have to be put in. They need a lot of material for that."

"Internals? But it looks like it has, well, just about everything."

"No, no. 'Internals' are what we call the stuff up here." He tried to gesture up at his head, but lacking any arms, had to settle for a meaningful shrug of his shoulders. "You know—intellect, personality, that stuff. That's what they're going to use me for."

"Why are you so all-fired anxious to get sent to some flying bucket of bolts and pretend to be me?"

He thought for a moment as the waldoes reached out to detach the smiling straw head. I was never quite sure if what he said before he was detached was "Because I like you" or "Because I'm like you." It didn't really make much difference when I thought about it. It didn't matter how much he liked me (if, indeed, he was capable of liking anything) or how "copacetic" our personalities were. With the personality adjustments I'd recommended for my replacement so that it would be content with its position on the *Enterprise,* my friend would be no more like me (or its old self) than Minnie-2 now inwardly resembled Minnie-1.

The realization bothered me a lot. It was as if I were responsible for taking all of that wonderful altruistic nonreality away from my poor Scarecrow, personally draining every last drop of kitsch he had. No more Oz for him. No more "singin' in the rain" for Minnie-2. If what C had said was true, the trans-droids didn't really care. I suppose if I'd had a lobotomy I wouldn't much care what was done with my life either. But that didn't make me feel any less culpable now.

I picked up a leftover handful of straw from the metal table and stared at it silently. It wasn't exactly the good-bye I'd had in mind. I'd pictured it more like the movie, with me telling him I'd miss him most of all and him standing there, sadly speechless. Very touching, guaranteed to wring a tear from all but the totally kitschless.

I suddenly remembered what Minnie-2 had said in the film library, about Dorothy having chucked the opportunity to fulfill every daydream she'd ever had. "And for what?" Minnie'd complained. "For *Kansas!*"

The corner of my mouth twisted upwards in a fleeting smile. Yeah, Kansas. Mundane old Kansas. As in, there's no place like . . .

Ah, what the hell. If there was the slightest possibility that I *had* overlooked something in my own backyard, maybe I could stand it for another few years.

So I chucked it and went back to my own backyard and the old mundane routine of Starfleet. It was predictably lonely out there. At least Dorothy had Zeke and Hunk and the others to welcome her back when she went home. All I had was a lobotomized Minnie Moskowitz, who'd become a much better yeoman third class than she'd ever been before, not to mention a very boring person. I kept the tape of the old one for a while, and on the most mundane of mundane days, it was a great temptation to pull it out and plug it in, but I always resisted. It would have gotten me too depressed. Besides, it was a dangerous record to keep around. You never knew who might happen to catch a peek of it and notice how different the psych profile based on the taped Minnie was from the one currently programming coffee breaks. So eventually I ended up tossing the tape into a disposal chute.

There aren't any recreational counselors on the *U.S.S. Enterprise.* On those irrelevant Saturday nights when someone like Angie would ask his friend what he wants to do tonight, Marty, I end up going down to the video library and spending the evening hours there all alone, systematically viewing every film we've got on file. Every now and then I run across a piece of Gene Kelly celluloid, or something equally inspirational, and I feel this twinge, but I tell myself, hey, Doc, it's not meant for you. You can be content with just two weeks of fantasy a year. Some people just aren't cut out for more than that. After all, if God had meant for you to soar, he'd have given you Gene Kelly's feet.

Afterwords

My First Story

John J. Ordover

The first story I ever wrote was a *Star Trek* story. Not the one in this book, which was written several years ago when Kevin Ryan first told me that Pocket Books might publish a *Star Trek* anthology. My first story was written in the summer between eighth and ninth grades, scrawled out in my terrible handwriting on page after page of a yellow legal pad.

I wish I could remember what it was about. All I can remember is that it starred Kirk and Spock, and that they beamed down to a hostile planet. Oh, and then suddenly a force field snapped up that wouldn't let them beam back to the ship.

I don't remember the rest of the story—who the bad guys were, what the problem was, or how Kirk and Spock were going to get out of this one. But I do remember what it felt like to write a *Star Trek* story. Because I remember it, as soon as I could, I gave fans who write *Star Trek* a chance at having their stories professionally published.

I've written lots of things now. Dozens of short stories published everywhere from *Amazing Stories* to *Penthouse* magazine, and even an episode of *Star Trek: Deep Space Nine* ("Starship Down," with my pal David Mack), but I'll never forget lying on my bed in a hot summer room writing dialogue for Kirk and Spock, and what it felt like to write phrases like "Kirk to *Enterprise*" and "Captain, I canna do it!"

To all of you who wrote stories that were not chosen for this anthology, think about this: You've done more than ninety-nine percent of the people who say they want to be writers do. You wrote something and sent it in. We're going to run this contest again next year (see the back pages for details) but this is hardly the only place your writing can appear. Check the science-fiction magazines like *Analog, Asimov's,* and *Fantasy and Science Fiction*. They publish great stuff (even if it isn't *Star Trek*) and someday your name could be on one of their covers or in one of their tables of contents.

And to all of you whose first professionally published story appears in this volume, congratulations. Your goal is to make sure your first story isn't your last.

A Few Words . . .

Paula M. Block

Just so you know, I watched first-run *Original Series* episodes of *Star Trek* while I was attending high school. I'm *that* old. And, in fact, I wrote "The Girl Who Controlled Gene Kelly's Feet" twenty years ago, during a period when I was deeply entrenched in *Star Trek* fandom. Although I loved *Star Trek,* I didn't know anything about fandom until around 1974, when I saw a classified ad in the school newspaper at Michigan State University mentioning a *Star Trek* club. I went to a meeting out of curiosity and met a lot of people who could actually identify episodes by looking at a picture of Mister Spock's left ear. I was impressed. I didn't even know there *were* pictures of Mister Spock's ear.

There was hardly any merchandise in those dark days. I had a well-thumbed version of Stephen Whitfield's *The Making of Star Trek,* and some of the James Blish books, and that was about it. But these people had a lot more. They had been to *Star Trek* conventions. I vaguely recalled reading an article in *TV Guide* about a *Star Trek* convention that had been held in New York and had thought at the time that it might be cool to attend one. I had no idea that I would someday be working on con committees, writing and editing fanzines, and becoming good friends with many of the people who were the BNFs (Big Name Fans) of *Star Trek* fandom.

Those were really fun days. Fandom was like the extended family I'd never had. Everyone was warmly accepted into its ranks, no matter what race, creed, religion, or dress size you had. And fanzines—those hand-mimeoed or offset printed pamphlets of amateur fiction—were the training ground for my future career in publishing. I met a variety of incredibly talented writers, artists, and intellects along the way. Lori Chapek-Carleton and Gordon Carleton and the rest of the Landing Party crew in East Lansing; Paula Smith and Sharon Ferraro in Kalamazoo; Connie Faddis in Pittsburgh; Joyce Yasner and Devra Langsam in New York; Judi Hendricks, Jan Lindner, and Jackie Paciello Truty in Chicago. There are a lot more, but John said to keep this under five pages. (However, just for the record, I will mention that I also met my wonderful husband through fandom, although he wasn't actually a fan. It's a long story.)

I wrote a lot of *Star Trek* stories for the fanzines, and the feedback that I got from the editors and, more importantly, the readers, helped me to polish my rough skills considerably. ("Gene Kelly's Feet" was for Paula Smith's fanzine, "Menagerie," so thank her if you like it.) It was on the basis of a fanzine story that I got my first professional writing assignment, a series of humorous diet columns for the *Chicago Sun-Times*. And long after I had stopped writing for fanzines, it was my experience in fandom that helped me to get my job at Paramount Pictures.

By 1989, there was a *lot* of *Star Trek* merchandise out there, particularly books, and Paramount's licensing division needed someone with a professional publishing background who was familiar with *Star Trek,* to review the books, comics, and magazines being produced by their licensees. The old adage about being in the right place at the right time (and with the right qualifications) proved correct, and I was offered the job. Eight years later, I'm still here. It's a crazy world, all right. Over the course of my professional career, I've written diet columns, biotechnology updates, and automotive trend reports; I've also headed up the international section of a trade magazine and been the staff editor for *Chemical Week* magazine. And I can firmly state that my present job is definitely the most fun (although the folks at *Chemical Week* were a wild and crazy bunch!).

Some of you may be wondering just what it is that we do over here in licensing. It's very simple. We try to make sure that each and every product is true to the spirit of the movie or TV series it is based upon, because we know that if we don't, you folks will notice. In the case of *Star Trek* publishing, we make sure that Captain Kirk sounds like Captain Kirk, that Data employs the appropriate technology when he does something to the ship's computer, that the stardates referenced match up with the ones we heard in episodes, that the story lines seem like something that actually could happen on the series, and so forth. I followed those same guidelines while reviewing the submissions to this book, and was very pleased with the quality of the stories. But then, having come from the same "gene pool," so to speak, I expected no less!

I have to point out that my story, "The Girl Who Controlled Gene Kelly's Feet," breaks all manner of rules. It doesn't contain a regular *Star Trek* character. It sets an unestablished precedent (the idea that an android is serving on the Original *Enterprise*). It's implausible (the fact that this android would remain undetected by someone as astute as McCoy). It's way too focused on certain 20th-century movies and personalities. And it goes way over the specified word count for the contest. So if this were a submission, I'd have some problems with it. But you'll notice that it's in a special section devoted to rule-breaking. I hope you enjoy it all the same.

The real reason I had for writing this "Afterword" was partly to thank Lori for running that ad in the *Michigan State News,* and more importantly, to let you all know that the things you do now can influence your life later on. So keep on writing, or drawing, or making costumes, or whatever it is you like to do. Get good at it. If you really like it, make it your profession. Think about doing things that *aren't* about *Star Trek,* too.

Ironically, if I hadn't learned how to write about recombinant DNA and the gross national product of Finland, I wouldn't have had the professional background that I needed to get this job. Just remember, *Star Trek* is a way of life, but it isn't the only way of life. It's a big universe. Be open to everything. And keep reading. Everything. Be literate—it's the true key to the future, and it's already in your grasp.

STAR TREK®

Strange New Worlds II
Contest Rules

1) ENTRY REQUIREMENTS:

No purchase necessary to enter. Enter by submitting your story as specified below.

2) CONTEST ELIGIBILITY:

This contest is open to nonprofessional writers who are legal residents of the United States and Canada (excluding Quebec) over the age of 18. Entrant must not have published any more than two short stories on a professional basis or in paid professional venues. Employees (or relatives of employees living in the same household) of Pocket Books, VIACOM, or any of its affiliates are not eligible. This contest is void in Puerto Rico and wherever prohibited by law.

3) FORMAT:

Entries should be no more than 7,500 words long and must not have been previously published. They must be typed or printed by word processor, double spaced, on one side of noncorrasable paper. Do not justify right-side margins. The author's name, address, and phone number must appear on the first page of the entry. The author's name, the story title, and the page number should appear on every page. No electronic or disk submissions will be accepted. All entries must be original and the sole work of the Entrant and the sole property of the Entrant.

4) ADDRESS:

Each entry must be mailed to: STRANGE NEW WORLDS, *Star Trek* Department, Pocket Books, 1230 Sixth Avenue, New York, NY 10020.

Contest Rules

Each entry must be submitted only once. Please retain a copy of your submission. You may submit more than one story, but each submission must be mailed separately. Enclose a self-addressed, stamped envelope if you wish your entry returned. Entries must be received by October 1st, 1998. Not responsible for lost, late, stolen, postage due, or misdirected mail.

5) PRIZES:

One Grand Prize winner will receive:

Simon and Schuster's *Star Trek: Strange New Worlds* Publishing Contract for Publication of Winning Entry in our *Strange New Worlds* Anthology with a bonus advance of One Thousand Dollars ($1,000.00) above the Anthology word rate of 10 cents a word.

One Second Prize winner will receive:

Simon and Schuster's *Star Trek: Strange New Worlds* Publishing Contract for Publication of Winning Entry in our *Strange New Worlds* Anthology with a bonus advance of Six Hundred Dollars ($600.00) above the Anthology word rate of 10 cents a word.

One Third Prize winner will receive:

Simon and Schuster's *Star Trek: Strange New Worlds* Publishing Contract for Publication of Winning Entry in our *Strange New Worlds* Anthology with a bonus advance of Four Hundred Dollars ($400.00) above the Anthology word rate of 10 cents a word.

All Honorable Mention winners will receive:

Simon and Schuster's *Star Trek: Strange New Worlds* Publishing Contract for Publication of Winning Entry in the *Strange New Worlds* Anthology and payment at the Anthology word rate of 10 cents a word.

There will be no more than twenty (20) Honorable Mention winners. No contestant can win more than one prize.

Each Prize Winner will also be entitled to a share of royalties on the *Strange New Worlds* Anthology as specified in Simon and Schuster's *Star Trek: Strange New Worlds* Publishing Contract.

Contest Rules

6) JUDGING:

Submissions will be judged on the basis of writing ability and the originality of the story, which can be set in any of the *Star Trek* time frames and may feature any one or more of the *Star Trek* characters. The judges shall include the editor of the Anthology, one employee of Pocket Books, and one employee of VIACOM Consumer Products. The decisions of the judges shall be final. All prizes will be awarded provided a sufficient number of entries are received that meet the minimum criteria established by the judges.

7) NOTIFICATION:

The winners will be notified by mail or phone. The winners who win a publishing contract must sign the publishing contract in order to be awarded the prize. All federal, local, and state taxes are the responsibility of the winner. A list of the winners will be available after January 1st, 1999, on the Pocket Books *Star Trek* Books website, www.simonsays.com/startrek/, or the names of the winners can be obtained after January 1st, 1999, by sending a self-addressed, stamped envelope and a request for the list of winners to WINNERS' LIST, STRANGE NEW WORLDS, *Star Trek* Department, Pocket Books, 1230 Sixth Avenue, New York, NY 10020.

8) STORY DISQUALIFICATIONS:

Certain types of stories will be disqualified from consideration:

a) Any story focusing on explicit sexual activity or graphic depictions of violence or sadism.

b) Any story that focuses on characters that are not past or present *Star Trek* regulars or familiar *Star Trek* guest characters.

c) Stories that deal with the previously unestablished death of a *Star Trek* character, or that establish major facts about or make major changes in the life of a major character, for instance a story that establishes a long-lost sibling or reveals the hidden passion two characters feel for each other.

Contest Rules

d) Stories that are based around common clichés, such as "hurt/comfort" where a character is injured and lovingly cared for, or "Mary Sue" stories where a new character comes on the ship and outdoes the crew.

9) PUBLICITY:

Each Winner grants to Pocket Books the right to use his or her name, likeness, and entry for any advertising, promotion, and publicity purposes without further compensation to or permission from such winner, except where prohibited by law.

10) LEGAL STUFF:

All entries become the property of Pocket Books and of Paramount Pictures, the sole and exclusive owner of the *Star Trek* property and elements thereof. Entries will be returned only if they are accompanied by a self-addressed, stamped envelope. Contest void where prohibited by law.

About the
Contributors

Landon Cary Dalton ("A Private Anecdote") was born on August 7, 1963, in the city of Bowling Green, Kentucky, where he still resides. He graduated from Western Kentucky University in 1986 with a bachelor's degree in religious studies. He is extensively involved in local church work and is an avid comic book collector.

Keith L. Davis ("The Last Tribble"), forty, is a family physician currently residing in Wellington, Ohio, with his wife, Lori, and their two children. He attributes his interest in writing to his educators at Fairview High School and Hiram College. He is presently working on novels within and outside the *Star Trek* universe.

Phaedra M. Weldon ("The Lights in the Sky") has worked in the printing industry for over thirteen years. Seventy percent of her weekly life is spent in front of a Mac, whether at work or, in the evenings, writing. The other thirty percent is divided between reading and Colin, with Colin getting first dibs.

Dayton Ward ("Reflections"), a Florida native, was transplanted to Kansas City during his career with the Marine Corps. Now he's a computer systems engineer there, living with his wife, Michi, along with a cat that thinks she's a dog and a dog that thinks he's human.

Dylan Otto Krider ("What Went Through Data's Mind 0.68 Seconds Before the Satellite Hit") has been a promotion assistant for a TV station, a movie theater spy, and owner of a video movie and arcade game distribution business. He currently works as a promotions manager at the University of Chicago Press.

Jerry M. Wolfe ("The Naked Truth"), a longtime Trek fan, lives in Eugene, Oregon, where he writes science fiction and fantasy when not teaching mathematics at the University of Oregon. He is also a "Wordo," a member of the Eugene Professional Writer's workshop. *Star Trek: The Next Generation:* "The Naked Truth" is his second published story.

Peg Robinson ("The First") is forty. She has a wonderful husband and daughter, and four pushy cats. She was born in the former Panama Canal Zone and has lived in too many places since. She does the housewife thing, some amateur theater, reads, and works on her writing. The rest is silence. . . .

Kathy Oltion ("See Spot Run") became a *Star Trek* fan as a child in Rock Springs, Wyoming. She met her husband, author Jerry Oltion, in a creative writing class in college. They now live in Eugene, Oregon, where Kathy works in a medical laboratory and writes. She has also sold fiction to *Analog* magazine.

Bobbie Benton Hull ("Together Again, for the First Time") was born, raised, and currently lives in rural Yakima, Washington, with her husband and two daughters. She attended West Valley High School (1977) and has a bachelor's degree in soil science. She enjoys landscaping, her AOL True Trekker friends, performing in the Yakima Symphony Chorus, and is a 4-H volunteer.

Alara Rogers ("Civil Disobedience") has been writing since the age of four, and intends to be a household name by the age of forty, or at the very least have a Nebula or two. She has a background in psychobiology, has studied Japanese, assembles computers and plays with the Internet in her spare time, and has a job that calls for none of these skills, except maybe the Internet, occasionally. This is her second professional short-story tale. She lives in Philadelphia, Pennsylvania.

Franklin Thatcher ("Of Cabbages and Kings") is a software developer by vocation, a writer by avocation, and bishop in the Mormon church by dedication. Though he has sold several planetarium starshows, he prefers to write science fiction and fantasy. He and his wife, Laura, live in Orem, Utah.

Christina F. York ("Life's Lessons"), aspiring writer, self-published at the age of ten, then retired. After raising a family, she returned to writing non-fiction. "Too old" for the original series, she quickly became a fan of *Star Trek: The Next Generation.* She lives in Eugene, Oregon, with her husband, SF writer J. Steven York.

Vince Bonasso ("Where I Fell Before My Enemy") lives in Memphis, Tennessee, where he flies jets for Federal Express. He enjoys traveling and spends most of his free time in southern California. He is a Clarion West 1992 graduate.

Patrick Cumby ("Good Night, *Voyager*") lives with his wife, kids, dog, cat, and fish in the 'burbs of Atlanta, where he manages a team of tech writers and Web developers. When asked to sum up his life in fifty words or less, he ceases his furious typing, looks up from his keyboard, and wonders, "Does that count include punctuation?"

J. A. (Joe) Rosales ("Ambassador at Large") is a freelance comic book artist living in San Antonio, Texas. He is a fan of many media and genres. In his free time he enjoys reading about the Victorian era, trying to figure out what happened to the Andorians, and looking for inside jokes in science fiction.

jaQ Andrews ("Fiction"), nineteen, is studying creative writing at Simon's Rock College of Bard in Great Barrington, Massachusetts. His current career whim is to become a fiction- and songwriter as a side art to a janitorship at a yet-to-be-determined elementary school.

Jackee Crowell ("I, Voyager") was born with a love of science fiction, especially *Star Trek.* Being a writer has been a dream since age eight, when she "penned" her first story. These days she's a busy wife and mother of three, but finds time to visit with fellow pond members.

Craig D. B. Patton ("Monthuglu") grew up a science fiction fan in Chelmsford, Massachusetts. After a stunningly short-lived career as a filmmaker, he sought refuge (read "income") in the computer industry, where he found success as a marketer. "Monthuglu," his first published story, marks his return to the creative arts.

Printed in the United States
31793LVS00003B/265-273